Also by Marie Rutkoski

The Cabinet of Wonders
The Celestial Globe
The Jewel of the Kalderash

THE SHADOW SOCIETY

MARIE RUTKOSKI

The Shadow SOCIETY

FARRAR STRAUS GIROUX

NEW YORK

Farrar Straus Giroux Books for Young Readers
175 Fifth Avenue, New York 10010

Copyright © 2012 by Marie Rutkoski
Printed in the United States of America
Designed by Jay Colvin
First edition, 2012
1   3   5   7   9   10   8   6   4   2

macteenbooks.com

Library of Congress Cataloging-in-Publication Data
Rutkoski, Marie.
   The shadow society / Marie Rutkoski. — 1st ed.
       p.   cm.
   Summary: Sixteen-year-old Darcy Jones knows little about her past
except that she was abandoned outside a Chicago firehouse at age five,
but when the mysterious Conn arrives at her high school she begins to
discover things about her past that she is not sure she likes.
   ISBN 978-0-374-34905-9 (hardcover)
   ISBN 978-0-374-36757-2 (e-book)
   [1. Identity—Fiction.   2. Foster home care—Fiction.   3. High
schools—Fiction.   4. Schools—Fiction.   5. Illinois—Fiction.
6. Science fiction.]   I. Title.

PZ7.R935Sh 2012
[Fic]—dc23   2011033158

This book is dedicated to dear friends:
Becky Rosenthal, Dave Elfving, and Donna Freitas

THE SHADOW SOCIETY

PROLOGUE

Knowing what I know now, I'd say my foster mother had her reasons for throwing a kitchen knife at me. It flashed across her faux-wood-paneled living room, straight toward a fairly vital body part of mine, yet didn't touch me one eensy bit. Instead it struck the fish tank with a great kerRRRASH, like in a comic book, though whether I get to be the hero or the villain remains to be seen. The water gushed, and silvery black striped fish flopped all over the ratty shag carpet. I liked those angelfish, but I let them die their airless deaths and ran out of there, fast.

Conn was right behind me. I heard him chasing me down.

Other girls might have been afraid of their knife-wielding foster mother. Me, I was more afraid of Conn, and most afraid of myself.

But this isn't the story of how Marsha smashed her precious fish tank, though that little episode certainly played its part. This is the story of how I met Conn, got arrested, and discovered the truth about myself.

1

My first day back at Lakebrook High seemed innocent enough. I walked toward the beginning of my junior year in a fine spirit, scuffing my combat boots along the hot pavement. I was happy for a simple reason. For once, I wouldn't be the new girl, and I had friends. Sometimes being able to scrape a hard red chair up to a lunch table with the handful of people who accepted me was all I wanted. It was my second year at the same school. It was a personal record.

Little did I know that someone would try to take this and so much else away from me.

I liked Lakebrook. Sure, suburbia is soulless, but Lakebrook is a thirty-minute train ride from Chicago, with its skyscraping steel and wide pavements that feel like freedom. And, very important, Marsha had agreed to renew my stay with her for another year. This decision might have been inspired by the money the state sent to keep me clothed and fed. I wasn't complaining. Marsha was a little kooky, but she was also the only foster parent who hadn't gotten rid of me at the first opportunity.

I followed the yellow buses wheezing their way into the Lakebrook High parking lot and watched students swarm by the entrances. The air was heavy with the tarry smell of fresh asphalt as I walked up to my little clan.

"Daaaarcy!" Jims waggled a pack of Slim Jims—hence the nickname—stuck one tube of beef jerky in his mouth, and offered the rest to me. "Want some?"

"Um, gross," I said. "Vegetarian here, remember?"

"I thought maybe you'd come to your senses over the summer."

Lily lit a cigarette, inhaled, exhaled, and passed it to me, lipsticky pink. "Want some?"

I rolled my eyes. I hate, hate, hate smoke, and Lily knows it.

"Want some of this, then?" Raphael rested one finger on his chest in deliberate imitation of the Spanish soap operas we watched at his house. He looked the part of a lead: cinnamon skin, wavy dark hair. But the gesture was a joke. A bluff.

I stared him down. "Why do you all insist on giving me things I don't want?"

Raphael pretended to look wounded, Lily shrugged, and Jims said, holding his Slim Jim like a cigar, Groucho Marks style: "Because no one knows the square root of pi, because a stegosaurus is no match for a tyrannosaurus, because we always tease the ones we love, and you, Sunshine, we love. Some things are universally true."

Lily tilted her head, inspecting me. "Darcy doesn't look like sunshine. More as if someone drew her with pen and ink. Straight black lines. Pale features."

"I was using irony," Jims said. "It's *meant* to be inappropriate. The opposite of what you expect. You know, like getting hit by an ambulance. Or like a hot dog vendor drowning in a vat of ketchup."

"Your mind lives in strange places," I told him.

"True. But you all enjoy visiting."

"I also enjoy a jaunt through a haunted house once a year, come Halloween."

Lily tapped her Hello Kitty watch. "Ten minutes till the bell. Time to get down to business."

Raphael reached into the back pocket of his jeans and pulled out a folded white card. "Here's mine."

We passed around our schedules, except for Jims, who, being a senior, shared no classes with the rest of us. I was taking Art II and Biology with Lily and Pre-Calc with Raphael. PE, European History, and AP English were wide, vast deserts with nobody.

Right before the bell, when the noise of hundreds of people laughing, talking, squealing, and bickering had swelled into waves, I felt the back of my neck prickle. I was being watched. I knew this even before I slowly turned around, knew it like I knew I had ten fingers and ten toes.

There was a boy standing in the shadow of an oak tree. His

stance seemed easy, even lazy. But his expression was electric, tense, taut as a corded wire I could tightrope-walk across.

He was dressed simply. Jeans and a white T-shirt. If he intended to blend in, he utterly failed. His beauty wasn't my type, but it was undeniable. A cool, angular face. Hair the color of golden wheat, shorn brutally short. Lips so defined they could have been carved by a deft knife.

He lifted his chin a little, acknowledging that I had caught him mid-stare. A smile flickered at the corner of his mouth. Some might have interpreted this as flirtation. I knew better. It was a warning. The smirk of a gunslinger in one of those old orange-brown westerns, as if tumbleweeds were skittering down the parking lot between us and he was daring me to fire the first shot.

Anxiety twisted in my stomach. I had no idea why I had caught his attention. But whatever the reason, it meant trouble.

2

The bell shrilled. I yanked my gaze away. With my friends at my side, I merged into the river of bodies that flowed through the school doors. I left him behind, whoever he was.

"Well, that was interesting," Raphael muttered with a sidelong glance, making clear that my staring contest with the stranger hadn't gone unnoticed.

"You all right, Darcy?" said Jims. "You look like James Bond's martini."

Lily raised one thin eyebrow.

"Shaken," I told her. "Not stirred."

"You seem plenty stirred to me."

"Actually," Raphael said, "you *do*."

I tugged Lily away from the boys. "We're going to be late."

We took the flight of stairs up to the art department. She

paused before we entered the classroom. "Did you know that guy?"

"No."

"Because he acted like he knew *you*."

I almost asked Lily if she'd noticed the hostility lurking in every line of his body, then got paranoid I'd sound paranoid. I shrugged, so Lily dropped the subject and opened the door.

I breathed in the familiar smell of the art room. It helped calm me: Conté crayons, wet clay, spilled acrylics.

I had met Lily here last year, in Art I. For months, I had watched her out of the corner of my eye, curious that someone so quiet would dress in such a riot of color. Lily was a kaleidoscope that shifted every day into a new pinwheel pattern. She wore striped tights, red Chinese flats, blue nail polish. Her hair might be green. The next time I saw her, pink. She kept to herself, tucked into a corner of the classroom, her materials spread around her table like a protective wall.

We were working on our self-portrait projects when everything changed.

Mr. Linden had said we could choose our own medium. I peeked at Lily and wasn't surprised to see her with a set of watercolors. Me, I kept scrapping whatever I tried. I had crumpled yet another sheet of paper into a ball when I heard the sound of a fallen glass and something spilling. I glanced over and saw water flooding onto Lily's self-portrait. She kept her head down, shoulders stiff. A purple mascara tear ran down her cheek. Then she lifted her face and looked at me.

I smiled. It was a small smile of sympathy, and anything but spontaneous. It took several seconds for me to do it, which may not sound like a long time, but in my head I spent an eternity screwing up the courage to make my mouth muscles work.

Lily stood, crossed the room to my table, and said, "Etch-board."

I blinked. It took me a moment to realize she was offering advice—*good* advice. Before she had returned to her seat, I had snatched some etchboard and India ink from the supply closet. I started to work again on my self-portrait, and by the end of the period I had something that didn't look like a total waste of energy. And I had my first friend at Lakebrook High.

Now Lily and I shared a table in Art II. We sat quickly. I was eager for class to begin. I was eager for anything to distract me.

Mr. Linden liked to perch on a stool by a podium. He began speaking softly, and everyone settled into silence. "You will have one project in Art II." He stood and walked to the blackboard, a piece of chalk gripped in his stubby fingers. "Here it is."

He wrote: *Do Whatever You Want.*

God, I loved Art.

So I should have gotten busy right away, spinning ideas about my Whatever I Wanted. Instead, the image of that boy's face slipped into my mind. *He acted like he knew you,* Lily had said.

Was that possible?

There was so much I didn't know about my own past, so

much I didn't remember. And then there were the many towns I had blown through like a scraggly leaf. Maybe I had met him, somewhere, sometime.

I felt jittery again. Fizzy, crackly. I glanced down and saw a stylus clenched in my hand.

It had never occurred to me before that a stylus could be used as a weapon. But it could. Easily. It was long and thin—more or less a pen-sized needle with a wicked point.

This was the tool I had used last year for my self-portrait. Etchboard is heavy white, glossy paper. I had painted over the entire surface of one sheet with India ink. The wet ink gleamed—black as my eyes, black as my long hair. When it had dried, I scraped at it with my stylus, revealing the white paper below. Listening to the *scritch-scritch* of the tool, I watched the features of my face emerge. A ghost, rising out of the night.

Etchboard art works not by adding color but by taking it away. Lily, even though she didn't know me then, had chosen well.

I was abandoned outside a Chicago firehouse when I was five years old. I had no memory of whatever my life was like before that morning—only of the rosy dawn, the frigid cold, the weary face of the firefighter who found me, and how the social worker in charge of my case handed me a styrofoam cup of hot chocolate. I didn't even know my own name. "Darcy Jones" is what the social worker chose to scribble on my file. I guess "Jones" is proof of her total lack of imagination. As for "Darcy," well, she named me after her black cat.

Silly. I made myself drop the stylus to the table. *You're acting crazy,* I told myself. *Loony, loopy, mad as a hatter.* So a boy had stared at me. It didn't happen often, but it wasn't earth-shattering either. It was stupid to feel vulnerable. And if I had met him before and had forgotten, no big deal.

Still, how can you trust your memory when it has so many holes?

How can you interpret the behavior of others when you're a mystery to yourself?

3

As the morning went by, I didn't see him again. I began to breathe more easily, and my eyes stopped darting up and down the halls.

Bio was fine, though Lily and I gagged when we found out we'd have to dissect a fetal pig. Pre-Calc was worse, *much* worse, but Raphael and I weren't too worried because we had Jims's notes from last year.

I was feeling iffy about lunch. As Raphael and I pounced on one of the small round tables, I couldn't help doing a visual sweep of the cafeteria. He wasn't there. I let out a slow breath and unpacked my crinkly brown lunch bag.

Jims and Lily joined us, Lily looking slightly traumatized from her PE class last period. The four of us slipped into the usual dance of our conversation as if three months hadn't gone by. Lily and Jims had spent the summer at a Young Scientists camp in Wisconsin. Never mind that they liked science about as much as I'd like to lick the inside of a used petri dish. Mr. and Mrs. Lascewski (Jims's parents) and Mr. and Mrs. Chen (Lily's) worked at a Department of Energy lab, and were practically clones. They lived next door to each other. They carpooled. And they ignored what their children wanted with pretty much the same level of intensity.

As for Raphael and me, we'd been working fifty-hour weeks—him at his parents' gas station, me at the Jumping Bean Café. He sometimes came by for a black Americano, and twice we took the train to Chicago for the day. We had fun, but it wasn't like when we were all together. It wasn't the same.

"New Boy's a senior," Jims announced, jerking my attention right back to where it had been for most of the day.

"I didn't ask you to do recon on him," I said.

"You didn't have to." Jims waved a lazy hand. "I know you're curious. I'd be, too, if he'd locked eyes with *me* in front of the entire student body. He's a quiet kid. Dull as dishwater, if you ask me." Catching Lily's disbelieving look, Jims rolled his eyes. "Oh, all right. *Pretty* dishwater."

And that was when, just as I was about to laugh, the very subject of our conversation walked into the cafeteria. The laugh caught in my throat. My pulse stuttered.

He eased across the cafeteria smoothly, as if on ice, and never once glanced my way. Taylor Allen raised her slender hand in a flirty wave, and he was gone—sucked into a seat at the long, rectangular table owned, stamped, and certified by the elite of Lakebrook High.

My friends, of course, missed none of this.

Jims shook his head. "We are the Borg. Resistance is futile. Your life as it has been is over. From this time forward, you will service us."

"Jims," Raphael moaned. "No Star Trek references while we're eating."

"Listen, the Borg isn't simply an alien cyborg race that roams the universe in search of people to conquer. The Borg is really about human society."

Lily raised her eyes to the ceiling, begging it for patience.

"Seriously," Jims said. "The Borg is a commentary on the way humans form cliques, and how cliques, when they find someone they like, do their best to make him just like them. See? The popular crowd is the Borg."

"He was like them already," said Raphael. "That's why Taylor invited him to sit at their table. Birds of a feather."

"Catch avian flu together?" Jims supplied. "We can hope."

"Misanthropy suits you," I said, doing my best to keep up with the conversation—and, above all, act as if what had happened didn't matter one bit.

"Misanthropy. Is that, um, turning into a werewolf?"

"That's *lycanthropy*. Misanthropy is the hatred of people."

"I don't hate Taylor's followers. I just like avian flu more. Is it so wrong of me to want it to thrive and prosper? Viruses are living things, too."

Jims launched into a tirade about how we were virus-phobes, how he bet we used antibacterial soaps, too, and did we ever stop to think that flu shots meant that, every year, sad viruses had to watch their babies suffer? I was the worst, he said. "Darcy never gets sick. She's where the common cold goes to die."

I let his words wash over me. I smiled when it seemed appropriate. I tried to never once show on my face what I was thinking, which was this:

Typical. This was just typical of me. A normal girl would have been giddy at the thought that a beautiful stranger had noticed her. Me, I had felt instantly threatened. And now it seemed that I had made a huge drama over nothing.

I told myself I was relieved. But relief doesn't feel like a chunk of lead in your heart.

That's disappointment.

4

I was stepping through the door of AP English, weary and glad that this was the last class of the day.

Then I froze.

He sat in the exact middle of the class, tracing a long finger across his desk, lost in thought. He frowned, then raised his dark blond head. His eyes flashed to mine.

My nerves sparked and flared. I should have been prepared, I thought. I should have guessed he might be in a class that mixed juniors and seniors. If I had, maybe I wouldn't have been so easily snared by the intensity of his gaze.

Then his eyes skipped away. His expression cooled. Gone was the gunslinger from this morning. Gone was that curled smile. He looked, if anything, bored.

I edged toward the back of the room, sank into a seat, and barely listened as Ms. Goldberg asked us to introduce ourselves. I wasn't the only girl staring at him, and maybe they, too, had noticed that he wasn't quite so perfect up close. His nose had been broken.

Somehow, though, even that—that slight crookedness—was appealing.

And then it was his turn.

"My name is Conn McCrea." He spoke in a low voice, as if those three syllables were the most unimportant on earth. Despite the spelling, which I saw at a much later date, his last name was pronounced "McCray."

Taylor Allen, who was sitting right next to him, gave him a coy look. He didn't seem to notice. He slouched at his desk, but there was something a little calculated in his slumped shoulders and stretched out legs. I got the impression that he had riffled through his closet, found his Typical Teenager costume, and was trying it on.

And now we come down to it. My suspicion: Conn McCrea wasn't exactly normal.

My reasons? Let's just say it takes one to know one.

Ms. Goldberg leaned against the blackboard, ignoring the chalk that dusted her clothes, and said, "Our first text will be 'The Love Song of J. Alfred Prufrock,' by T. S. Eliot."

"Great. A *love* poem," muttered Jason Sloane. He added in a falsetto, "Smooooochics!"

The class tittered.

"Do you have a problem with that, Mr. Sloane?"

"Nope. I like smooches."

"Then you may be disappointed to know that there are none in this poem. You might wonder, in fact, if there is any love at all. The main character, J. Alfred, can't decide if he should tell a woman how he feels about her, but he's just as concerned about whether he belongs to a world of dirty one-night hotels or to the chic society of tea parties." Ms. Goldberg opened a slim book and began to read:

> *"Let us go then, you and I,*
> *When the evening is spread out against the sky . . ."*

I wish I could say I was instantly wowed by "The Love Song." But the truth is that I was inventing a poem of my own:

> *I will not think of Conn McCrea.*
> *I will not, cannot, in any way.*

Gradually, though, "The Love Song" crept under my skin. I listened as J. Alfred Prufrock wandered down deserted streets. I didn't forget about Conn, but I forgot to forget about him, and let myself study him as Ms. Goldberg's voice rose and fell.

I was in the back. He couldn't see me.

Why, then, would I have bet anything that he could *feel* me, could sense my stare on the nape of his neck like I had his in those minutes before the first bell?

"So, what do you think of him?" Ms. Goldberg closed the book. "What kind of man is J. Alfred?"

"He really likes tea," someone offered.

"He likes Michelangelo? Or hates Michelangelo? I don't know."

"He repeats himself a lot."

"Why doesn't he quit moaning? J. needs to man up."

"He cares about the way he dresses."

"He's a *loser*."

When Ms. Goldberg came to Conn, he hesitated. Finally, he said, "He's uncertain."

I couldn't help puzzling over Conn's answer as if it were a clue to his character and he was a poem that needed to be interpreted. Uncertain? About what?

"Ms. Jones?"

Startled, I glanced at Ms. Goldberg. The awkward silence told me she had been calling my name for some time. I might have blurted out something random, but then I noticed that Conn had tilted his head slightly. Like a listening hawk.

I thought of J. Alfred walking on the beach with the bottoms of his trousers rolled, and how these lines of the poem weren't the last, but might as well have been:

I have heard the mermaids singing, each to each.
I do not think that they will sing to me.

"He's lonely," I said. "And he's given up."

Conn didn't turn around. He didn't look at me.

Taylor, however, did.

Freak, she mouthed.

Who would have guessed it? As things turned out, Taylor was absolutely right.

5

The last bell rang. Jason slapped Conn on the shoulder, saying, "C'mon," and the two of them strode out the door with Taylor leading the way.

I walked home. Where there weren't trees or raised-ranch homes, I could see far and wide around me. The land here is as flat as the palm of my hand. Illinois is tornado country.

I always stayed outside in a tornado long after anyone sensible had gone down into a basement. I loved to watch the sky go green and brown and dangerous. The wind thrashed the trees, and sometimes, if I was lucky, I'd spot the cyclone twisting in the sky. Afterward, I'd walk around and survey the damage: willow branches lying in whips across the sidewalk, and gutters rushing with leaves and the stringy bodies of drowned worms.

The arrival of Conn McCrea at Lakebrook High made me think of a tornado—of the aftermath, and how the world looked as if it had been spun in a blender. Most of all, it reminded me of the very start of a storm. Of the alluring risk, the winds muscling against me as I waited to see if that cyclone would touch down, and where, and when.

WHEN I GOT HOME, I unlaced my boots and lined them up by the door.

Marsha's place was your typical ranch home. The front door opened up into a living room that connected to the kitchen, with nothing to separate the two spaces except a brassy metal strip on the floor that marked the border between the carpet and the linoleum.

The house was cozy. And cutesy. An oil portrait of a raccoon hung over the television. There was a wall rack of forty-nine silver spoons with a different state bird painted onto each handle. Marsha had told me with great satisfaction that she had bought only one: the spoon with the Illinois cardinal. "The rest are gifts from friends," she explained. "Once I get the willow ptarmigan from Alaska, my collection will be complete."

Her pride and joy was the fish tank, which stood by the hallway leading to the two bedrooms. It had a bed of blue rocks, a treasure chest that burbled open every few minutes, and a crew of angelfish. Marsha called them each by name, though if she was too busy for individual hellos she might simply wave and say, "Good morning, my angels."

I fed the angelfish, watching them dart after rust-colored food flakes. Then I launched myself onto the leatherette sofa and called Jims.

"Hey, sister." He was chewing on something. "What'cha building?"

"A garden that grows ninja warriors." I swung my legs over the armrest. "You?"

"A rocket ship fueled by chocolate sauce. No! A rocket ship that *delivers* chocolate sauce."

For endless conversation about nothing at all, Jims was the best.

He began pestering me to see a band called the Flippin Idjits play in the city that weekend.

"Not sure." I wagged my feet. "They sound a little too dance-y to me."

"Nuh-unh. They sound like men with lean hips who know how to shake 'em."

For pure distraction, Jims was the best.

He added, "Just like Conn McCrea."

Or not.

"He's in my American History class," Jims said. "Right after lunch. The boy knows jack about the presidents. He said JFK died of a brain tumor!"

I pushed myself off the couch and strode into the kitchen. "I don't care."

"You don't care because you prefer your men sweet and empty, like one of those hollow gumballs you can buy for twenty-five cents from a dispenser in the grocery store."

"No." I paced the linoleum floor and lied through my teeth. "I don't care because I'm thinking about my art project, and want your advice."

"Yeah?" I could almost hear him rubbing his palms. "Sure thing, young grasshopper. You want wisdom, you've come to the right place. Jims to the rescue. So, what're you planning?"

"Um . . ." Since up to that moment I'd been planning a big, fat Nothing, I scrambled for a response. I reached past the butcher block of knives resting on the counter, opened a cabinet, and rummaged through Marsha's baking supplies. I looked at a green bottle. "Maybe something with vegetable dye?"

"Ah, avant-garde. I like it, I like it."

I reached for a tea canister. "Or tea leaves?"

"I sense a food theme. I am an expert on that topic!"

I opened the canister. Inside was a thick roll of money.

"Jims. I've got to go."

"But we're just getting started—"

I hung up.

The label on the tin was for Lapsang souchong tea, which tastes like charred wood. Even the smell of it made me want to throw up. And Marsha knew it.

What she didn't know was why. I was terrified of fire. I always had been, though I did my best to hide it. It was embarrassing, because it wasn't only fire that set me on edge. It was everything that had anything to do with fire. Cigarettes. Smoke. Even stupid smoky-tasting tea.

I unwrapped the rubber band around the money. Most of it

was small bills, but there was a lot of it. Hundreds of dollars. Maybe even a thousand.

What was Marsha saving for? And why was she hiding it from me?

I fanned it out and couldn't help wondering if she'd miss a twenty. Then I quickly tapped the cash against the countertop like a deck of shuffled cards.

She was hiding it from me because it was none of my business. I was just her foster kid.

Who didn't need to give her a reason to kick me out.

I put the money back into the tin, clamped the lid shut, and shoved it into the cabinet—not a moment too soon. Marsha's car pulled into the driveway. She walked into the house, her hands rustling with plastic bags, and let the door bang shut behind her. "Hi, Darcy. Did you have a good day?"

Had I? Even I didn't know the answer to that question. "It was okay."

"Well, *I* am dog-tired." Marsha plopped down on the couch and propped her feet on the coffee table. She was still wearing her name tag from the bargain clothing store where she worked as an assistant manager. "I think we both deserve a treat." She dug through one of the bags and pulled out a pack of multicolored chocolate-covered marshmallows. She ripped it open and offered it.

"No, thanks," I said.

"Go on, have a pink one. I love the pink ones."

"It's just dye. They all taste the same."

"I know. But the pink cheers me up." She wriggled her fingers above the marshmallows and picked out her favorite. "Are you working at the Jumping Bean tonight?"

"Yes." I sighed.

"Keep interested in your career," she said. "However humble."

Marsha enjoyed quoting from a plaque that hung above the toilet in her bathroom. It was inscribed with a letter called "Desiderata," which means "Desired Things." It's full of impossible advice, such as the idea that you could get along with everybody without giving up pieces of yourself, and that even a minimum wage job should be thought of as a worthy "career."

"Here." She handed me a plastic bag. "This is for you."

Inside was something soft: a ruby cardigan. "Marsha, you didn't have to—"

"I sure did. You look like you're going to a funeral. I want to see you wearing something other than black, black, and black. Go ahead, put it on. It's part cashmere."

Even though the sun was going down, it was still shaping up to be a steamy evening. "But—"

"No buts. It was on sale, plus I got my employee's discount. And that itty-bitty thing isn't going to fit *me*."

I touched the red sweater. It had been a long time since I'd received a gift. "Thank you."

"You'll look pretty in it," she said.

Would I? Could a red sweater change so much?

It was as if she'd read my mind. "You're the artist, Darcy. Don't you think a little color packs some punch?"

I smiled, not only because it would please her, but also because I wanted to. Then I took a pink marshmallow, pulled on the cardigan, and left for work.

At the coffeehouse, I focused on cappuccinos, lattes, and double-shot espressos. My hands steamed milk and ground beans. I paused only for enough time to peel off the red cardigan. It was too hot. More than that—wearing the sweater felt too hopeful. Like I wanted to look pretty for someone, and that someone wasn't Marsha.

Inside, I recited my poem and matched its beat to the rhythm of my work:

I will not think of Conn McCrea.

Easier said than done.

When I locked up the café, I looked out at the dark parking lot, reminding myself that Conn was already liked. Already adored. And I was a misfit.

That's right, a voice whispered inside. *You don't fit in. You don't belong in this world.*

I frowned. That was a weird thought. I didn't belong in *this* world?

It wasn't like there was any other one.

6

It took me a couple of weeks to wear the sweater to school. I kept blaming the heat for this, but then one day, in that schizo way Chicagoland weather has, it was suddenly autumn. The air was apple-crisp, and I had run out of excuses.

Lily's jaw dropped when she saw me wearing the cardigan. She whirled us into the girls' bathroom, demanded I put on her lipstick, and swept the loose hair off my face. She produced a handful of bobby pins as if by magic.

"Lily, what are you doing?"

"Finishing what you started." Her eyes met mine in the mirror. "This is the first time you look as if you're not trying to disappear." She swiftly did something complicated with my hair. "There. Now everyone can see what a lovely, slender throat you have."

I tightened my mouth. "They can see *this*." I pointed to the scar at the base of my neck, where the skin sloped toward my shoulder. It was an old, white slash.

Lily lost her imperious air. "You still don't remember how you got that?"

I looked at her.

"Sorry," she said. "I shouldn't have asked."

I shrugged. It wasn't her fault I was a messed-up amnesiac.

"Well, what're you going to do, hide it forever?" She gave me a gentle push out the bathroom door. "Go."

Luckily, the boys made little comment on my new and supposedly improved appearance. Jims just said "Ooh la la" when he passed me in the hall, and Raphael gave me an incredulous stare in Pre-Calc. I tried not to take offense, since Raphael was fizzing with anxiety and barely able to pass for a normally functioning human being. Auditions for the fall play were that afternoon.

In English class, I did something different. That moment of walking through the door was always agonizing, always the best and worst part of my day. So over the past week, I had developed a ritual. It was a simple one: eyes down, feet steady. Walk.

And don't look at him.

But that day, I did.

The effect was instantaneous. Conn's eyes were on me. His mask of boredom slipped away, and it was only then that I knew that it *was* a mask, that it had to be, it had to be fake, because what I saw underneath was too real. His face was fierce, filled with something hot and strange.

And resentful.

I slunk to my seat. I had to get to English earlier, I thought shakily. He always beat me there. He always sat in the middle, so that if I sat anywhere else than in the back I'd feel like a target in his line of sight. Even sitting in the back wasn't the perfect solution, because I had to push myself past him. Every day.

I ignored most of the lesson, at least until Ms. Goldberg said, "'I am no Prince Hamlet.'" She was reading from her book. "What does J. Alfred mean? Why does he say he's 'an attendant lord, one that will do / To swell a progress, start a scene or two'?"

I had a pretty good guess, but I sure wasn't going to raise my hand. I already felt enough like a fool.

"Well?" Ms. Goldberg waited, and the entire class hardened into stubborn silence.

Deep down, she must have been a very perverse person, because she grinned. "Isn't that appropriate," she drawled, "since J. Alfred spends the entire poem debating whether to profess his love, and chooses silence. Here is one question you *will* answer, or fail my class." She turned to the board and wrote:

Do I dare
Disturb the universe?

"This is J. Alfred's question," she said, "and it is yours. Your assignment is to decide what it means. I will give you a month to prepare a presentation of your findings to the class. You may work alone or with a partner."

Well, that was fair. At least she wasn't going to force me to find someone to pair up with. I listened to the squeal of desks dragged across the floor. To loud voices bouncing off white concrete walls as people sought and found partners. I opened my sketch pad and kept my head down, doodling a cityscape, though it was no city I had ever seen. The skyscrapers were slender and curved. They looked like a wind could knock them down.

"Darcy?"

That voice. Quiet. Deep. I knew before I lifted my eyes who owned it, but I couldn't believe he was speaking to me.

"Will you be my partner?" asked Conn McCrea.

There was only one possible answer. "Yes." I shut my sketchbook, but not before his gaze fell on my drawing. I could have sworn I saw a flash of recognition in his eyes. Then it was gone, and I doubted what I had seen, for how could he know a city I had invented only moments before?

Conn pulled up an abandoned chair and sat down next to me. He was tall, yes, but broader than I'd thought, not as lean as he'd seemed from afar. He looked like he trained for something.

It troubled me more than it should have. I instinctively touched the scar on my neck. His gaze flickered to it, and lingered.

Then his eyes met mine. They were a fitful color, the kind that changes according to mood or the light. Gray, blue, green. Like pieces of glass washed up on the shores of Lake Michigan, polished by waves almost as big as the sea's. My pulse sped along the scar beneath my fingertips.

"Did you know the answer to Ms. Goldberg's question?" he asked. "About Prince Hamlet?"

I went for nonchalance. "I suppose there could be several theories. What's yours?"

He gave me an inviting smile. "I'd like to hear what you have to say."

I played with my pencil. "J. Alfred's decided to be unimportant. No one's going to notice him."

"Yes," said Conn. "He is very different from you."

The pencil spun out of my fingers and clattered to the floor. Conn picked it up and set it neatly on my desk. His words had sounded like a compliment. But his voice hadn't.

The bell rang, and turned off any hint of friendliness in him. Now he looked at me clinically, as if he were wearing night-vision glasses and I had stopped being a person and had become just an interesting pattern of heat.

"I'll see you tomorrow," he said shortly, and even though that was a promise of some kind, I felt dismissed.

He stood. I stayed in my seat, watching him go, and pulled the cardigan's cuffs over my fingers. A little bit of color, and Conn had asked me to be his partner.

Could things really be so simple?

7

The next day, we learned that Raphael got the part of Hamlet. Taylor Allen was cast as his mother, Queen Gertrude, which led to a lot of "your mama" jokes from Jims.

At lunch, Raphael seesawed between excitement about the play's fencing scenes and misery about the cafeteria food. Finally, he dropped his taco pizza to his plate. "Why am I even eating this? It tastes nasty."

"Just like your mama," said Jims.

We cracked up.

"Why is it funny that James insulted Raphael's mother?"

We blinked, startled that A) someone was using Jims's real name, and B) that someone was Conn. He stood expectantly, a lunch tray balanced on one hand.

"I doubt you'd understand," Raphael told him.

A smug smile tugged at the corner of Conn's mouth. "I know more than you think."

I became acutely aware that this—this small lunch table, my three friends—was *my* territory. Conn had already invaded my mind. I felt nervous about having him so close to the rest of my life, too. And yet—

"May I sit with you?" he asked.

And yet, I wanted him close. Close enough to touch.

The thing about wanting, though, is that it had never gotten me very far.

"Why are you interested in slumming it, Conn?" I tore shreds off my lunch bag, examining them as if they were the Dead Sea Scrolls and I was a very brainy scholar who had no time for gorgeous boys. "Haven't you figured out that people like us will depreciate your social value?"

Lily gave me an odd look, the kind you might give to someone who was about to eat her winning lottery ticket after slathering it in chili sauce. "Sit down, Conn," she said. "We won't bite. Not even Darcy."

Jims warned, "But we might pelt you with questions."

Conn sat and leaned back in his chair, arms crossed. Amusement colored his expression, but also a quiet arrogance he didn't quite bother to hide. No question, he seemed to believe, could rattle *him*. "Pelt away."

Jims pretended to straighten an invisible tie. "You see, we know so little about you, and we'd like to make certain you're a decent sort of fellow. What brings you to our humble table?"

"Darcy's my partner for a class project," Conn said. Three pairs of curious eyes turned toward me. "I hoped that she'd be free to meet me after school today to work on it."

"So ask her," said Raphael, knowing full well the answer.

Conn looked at me, and for a moment I was in danger of drowning in his lake-colored eyes. But I knew my priorities. "I can't."

"Really?"

Conn's tone was mild, yet I sensed that beneath it lay something frustrated. And *pushy*, which set some steel into my spine. "Yes, really," I told him.

He narrowed his eyes. "Why not?"

Somehow, Conn's questions were evolving into an interrogation. I didn't like it. Judging by the looks on my friends' faces, *they* didn't like it either. "Because I'm busy."

"With what?" He let his irritation show. "I doubt your social calendar is completely full."

The sting of insult wasn't as strong as the sense of my friends silently closing ranks. Lily's expression didn't change, but Raphael glowered, and all the humor bled out of Jims. "Darcy," he said, "why don't you show your guest to the door?"

"No need." Conn stood, and I wished that I had, too, because the way his gaze swept down on me from above was unsettling.

As Conn walked away, Jims said, "You sure know how to pick 'em, Darcy."

"He chose her," said Lily.

* * *

LATER, AFTER THE BELL announced the end of English class, Conn approached.

He wasn't *that* attractive, I told myself.

He cocked his head, and his smile was charming. Brilliant. A sweet knife that sank into my heart and slashed my lie to pieces.

"Lunch didn't go the way I'd planned," he said. "I was too nosy, wasn't I? And rude."

I slid books into my battered backpack. "A little."

"Sorry." His brow rumpled into a rueful, slightly helpless look. "I'm worried about my grade, and want to get a jump-start on our project. College applications are coming up."

I understood. I had hopes of going to art school, and no way to pay for it beyond my crap job and, maybe, a merit scholarship.

"I liked your answer the other day, about J. Alfred's loneliness," he continued. "I think you really understand the poem, and I could use your help. Can we meet soon?"

The mystical powers of the red sweater were, it seemed, nothing more than Conn's very ordinary grade grubbing. I struggled against a sudden unhappiness and told myself that at least I was on familiar ground. "I'm free tomorrow after school."

"Perfect." He beamed.

Something about Conn made me feel in between every-thing—in between wariness and yearning, self-preservation and attraction—which gave me an idea. "We'll need a car," I said.

"I can arrange something."

IF I WERE NORMAL, I would have fled school the instant classes were over, along with everyone else. But I slipped into the art room. Mr. Linden didn't mind if I stuck around while he packed away the supplies.

I opened my sketchbook and began to draw.

I chose a thick-leaded pencil, so the lines were heavy, almost fuzzy. I sketched like someone obsessed, which was sort of absurd, since what I was drawing shouldn't have stirred so much feeling. It was just a building. And yet . . . creepy. Or maybe it wasn't the building itself that was creepy, with its twenty-seven steps and neo-Gothic touches. Maybe it was the way I recognized it, yet had no idea what it was.

I found myself gripping the pencil very tightly. I set it aside and reached into my case for a thinner one.

There should be an inscription on the building, I thought. I set the pencil to paper and felt a sensation inside, like something unbuttoning. Opening. I couldn't name it. But it stole my breath.

Then my hand flickered. For one insane second, it seemed like I could see *through* it. I blinked, and breathed, and there were my fingers. Solid. Clutching the pencil so hard that it snapped.

Mr. Linden stepped out of the storage closet. He studied my face. "Darcy? Is something the matter?"

"No." The broken pencil halves chopsticked in my hand. "Or . . . I don't know. I guess I feel a little faint. Or something." I forced a smile. "I've been staring at my sketchbook too long. My eyes are playing tricks on me."

"That happens sometimes," he said kindly. "Take a break."

I nodded, but couldn't tear my gaze away from the drawing. I didn't know anymore what name I'd been about to give the building. But now I could name that feeling growing inside me.

Fear.

I shut the book.

I GLANCED AT JIMS'S HOUSE before knocking on Lily's door, but it was almost four o'clock, the hour of his online role-playing game, and we were under strict orders not to interrupt.

Lily's mom pointed to the basement, where I found Lily in front of a stretched canvas, gobbing on oil paint. She flipped the brush in her hand, sliced the wooden end across the paint, and looked really pissed off.

"What's that?" I nodded at the painting.

"A waste of an entire tube of Prussian Blue." She turned to the pool table, reached for a wooden triangle, and began to rack the pool balls. "Whatever You Want is harder than you'd think. What have you been working on?"

I hesitated. "Sketches. Of a city."

"And you seem *so* thrilled about it. Problems?"

The first sketch had been the skyline I'd drawn the day Conn had asked me to be his partner, and the last was the government building today. But there had been plenty in between, all city scenes. My notebook was filling up. I looked at Lily, searching for a way to explain that the images I'd drawn recently looked familiar, yet I couldn't identify them.

Except one. "I drew the Water Tower," I told her. "You know, the old pumping station in Chicago that survived the Great Fire? My Water Tower looks like the real Water Tower. But everything around it is different. There's no university campus. Instead, the tower's surrounded by a park. When I sketched, it didn't feel like I was making stuff up, but drawing from memory, and not a memory from last summer. A much older one." I shook my head in frustration. "The cityscapes are strange. When I look at them, I'm sure they're some imaginary city I've dreamed up. Then I blink, and I'm convinced I've drawn parts of Chicago. Which is impossible. None of the images completely matches up with anything I've seen." I decided not to mention the knowing expression on Conn's face when he'd seen my first drawing, or the way my hand had seemed to . . . vanish. To dart in and out of existence. Like lamplight from a dying bulb, going on and off and then on again.

Saying all that would make everything seem even weirder than it already was.

"Raphael could probably make sense of the drawings," said Lily. "He's such a Chicago history buff. Maybe you should show him your sketchbook."

"Maybe," I said, meaning "no."

"Would you like me to look at them?"

The truth was, the sketches felt too personal, too unnerving to share with anybody. When Conn had glanced at my open notebook, I'd felt defenseless. Small.

"It's okay." Lily quickly interpreted my silence. "You don't have to show me."

"It's just . . . I don't think they're good enough to be Whatever I Want."

"Speaking about what we want . . ." Mischief crept into Lily's voice. "Are you and your class partner making any, hmm, progress?"

"No." I told her what Conn had said after English. "It's all about his grade."

Lily lifted the rack, leaving a perfect triangle of pool balls. She offered me a cue. "Want to break?"

I shook my head. "Go ahead."

She lined up the white cue ball. "I know what I saw in his eyes, that first day of school."

I couldn't help myself. "Really? What?"

The white ball punched into the triangle, shattering it. Colored spheres spun away and slammed into each other like this was the Big Bang, and the start of the universe.

"Fascination."

8

Conn had a motorcycle. Of course.

It was sleek and gray and, as far as these things go, quiet. Not to mention dangerous. I stared at Conn, trying to remember what, exactly, I'd done to earn the dubious honor of riding with him on his rumbling, wheeled death contraption.

"Don't pretend you're nervous," he said.

"Fine. I'll be genuinely nervous."

"I don't believe you."

"Cross my heart and hope not to die," I said, though a little proud that, somewhere in the course of our short acquaintance, I had convinced him that I was a toughie.

"You wanted transportation," he said. "This is what I've got."

I took a deep breath and held out my hand. "Helmet?"

He gave me a look of surprise mingled with reproach. Apparently, he had decided my fear was a total charade, and now I was taking it too far. "You don't need a helmet."

"Like hell I don't."

"Illinois state law doesn't require that drivers or passengers of motorcycles wear helmets."

"Yeah, but the law of common sense does."

He seemed unnecessarily confused for someone suggesting I risk splitting my head open like a ripe melon. "Darcy, you won't get hurt. And I won't let us crash."

Well, I wasn't the first girl to let a boy talk her into doing something stupid.

The engine continued its low growl as Conn instructed, "Wait until I'm ready, then hop on using the pegs above the rear wheel as if they're stirrups and this is a horse."

I climbed up behind him, touching his shoulder for balance. It went rigid under my palm.

I quickly let go, my fingertips slipping from the smooth brown leather of his jacket. I shifted on the seat and decided to focus on not falling off.

He cleared his throat. "As we ride, keep your feet on the pegs."

And my hands? If this were a Spanish soap opera, for sure I'd be expected to wrap my arms around this muchacho's warm waist. Conn, however, was obviously not thinking along *¡Ay, caliente!* lines. "There are bars for your hands on either side, just behind you."

I tried not to feel like I had been reprimanded. And for what? Touching his shoulder? That had been innocent enough.

I gritted my teeth. I gripped the bars, and we were off.

My nervousness disintegrated into exhilaration. Trees blurred by in a smear of autumnal gold. As I shouted directions in Conn's ear, we hit the highway, and he opened up the throttle.

The wind buffeted me, strong and cold. The only shelter from it was Conn—whom I wasn't supposed to touch, whose body radiated heat. I tried not to want to press myself against his back. My fingers tightened around the freezing bars.

When we finally slowed and Conn parked at the commuter train station, my skin vibrated from the motorcycle's engine. I jumped off. If one small part of the ride had been difficult, if a sliver of me felt the pain of impossible things, the rest of it had been thrilling. "That was fast!" I said.

"Not really." Conn killed the engine and dismounted.

I laughed. The sound began as self-mocking for having been afraid of a motorcycle, for thinking something was fast when it was slow, but then my laugh changed of its own free will. It grew heady, throaty . . . happy. It startled me.

It startled him. He looked at me, really looked at me, and caught his breath.

"What?" My pleasure shrank. "What's wrong?"

He shook his head. "Nothing."

I touched my chilled cheeks, sure that there must be the remains of a dead bug somewhere, then reached for my ponytail. The tie had vanished, leaving a snarled disaster in its wake. "Whoa. Banshee hair. I bet I look like a member of an eighties post-punk boy band."

"Post-what?"

Jims was right: Conn was oddly clueless about obvious things. I was about to lecture him on the revolutionary significance of punk, but he asked, "What are we doing here? You don't want to take the train to Chicago, do you? I can drive us to the city."

"This is our destination. Actually, *there* is." I pointed at the tracks. "Follow me."

I led the way down the rails, over the rubbly white rocks. "Usually the tracks are kept clean close to the stations, but in between stops on the line you can find a lot of useful junk."

He raised one skeptical brow. "Useful."

I picked up a tube of rusted metal. "Like this."

"I don't see how that's useful for our class assignment."

"That's because you lack vision."

"I lack many things." He kicked at the rocks. "But not my sanity."

I unzipped my backpack, tucked the tube inside, and tried to explain. "J. Alfred spends the entire poem wandering around, talking about cheap hotels and chimney soot. He thinks about dirt. Trashy stuff." I crouched to uncover a pile of springs.

He looked down at me with an expression of growing wonder, so I continued. "Also, J. never actually *goes* anywhere. He's always between places, and takes forever to make up his mind. So I thought of this"—I swept my hand at the tracks— "because it's in between stops and littered with trash. I don't know where this junk comes from. I guess it falls off the trains, which doesn't really boost my confidence in the safety of Chicagoland commuter rails. But why not build a sculpture about the poem from what we collect here? The junk from an in-between place?"

He knelt next to me, right on the rocks. "You noticed that much. About a *poem*."

"Do you still think I'm crazy? If not, do you know how to solder?"

He laughed a short laugh that was more like the sound you make when you get punched in the gut. "You're not exactly what I expected."

Hanging out with Taylor's crowd no doubt gave him total access to the Lakebrook High rumor mill. "What did you expect?"

He toyed with a rusted spring. "I heard you were a bit shy . . ."

I suspected he was politely editing the information he had received.

". . . and socially dysfunctional."

Or maybe not.

"I also heard"—he dropped the spring—"that you were cursed."

That was new. And it stung. I snatched up the spring and fought the prickle in my eyes. "Be careful. This spring might not look like much, but it's good material." Jamming it into my backpack, I stood and stalked away from him, down the tracks.

He caught up with me, offering a shiny railroad spike. "What about this?" He spoke so humbly that I paused and forced myself to look at him.

"Cursed?" I tried to keep my voice light. "Cursed, like how? Like someone's using a voodoo doll of me as a pincushion?"

But I had guessed what he had meant, and I was right.

"People say that you've lived in as many foster homes as years of your life. They say that no one wants to keep you."

"People are wrong," I said, and a tear spilled over.

Astonishment flashed across Conn's face, then a kind of hesitancy crept in, one that reminded me of someone who has broken something and has no idea what to do with the pieces. "Darcy . . . I didn't mean to make you cry." He lifted a hand. He stretched it out slowly, as if I might bite him. He touched my sleeve. "I'm sorry. Truly."

I swiped at my wet eyes. I felt a surge of frustration—resentment, even—that just a few words from him had stripped me bare. I didn't even really know Conn, yet still he made my most intense emotions simmer to the surface.

"People are wrong," I began again. "I'm sixteen, and I've lived in *nine* foster homes. Plus two years in a group home when the DCFS couldn't place me."

"Why so many?"

"There was always a reason. An excuse the foster parents gave for not keeping me. I got kicked out of my first home for poking a wire hanger into an electrical outlet. My foster mom caught me, shrieked, and called the DCFS to come cart me away, because I was clearly suicidal and no one had told her that I was a child with 'special needs.'"

"Were you? Suicidal?"

"I was *five*."

"Still."

"No, I wasn't trying to off myself. I was curious. Little kids spend half their waking hours being warned not to do things. Don't run with scissors. Don't lick a flagpole in winter. Don't stick anything into electrical outlets. Those three little holes looked so mysterious. I had to know if they were as dangerous as everyone said."

"What happened?" A smile curled the corner of Conn's mouth, indicating he'd already guessed the answer—which wasn't exactly *hard*, given that I was standing right there in front of him, and not buried in an early grave with the tombstone *Here lies Darcy Jones, electrocuted orphan*.

"Nothing happened," I said. "Just a jolt. My foster mom freaked out over nothing."

"It *does* seem like an insufficient reason to send you back to the DCFS."

"It was a better reason than others. My second set of foster parents canceled my stay with them because I brought a bat inside the house."

It seemed like every word I spoke surprised Conn more. "Why did you do that?"

"It was dying. I found it on the ground outside, struggling to lift its wings. I just wanted to give it some water, but my foster parents thought that what I really wanted was to give their kids rabies. They declared me a danger to their children."

He paused. "It sounds to me more like there's something wrong with your ex–foster parents."

"All nine sets? No. They were nice people. Maybe a little hysterical where bats and electrical outlets were concerned, but, with one exception, they tried to be nice to me."

His gaze sharpened. "One exception?"

I wished I hadn't said that. But now Conn was standing in front of me, feet planted on the tracks in a way that made clear he wasn't going to let the matter lie. "One foster father," I said. "When I was twelve."

"What did he do?"

I shrugged. "What does it matter?"

Conn's eyes were hard. "Tell me."

"He didn't do anything. I punched him in the face first. Broke his jaw in three places."

"Right. Of course he didn't." The tension drained from Conn's body. "Of course you did."

Believe me, I was glad, too, that that story had a happy ending. But it got even harder for the DCFS to place me once I had 'Violent' and 'Behavior Disorder' stamped on my record. Hence the two years spent in the Ingleside Home for Girls.

I probably should have thought a little more carefully about why a twelve-year-old girl had been able to put a grown man in the hospital, but that would have meant mulling over the whole incident, and it's hard to think too much about things that hurt. So I didn't.

Still, a needle of unease slid into me. For a moment I sensed the suspicion that must have touched every single one of my ex–foster parents.

"Have you ever read Sherlock Holmes?" I asked Conn.

"Yes . . . although I'm having some difficulty figuring out what he has to do with the topic at hand."

"He once said that, when solving a mystery, you have to consider all the possibilities and eliminate them one by one. Whatever's left, no matter how strange it seems, must be your answer. What makes more sense? That *all* eighteen adults vetted and interviewed and trained by the DCFS to be foster parents were awful people, or that there is something wrong with me? Something deep inside. Something they didn't notice right away, but eventually couldn't live with."

Conn didn't reply.

"So maybe I *am* cursed," I said. "It's the most straightforward answer."

He turned away. The sun had lowered on the horizon, pouring amber light over his skin, turning it the color of honey. In a wild, dizzying flash, I wondered if he tasted like that, too.

Softly, he said, "I'm beginning to think that nothing is straightforward."

9

It's rare when you see your life is changing. Usually it simply changes and you're left blinking at the aftermath, wondering how you got there. I knew, though, that Conn's arrival had already changed me. For years I had ignored my own mystery. Now ignoring it was a luxury I couldn't afford, because even though I *knew* I had never seen Conn before the first day of class, he did remind me of something, like my drawings reminded me of something. With every day, I seemed to get closer to it. Strange things were happening.

One night, after I'd kicked the espresso junkies out of the café and cleaned up the wet swizzle sticks and torn sugar packets, my eyes snapped up and stared out the glass door even before my heart had a chance to constrict with fear. I couldn't see anything. The café was bright, and it was black outside. But I was certain that a face had been peering in at me.

I turned off the café lights and looked out into the parking lot. No one was there.

I was losing my mind. First I thought I saw my fingers disappear, and now this? I shook my head. There was no reason to do anything different from what I always did, which was walk home along a well-lit road. Lakebrook was safe.

I locked up. The empty parking lot was shadowy, and a fallen leaf scratched across the concrete. I curled the keys between my fingers so that they stuck out past my knuckles like short knives.

A young man curved around the corner of the café. He had a bulky body. Dark hair. A forgettable face—forgettable, except for the leer that split his mouth. "Hi," he said. "Can you help me?"

"Don't think so." My fear was instant, jagged. I turned back toward the door.

He squeezed between it and me. "Yes, you can," he said, and grabbed me.

I punched him in the stomach with my fist full of keys. He doubled up, groaning. I shoved myself back, ready to sprint away, but his hand lashed out and seized my wrist. "You're still here!" He laughed breathlessly. "Playful little thing."

Anger threaded through my panic, and I swung my free arm back to strike. That only made him smile more brightly.

"Hey!" someone shouted. It was Conn, striding across the parking lot.

My fear melted. I teetered on my feet, and it took me a second to realize it was because my attacker had let me go. "Why not now?" he said to Conn.

"Back off," Conn told him. He stood next to me, shoulder to shoulder. "Back away."

"Why should I?" the guy snapped. "You're so *slow*."

"You heard what I said. Get out of here."

He shot a surly look between the two of us. "Yes, sir," he snarled at Conn, and stalked off into the darkness.

I let out a shuddering breath. "What a psycho."

"Yeah." Conn frowned into the distance, even though the other man had already disappeared.

"What was he talking about, 'Why not now?' Did you understand that?"

"No." Conn seemed rattled, even more than me. "Let's get out of here."

"Why did he call you *slow*?"

"I don't know. I guess . . . I guess he meant that, if it came to a fight between him and me, he didn't think much of me."

I looked at Conn. "That doesn't make a whole lot of sense."

He gave me the ghost of a smile. "Well, then: a psycho. As you said."

"When I hit him, he *laughed*. He said, 'You're still here.' Like I'd be anywhere else. And, actually . . . what are *you* doing here?"

He ran a hand through his short hair. "I came for some coffee." He looked at the dark café. "Too late, it seems."

I shook my head. "In the nick of time is more like it."

"To tell the truth . . . I came to see you."

"Oh," I murmured. "Thanks. For helping me."

"Don't." The word was curt. Then, in an even voice, he said, "There's no reason to thank me. I didn't do anything. Anyway, it looked like you were holding your own."

Now that the adrenaline was draining away, I realized that I had pulled that punch to the gut. I could have hit a lot harder. I don't know what worried me more—the fact that I could have done more damage, or that I hadn't.

"He didn't hurt you, did he?" Conn said. "You're okay?"

"Yeah. Just wobbly on the inside."

At that, his edginess faded. "Of course you are. Let me give you a ride home."

We walked to the far corner of the parking lot, to his motor-cycle. He got on first, started the engine, and backed it up with his feet, balancing the loud machine. He nodded, and I climbed on, reaching for the bars behind the seat, a little lower than my hips.

"You trust me, don't you," Conn said, and I couldn't tell whether that was a statement or a question.

"Sure," I said, startled. "You just did this impressive knight in shining armor thing. And we—we're . . . friends, right?"

"Yes." His voice was husky. He reached back for my hand and drew it around his waist. "Ready?"

I felt the hard, warm plane of his abdomen against my arm. "Um."

He drove.

I didn't sink against him. I didn't press my cheek against

his leathered back. I held my breath and wished the ride would last.

When he pulled up in front of Marsha's, I said, "I suppose you came by the café to talk about the project."

"Yes, but . . ." He unzipped his jacket, rummaged inside an inner pocket, and pulled out a scrap of paper and a pencil. He gave me his phone number. "It doesn't have to be about the project. If you need a ride someplace, or want to talk . . ." He smiled. "Call me."

10

Do you think about your parents?" Conn asked me late one night on the phone. There was a hesitant note in his voice.

It was thundering outside, and I could hear Marsha snoring through the walls. I lay on my waterbed, thinking about how to answer him.

It had been more than a week since the incident at the café, and Conn kept asking me questions. On the phone, in the few moments before or after English class. It was a thrill to hear Conn's voice lift at the end of a sentence, and a comfort to answer him, because even though a question might be a hanger waiting to be jabbed into an electrical outlet, it can also be an outstretched arm, ready to curl around you and tug you close.

"No, I don't," I told him. My ears hummed with the sound of rain, a car hissing down the street, and Conn's listening silence. "I don't remember my parents. The DCFS was never able to track them down. Anyway, they're dead."

"How do you know that?"

"I was left outside in the middle of winter without a coat. Either my parents are dead or they should be."

That kind of killed the conversation. Now Conn's silence on the other end of the phone was stony, as if I'd said something unforgivable.

"It's late," he said. "See you tomorrow."

It was pretty obvious he was going to hang up on me. I felt a flare of resentment. "Who are you to judge? They're my parents, not yours. You don't know what it's like."

I turned off my cell phone. On the other side of the bedroom wall, Marsha's snores stuttered, stalled, then kicked into gear again.

I wasn't sorry for what I'd said. Lily once told me that her earliest memory was the sound of bells, because her mother had sewn little silver jingle bells onto her dresses. That filled me with a huge longing, though Lily, when she saw my face, added that she had been about three years old then, and it was probably the last time her mom had any idea about what made her happy.

"She doesn't understand me," Lily said. "I wish she'd leave me alone."

I thought it might be nice to be misunderstood by a mother. Because if you snap at her and she's still there in the morning to pour you coffee and say she hates your green hair, that's something special. It's forever.

I listened to Marsha's snores, remembering how I'd huddled with cold outside the fire station as a five-year-old child. And even though Conn made my heart race as I lay in the dark, and even though I knew I had crossed some line with him by wishing my parents were dead, I could never take back what I'd said.

I closed my eyes, and my mind nuzzled its way into sleep. I had one last conscious thought, and it was sharp.

Tomorrow, he will avoid me.

11

I was wrong.

Conn was leaning against his motorcycle, parked by the last street corner I always passed on the way to school. A gust of wind blew through the trees, showering red and gold leaves. He walked up, close enough that I could see the hollow of his throat. He plucked a maple leaf from my hair and twirled it between his thumb and forefinger. It was a red, delicate, pointed star.

I had been angry with him the night before. Really angry. I only fully realized that now, as a knot in my chest disintegrated.

"I have a gift for you." Conn let the leaf fall. He reached into his jacket pocket and pulled out something. His hand opened, and resting on his palm was a gleaming metal object the size of a plum. It was round, silvery, and looped by a brass ring. "It's a planet," he said. "For the sculpture. I thought of it because J. Alfred wonders what it would be like to squeeze 'the universe into a ball / To roll it toward some overwhelming question.'"

" 'To say: "I am Lazarus, come from the dead," ' " I quoted the next lines. " " "Come back to tell you all, I shall tell you all." ' "

"Do you like it?" He tipped the planet into my open fingers.

I traced the cool, smooth, silver surface. "It's beautiful. How did you make it?"

He grinned. "I'm good with my hands."

Those words left me a little breathless.

"I stayed up late last night making it," he said.

"I thought I had offended you."

"Of course you didn't." He looked straight at me with an innocence so convincing it had to be fake.

"Conn, I may be socially dysfunctional, but I can tell when I've upset someone."

"All right," he said slowly. "Maybe you did. It seems like you hate your parents without knowing anything about them. Mine are important to me, so I couldn't ever agree with your perspective. But I can't fault how you feel when I don't know much about you. And"—he paused—"I upset you, too."

I was used to people disagreeing with the way I saw the world. That's why my DCFS file was brick-thick and I would never be voted Prom Queen or Most Likely to Do Anything. I considered the idea that Conn could disagree with what

I had said but would still try to understand how I felt. This seemed as rare and lovely as the planet I cradled in the palm of my hand.

"Let's ditch school," he said.

"Ditch?" I glanced at my watch. If we began walking now, I wouldn't be late for first period. "I don't know, Conn. I *like* Art."

"I thought you were supposed to be working on Whatever You Want. Maybe you want to spend the day with me."

I looked at him. Why did he have to speak so seductively, when he couldn't mean it? Carefully, I said, "I don't want to miss English. I also like English."

"Ah, but you hate Pre-Calculus."

He had a point. "What about lunch? My friends will be looking for me."

"Your friends monopolize you."

"That's not true."

"It is. They're like a fortress with a sign that says TOUCH DARCY JONES AND WE WILL DESTROY YOU. I find it surprisingly . . . touching, actually. I admire loyalty."

"Destroy," I scoffed. "They would never hurt anybody."

"There are different ways of hurting people. Raphael would go the most obvious route, of course. He would fight with fists. James—no, you call him Jims, don't you?—has a gift for psychological warfare. As for Lily, she is perhaps the most dangerous of the three, because she's the decision maker, and the others will follow her lead. You couldn't have chosen a better army."

I stared. I had never thought about them in this way. "That's not why they're my friends."

"Maybe not. But they can do without you for one afternoon."

I shook my head and began striding toward the school. "My foster mom would have a litter of kittens if I ditched."

He stepped in front of me. "Your foster mother need never know." He pulled two pink slips of paper out of his back pocket. "These are dated and signed excuse slips from the nurse's office. You can go to Art, then meet me by Door 6. We'll slip out for a very leisurely lunch, return in time for English, and as far as anyone official is concerned, we were in the nurse's office for second to sixth periods."

"Exactly how are we supposed to get back into the school? The doors are locked from the outside, except the main entrance, and I hope you don't think we'll be able to make the security guard believe that the nurse's office is located off-campus." The Ingleside Home girls had taught me how to jimmy open locks, but it had been a long time since I'd practiced.

"Door 6 *is* unlocked, inside and out," said Conn. "I've checked. It's left that way for the maintenance workers. Come on, Darcy." His voice grew alluring. "Please."

Everything in the world suddenly distilled down to that word and this truth: he wanted me to come. *Why* didn't matter. The wanting was enough.

"Fine," I said. "But since you've already planned our escape route, I get to pick the destination."

That's how we ended up at a diner by the interstate. It

wasn't exotic or hip or filled with zippy roller-coaster rides or anything fun like that, but it was close enough to Lakebrook High that we'd easily make it back in time for English class.

As we slid into a booth, I said, "Did you get kicked out of your last school?"

He blinked, clearly surprised. "No."

"Reform school," I guessed again.

"What?"

"You used to go to a reform school."

He laughed. "Of course not. What makes you say that?"

"Those pink slips from the nurse's office. You must have stolen them. Plus, you knew Door 6 was unlocked from the outside, which *I* didn't know after more than a year at Lakebrook High. There are at least thirty doors in that godforsaken school. Did you check every one? Did you transfer here to case the joint?" I began to tease. "Are you planning some big heist? There are diamonds in the principal's office, aren't there?"

He shook his head. "You couldn't be farther from the truth. I attended a kind of . . . military academy. And I was an excellent student."

That explained a few things. Conn's clean-cut look. The athletic build. A certain amount of fearlessness.

The waitress came to take our order, and after we handed back our vinyl menus, Conn repeated, "*Reform school*. You really thought I was some kind of criminal?"

"Don't take it personally. I'm the one with a DCFS file that says I'm violent, disobedient, and impertinent. Oh, and strange."

His brows lifted. "Strange?"

"'Eerie' was the exact word."

"That's not the word I'd use."

"Oh?" I asked while my courage was high. "And what's that?"

He murmured it. "Ethereal."

Such a beautiful word. It thrilled through my veins. Yet he had sounded so bitter. He fell silent, and seemed to regret having spoken.

"To be honest," I said lightly, "I *am* kind of strange." Somehow I began telling him exactly what I had been trying to forget for more than two weeks: that I thought I'd seen my hand vanish. What a ridiculous thing to imagine, right? I told it all as one big joke. I'd meant to make him laugh, because he laughed so rarely and when he did it could become a deep and free music that I couldn't help longing to hear. But he stayed serious. Pensive. His gaze wavered over me.

The waitress came, plunked down pancakes and a carafe of coffee, and slouched away. I filled my cup and took a sip. The silence stretched. It occurred to me that Jims must have a heart of steel, to always try so hard to be funny. I cast around for some way out of the awkward silence. "Doesn't your mom worry about you riding a motorcycle? I mean, it seems like something a mother would do."

He seemed to consider his answer carefully. "No. She doesn't. She's . . . used to that sort of thing. My dad and I tinker around in the garage, rebuilding engines. Sometimes . . . sometimes my little sister sneaks in and plays with the parts."

Conn's voice took on a dreamy quality, and I could hear, in every syllable, how much he loved his family. "We live in a big house—old, beautiful—and my mom always complains that we get grease everywhere. But part of her likes it, too, because it's a reminder that we're there."

"That sounds . . . perfect."

He looked at me. I hadn't been able to keep the wistfulness out of my voice. "It is," he said softly, and the sudden certainty that sharing this with me meant something to him pressed a finger right on my heart.

Then he asked, "What's your foster mother like? The one you have now."

I described my first meeting with Marsha, how I'd turned up at the DCFS-organized "date" at McDonalds to find that she had already ordered for both of us: two quarter pounders, large fries, and shakes. In my snottiest tone, I informed her I was a vegetarian. She chirped back that she'd eat both burgers then, and I could have the fries. And the shake, she added. I must love shakes. Everyone does.

Conn said, "You like Marsha, don't you?"

I'd always thought that what you saw was what you got with her: someone cheerful and a bit goofy. Her hidden wad of cash did make me wonder, though, if she really was so simple, and if I knew her as well as I'd believed. But one thing was sure. "She's got a good heart."

He paused. "I think you do, too."

I let that sink in like heat from the first sip of hot chocolate on a snowy day. And since I was thinking about sweet things,

I asked, "Why does J. Alfred say, 'Do I dare to eat a peach?' The poem's supposed to be about whether he'll tell a girl he loves her, right? Not about *fruit*."

Conn laid his hands on the table, and I noticed that his nails were cut to the quick, his knuckles nicked with tiny white scars. He folded his fingers, hiding them behind each other. "Peaches are messy," he said. "Sticky. I suppose all his questions boil down to the same thing. 'Do I dare disturb the universe?' and 'Do I dare to eat a peach?' are the same as 'Do I dare to tell her the truth?' Because *that* question will change his world, and the consequences . . ."

He didn't finish. He didn't have to. I got it.

The consequences would be messy.

WE MADE IT back in time for English class. After English, I was kidnapped.

Conn and I were walking down the hall, side by side, when I heard heavy footsteps racing behind us, coming closer. Conn glanced back in alarm. He almost reached for me, then checked himself. I had enough time to see his face melt into amused resignation before a pair of hands seized and scooped me up.

"Sinner!" Jims took off down the hall with me in his arms.

"Hey!" I thumped his shoulder. "I'm not a sack of potatoes!"

"No, you're a *sinner*." He jogged down the stairs and ran up to Lily and Raphael, who were waiting with folded arms.

"I told you so," Lily said to the others. To me, she said, "I can't believe you walked out of Art without mentioning you were going to ditch."

"With *McCrea*." Jims set me down onto my feet.

"It was just a little ditch," I said. "What do you care, Jims? You've been trying to talk me into cutting class for as long as I've known you."

"Exactly. Yet you have always denied me. Then along comes a boy who crooks his sexy finger at you, and you ditch at the drop of a hat."

"Leaving me alone in Pre-Calc," Raphael added.

I winced, but defended myself. "You're making a big deal over nothing."

"What if you'd been caught?" Lily demanded.

I told them about the excuse slips. "Conn had a plan."

"Screw Conn's plan," said Lily. "You still could have gotten into trouble."

Jims fell to his knees and lifted his hands in prayer. "I'm begging you, Darcy: don't become a cliché."

"*Which* cliché?"

"The one who abandons her friends for some guy," said Lily.

12

After that day, Conn sought me out at school. He would walk with me in the halls and wait outside my classroom doors as if he had no place else to be except at my side. Meanwhile, Jims inquired when I was moving to Connland. "Are you boning up on your Connish?" he asked. "Because I hear that language is a hard tongue to master."

Lily went quiet on the whole subject, but her silence had a determined edge to it, as if she'd taken a personal oath Never to Speak His Name. As for Raphael, he looked gloomier and doomier. My friends probably would have liked Conn better if I'd told them about the attack outside the café, but I kept that to myself. They'd pester me to report it to the police, and insist on being my personal bodyguards. The last thing I needed was a fuss over something I wanted to forget.

I knew that my friends were beginning to see Conn as an unhealthy addiction, and that at some point one of them was going to try to stage an intervention. But I didn't expect it to be Raphael. At least, I didn't think that Taylor Allen would be with him when it happened.

Taylor sailed ahead of him through the coffeehouse door and zeroed in on the best seat: a paisley sofa that still had most of its stuffing, tucked in a far corner. She dropped a snakeskin purse on the table in front of her, gave Raphael a meaningful look, and got comfy.

Raphael approached the counter with an expression so sheepish that a sheep would be jealous. "Hey, Darcy. Can I have the usual and, um, a mocha latte with extra whipped cream and sprinkled cocoa on top?"

I stared. "Are you on a *date* with Taylor Allen?"

"Are you on crack?" He pitched his voice low, to match mine. "No, I'm not on a date with her."

Here's what I haven't mentioned about Taylor. She was gorgeous. Not even in a plastic doll kind of way. She was a long-limbed brunette who looked ready to drink down your soul like a shot of tequila, with a bite of lemon and an extra lick of salt.

"We're studying our lines for the play," Raphael said. "She's really serious about giving a good performance."

"I bet." I poured beans into the grinder. "Taylor puts on quite the act."

Raphael gave me a narrow look. "She's not that bad, actually. And, speaking of putting on acts, how's Mr. I Wear a Cologne and It's Called *Mysterious*?"

"Mysterious?" I ground the beans into dust. "Jims thinks Conn's the most boring thing since baked potato chips."

"I'm not Jims. My head's not buried in sci-fi craziness where humans grow superpowers and extra robotic limbs. I see things for what they are. I see *people* for *who* they are. Have you ever seen McCrea angry? Happy? No. He never shares what he's thinking. There's something about him that's . . . I don't know. Calculating."

"Maybe I know him better than you do."

"Then what *do* you know about him?"

I wanted to tell Raphael that his first impressions of Conn were wrong, as mine had been. That Conn was kind, thoughtful. A good listener. If he kept his feelings close to his chest, who was I, of all people, to blame him? But instead of saying any of this, I focused on preparing the drinks.

"Darcy," Raphael said in a gentler tone. "We don't want you to get hurt."

I slammed down the tamper. "Well, maybe it hurts that you think I'll get hurt."

Raphael held up his hands in surrender. "Okay. Forget I said anything. I'll leave you alone." He started to walk back to Taylor.

"Wait," I called. He turned, and I saw how worried his eyes were. "I spend a lot of time with Conn because of our project."

"I sincerely doubt that."

"Also . . . he helps me."

"Helps? With what?"

"I've been thinking a lot lately about who I was before the

DCFS picked me up. Conn wants to get to know me. Is that so bad? *I* want to get to know *myself*. When he asks me questions, I want to know the answers. I want to *remember*, Raphael."

He reached across the counter for my hand. "I know you don't remember a lot about your childhood, but maybe that's for the best. Maybe there's a good reason for it." He let go. "Will you at least tell me what this morning was all about?"

Conn had been waiting for me outside the school entrance. He had waved, beckoning for me to leave my friends and join him. His chameleon eyes had been green with sunlight and excitement.

"It was about our class assignment," I told Raphael. "No, really," I spoke over his sputter of disbelief. "We're building a sculpture about the meaning of 'The Love Song of J. Alfred Prufrock.' Conn had an idea. In the poem, J. Alfred repeats 'there will be time.' So, this morning, Conn suggested that we build a sculpture that's also a working clock. Because of phrases like 'time for you and time for me.'"

"He does take up a lot of your time," Raphael muttered. "He's always hanging around you. We miss you, Darcy. We were your friends first."

"I know," I whispered.

"Do you remember this summer, when we went to the Water Tower?"

Usually when people talk about the Water Tower, they mean Water Tower Place, the mall that's right down the street from one of the oldest monuments in Chicago. But Raphael was referring to the nineteenth-century pumping station, which looks like a miniature cathedral surrounded by concrete pavement. In the summer, the pavement is covered with tables and chairs where sharply dressed business people take their lunch breaks. Musicians play and kids in sweatpants break-dance on cardboard.

"Your chalk art was beautiful," Raphael continued, "swirling over that plain concrete. You signed your name and made me sign mine, too, even though I hadn't done anything but keep you company. Darcy Jones and Raphael Amador."

"I remember."

"Hey!" Taylor called. "Where's my mocha latte? How long does it take to foam milk?"

Raphael shrugged helplessly and reached for the drinks.

I raised one brow. "Do you really want to have a chat about keeping bad company?"

"Maybe not." He smiled. "See you later, Darcy." He headed back to Taylor, who snatched her mug from him. Brown froth sloshed onto her skirt.

I tuned out her outraged cry and Raphael's protest of innocence. My attention was drawn to something else: the rack of tiny demitasse spoons to be served alongside espressos. J. Alfred says, "I have measured out my life with coffee spoons," and it struck me that they would make perfect hour and minute hands for the clock sculpture. I stuffed two of them in my pocket.

Riding around on a motorbike. Cutting class. Petty thievery. I was well on my way to becoming a juvenile delinquent.

Though that wasn't what got me arrested the weekend before the English project was due.

13

Conn stopped me in the halls. It was Friday, and our project was due on Monday.

Rushing students flowed around him like he was a sharp rock and they were water. He started to say something, then peered at me. "Have you been sleeping all right?"

No. Pretty much as soon as I admitted to Raphael that I wanted to know more about who I was before becoming a constant headache for the DCFS, I began to have nightmares. They weren't about anything specific, but I woke up choking back screams of terror, my heart leaping like a wild beast. I could only remember fire and a horrible smell I couldn't quite identify.

"Sure," I said. "I've been sleeping fine." But I knew there were violet smudges under my eyes.

Conn's expression turned skeptical. Then he shook his

head slightly, as if trying to clear his vision. "When can I see you in private? Later this afternoon?"

"I can't," I said reluctantly. "I work."

"Tonight, then?"

"The same."

He said nothing, but bit his lip.

"Conn, everything will be okay. I promise."

"How can you say that?" he whispered.

"Because it's just one grade. It's not the end of the world, whatever happens. You've done your part for the English project, right?"

He gave a short nod.

"I've done mine. We'll put them together this weekend. Marsha works on Saturdays. Come by tomorrow afternoon, and we'll have the house to ourselves to finish the sculpture. How does that sound?"

"Ideal, actually." Yet he didn't smile. "Your hair is damp," he said abruptly. He raised a hand and I stood perfectly still, holding my breath as he touched the air an inch from my face. He let his hand fall, but my skin tingled all the same.

I forced myself to breathe. "Well, that's what happens when you take a shower after gym class."

"Hmm." He gave me a long look. "I imagine so."

Wait. Had I brought up the subject of nudity? With Conn? Was I *insane*?

I couldn't take any more of this conversation. It was tugging my emotions in too many different directions. "I'm going to be late for my next class."

"One more minute. Darcy, I have to tell you something. I mean, I have to ask you something. I . . . I don't really care about the project."

"You don't?"

"What I need to know is this: will you still want to see me after Monday?"

That was the moment I allowed myself to hope. The feeling was beautiful: a rainbow soap bubble expanding inside my chest. I thought about seeing Conn the next day, and I knew I wouldn't be able to sleep that night. Not because of my nightmares, but because of my dreams.

"Yes," I told him. "I will."

14

That night there was a cold snap, and when the dawn came the dry grass glittered with frost.

I rubbed my eyes and pushed myself up from the waterbed, which gurgled as I stood and searched for my slippers. Finally, too tired to care if my feet were cold, I gave up the hunt and was walking through my bedroom door when I stumbled over one of those sneaky slippers and whacked my wrist against the doorframe. Not a great start to the day.

Marsha was in the living room, watching Saturday morning cartoons and dusting sugar over her cereal. "You're up early," she said.

"Coffee," I mumbled.

"Big plans for the day?"

"Yes. Coffee."

"If you want some, you'll have to make it yourself. I'm leaving in five minutes. We ran out of that fancy stuff you brought back from work, but there's some instant coffee."

I tried to take this news bravely.

"You're not going to the café today, are you?" Marsha said. "We agreed you would work only part-time once the semester started. You've got to keep your grades up."

"That's what I'm going to do." I filled a mug with water and stuck it in the microwave. "Me plus free time equals homework." It probably wasn't wise to mention that Conn was part of this equation. Marsha hadn't exactly forbidden me to have boys over, but probably only because the thought of it had never entered her head.

I glanced at her and fought a foolish urge to tell her everything. I remembered how it felt to *not* feel Conn's fingertips touch my hair. And I knew the exact nature of my hope. I saw its shape. I saw its size.

The microwave chimed. Marsha slurped down the milk at the bottom of her bowl and switched off the television. "Oh!" She looked at the clock. "I'm running late. Bye, Darcy."

I lifted a hand and made myself wave. "Bye," I said as she hustled out the door.

Alone in the sudden quiet, I dumped the remaining contents of a jar of coffee crystals into my mug, stirred, and choked it down.

Then I waited.

Stage One of waiting for Conn was a hot shower, during

which I was so sleep-deprived and nervous that I used Marsha's purple shower gel and emerged from the bathroom smelling flowery and way too flirty.

Stage Two was selecting clothes that would make me seem unimpressed by Conn's presence. Something simple, careless. Black cargo pants and a long-sleeved black T-shirt. Done.

Stage Three was revising my strategy. Maybe I *should* look like I cared, a little? I tried to reproduce the elegant hairstyle Lily had concocted for me in the girls' bathroom.

Stage Four: I failed. I looked ridiculous. I tore the pins from my hair and brushed it loose and smooth.

Stage Five: I curled up on the sofa with my sketchbook and cracked it open to a bare page. I drew a low stone house framed by a wrought-iron fence. The lines came heavy, hard, and fast, and I began to relax until I realized that this house, like everything else I'd been sketching lately, looked familiar yet impossible to recognize.

Stage Six: I threw the sketchbook onto the shag carpet.

Stage Seven: there was a knock at the door.

I stood slowly, moved toward the door slowly, and opened it slowly—not just because I didn't want to seem eager, but also because I sensed that the moment Conn came inside, everything would change.

He held a cardboard box in his arms. Conn's face was grim, and his breath fogged the air.

When he stepped into the living room, his gaze flickered,

pausing on the three closed doors down the hallway: the bathroom, Marsha's room, my bedroom. He raised the cardboard box, which ticked like a bomb. "Where should I put this?"

"The rest of the sculpture is in my bedroom." I led the way. Determined to speak lightly, I added, "Marsha doesn't like art to get all over the house, unless it comes in the form of an adorable portrait of a furry woodland creature."

My room was small, but I kept it neat—except for the desk, which was strewn with pencils, a stylus, and an X-Acto knife, everything clustered around a tall, rectangular object I had sheathed in a pillowcase.

Conn set the box on the bed, and when the mattress sloshed he lifted his brows. "Is that . . . filled with water?"

"Very 1970s, isn't it? Marsha was so proud when she first showed me this room. She thinks everybody wants a waterbed."

Conn pressed his fingers against it, bewildered, as if he'd never seen a waterbed before. Then he shrugged and turned to shut the bedroom door. The sound thumped somewhere deep inside me.

He pushed up the sleeves of his gray sweater, revealing the tight muscles of his forearms, and slipped both hands into the back pockets of his jeans. "We should get started," he said, his tone all business. He nodded at the pillowcased object on my desk. "Is that it?"

Grateful for something to do, I unveiled the sculpture.

It was a glass box encasing a human figure made from plaster, pinned by its feet to a wooden bottom. It was J. Alfred, and he could barely be seen through the ocean I had painted on the glass panes. Above the water, the glass walls were clear and speckled with tiny, gold-colored watch gears that I had wheedled out of the manager at the local jewelers. I had superglued the gears, one by one, into constellations above the ocean. The box had no lid.

Conn stepped closer and touched the painted mermaids swimming in the waves, their tails flowing like long dresses. "'We have lingered in the chambers of the sea,'" he quoted the poem's final lines. "'By sea-girls wreathed with seaweed red and brown / Till human voices wake us, and we drown.' Darcy." He looked at me. "This is beautiful." His gaze held mine so fully that I felt as if his hands had cupped my face.

I forced myself to speak. "The shadow box isn't sturdy. I used a hot glue gun to fit the four panes of glass into a rectangle, so the box won't last forever, but I reinforced the base with copper wire. We'll do the same to the top once you've inserted the clock mechanism. I should have used a small propane torch to fuse the glass together, but I don't have one, and anyway, open flames make me twitchy. I don't like . . . that is, I'm . . ." I trailed off.

"You're afraid of fire," he said gently.

"Yes," I muttered, embarrassed.

"Don't worry. We all have our weaknesses. I think the sculpture is perfect."

"No, it isn't." I opened Conn's cardboard box and lifted out a small, narrow machine. "But it will be."

Reluctantly, Conn removed his hands from his pockets and

took the clock. Once he held it, though, his shoulders relaxed. Maybe, like me, he was grateful to have something to do. He sat at the desk, lowered the clock into the shadow box, and began to attach it by squeezing metal clamps onto the glass edges. His fingers were quick and sure. Gifted. I watched them dance, and it was easy, too easy, to fall under their spell.

A bad idea. I tore my gaze away. I looked at the clock instead. As I studied its intricacy, I realized that Conn was an artist, too.

Then he leaned back, and I could see what we had done together. There were the coffee spoons, one painted and one plain, measuring the hours and minutes. There was the clock's pendulum: the rusted spring we'd salvaged from the train tracks, dangling over J. Alfred's head in a spiral like a strange halo. There was everything we had planned for a month, everything except—

"The planet," I said. "Where should we put it? Maybe we could fix it to the top of the box, tilted at an angle? Or—"

"You should keep it for yourself."

"But you made it for the sculpture."

The sharp angles of his face softened. "I made it for you."

I became acutely aware of the ticking of the clock, and another sound: my heartbeat, skipping in a quick rhythm. I nodded, and knew that now I needed the spool of copper wire, and should get it, I really should, but it was in the desk drawer and Conn was sitting in front of it like a lion I'd have to creep past. I hesitated, then stretched out my arm and reached for the drawer.

His hand caught mine. "What's this?" He eased back my sleeve, exposing the black and blue mark on my wrist.

"Just a bruise."

"A bruise," he repeated.

"Yeah. Really clumsy of me. I got it this morning." Conn was examining my skin with wonder. His dark golden head bowed over my hand in his as I stood before him, begging my body not to tremble, begging my voice not to break. "What's the big deal?" I tried to sound nonchalant. "Everybody gets bruises."

"Not you. Never you. You shouldn't allow it."

Which was, obviously, a bizarre thing to say. But before I could make a comment to that effect, Conn grazed his thumb over the bruise and swept his fingers up the tender skin of my inner arm. I forgot to speak. I forgot to breathe.

Still seated, still caressing the pale hollow of my elbow with a palm as rough as a cat's tongue, Conn looked up at me. His eyes were the color of storm clouds, and alive with a question.

My answer?

I kissed him.

He sighed. It was a tired sound, and so brief that I might have imagined it if that breath hadn't brushed against my mouth. If I hadn't inhaled it, tasted it, and made it mine. Then Conn pulled me into his arms, and I was invaded by an emotion as fierce as fear. I touched the prickle and velvet of his shorn hair. *This is what it means to kiss,* I thought. *This is what it means to—*

Conn shifted. His lips hardened, grew eager. Almost angry.

He grasped my fingers, lowered them to his waist, and seized my upper arm. Gripped it to the bone.

Yet I didn't pull away. I couldn't. He crushed me close. I strained closer. Our kiss was a deep, dark well, and I fell into it, and never wanted to see the sun again. It didn't matter that my arm hurt. It didn't matter that Conn's other hand was reaching behind him, searching for something in his back pocket.

Something that flashed through the air and bit into my wrists.

A pair of handcuffs.

"You're under arrest, Shade." Conn tightened the cuffs. "You have no rights."

15

What had he called me?

Why was he acting like a cop?

Were those handcuffs made of *glass*?

My mind groped for something that made sense. Nothing did. I lifted my cuffed hands and stared at the transparent device that chained them together. An orange light coursed through the cuffs and the links between them. "What the *hell*," I hissed.

Conn was silent. Stony. A suddenly menacing stranger.

I wrenched away from him and raised my hands high.

"No!" Conn's eyes filled with horror. He moved to stop me.

Too late. I smashed the handcuffs against the edge of the desk.

My hands burst into flames.

I screamed. My fingers curled into fists of agony. The ends of my hair caught on fire. An acrid smell filled the air, and I remembered it from my nightmares. Now I knew what that stench was. The smoke of burning hair, of burning flesh.

Conn snatched the X-Acto knife from where it lay on the desk. He barreled into me, shoving me onto the bed.

"Don't!" I cried. "Please!" My breath came in heaving sobs as he tried to pin me down and the waterbed rocked beneath us. I struggled, but struggling didn't help. He was heavy, and I was on fire.

Conn raised the knife. Terror beat its wings inside me, and I heard my voice begging him not to do this, to let me go, to stop, please stop—

He drove the knife down, slashing into the mattress.

Water gushed over us. Conn flung the knife away, ripped the mattress wide open, and pressed my body into the wet ruins of the waterbed.

I choked, coughing up water that tasted like moldy plastic. The fire was gone, but I still twisted beneath Conn. His chest was a hard weight against mine.

"Darcy?" His face dripped water onto my cheeks. "Are you all right?"

His hold loosened.

I hitched up my knees and kicked him in the stomach. He slammed onto the sodden carpet, and I was up, I was free, I was careening toward the door.

He seized my ankle, but before I fell against the desk I wrapped my scorched fingers around a weapon: the stylus.

Conn scrambled to his feet, but so did I. He inched closer, hands empty and low, signaling that I should calm down and drop the stylus. Some of my fear had burned out with the fire, and the thick smoke in my lungs began to taste like anger as I listened to him gasp, trying to speak. I had knocked the wind out of him.

Well. That wasn't much, but it was a start.

I swept my arm against the sculpture and flung it at him. The four glass panes split apart, the plaster man broke. Conn reeled as I drew my hand back and drove the stylus deep into his bicep.

He cried out. As much as I hated him then, I hated myself more, for my last move had been stupid. I had just given him possession of my only weapon.

But maybe he was stupid, too. Shuddering, he yanked the stylus from his arm and tossed it into a far corner of the room. Blood seeped through his sweater.

"Listen," he rasped, but I had already thrown open the bedroom door.

I ran into the living room and had made it halfway to the front door when Conn snagged the waist of my pants and hauled me back.

"Listen," he said again, this time into my ear, his breath hot against my neck.

Depending on your point of view, this was either the best or worst time for Marsha to come home early.

Conn swore, but didn't let go. He snaked an arm around my waist and cinched me close.

Marsha let the front door swing wide until it banged against the outside of the house and cold air poured into the living room. She stood, staring. She sucked in a huge breath, and I could feel uncertainty in Conn's body against mine. Then Marsha did something very sensible. In a voice as shrill as a train whistle, she yelled, "*HELP! POLICE!*"

Maybe a neighbor would hear. In the meantime, I rammed my elbow into Conn's ribs as hard as I could, and heard something crack. He staggered back, and everything might have turned out differently if Marsha hadn't done something very *not* sensible, which was to run into the kitchen, grab a knife from the butcher block, and throw it.

I knew she meant to hit Conn, yet even though the knife spun through the air like it had been thrown by a ninja, Marsha's aim was really, really bad. The blade was whirling straight toward my chest.

For a moment, every sensation and thought was a sharp, clear crystal. The sound of Marsha's scream. The blistering ache of my hands. A bitterness on my tongue. Conn stumbling toward me. The shining blade.

My heart shrank, curling into itself. But a knife couldn't hurt it more than it already had been.

Then, just as the knife should have pierced my skin, I vanished.

I had been looking down, unable to tear my eyes away from my soaked shirt and the blade about to rip through it, when suddenly I wasn't there anymore. I was gone. I was air. I was nothing.

The knife cracked into the fish tank behind me. The glass broke, spilling water and panicked angelfish onto the patch of carpet where my feet had been.

"No." Conn whispered. "No, no, no."

Was I insane? Had my mind snapped during Conn's attack? Maybe my five missing, forgotten years, and the ones that came after that, the times when I appeared in one foster home only to disappear months later, had led to this. To believing that I had truly become a ghost.

Conn stared at the place where I should have been. Not in disbelief. More as if everything was lost.

"Darcy?" Marsha's voice wavered. "Where are you?"

I didn't understand what had happened. But I knew this: I needed to get away from Conn.

Could I run? Could I do that, without legs?

Yes.

I leaped over the sofa and rushed out the front door. I had made it to the street when something dragged me down. My own feet. They flickered into being: solid, heavy. I tripped, and fell onto the heels of my brutalized hands. Shrieked.

I tried to bite back the sound, but Conn had heard me. He had seen me. He was racing across the brown grass.

Get up. *Get up.*

Then I was running again, slightly ahead of him. My legs blurred and vanished once more.

It was dizzying, being invisible. Staring at the ground as I ran gave me vertigo, and I didn't have the courage to look back at Conn, so I kept my eyes trained on the wide streets. The pastel houses. The cars parked neatly in their driveways.

The neighborhood was deserted. Everyone was tucked inside on this chilly Saturday, playing video games or watching TV or doing anything except noticing a bloodied young man chasing nothing at all.

The quick thud of Conn's footfalls stopped. I glanced over my shoulder. He wasn't there. Had he given up?

The roar of a motorcycle.

No. He hadn't.

I sprinted through the narrow spaces between houses, zigzagged through backyards littered with toolsheds and swing sets. I turned a corner, and an unexpected fence loomed in front of me. I tried to slow and stop, but apparently that wasn't necessary. I flew through the wooden wall.

Some small kernel of me was fascinated and thought that maybe Conn didn't have a chance if I could zoom through solid objects. But I remembered how my feet had materialized beneath me, and realized that I couldn't control this. This thing. Evaporating. Ghosting. Whatever it was, I didn't want to be in the middle of a wall when it stopped working. So I skimmed through open spaces.

Then it happened: quiet. No more motorcycle. Only the scratchy rustle of a squirrel stealing from a bird feeder.

Maybe Conn had driven off in the wrong direction.

Or maybe he had parked somewhere and was hunting among the houses.

I skirted an aboveground swimming pool and slipped

through an open gate to a front yard. Hugging the driveway, I moved slowly toward the street. I looked left. I looked right. I didn't see Conn or his motorcycle.

I felt weak and heavy with relief.

No, not *felt*. I *was* heavy. Heavy, solid. *There*. My body had returned. My damaged self. The misery of my burned fingers.

I saw my reflection in a car window. This was what Marsha had seen when she'd come home, when she'd parked her rusted Camry and strolled toward the front door, completely unaware of the wreckage inside. She had seen a girl soaked from head to toe. A girl with burned, jagged hair. Torn clothes. Hands red, puffy, blackened in some spots and oozing blood in others. A welt on her chin from where it had hit the desk. Neck smeared with Conn's blood. Eyes wide, black, animal.

Shaken by the sight of myself, I had nearly turned away when I noticed something. There, lying on the passenger seat of the car, was a cell phone.

I should hide. Now that Conn might see me, I should hide.

I weighed temptation and risk. Call for help? Or find some dark corner to hole up in?

First get the phone. Then run and hide.

Holding my breath against the pain, I tugged at the handle of the passenger door. Locked. The windows were closed.

I scoured the area for some kind of tool, and my gaze fell on a stone garden gnome in the front yard, dressed in a painted blue coat and hat. I scooped up the gnome and hurled him through the car window. It smashed, the car alarm blared, and I reached through the shards to grab the phone. Then I ran down the street, away from the scene that would surely catch Conn's attention if he was still nearby. I ducked into a backyard and saw that the door of a toolshed had been left wide open. I hurtled into the shed, slammed the door behind me, and took stock of what was inside. Bags of dirt. Fertilizer. And weapons: a rake, a shovel, a trowel.

A good place. A safe one. Safe enough, at least, for now.

Wishing the door had a lock, I peeked out its tiny square window. I saw nothing, so began to punch numbers into the cell phone. My fingers shook as they bled onto the keypad. I looked at them and realized that my hand really *had* disappeared, that day in the art room. I remembered telling Conn. I remembered how he hadn't laughed.

Because he had believed me.

I pressed the phone to my ear and listened to it ring. And ring. And ring.

"Hello?" Lily's voice had that suspicion everyone gets when an unknown number appears on her cell phone.

"Lily, I need your help."

"Darcy?" Her tone instantly sharpened. "What's the matter?"

"It's Conn. Raphael was right. I don't know Conn. I never did. I didn't know anything about him. He attacked me, and—"

"He *attacked* you? Are you hurt?"

I touched my mouth, still swollen from that rough kiss. "Yes."

"Have you told anyone else?"

"No."

"You need to call the police. I'll help you, I promise. I'll do anything I can. But you've got to hang up right now and dial 911. Then talk to Marsha before you call me back. I'll be waiting."

"No!" I began to pace. "I can't talk to Marsha. You don't know what happened. You don't know what she saw. She must think I'm some kind of . . . demon. I broke things. Her fish tank. She loves her fish. And I destroyed her carpet. And then . . . I disappeared," I finished, unsure how to explain what had occurred in Marsha's living room. "I can't go home."

"Wait. You're not there now?" Her voice took on a new urgency. "Whose phone are you using? Where *are* you?"

"In a toolshed in somebody's backyard. Conn chased me, but I vanished, and I ran, but I'm sure he's still out there, searching—"

"Tell me where you are," Lily demanded. "The exact address. I'm coming for you. Then hang up the phone and dial 911!"

I turned away from the door and leaned against the wall opposite it. I pressed my forehead against the wooden surface, racking my memory of the past several minutes, trying to figure out precisely where I was. "I think—"

The door flung open behind me. Before I could wheel around, something struck the back of my head.

I blacked out.

16

When I woke up, I was lying on my side, my cheek pressed against a rattling metal floor. I opened my eyes and winced.

I was stuffed in the back of a large, moving vehicle with padlocked doors, and my bandaged hands were handcuffed. *Again.* My ankles were also bound, with one of those chains usually reserved for cannibalistic serial killers. Except this chain, like my handcuffs, was made of glass. I watched the flames flicker inside the cuffs and decided that I wasn't going to question this bizarre technology that seemed designed to contain me—*me specifically*, with my terror of fire.

No. No questions. I didn't dare open my mouth. I wouldn't even move. If I did, that would definitely catch the attention of the three hulking men in gray uniforms who surrounded me, armed with dull metal tubes shaped like nightsticks.

And then, of course, there was Conn.

My nerves sang with fear. Conn stood as far away from me as possible, back turned, facing someone who sat before him on a long bench screwed onto the wall. Conn's body blocked him from sight. I could see only the sitting man's hands as he riffled through a thrown-open medical kit stocked with syringes and gauze.

Conn hadn't noticed I was awake, yet the mere sight of him made every weary inch of me instantly alert and ready to flee—except there was nowhere to run, no obvious escape, unless I managed to ghost my way free. But guess what? My vanishing skills were on vacation. Wouldn't return my calls. Pretended I didn't exist.

I felt tattered and ragged and raw. All I could do was consider the disaster at hand. To see that I had been hunted and trapped, and to know that the handcuffs meant that Conn's kiss was a lie.

And the ache deep inside me told one great truth:

Conn McCrea was my enemy.

So I swallowed my fear. I slitted my eyes. I watched, and waited for an opportunity.

Conn's body shifted. I saw who was sitting before him and caught my breath.

"You sure took your sweet time, McCrea," said the guy who had grabbed me outside the café. My mind flung back to that night and began to understand things very, very differently.

"It worked," Conn said. "I made the arrest."

"And got yourself mauled in the process. My way would have been better."

"It's done, Michael. Leave it at that." Conn reached for the hem of his ruined sweater.

"Don't." I watched Michael cut at the fabric until it fell away from Conn's chest. Once upon a time, the sight of Conn's bare torso would have filled me with a kind of sore joy. Now it was a slap in the face. His tawny skin mocked me. It reminded me of how stupid I had been.

To desire him.

To trust him.

"Too easy." Michael glanced dismissively at the bloody hole I'd bored into Conn's arm. He shook what looked like a can of hair spray and pumped a fine mist over Conn's bicep. The blood fizzed and evaporated, leaving a clean wound that began to glue itself together. In a matter of seconds, there was a round, white scar.

"Breathe." Michael pressed his fingers along Conn's naked, bruising rib cage. Conn gasped. "Thought so. Not much I can do here." Michael began to unwind a roll of gauze around Conn's torso. "She broke some ribs. They'll have to heal on their own."

Conn grabbed the gauze out of Michael's hands. "I'll do that."

"Sir," said one of the three lumpy ogres guarding me.

Conn turned toward our corner of the truck. My eyes slammed shut.

"The Shade's waking up," the guard muttered.

There was a rustle, then the thump of boots on the metal floor, growing closer. My chest began to heave uncontrollably. The footsteps were measured and firm, so different from the rhythm of my shallow breaths. I could smell Conn's sweat.

There was no use pretending. I opened my eyes.

Conn was buttoning a gray shirt, a piece of the same uniform the guards and Michael wore, with a high collar and thick, stiff material. But his shirt, unlike the others, had a dime-sized red knot stitched onto the collar.

His frosty gaze flitted over me. I wondered if he could see the hate in my eyes, if I could squelch it, hide it for a few moments, for just long enough to surge to my feet and break my fire-filled chains right across his face.

Conn stepped back. "Hold her."

The guards seized me.

"Knock her out, Michael," said Conn.

"Gladly." He flexed his hand.

"Use a *match*," Conn snarled.

"*You* got creative with her. Why can't I?"

Conn stormed across the jolting truck, rummaged through the medical kit, and pulled out something that looked like a needle. He flicked a finger against its point and it glowed.

Then he was striding toward me, and I was straining away, pressing against the guards, who seemed safe in comparison with Conn and his smoldering needle. After a quick touch of my neck, he found the jugular and darted the needle in.

A bee sting. A roaring buzz in my ears, and I was smothered by dark, fuzzy sleep.

* * *

"Darcy. We're here."

The truck had stopped. Conn spoke again, and his voice was unyielding. "Look at me." He was crouched at my side, his elbows resting on his knees, hands dangling down.

"Why are you doing this?" I hadn't meant to speak to him. I certainly hadn't meant my words to sound so weak and tiny.

From his corner of the truck, Michael answered, "Because it's fun. And we get paid."

"Who is *he*?" I said to Conn.

"My partner."

"So what was *that*, that night at the café?" I remembered Conn's words to me, afterward: *You trust me, don't you*. I drew my breath so sharply it seemed to cut. "You staged the attack. It was a trick. To make me like you."

"Smart girl," said Michael.

I looked straight at Conn. "Tell me," I said thickly. "Tell me what is going on."

He paused, then said, "If you really don't know why you're under arrest, I don't have the authority to explain it to you."

"*If* I don't know? How would I—" I started to struggle to my feet.

A guard held me. "Sir? Another match?"

Conn shook his head. "She needs to be questioned. She'll be fine. Won't you, Darcy? You don't want us to drag you out. Now, your firecuffs." He tapped my glass chain. "You remember what they can do. You may not know, however, that they have different settings. When I cuffed you the first time, I used the lowest setting, for a small fire. Your chains are now set at the highest level. These"—he pointed at a guard's silvery tube—"are flamethrowers. I want to make something very clear before we walk out of this truck. If you try to break your cuffs, if you try to escape, if you try to do anything that might make us think that you will be a danger to others, you will die. Do you understand?"

Silence.

"Answer me." Fiercely.

"Yeah, I *get* it."

"Good. Help her stand," he told the guards.

Conn flung open the back of the truck.

17

I stepped outside, and staggered.

It wasn't the chains that made me lose my balance, or that a guard jerked too hard. It wasn't even the crowd in front of a huge building, a uniformed crew of men and women gathered, it seemed, for the sole purpose of glaring at me with such rage that it throbbed from them like heat off asphalt.

It was the building.

An old monstrosity with columns. These words were carved into the marble above the entrance: *The Interdimensional Bureau of Investigation.*

Even crazier? I recognized it. I recognized everything. The globe-topped street lamps. The marble archway. I knew that there were exactly twenty-seven steps leading up to the main entrance. And I *should* know, because I had drawn this building in great detail, down to the chipped ear on a stone gargoyle. It was all in my sketchbook. Everything except the inscription—which, unlike everything else, I didn't recognize from the sketch I'd drawn that day in Mr. Linden's classroom.

I recognized it from my memory. I had been here before. If I didn't know how or why, that could only mean I'd seen it sometime before being abandoned outside the Chicago firehouse.

My memory was so untrustworthy. Maybe I *had* done something to deserve these people's anger. Something awful. But what?

I could never kill anyone.

Some things you just know for sure, right?

But then, I also used to think that the world was solid and governed by certain laws. That people don't disappear—unless we're talking about parents dumping their kids on the DCFS and saying, "Ta. See you never." Nobody *actually* vanishes into thin air.

Except me.

I remembered slamming a fist into my ex–foster father's face and feeling his jaw crunch under my knuckles. It had felt good.

Maybe I was dangerous after all.

Maybe I had no idea who I was, or what I was capable of.

My thoughts were swirling, tumbling like a load of dirty laundry. I barely noticed my surroundings as they marched me up those twenty-seven steps and through the entrance. My three personal guards were dragging me toward a guarded gate that crackled with energy, when Conn caught Michael by the shoulder.

"This is my arrest," Conn said.

Michael's eyes narrowed. "Yours?"

"You weren't there when it happened. And I outrank you."

Michael shrugged off his hand. "Well, screw you, too," he spat, and stalked away.

"McCrea." One of the guards at the gate grinned at me. "Nice catch."

"ID," the other guy droned.

"I lost it," said Conn.

"What?" said the first guard. "Prince Connor the Perfect, valedictorian of the IBI Academy, lost his badge? Well, I am truly sorry to say that I don't think we can let you in without proper identification."

Conn snapped at him with the irritation of somebody at the end of his rope. The first guard kept teasing him while the second one picked at his teeth with a thumbnail. Things carried on like this for some time. I had an almost serious thought of breaking my chains, just to make Conn and his old school buddy shut up, when a uniformed girl rushed toward us. She gazed at Conn with syrupy hero worship. "Chief Ivers wants to see the Shade right away."

"Ivers?" The first guard's eyebrows shot up. He pressed his fingerprint against a shiny square embedded in the nearest post of the electrified gate. The zing and crackle was sucked out of the air in front of us, and Conn swept through the gate without a backward look, letting me and the ogres trail behind.

Their boots rang down a hall that smelled old. Slightly dank and booky, like a library or a church. Then a door was flung open and I was ushered into a room with two chairs, one of which was made of iron and bolted to the floor. In the other chair, which looked infinitely more comfortable, sat a gleeful middle-aged man rubbing his mustache. Ivers, I assumed.

"Agent McCrea." Ivers stood, and pumped Conn's hand. "Fine work you've done here. Back from the Alter in record time, with barely a scratch on you." He smiled widely, showing a set of perfect teeth. "You'll get a commendation for this, I assure you."

Conn shrugged. "I was doing my job."

"Don't be so modest. I know you. You're ruthless, kid, and it suits you. God knows that it's helped you bag more Shades than anyone else your age." Ivers clapped his large hands once and then spread them apart like a showman. "Let's unwrap your present."

The guards dragged me to the narrow, iron chair and shoved me down, shackling my chains to the arms and legs. Ivers settled his well-fed frame into the chair across from me and dismissed the guards. He peered at me with a hard twinkle as he did it, apparently to communicate that he wasn't afraid to be left alone in my oh-so-savage company.

"Wanna stick around, McCrea?" he drawled.

"I would, thank you." Conn leaned into a corner of the room, arms folded across his chest.

Ivers shifted in his chair. He was built like a brick house. Big yet trim, with not an ounce of fat on him. He tugged at his uniform jacket and smoothed the fabric around his neck, drawing attention to the red knots stitched along his collar. There were a lot.

"Bewitching, isn't she?" said Ivers. "Too bad she's not human."

Conn's mouth twisted in a way that could have meant anything.

"Hello? I'm right here," I said. "Why doesn't someone talk to *me* and tell me what's going on? Me, the human."

Ivers laughed.

"I'm totally human," I insisted, though honestly I was beginning to have my doubts. "And I want a lawyer and a phone call," I added, since that's what people always say in movies.

"You have no rights." Ivers almost sang the words. "Besides, we're simply having a friendly chat. I even paid you a compliment, like the gentleman I am. See how nice I'm being?"

" 'One may smile, and smile, and be a villain,' " I told him.

He crinkled his brow. "What?"

"Shakespeare," said Conn from his corner. "It's a line from *Hamlet.*"

Ivers craned his neck to look at him.

"Her friend's in the school play," Conn explained.

"Her *friend*?"

"Her human friend. In the Alter."

I didn't think Conn could betray me more than he already had, but his confirmation that I *wasn't* human stung. "I'm a *person*," I said. "You keep calling me a Shade, but I've no idea what that is, or what the Alter is, or where I am. All I know is that I've been abused and kidnapped and drugged." I flung those last words at Conn. They didn't touch him. His face was impassive.

"I want an explanation." I heard my voice and wished I'd never spoken. That hadn't been a demand. It had been a plea.

I was begging.

Ivers unbuttoned his jacket, reached in, and pulled out a lighter and cigar. "This is a good day for the IBI, a day for celebrating." He flicked the lighter open and I jumped at the sight of its tiny flame. Ivers lit the cigar, puffing, and blew a cloud of smoke into my face. I choked.

"The Alter is our word for your world," Conn said suddenly.

"McCrea," Ivers warned.

"You're in Chicago, but another version of the city you know. One where the Great Chicago Fire of 1871 never happened. That's what caused the interdimensional split."

"*McCrea*. Do I need to ask you to leave?"

A pause. "No, sir."

"Good. Because the only explanation *you* need"—Ivers stabbed a finger in my direction—"is that that chair is made of iron so that if you catch on fire, you won't burn the whole place down. But you will burn, sweetheart, oh, you will, if you don't answer my questions." He growled, "Exhibit A."

An image glowed on the wall behind him. My name, dashed in colorful chalk on concrete. Alongside it in different handwriting was another name: Raphael Amador.

"Exhibit B."

The image was replaced by another one: Raphael and me laughing as he tried to draw a daisy on the back of my tank top.

"What was your mission in the Alter?" Ivers demanded. "Why did the Shadow Society send you there?"

"You've been stalking me!" I stared at Raphael's face as if he could help me out of this horrible, senseless mess.

"Surely you wanted us to see you," said Ivers. "Flaunting yourself, flirting with a human"—he didn't bother to suppress a shudder—"in front of a known portal between worlds."

"We were at the *Water Tower*. It's not a 'known portal between worlds.' It's a *mall*!"

Ivers sucked on his cigar. "Don't lie."

"Fine, okay, the mall's like a few blocks away from where we were. But we were just hanging out. I drew on the sidewalk, and then we went to the food court for smoothies. Wait . . . have I been arrested for *graffiti*?" I glanced between Ivers and Conn. "Am I being treated like this because of some chalk art? It's *chalk*. It washes out in the rain!"

"Playing innocent is a stupid move," said Ivers. "Because if you don't play nice with me, like I'm playing nice with you, we'll have to vox you."

Vox? Something tugged at my memory. I knew this word. It's Latin. It means "voice."

"Only if you want to," said Ivers. "You're acting like you want to. Do you? I can do it myself, if you like."

"No," said Conn. The word was sharp. "That's a bad idea."

"I didn't ask for your opinion. You'll be debriefed later, McCrea."

Vox. Voice. A swirl of memory twisted inside me like a curl of that nasty cigar smoke, telling me that I *did* know what Ivers was talking about. I *did* know what it meant to vox someone.

They were talking about *making* me speak.

Torture.

"I was the senior ranking officer at the time of her arrest." Conn stepped between Ivers and me. "I'm responsible for her. At least until I *have* been debriefed, and therefore relieved from this mission."

Ivers looked at him disdainfully. "She's a tasty bite, Mc-Crea, but *she's a Shade*. I don't know what happened to you while you were playing school in the Alter, but you are seriously deep-sixing my respect of your objectivity."

Conn took a deep breath. "I hate Shades. You know that, sir. That's why you assigned me to this case. I *am* being objective. Voxing won't work on her. I have reason to believe that she doesn't actually know that she's a Shade."

"Impossible."

"Then debrief me. Listen to my report. Decide for yourself. Or ask Director Fitzgerald what she thinks of the IBI rules and regulations."

"Fitzgerald." Ivers repeated, sour. "Fine. Fine, McCrea. I'll debrief you. And in the meantime, you sweet little witch"—he tossed his burning cigar at my feet—"solitary confinement."

18

I'll take her," said Conn.

"Yeah, I bet you will," said Ivers.

Conn unshackled me from the chair, giving me a look that ordered me not to struggle. I didn't, if only because he'd left the firecuffs on my ankles and wrists.

He pushed me down the halls. "We don't have much time," he said, casting a wary look at the guards we passed every few minutes. "Can you walk faster?"

"No, I can't. Know why? Because I'm *chained at the ankles*."

"I can't do anything about that. Not now. Listen, about solitary: it's not as bad as it seems."

"No complaints here. At least it will get me away from you." Compared to everything I'd been through recently, a stint in solitary confinement would be a walk in the park.

"Your chains will be deactivated once you're inside the box," he said. "Just remember that nothing there can hurt you. Try to distract yourself. Think about . . . think about your art project. Or about how much you hate me."

With that, Conn stopped in front of a pair of guards standing outside an iron door. "Indefinite solitary confinement," he told them. "Ivers's orders."

To me he said, "I'll be back for you. I promise."

"Please. Take your time."

He gave me an inscrutable look, then turned and strode away, almost at a run.

The door clanked open and the guards pushed me into a dimly lit chamber lined with iron on every side, even the ceiling. Standing in the center of the room was a large glass box.

For the first time since I heard the words "solitary confinement," a worm of worry began to nibble at me. In my limited experience in the world of exploding handcuffs, glass was usually not a good sign. I dragged my feet, but the guards wrapped careful hands around my chains. "Don't fight it," one of them said. "You'll break your cuffs."

So I let them lock me inside the box, repeating Conn's promise to myself as if he weren't a mastermind liar. Nothing in here could hurt me.

I shifted my feet. I could walk two paces in each direction. The sounds I made were small and muffled—the scrape of my shoes, the short beat of my breath, the clack of my chains. I watched, but could not hear, the guards leaving the iron chamber.

I congratulated myself that I wasn't the claustrophobic type. Conn was so condescending. Solitary confinement wasn't so bad.

Then I heard a hiss and a click and my world burst into flames.

I reared back. Pure terror sucked the scream out of my throat. Fire was everywhere, flaring at me from all sides, driving away every rational thought. There was only heat and orange and red and fear fear fear. I beat against the glass walls, not caring that I might break my chains. Then I did break my chains, and ground my skin against their shards.

It was those thousand little cuts that began to slice through my insanity. They hurt. *Nothing there can hurt you.* Just one more of Conn's lies.

But if I was burning alive, shouldn't the pain be greater?

I glanced down at my wrists and saw smears of blood, but the flames weren't touching my skin.

The fire was outside the box.

It was a trick.

A psychological game, designed to make me crazy.

And it worked. Even now that I recognized that this was only mental torture, I couldn't stifle my panic.

Think, I told myself. *You're supposed to think. Distraction. Conn said.*

He said he would come back.

Yet . . . how could I be so desperate as to trust anything he said?

My sudden anger at myself reminded me of myself. Of who I was. Self-sufficient. Strong. Able to deal.

So deal.

Sweat oozed down my forehead, and I took a shaky breath. Everywhere I looked, flames blazed. I closed my eyes.

Think about how much you hate me, Conn had said. Now *that* was a topic that could occupy my mind for a long time. Thinking about him, though, only made me furious, and anger couldn't stop the earthquake inside me. I needed to be calm.

And the afternoon, the evening, sleeps so peacefully!

The words floated out of nowhere. Where had they come from? I grabbed on to the rhythm that strung the words together.

And the afternoon, the evening, sleeps so peacefully!
Smoothed by long fingers . . .

They were lines of poetry. From "The Love Song of J. Alfred Prufrock." Yet they were more than that . . . they reminded me of something. Of a warm day last summer. A kitten carried by the scruff of its neck, hanging from its mother's teeth.

Marsha had wanted to go on a road trip to Michigan. "You'll love it," she said. "Aunt Ginger lives on a blueberry farm. You can eat all the blueberries you want."

"I'd rather stay here."

"It'll be fun!"

"I'm not in the mood for fun. I'd like lots of non-fun."

"Well, too bad. We're going."

Then hours in the steamy car, with its broken air conditioner and broken tape deck. "Tell me again why we're doing this?" I had groaned.

"Aunt Ginger's sick. I spent every summer on her farm when I was growing up. This might be my last chance to see her."

And see her we did. She greeted us with a double-barreled shotgun.

It took some time for Marsha to calm her down, to remind her that she was her niece, and to explain that the stranger in the car was her foster daughter. Finally, Aunt Ginger lowered the gun and hugged Marsha with scrawny arms. She led us up the path to the peaked farmhouse, her white pouf of hair glowing in the sun. It was only then that Marsha whispered that Aunt Ginger was dying of Alzheimer's.

Also, we were going to clean her house and spend the night.

"Don't worry," she said. "I packed a bag for you. You'll adore sleeping in the attic, like I did when I was little."

I said she'd tricked me, and that sleeping over was a really bad idea (one word: shotgun).

But she badgered me into the house and then into the kitchen, which I had to admit was kind of cute with its frilled curtains and a lime green refrigerator that was all curves and chrome details like a 1950s Cadillac. Aunt Ginger forgot my name every five minutes, but she also made us chamomile tea and showed me the kittens in a cardboard box under the sink.

Then Marsha shooed me outside, telling me to explore while she gave Aunt Ginger a bath. I certainly didn't want to stick around for that. I wandered around the farm, checking out the blueberry fields. They probably hadn't been harvested for years. They were a vast thicket.

In the burning glass box, I tried to focus on the memory of tasting those blueberries. Soft beads cloaked in violet skin. The flesh green and pink and pale and slippery and sweet.

I remembered heading back to the house, where I helped Marsha with the cleaning while Aunt Ginger conked out on the couch. When night fell, Marsha led me to the attic, and she was right: it was awesome. Huge, with a view of the pond. A high, slanting ceiling and rows of beds on either side—at least twelve beds, in several shapes and sizes. Marsha plopped down onto a saggy feather mattress, said, "Take your pick," and promptly fell asleep.

I tried out the other beds, but none of them felt quite right. Finally, restless with my own restlessness, I gave up and tiptoed downstairs. I thought about raiding the refrigerator.

I slipped toward the kitchen through the living room, which flickered with light from the television. I glanced at Aunt Ginger asleep on the couch. Her twiggy hands lay almost gracefully on an afghan.

And the afternoon, the evening, sleeps so peacefully!
Smoothed by long fingers,
Asleep . . . tired . . . or it malingers . . .

Aunt Ginger's eyes sprang open. "You, girl!" An ancient finger crooked. "Come here."

I did.

"You're spooky, you know that?" She looked me up and down. "Your eyes are great black pools of need. You're hankering after something. Yes, you are. It makes a body uncomfortable, seeing all that want in your face and not knowing why. Go on, tell me what you want."

"Nothing."

"Don't be shy. Who knows? Maybe if you tell me your heart's desire, it'll come true. If not"—she grinned, flashing a full set of dentures—"I'll forget it anyway."

I thought about the disease creeping up the walls of her mind like the blueberry thicket coming closer and closer to the house. She was right. My secret would be safe with her.

I leaned forward and whispered in her ear.

Then I heard the crack of a door opening and fell on my face.

I opened my eyes. I wasn't in a Michigan farmhouse with Marsha snoring upstairs. I was in another world. I was in prison.

Or out of it, it seemed. I'd been let out of my glass box. The fire was gone. I blinked against the iron floor, then shoved myself up.

I stood face-to-face with a tall woman. She had a sleek cap of silver chin-length hair and was dressed in the IBI's gray uniform. I searched for the stitched knots that would give me an idea of her rank, but her collar was a band of solid scarlet.

"I'm Director Fitzgerald," she said.

I stared, still spinning in the memory of blueberries and Aunt Ginger.

"Can you speak?" Fitzgerald asked.

"Yes," I croaked.

"Good. I've just come from Agent McCrea's debriefing, which I found highly interesting. I understand that you are confused about your arrest, or that you're pretending to be. I'd like to hear things from your perspective. Who exactly are you, Darcy Jones, and what were you doing in Lakebrook, Illinois?"

Once upon a time, I wouldn't have been willing to spill my guts to her. But I was so tired, so shaken.

I told her about my five missing years, the DCFS, my collection of foster parents. Marsha and her silly bird spoons. My friends. Meeting Conn and not knowing what to think of him. I didn't (wouldn't, couldn't) tell her about the kiss. But everything else: his attack, how I vanished. Being afraid of him. Afraid of what I was. Or wasn't. I wasn't sure.

"I see," said Fitzgerald when I finished. "Of course, you might be a consummate actor. But I think you could be a golden opportunity."

"She is," said a voice from the shadows.

Conn.

He'd been listening the whole time. As soon as I'd thought he couldn't stab me in the back again, there he was, sliding in the knife, eavesdropping on my pathetic story.

"Darcy," Fitzgerald said. "Do you know what the Shadow Society is?"

"Obviously, *no*, I don't."

"It's a terrorist organization, made up of creatures like you. They look uncannily alike. They have different facial and bodily features, but the same black eyes, black hair, and pale skin. The IBI was startled to see you at the Water Tower, a portal regularly monitored to prevent unwanted traffic between our world and yours. We didn't know *who* you were—your face didn't match anything in our database. But one glance confirms that you are a Shade."

"Which is what, exactly?"

"A nightmare. Shades look human, but certainly are not. They can become incorporeal at will, and have used that against us, and more. Look: the May Day Massacre of 1916." An image of corpses with slashed throats lit up the wall behind her. I could see Conn clearly now. His features were harsh, almost black and white in the sudden light. "Gassing is one of their favorite techniques. The subway attacks of 1968." The image changed. "The Ravenswood Medical Center, 1997." More bodies, heaped up in hallways. "Hundreds of people, Darcy."

I felt sick. They believed that I had done this? *That?* "That's not my fault. All of that happened ages ago. You said the dates yourself." Only one, the last one, had happened during my lifetime, and that was when I was about five. Surely she didn't think that a *kid* had gassed the hospital.

"We're not accusing you," Fitzgerald said. "I'm simply telling you history that you apparently don't know." She swept a hand toward the last image. "This is a mere sample of the horrors the Shadow Society has perpetrated on humankind in the last century. The Interdimensional Bureau of Investigation was established with two related purposes: to patrol the borders between worlds, and to protect human society. It's a losing battle. Catching a Shade is difficult, for how can you catch what you can't see? How can you fight what you can't touch?"

"I'm guessing that this has something to do with your pyromania."

"Yes," said Fitzgerald. "Fire keeps you solid. It can hurt and kill you. It's our best weapon."

"Listen, I don't go around gassing people for fun. I'm not a terrorist. Before Conn dragged me here, I was living an ordinary life. Maybe it was a crappy one, but it was mine. Can't you just let me go?"

"That's exactly what I plan to do."

"You . . . do?"

"If what you claim is true—and McCrea's evidence supports this—then you were raised as a human with no knowledge of your origins. You are perhaps the one Shade who has no belief in the Society's propaganda of hatred and destruction. You must have sympathy for the human cause."

"My sympathy might be a little tarnished by abuse and kidnapping."

"Regrettable, but consider what we face." Fitzgerald pointed at the hospital scene, at the rigid limbs and bugged-out eyes. "There hasn't been a Shade attack in years, but recent intelligence indicates that one is in the planning stages. The IBI could keep you here forever, or we could take a risk. We could ask for your help. Infiltrate the Society. Make the Shades accept you as one of them. After all, you *are*. If you manage to gather useful information, the IBI will send you back to your world."

"How *much* information? How long would this take?"

"The IBI will determine that. Darcy, do you want more people to die?"

"No."

"Do you want to remain a prisoner of the IBI?"

"Yes. It is my one true ambition in life."

Fitzgerald made an impatient noise. "Do you want to go home or not?"

Home. I wasn't sure what that meant anymore. After the freak show on Saturday afternoon, Marsha would probably be glad to have her spare room back, and I'd have a short return trip to the DCFS. I'd stay in a group home until I was eighteen. Then the DCFS would cut me loose. Lily, Jims, Raphael . . . maybe we'd stay in touch. Or they'd forget about me. They'd have each other.

I remembered leaning toward Aunt Ginger and whispering my secret in her ear. "I want a family," I had told her.

Aunt Ginger had thrown back her head and laughed. "Why, make your own!"

Now, in the iron-walled cell, I considered Fitzgerald's proposition. I doubted there was much left for me in Lakebrook. As for the Shadow Society, it was possible they had done the horrible things Fitzgerald claimed, but I had only her word, and I didn't exactly trust the IBI to tell me the truth. Could Shades really be so evil? I wasn't evil.

And I was a Shade.

This was a chance. A golden opportunity, like they said. I could find out more about my past. I'd judge the Society for myself. Maybe I could find my parents and tell them exactly what I thought of them.

And maybe, just maybe, I'd find a place where I belonged.

"Yeah, okay," I told Fitzgerald. "I'll do it."

19

Excellent," she said. "McCrea will be your handler."

"My *what*?"

Conn's eyes cut to Fitzgerald's. When she nodded, he said, "You're to report to me, Darcy. We'll meet on a regular basis but at irregular hours, and in different locations. You'll pass along any valuable information about the Society. Meanwhile, if the IBI needs something else from you—either based on your intel or on its own agenda—I'll give you instructions."

"No way," I told Fitzgerald. "Not him."

"You have no choice," she replied. "You need a liaison within the IBI. If you don't like it"—she tapped the glass box—"you know your alternative."

"Give me someone else!"

But she was already heading toward the iron door. "McCrea

is best equipped for the job. And quite frankly, no one else would be willing to work with you."

She left me alone with Conn.

With a slight shake of his head, he began talking. Rules and regulations of our partnership. Standard operating procedure. Et cetera. I couldn't believe it. I couldn't believe he was acting as if he had done nothing wrong.

"Darcy, are you paying attention?"

Silence.

His mouth tightened. He stood, jerked the door open, and slammed it shut behind him.

What was I supposed to do now? Maybe I'd gotten lucky and Conn was out there shanghaiing somebody else into working with me. Or maybe the deal was off.

He wasn't gone long. He came back with a glass of water. He handed it to me. "In training, we're told that Shades don't need to eat or drink. But I know *you* do. I've seen you. After everything . . . I should have thought of this earlier. This water's balanced with electrolytes, sugar, protein, and vitamins. It's essentially a full meal."

I drank. "What about a shower? I'm a mess."

He shook his head. "You look authentic like this. Like you were brought into IBI custody and escaped. That's your story. There's more to it, of course, but we'll go over that later." He hesitated. "Darcy. I have to take off your bandages." His hand reached for mine.

I flinched away. "Don't touch me."

"I won't hurt you."

"You heard what I said." I gripped the empty glass, wondering if Conn realized that he had handed me a weapon.

He closed his eyes. Briefly. When he opened them, they were weary. "I don't want to take off your bandages, but it would look suspicious to the Society that the IBI healed your wounds."

And if I bashed the glass against his cheek, what then?

I'd face a swarm of people itching for the excuse to do their worst.

"Please," Conn said.

"Fine." I set the cup on the floor. "Go ahead."

He was gentle. The gauze unwound with a whisper, coiling onto the floor. My skin emerged: pink, crinkled. But healed.

Conn touched the back of my hand. I felt a spike of desire, then a gush of disgust. I wanted, more than anything, to disappear. At least then my body couldn't betray me.

"Michael did a good job," he said. "He has some medic training."

"Whose idea was it to jump me in the parking lot?"

At first, he didn't answer. "Mine. But the plan was laid before I really knew you. After we went to the railroad tracks, I couldn't figure out if you were pretending to be human or genuinely thought you were. The plan was a test. To see what you would do. At the very least, I hoped it would make you trust me."

It was hard, very hard, not to pick the glass off the floor and break it against him.

Conn said, "That night, when you didn't disappear in front of him, Michael wanted to arrest you then and there. It was the smart move. It would have been easy. But . . . I didn't want to do it."

"Oh, but you did. You *did* arrest me. Eventually."

Conn looked away. He nodded, and when he spoke, his tone was empty and official. "Tell the Society that you were burned when the IBI arrested you, and that you were imprisoned for at least two weeks. Then they'll think that time healed your burns. You got these"—he pointed at the small cuts etched around my wrists—"when you escaped."

He put another pair of firecuffs on me (yes, again!), swearing that they weren't turned on; they were for show, so that the entire IBI force didn't freak out at the sight of a free Shade strolling its halls. Then he led me through the IBI labyrinth until we reached an underground garage. He uncuffed me, unlocked a car with tinted windows, and then we were inside the car, up and out onto the street, driving along the lake.

"Where are we going?" I asked. A heavy fog cloaked the city, and all I could see was the road and the lake and the white sky.

"North. Closer to where the Society lives. Or that's what we think, anyway."

He outlined his master plan to get me inside Society headquarters. It seemed hopeless and dumb. I didn't care. At least I'd be free.

"It's quiet," I interrupted.

"It's Sunday. The streets are often empty on Sundays."

"No, the car. The car is quiet."

His face lit up. "That's because it runs on internal magnetic energy. You really should have that technology in the Alter. It causes less wear on the transmission, there's no messy oil . . ."

"Do you honestly think I care? I just found out I'm not human. I've got a few more things to care about than the transmission of a *magnetic car*."

He shut up.

I gazed out the window at the lake and the boats rocking by the piers, their masts fuzzy in the fog, as if they were being slowly erased. The sky was heavy with weather. I felt like the giant cloud sagging over the city—full, full almost to bursting, because even though the last thing I wanted to do was chat with Conn, I also was dying to spill out a thousand questions.

I settled for the one that seemed most important. "Fitzgerald said you presented evidence that convinced her I didn't know I was a Shade. What evidence?"

Conn took an exit and turned onto a small road. "From the beginning, you—you were complicated."

"Complicated."

"Mysterious. Shades don't exist in the Alter, and one has never been seen on surveillance of the portals. You looked happy. Happy with a human." He shook his head. "Impossible. And the name you signed wasn't fake. We traced it to Lakebrook High within seconds. I thought you were taunting the IBI. Showing us how powerless humans are, how we couldn't stop you from doing whatever you were there to do, even if we could easily track you down." He paused. "But there is another interpretation: that you had nothing to hide."

"And that convinced Fitzgerald." I raised my brows. "An interpretation?"

"There's also the way you reacted when I arrested you. The arrest . . . I didn't—it didn't go as planned. You broke your chains. I never thought you would do that. No rational Shade would—unless she didn't know what firecuffs were."

"Maybe I knew, and gambled. I could have bet that the cuffs were set to a low flame. Or maybe I wanted to go out in a kamikaze blaze of glory."

The car slowed. "We considered those possibilities."

"Then what proof did you have? I'm a monster. Why would Fitzgerald even think about letting me loose?"

Conn stopped the car. "It was your file."

"My *file*?" I had the strong suspicion that I was going to have to kill him.

"Your DCFS file. I showed it to her."

Psychological and medical evaluations. Report cards. IQ scores. Complaints from foster parents . . . even *I* didn't know everything that was in my file. "You stole it," I finally choked out. I felt as if Conn had seen me in nothing but my oldest, ugliest underwear. "When?" I demanded.

His hands fell from the steering wheel. "After we cut class and you told me about how your fingers had disappeared while you were drawing."

"Why did you do that? *Why?*"

"I was confused." He kept staring at the windshield. The weak light traced his profile, his crooked nose. He rubbed his eyes, and I found myself wondering when he had last slept. Then I wiped that thought from my mind. "It was obvious that you had no idea what happened," he continued. "You seemed so innocent. I'm trained to look for deceit, Darcy, but when I met you I had to rethink everything. It was possible that my training meant nothing and that you could lie without the tics and tells humans have, but then why would a Shade share anything about her past with me? Why would you welcome my friendship? Or seem to. Why would you—?"

He stopped right there, and it was a good thing that he did. The memory of our kiss paced between us like a dangerous animal. Neither of us wanted to touch it.

Conn leaned back in his seat and winced. I had forgotten about his ribs. He stared out the windshield and didn't speak.

When he finally did, his voice was crisp. "Don't deviate from the plan. Remember that the most insidious thing about Shades is that they can be anywhere, anytime, unseen. They may already know you're working for the IBI. Even if they don't, they might come to suspect you." He handed me a backpack. "Good luck. I'll see you on Tuesday at 3:23 p.m., at the corner of Michigan Avenue and Van Buren Street."

We'll see about that, I thought. I opened the car door.

"There's something else," he said.

I looked at him. I didn't know how much more "else" I could take.

"A photograph," he said. "Of a little girl. I found it in the IBI database, before I left for the Alter. There's no definite match, but she looks like you."

"All Shades look alike. That's what Fitzgerald said."

He shook his head. "They have the same coloring, but there are differences. Believe me. She looks like *you.*"

"Then give it to me." When he didn't respond, I raised my voice. "Conn, I want that photograph."

"I know you do. I'll bring it with me to our meeting."

For a moment, I held the door handle, shocked at how easily he had manipulated me. *Again.* That photograph was bait. Now I *needed* to see him again. I got out of the car, slammed the door shut, and walked away.

I didn't get very far before I heard the first scream.

Stage One of Conn's plan was for me to parade myself in full view of everybody: a nightmare walking around in broad daylight. If I caused enough commotion, an invisible Shade might notice. Brilliant, right? I mean, if I didn't get killed first.

I had had just enough time to register that the fog had lifted and that it was wickedly cold. I looked around at the low row houses and caught the smell of cinnamon rolls from a bakery. I guessed that maybe I was in Andersonville, the Swedish part of town. At least that's what it looked like, except that this street had an odd metal rail running along both sides, tacked high onto the walls of the buildings, sort of like a sideways roller-coaster track, except with a single rail. And in this world, there were more trees. The streets were cleaner. Also, everyone was dressed very formally, in a mix of tailored coats and strikingly modern accessories, like caramel-colored sunglasses and high-top boots with cutout patterns. No one wore even a trace of black.

A man strutted by in a fedora and striped suit, then skidded to a halt when he saw me. He shrieked. A few women in cloche hats were more composed, though they clutched each other and yelled for someone to call the IBI. I stood there, hoping that this was enough of a commotion, when a mob rounded the corner, carrying torches and calling me names.

It was almost as bad as high school.

I ran.

But I was running on empty. I didn't get far. The mob cornered me in a blind alley. I wondered if Shades got last requests, and if someone would give me a cinnamon roll before going completely Spanish Inquisition and burning me at the stake.

Then I heard a pair of light feet land next to me.

It was a boy.

"You," he said, "look like hell."

20

A nd suicidal," he added. "Are you suicidal?"

Our eyes locked. We were the exact same height. We were almost the exact same everything. "Um, help?"

The mob hung back. Two Shades was maybe too much.

"Just ghost," he told me.

Ghost. That was *my* word. "I can't."

"Really?" he said with amused curiosity. "Why not?"

"Sometimes it works, sometimes it doesn't. Like *now* it doesn't. Like *now* I could use your help."

He looked at the crowd. They were backing off, muttering that they should probably wait for the IBI, though I knew that they had been ordered by Fitzgerald not to arrive at the scene. "Very well." The Shade shrugged. "Shall we kill them all?"

Torches dropped to the ground. People shoved each other in their haste to run out of the alley. They were gone.

He chuckled. "My name is Orion. Who are you, and why are you playing cat and mouse? Or rather, why are you the mouse?"

"I'm Darcy Jones."

He pulled a sour face.

"What?" I asked.

"That's a human name."

Now that we were alone and I wasn't about to be barbecued, I had time to see that he wasn't exactly my male mirror image, as I'd first thought. There were differences. Orion's eyes tilted up at the corners. My chin is pointy. But he wore what I always wore—simple black—and looking at him was like looking at myself from a stranger's perspective. Slender frame. Hair like an oil slick. Winter skin.

Orion picked up the backpack that had dropped at my feet. He handed it to me.

"Thanks." I unzipped the backpack and dragged out a blue wool coat with a large hood. It looked like it was going to snow.

"What else have you got in there?" He yanked back the bag and rummaged through it as I put on the coat. "A brown wig. Makeup. Sunglasses. Things to help you pass as a human. Where did you get them?"

"I stole them."

"I don't think you're very bright, Darcyjones." That's how he said my name: in one big blur. "If you can't ghost, why weren't you wearing any of this? Or that?" He pointed at my coat as I tried to tuck my hair under the hood. "Of course the humans attacked you."

Stupid Conn and his stupid plan. "I was trying to find you."

"*Me?* Why?"

"Not you specifically. Someone like you."

"Someone like me," he repeated.

"I wanted to find a Shade. But invisibility makes it kind of hard to see you."

"A fair point."

"So my best hope was to make a screaming target of myself and catch a Shade's interest."

"Ah." He returned my backpack. "That's quite daring. Probably the swiftest solution. Not bad."

Huh. Stupid Conn and his apparently not-so-stupid plan.

Orion tucked a stray lock of my hair into the hood.

I pulled away. Was he flirting? No more flirting. Ever. Look where it got me the last time.

"I can do that," I said.

"You asked for help." Then he glanced down at my burned hands and his smile vanished. "What happened to you?"

A snowflake touched my wrist and disappeared.

It came and went silently. I was silent, too. I hadn't practiced this, how to tell Conn's lies. But the snow helped. A snowfall softens all the hard noises and hard corners. It's a natural liar. I saw the sky sprinkle down a hundred, a thousand little white lies, and decided that I didn't owe Orion anything.

Okay, he *had* saved my life. But saving someone and knowing her are different things. I had my reasons for following Conn's advice.

I needed time to decide if I even wanted to go home to Lakebrook. I needed information.

I also needed Conn's photograph. It could be the key to my forgotten years.

So when Orion said, "Let's walk. You can tell me all about it," I was ready.

TALKING WITH ORION MEANT talking to thin air. He strolled invisibly by my side while I muttered to myself like a crazy person. Every so often, I saw Orion's fingers flash in and out of being. He nipped at my elbow, tugging me in one direction or another.

When I asked, he explained (with some surprise that I didn't know already) that it was easy enough to make specific body parts appear and disappear, though harder to talk as a ghost.

"What about your clothes?" I asked.

There was a pause, then a wicked chuckle. "What *about* them?"

"They disappeared when you did." That's how it had worked for me, at Marsha's house.

"When Shades ghost, we produce a kind of energy, like body heat. Anything small or light enough and in direct contact with our skin—such as clothes, or a book—comes along for the ride."

"I assume your clothes will reappear, then, when you do."

Another laugh. "I suppose so."

It was snowing hard by the time he pulled me north along Clark Street, one of my favorite parts of Chicago. This was where (in my world) Lily and I stocked up on art supplies. Then we'd pile into a booth at the Melrose Diner with Jims and Raphael and order a huge plate of mozzarella sticks. We'd swear that the next time we took the train into the city we'd do something different. But we never did.

Orion's Clark Street was too clean. The apartment buildings were all very nicey-nice. Even the fire escapes were painted in pastel colors, though the strange rail that ran along the buildings was left alone, just plain silver.

Orion led me into a park and under a cluster of trees. The bad weather seemed to have chased everyone inside, so we had the place to ourselves. By then, I had told Orion almost everything, aside from the kiss (which might actually cease to exist if I ignored it hard enough) and how I really got away from the IBI.

Orion appeared. "So you ghosted out of IBI headquarters? I thought you didn't know how to do that."

I remembered Marsha throwing the kitchen knife, and the fear that had crept over me while drawing the IBI building. "If I'm startled or scared or about to die I can do it."

"Half an hour ago, you were being chased by humans. Weren't you frightened then?"

"No." I realized that this was somewhat true.

"They had torches."

"Yeah, but after firecuffs and solitary, the torches seemed kind of charming."

"The IBI put you in solitary confinement? You are a brave Shade, Darcyjones."

"Just Darcy." He looked at me quizzically. "Jones is my last name. You don't have to say it all the time." He was still confused. "Okay, I get it. Shades don't have last names, do they? Still, don't you spy on humans?"

"Of course."

"Haven't you ever noticed how they speak to one another? How they use names?"

"We study humans for self-defense. You're talking about cultural habits. We don't care about that. You're home now, Darcy. You're one of us. You need to learn what matters."

"Am I home?" I looked around the park, and it hit me that it *wasn't* a park. It was Graceland Cemetery. "You're kidding."

He brushed the snow off a marble grave slab and pried up one edge. It lifted like a hatch, revealing an underground tunnel. "After you."

Give me some credit. I *did* consider the possibility that the underground tunnel wasn't going to lead to a party with streamers and balloons and a big banner saying, "Welcome home, Darcy!" But I went down anyway.

I dropped about fifteen feet. The shock of hitting the packed earth below made me stumble and really dislike Orion, who landed as lightly as a cat. He had probably ghosted his way down most of the tunnel. Cheater.

He reached into a tangle of roots and must have flipped

some kind of switch. The tunnel glowed with sudden light, illuminating a passageway where the earth merged into stone walls and floors.

"How do you get electricity down here?" I asked, peering down the tunnel. Yes, I was stalling. That fall had shaken some sense into my head, reminding me (now that it was too late, now that I was trapped in an underground Lair of Doom) that Shades were supposed to be mass murderers. Hadn't Orion threatened to slaughter that angry mob?

But no, that had been a joke. Or a bluff. Or both.

Right?

I kept babbling. "Doesn't the IBI notice power being sucked out of the city to a hole under Graceland Cemetery? You might as well set up a flashing sign saying 'We're here. Come and get us!' over one of the mausoleums."

"We use solar energy. Many of the gravestones absorb sunlight, and its energy is conducted, stored, and used here." He paused.

The funny thing about being alone with someone who was maybe an Evildoer with a capital E is that, no matter how attractive he is (in a gaunt, French runway model kind of way), a pause isn't just a pause. It's a heavy, sharp weapon. "You look nervous," he said.

"Me?"

"Is there something you're not telling me?"

"Nope. Nothing." Aside from planning to spy on you and report back to your enemy, whom I happen to hate.

"Perhaps I shouldn't have brought you to the Sanctuary.

This might go badly if you're not ready yet. I can return you to the surface."

"No. I'm . . . you're right. I *am* nervous. There's a lot I don't know. About who I really am. How to act. You said it yourself: I need to learn what matters, as a Shade. I hope that everyone else will be as nice as you."

That won me a warm look. Ah, flattery. How had I over-looked this very useful tool all my life?

Orion led the way down the tunnel. I followed, and stopped asking questions about how this place had been built. I didn't need to. Orion had taken my question about electricity as an invitation to give an eager lecture about the Sanctuary, which was built in the nineteenth century. Its halls were made from Illinois limestone, he said, and its running water was pumped in from Lake Michigan.

The echoing tunnel flowed into a spiraling staircase that sucked us deeper into the earth as Orion explained that Shades had constructed the Sanctuary when their society began to change from a close-knit community based solely in Chicago to a nomadic collection of clans that traveled far and wide. "Different groups within the Society have different interests. We don't always agree. Yet we have a common adversary, and a common history. These things will always bring us together, and the Sanctuary provides a home to all Shades, wherever they come from."

The tunnel opened into a chamber with soaring ceilings. High up—maybe hundreds of feet high—arcades lined the walls. Passageways with balconies looped overhead, and I was so busy wondering if anybody up there was looking down at us that I didn't notice the appearance of another Shade until I bumped into her.

"Idiot!" The young woman had tiny hands. Tiny or not, they felt pretty strong when she gave me a good shove. "Have you no manners? Orion, who *is* this filthy creature?"

"Well, it's a very interesting story—"

"Get to the point."

Orion described our meeting. "So you see, Darcy meant no disrespect. Of course she should have avoided physical contact with you, but she can't ghost. She has lived in the Alter almost her entire life—"

"Then she is no proper Shade! What were you thinking, bringing her here?"

He paused. "I shouldn't have to remind you that our law requires us to offer shelter to any Shade."

"This matter should have been brought before the Council first. And it certainly will be."

She vanished.

"The Council." Orion sighed that kind of sigh that tells you that someone is totally screwed.

That someone being almost certainly me.

21

I had traded one prison for another.

It wasn't long before Orion and I were surrounded by Shades. They flashed into being, their faces as pale as cold stars. No one laid a hand on me, but the threat in their eyes was clear, and Orion whispered that I should do as they said. This meant getting locked into a small cell with a narrow bed and a stockpile of bottled water.

"The water has a high caloric content," Orion said as the other Shades shut the door behind them, throwing the lock. "And it's full of electrolytes, so—"

"Let me guess. It's essentially a full meal."

"I'm sorry, Darcy. It's against the spirit of the Society to imprison you like this. No Shade should be kept in a cage."

Of course, most Shades *couldn't* be imprisoned, not in any

normal sense of the word. Which—I realized as I looked at the bolted door—meant that this room wasn't designed to hold them.

It was a cell for humans.

"Take heart," Orion said. "This is one of our nicer cells, and you won't be here for long. I'll plead your case with the Council."

Then he disappeared.

There wasn't much to the room, but I discovered that what I thought was a closet door actually led to a bathroom. I went weak-kneed at the thought of being clean. I stripped off my clothes, telling myself that things weren't so bad, that I should take heart, like Orion said. Sure, being dragged to another dimension and finding out you're not human is higher up on the scale of life-altering events than getting booted out by yet another set of foster parents. Maybe being in jail sucks a bit more than living in a group home. But I'd been through a lot. I could get through this.

Naked, I shivered. I looked down at this body that was mine and yet not at all what I'd thought it was. Then I saw my bruise.

I had a lot of them at this point, but this wasn't just any bruise. The one that caught my eye was a small purple smudge on my wrist.

"Hello, you," I whispered. The memory of Conn's touch welled up within me.

And Darcy Jones, the tough girl with the snide remarks, the one who had been broken and remade every year, in every new home, in every new school, and every new life, crumpled. Tears slid into my mouth and then fell onto my hands until I covered my face.

I didn't want to be a Shade. I didn't want to disappear. I hugged my arms to my chest. Stay, stay, I told my skin.

If I vanished, I might never find myself again.

OVER THE NEXT FEW DAYS, Shades came and went. They examined my injuries, asked me questions. By the time I started receiving visitors, I had sucked back my tears and scraped myself together, though I nearly lost it again when I found a hairpin lying on the slick shower tiles. The little stowaway. I must have missed it when I'd pulled apart my lopsided effort at elegant hair on that Saturday morning that felt like forever ago.

I flicked the pin into the corner of the bathroom.

When the Shades came, I told my story over and over again. That I didn't remember how I'd gotten to the Alter as a child, that I hadn't known what I was, that I'd been minding my own supposedly human business when an IBI agent hauled me into this world. I'd broken my firecuffs and ghosted out of IBI headquarters.

"But you say you don't know how to ghost and manifest," said one Shade with a short black beard.

"Manifest?"

"Appear."

"It just kind of happens. Or doesn't." I knew that sounded lame. I didn't need this guy's skeptical look to remind me. He gave me one anyway.

"Perhaps it's pure instinct." This came from a middle-aged woman with ropy arms and burns wrinkling half her face. "Think of her as a child, Veldt," she told the man. "One that has been raised by wolves."

It probably wasn't a great idea to scowl at one of the few people who seemed to be on my side. But when I did, she chuckled.

"There is no humor in this situation," Veldt snapped. "We have no proof that anything she says is true."

"Then what do you propose?" she countered. "Imprison her forever? Perhaps we should experiment on her. Cut her open to discover why she can't control her shadow."

That sounded like one of those fake, extreme things people say in order to sound snarky. But Veldt hadn't rolled his eyes. He hadn't told her she was being ridiculous. Fear zigzagged through me—not quite panic, not yet. But getting there.

"Is that what you think we should do?" the woman continued. "No. A thousand times no. She is one of us."

Veldt made a frustrated noise. "Now, more than ever, we need to be careful."

"We need to embrace the risks of who we are!"

They continued to bicker in a deadlocked way, and my fear ebbed when it seemed that there were no immediate plans for eviscerating me.

I hadn't missed the significance of what Veldt had suggested: something was afoot inside the Society. *Now, more than ever.* I wanted to ask him what he'd meant by that, but I figured that if the IBI was right and the Society was planning an attack, asking questions that came too close to that truth wouldn't help my Little Lost Lamb image.

One question seemed innocent enough. "Can you tell me what day it is?" I interrupted. "I'm losing track of time. No window, no clock. Trapped hundreds of miles below the earth's surface, you know?"

"Wednesday," said the woman.

Wednesday. My meeting with Conn was supposed to be yesterday. I wondered what he'd felt, waiting, and how long he'd stayed, and what his final thought had been before giving up and heading home. I imagined him pacing. Anxious, even if only for himself and the trouble he'd get into when he told Fitzgerald that the Shade had slipped through his fingers. I saw his face taut with worry.

It almost cheered me up.

I SLEPT. Drank tons of water. You might not think water has a taste, but it does—a kind of non-taste taste—and I got sick of it. Time stretched and bent and tied itself into knots and finally ceased to exist. I began to wonder if I was losing my mind, or if one of the several fires I'd been tormented with had damaged my eyes, because sometimes I saw dark blurs in the corner of my vision, flickering against the walls.

"Really?" Orion said when I told him during one of his visits. "That's wonderful!"

"Please tell me that the Society doesn't think that going blind is a holy rite of passage."

"Of course not," he said when he had stopped laughing.

"You're just coming into your own. Shades don't disappear completely. We leave a trace. A shadow. Most humans, however, never see it. The fact that you do means that you're starting to remember what it means to be a Shade."

This strange thought—that I was learning how to not be human—crinkled my brain, completely distracting me from an important significance of what he'd just said. Then I got it. "Are you saying that Shades have been in my room? *Spying on me?*"

He brushed aside my anger. "You're under observation, Darcy. What did you expect?"

"There are laws against that in my world!"

"*Your* world?" His black eyes narrowed, all laughter gone. "And in *your* world, is it unheard of for prisoners to be monitored by, say, video cameras?"

"But I had no idea! I never even thought . . ." I felt like I'd been dipped in slime, and it occurred to me that this was what people in this world had to deal with on a daily basis. The possibility of being surveilled. Never trusting that any moment was truly private. "No wonder humans hate you."

"Unbelievable." There was a dangerous curl to his mouth. "It's unbelievable how ignorant you are. Do you even know what caused the break between *your* reality and *ours*?"

"Yes." I drew myself up to my full height. "Yes, I do, as a matter of fact. It was the Great Chicago Fire."

"And who caused it?"

"Mrs. O'Leary."

He choked.

"I mean, her cow. Like in the song." I sang the rhyme every Chicagoland kid is taught in school:

"Late one night when we were all in bed,
Mrs. O'Leary lit a lantern in the shed.
The cow kicked it over, and Mrs. O'Leary said,
'It's going to be a hot time in the old town tonight.
Fire! Fire! Fire!'"

"That," said Orion, "is absurd. It was a witch hunt. A witch hunt burned down the city. Surely you must have been curious about the fact that there are no Shades in the Alter."

"Not really. It's hard to notice the absence of people you don't know exist."

"There are no Shades in the Alter because they were murdered. Every man, woman, and child. It was a genocide."

Words have different weights. This one would break any scale. It lay there, heavy and hard, between us.

"There were never very many of us," Orion said. "We don't know how we came to exist, though legend tells that the first Shades were born on the shores of Lake Michigan in a meteor shower, and that this is why fire can kill us. We came from fire, and so fire will return us to the darkness.

"Humans hated us, and we were afraid of our own shadows. Afraid to embrace who we were. Afraid of what humans might do. They did it anyway. They burned us from our homes. They set women on fire with torches made from the hair of their children. The fire swept out of control and raged through the city for three days. When the ash settled, the Society was gone and humans in the Alter insisted that nothing, not even a memory, should remain of it. It was forbidden to speak about Shades, and all evidence that they had ever existed was burned.

"Humans here revere the Great Fire. There are monuments to it in the center of town. Not a day goes by that the Society doesn't dread that this world will try to reenact what *yours* did." His eyes pinned mine. "The humans struck first. Anything else that we did later, we did in self-defense. Consider that. Consider it while you wait for the judgment of the Council. Given your current attitude, there will be time for you to think about it."

He vanished.

I hated Orion. Who was he to expect me to embrace the ways of people I didn't know? I hated the entire spying Society, for watching me while I wept. I hated Fitzgerald, for making me lie. Didn't she know how hard it was to fake it, to create a new me, every time I met a Shade? It was exhausting. It was horrible. So was she.

I even hated my friends, for not being there.

I hated Conn. For everything.

And I hated J. Alfred Prufrock.

Because he waits and wanders and dithers and can never make up his mind. Because he tells himself there's time to think and think and think. But there's not enough time. There never is. Not for anybody in this whole universe. We always want more. Why waste it doing nothing?

It was time to take matters into my own hands.

A brilliant thought crashed and shook in my mind like a gong. I raced into the bathroom, fell to my hands and knees, and snatched the hairpin from its dusty corner.

Know why jailbreakers and burglars in movies always use a bobby pin to unlock doors?

Because it works.

22

What they don't show you in movies, and what the Ingleside Home girls had showed me long ago, is that you also need a tension wrench.

I glanced around the room, searching for shadows that didn't belong there. I didn't see any, but they could appear any second. I grabbed my backpack and stuffed it with water bottles.

Now for the tension wrench.

After some thought, I attacked the bed. It was squeaky and old and—thank God—held together with screws. I twisted off a few and pulled away a metal bed slat. It would do.

I stared at the lock on the door. It looked simple enough. The Ingleside girls would laugh at this so-called security. But I figured that the Shades weren't super worried about me breaking out because A) they could probably tackle me in the halls, and B) I didn't know how to get out of the Sanctuary. I had a plan for Problem A. As for B . . . well, I'd worry about B later.

I bent the bobby pin into a right angle. Now I could use it as a pick. All I had to do was wriggle it into the lock and free the cylinder that blocked the whole mechanism. Little pins kept that cylinder in place.

I stuck my pick in the lock and raked it along the pins. My hand shook. But I set the pins, pushing them back on their springs. The cylinder slid in its chamber, the lock shuddered open. I was free.

And the Shade stationed outside my door noticed.

I snatched a water bottle from my backpack and threw it at his head. He vanished, and the bottle smashed against the wall behind him. I ran, gripping the bed slat in one hand.

Shadows swarmed behind me as I tried to retrace the steps Orion and I had taken to my prison. Sometimes a Shade would manifest at my side, and I'd lash out with the bed slat. Several of them tried to block my path. I fired bottles at them. I pounded into the Great Hall and had spotted the tunnel leading to the earth's surface when countless Shades erupted into being, surrounding me with their dizzying similarity. Their gleaming eyes and skin and fierce faces. I slung bottle after bottle at them until I had none left. Then I struck out with the slat. The Shades flickered away. Flickered back. Finally I hit one, cracking the slat down on his arm. He cried out, fell back, then lunged forward with a kick to my side. I hit the ground, and Shades poured on top of me.

They wrenched at my hands. The slat was snatched out of my fingers. They squeezed down on my chest, and I couldn't breathe. I couldn't do anything.

But at least I'd tried.

THEY DRAGGED ME into a courtroom that looked nothing like a courtroom. Waterfalls chattered and shushed in the corners. Ferns and orchids twined across the limestone walls.

So how did I know it was a courtroom and not an underground botanical garden sprouted by someone with serious heat lamps? My biggest clue was the curved, monolithic table and the five angry Shades sitting at it. My second clue was the doom that hung in the air. And the third?

That was when a young woman—*the* woman who had shoved me on my first day in the Sanctuary, who was sitting at the center of the table like she was the one in charge—said, "Who will speak for Darcy Jones before she meets the Council's judgment?"

"I will," I said. I took a deep breath to calm my hammering heart.

"You can't," said one of the five seated Shades, an elderly woman whose hair was still jet black. "It's not allowed. You must remain silent."

"She doesn't even know our laws," I heard someone mutter in the crowd of Shades behind me.

"Well?" The young woman smirked, templing her small hands. "Will anyone speak for her?"

No one answered.

Not at first. Then I heard the whisper of feet shifting behind me. Light feet. Graceful ones.

"I will," said Orion.

His voice did little to dull my fear. Sure, he'd promised to speak in my defense, but that was before the "Your World/My World" argument.

"Orion." The scarred woman who had interviewed me leaned forward, placing her hands on the table where she sat. "You can't be serious. Not after what she's done."

"And what has she done?" said Orion. "She fought for her freedom. Don't tell me, Meridian, that you wouldn't have done the same."

Meridian's face tightened, but into a pleased kind of frown.

"No." The young woman slapped the table. "Meridian would never have acted like that. Never. No cage can bind a Shade. But that's because a Shade will *ghost her way free*. She won't crash and blunder through our Sanctuary in a shameful display of *humanity*."

"She fights well," said a stocky man to her left. "She's fast, too fast for me to ghost out of her way. I have the marks to prove it." He raised a bare arm, which bore a welter from my bed slat.

I held my breath. It was a *good* thing that I had hit him?

"Your injuries cannot be part of her defense!" The young woman cinched her tiny hands together.

"Why not?" Orion faced her. "Zephyr, the Society can't rely wholly on its ability to ghost. We must also know how to fight. We need warriors. We always have. Darcy struck out against us, true, but what choice did she have? We should have offered her our protection and help, as our law demands. Darcy never should have been imprisoned to begin with."

"No one questions that Darcy Jones is a Shade," said the elderly woman. "But—" She glanced at Zephyr, who said, "She claims she was raised by humans, yet who knows what she hasn't told us? How are we to believe anything she says? She's a security risk. At the very least, she needs to be imprisoned indefinitely."

"I have to agree with Zephyr on this matter," said a serious-eyed man seated at the edge of the table. "We live in dangerous times. If what Darcy says is true, I pity her, but we cannot trust someone who knows so little of our ways."

"You won't even give her the chance to learn!" said Orion.

"Her escape attempt speaks for itself. She may be a Shade, but she acts like a human."

"Which is why you must believe she is telling the truth about her past," Orion insisted. "A Shade who can ghost and manifest would never go through such an elaborate, *physical* effort to escape. She would simply vanish. Instead, Darcy risked everything to break free the only way she knew how. This proves she has been honest with us and is worthy of our trust."

Not too long ago, I could have strangled Orion. Now his passion made me cringe. I was a liar. I wasn't even a good one, and still he believed me.

"You're blinded, Orion." The man sighed. "I'd like to know by what."

"By admiration." Orion's eyes flashed to mine. "She cheated the IBI. If the IBI thinks they can contain us, they will think of

Darcy Jones and think again. Yes, she has been raised as a human, and yes, the damage done is immeasurable. But all the more reason that she needs our help to reclaim her identity as a Shade."

"Impossible," said Zephyr.

"You know what your problem is?" That was my mouth, moving. Those were my words. It took a little while for my brain to catch up and realize that I was about to piss everyone off. "You're afraid of humans."

A collective gasp sucked all the air out of the room.

"You know what you've got here?" I jabbed a thumb into my chest. "A golden opportunity." My guilt about lying evaporated in the face of my sudden insanity. What was I *doing*? "I don't know much about this world, but I know that there's a war between humans and Shades."

"That's not what I would call it," said the man I'd hit.

"You will be silent!" Zephyr hissed at me. She glanced at the man. "You, too, Loam."

He bristled.

Was it possible that I was winning at least one of the Council to my side? I plunged ahead. "I know a lot about humans. I could help you."

Shades turned toward one another, and the chamber murmured with whispers. I wondered if my parents could be here, in this very room. If they were, they didn't seem eager to claim me. Not that I'd expect them to be. Not that the thought of them being here, and saying nothing, hurt.

Not at all.

"We are excellent spies," said Meridian. "We observe humans daily. There isn't much you could tell us about their ways that we don't already know. Besides, you grew up in another world. Humans are different there."

"They can't be that different," I said.

"This isn't a conversation!" said Zephyr. "This is a *trial*."

"But I know the way humans *think*."

"Darcy can even pass as one of them," Orion said.

The crowd muttered again. Something flashed across the elderly woman's face. The serious-eyed man leaned back in his chair.

"The Society has always been poor at disguising ourselves as humans," said Orion. "We need to be manifest in order to have a physical effect on the world. Yet how many missions have failed because a Shade ghosted the moment things got dangerous? Darcy's very inability to ghost could work to our advantage. And she *moves* like a human. Wigs, makeup, clothes rarely work for us. Not for long. Yet she was able to walk down the street in broad daylight with nothing more to hide her than a coat with a large hood. Any other Shade would have brought attention to herself. She would have been too agile. She would have walked too quickly. Airily. Darcy positively lumbers."

"I don't *lumber*," I said. Orion looked at me. "I mean, yeah. I'm slow. Total slowpoke. That's me."

"So she's quick when it's convenient to you"—the elderly woman glanced at Loam—"and slow when it's convenient to you." She nodded at Orion.

"I'm a multitalented girl," I said.

"Enough." Zephyr stood. "The Council has heard what it needs—*more* than it needs—to judge the fate of Darcy Jones."

"Agreed," said Meridian.

The five Council members vanished.

They were gone for a long time. How long, I couldn't say, but my feet began to prickle from standing and my body swayed. Many Shades watched and waited, their faces lit with an intensity that could have been for or against me. Others ghosted away for lengths of time and then reappeared for a few seconds, like people who don't really care about a football game on TV but occasionally stick their heads in the living room to check the score. Some Shades never showed their faces, not once during the trial. I could see several shadows against the courtroom walls cast by people who weren't there.

It was eerie. To be constantly scrutinized by invisible eyes. To have someone burst into being inches in front of my face. Sometimes a host of Shades disappeared at once like a flock of birds taking flight. I couldn't help flinching. I was startled every time. There was no way I could get used to this, even if I wasn't waiting for my fate to be decided.

I tried to catch Orion's eye. He stared straight ahead.

When the Council manifested around the table, Orion glanced at me. He knew, as well as I did, what they had decided. We could tell even before Zephyr opened her mouth. We could tell because of the way she looked at me.

Like she wanted to eat me alive.

"Darcy Jones is free to claim her rights as a Shade," she said, "and to call the Sanctuary her home. She may come and go as she pleases." Her next words were carved out with very precise diction. "She is truly one of us."

Orion gave me a half smile, triumphant but also cocky, like he had never doubted this outcome. But I'd seen the tension on his face and wondered if some hidden part of him, the one that had accused me of ignorance, was uncertain whether it was a good thing that we'd won.

I smiled back at him. I pretended I wasn't someone who would betray him.

I'd betray anyone in that room—the IBI, too, if I wanted. I didn't know what I wanted, exactly. Not yet. But I was going to find out, starting with finding Conn and snatching that photograph right out of his thieving hands.

23

This is something I have to do on my own," I told Orion. "It's dangerous to explore the city by yourself."

It was several days after my trial. Orion and I stood at the top of a long flight of stairs, just below a hatch that, above the earth over our heads, was covered by a gravestone.

"I'm not afraid," I said.

Orion's expression softened.

I'd suspected those words might work some magic on him.

"I understand," Orion said, and pushed open the hatch. Snow showered down onto us, biting at my skin, sneaking under my collar. I yelped.

"Brr!" Orion shook snow from his hair.

"Freezing," I agreed. "But *you* don't have to feel the cold. Ghost, if you want."

"No. There are certain advantages to having a body."

For a second, I could feel it: the chill of delight. Snow tingled on my cheeks. Then I realized that Orion's black eyes were too bright. "Without lips," he said, "how could I say goodbye to you?"

I took a step back. Buttoned my coat. Reached for the edge of the opening above me, ready to hoist myself into the pre-dawn sky. "Goodbye."

His face dimmed, yet he lifted his fingers to my neck and fastened the last button on my collar. "Goodbye. Be back by nightfall?"

I nodded stiffly, then pulled myself up, kicking a snowdrift down onto Orion's head.

He spluttered. "You'll pay for that."

I looked down at him, unsure if he was joking. He reached for the hatch. "By the way," he said. "You're welcome."

The gravestone shut.

For a moment I simply stood in Graceland Cemetery, surrounded by pearly gray light and lacy black trees. Then I walked away.

It should have been easy to thank Orion, but I never had, not once since he'd defended me at the trial. Not when he gave me a tour of the Sanctuary. Not when he showed me how to access the earth's surface.

I owed Orion. I would have to be very careful around him. But not today.

It was a Tuesday morning, two weeks since Conn and I were supposed to meet. I had the foolish hope that maybe Conn would show up at the meeting point: 3:23 p.m., at the corner of Michigan and Van Buren. That's what I'd do, if I were him. I'd go there every Tuesday, same time, same place. So that's what he should do, if he was smart.

If he thought I was still alive.

If he thought I hadn't decided to break my deal with the IBI.

As I said, it was a foolish hope.

My boots crunched on the snow. A sheer layer of ice had frozen over it, and I could feel it hold my weight for a fraction of a second, right before it cracked. And over and over, with every step.

It was strange to be so aware of my weight. Of the quiet miracle of gravity. That I had feet and that they touched the ground. But when I opened the cemetery gate, looked back, and saw my footprints in the snow beneath the pink line of the rising sun, I knew that this was how I wanted to be. Cold and heavy and *there*. A ghosted Shade wouldn't have left footprints, but I didn't want to be a ghost. I wanted to be myself.

The gate clanged shut behind me.

I knew where Michigan and Van Buren was. That part wasn't hard. It was in the Loop, the heart of downtown Chicago, just south of the Art Institute. At least, in my world.

The tricky part was getting there. I was so far north that I'd have to find some kind of ride. I adjusted my wig, letting the long brown curls trail out from underneath the raised hood of my coat, and slipped on the sunglasses. I headed west.

The streets were quiet. There were no buses. A car whizzed

down the street, Indy 500 style, and I was sure I'd hear a police siren, but none came.

I searched for the familiar steel frame of the elevated train. The skies were empty.

No buses. No trains. Only a few cars, as far as I could tell. But there had to be public transportation. I just couldn't see it.

I spotted a few early morning commuters, stepping outside of low houses so flashy it was hard not to stare. My Chicago was gritty, a city born out of steel, railroads, and meatpacking plants. It's big and brown and gray. But these homes were painted like gingerbread houses with candy-coated roof tiles. Slick pink window frames. Stained-glass windows. Lily would have loved it.

And then there were the people. Dressed in wraparound coats with fur collars, narrow-waisted jackets, long gloves, canes. *Everyone.* Even my coat, I realized, subtly fit the fashion.

I figured that one of these people had to be heading toward the L, so I followed a man with stovepipe trousers. He briskly turned the corner and dropped down out of view. The sidewalk seemed to have swallowed him up.

Of course. There must be a traditional subway. One tunneled underground, like most city metros.

I strode toward the spot where the man had plunged downward and saw nothing but a rectangular metal plate in the middle of the sidewalk. I tapped it experimentally with one boot, then stood on it.

And screamed.

It plummeted beneath me, hurtling down like an elevator

with cut cables. I looked for walls to hold on to, but there weren't any and it wouldn't have mattered if there were, because the plate had locked onto my feet with a force that held me completely rigid. I was frozen in place.

The plate slowed, then hovered above a long, metal box. I stopped yelling, and just in time, too, because the top of the box slid back, revealing several people standing in the box's bright light. My plate dropped through the opening.

I had been deposited directly into a subway car.

There were no seats. Everyone stood against the walls, chatting and ruffling newspapers. It crossed my mind that maybe I should lean against a wall, too, but I wanted to find the map that every civilized society puts in its subway cars.

The car hurtled sideways, flinging me against a wall. The same force that had held me to the plate now sucked my cheek against the metal side of the car. I tried to move. Couldn't. I was splayed against the wall in a crazy yoga pose. The other passengers stood calmly, having had the good sense to stand in comfortable positions before getting glued to the walls.

The car glided to a stop. I wobbled, suddenly unstuck. The roof slid open. Someone stepped onto a metal plate in the center of the car. He shot through the roof, which then sealed shut.

The car jumped forward, skewed left, and sang with speed.

After several stops, I still couldn't see a map and didn't dare ask for help. Finally, after being zipped around and shaken like a fancy Cuban dancer's maracas, I realized that either I was going to throw up my breakfast of highly caloric water or I had to get off this mad fun-house ride.

I got off at the next stop. I didn't care where the train spat me out.

It was somewhere along the river. I studied the skyline, searching for a black skyscraper with broad shoulders: the Sears Tower, the tallest building in Chicago. Seeing it would help me figure out where I was.

It wasn't there. The skyline bristled with buildings that stretched even higher than the Sears Tower, with shapes I recognized from my sketchbook. Thin, elegant curves. They gleamed in the dawn like ice sculptures.

Since I couldn't have the Sears Tower, along with a fair number of other perfectly reasonable things, I had to be satisfied with the fact that at least the sun told me I was west of the river. The center of this city seemed to be where my Loop was, even if these new skyscrapers had been designed by some fairy tale architect.

I set out to cross the river when my boot touched a brass disk set into the sidewalk. I jerked my foot back. This disk wasn't a subway plate, though. It was round, much smaller and brighter, and etched with the symbol of a flame. It didn't seem to *do* anything. Then I saw another one in the ground, several feet ahead, and another one just after that. It was a trail.

It didn't lead exactly where I wanted to go, but it was morning, 3:23 p.m. was still many hours away, and even if I had to see Conn, I dreaded it. I dreaded seeing the fine, awful angles of his face again, and eyes that managed to be so clear even when his mouth was full of tricks and lies.

Maddening, to have to work with him. Sickening, that he

had fooled me. Impossible, that he was the key to my return home, and my past.

Impossible.

I followed the brass disks. This would be a distraction, something to unknot my nerves. It would also be a weapon. I refused to be so much at Conn McCrea's mercy, and if there was anything I could do to hold my own against him and not rely so much on the whims of the IBI, it was to learn more about this world.

The disks led to a house that was simple and old, but in pristine condition. I recognized it from my sketchbook, and this alone—that shiver of recognition, with no memory to explain it—drew me closer.

The house was a tourist attraction. Scores of people milled around, talking excitedly. A group of schoolchildren seemed to be on a field trip, and oohed and ahhed as they listened to their teacher, who stood in front of the door. A group of adults gathered in the front yard around a bronze statue of a man raising a torch that burned with a small, living flame. I heard the teacher's voice rise and fall with authority.

". . . Cecil Deacon," she was saying, "who led the 1871 crusade against the Shades in the Alter where, of course, this house burned down and he tragically died. Hundreds of human lives were lost and the fire left many homeless, making the Alter's Great Chicago Fire the most traumatic event in the city's history. Yet it was also ultimately uplifting. We must remember the heroism of Deacon and his followers. They accomplished the unthinkable. They rid their world of Shades."

"We should do the same," I heard a man mutter.

"Notice," the woman continued, "the wooden sidewalks that lead from Deacon's house. They date back to the early nineteenth century, and very few remain in the city. They are a Chicago Heritage monument, and can be traced back to this house, almost"—she smiled—"almost as if Cecil Deacon is the origin of everything that makes Chicago special."

So Orion had been telling the truth about the Great Fire. I stared at the woman, shocked that anybody could be so enthusiastic about the deaths of so many people. And maybe I would have spoken up, but I noticed something.

One of the schoolgirls had an extra shadow. It was the vague shape of a person, longer than the schoolgirl's, and cast by no one. No one, anyway, that I could see.

I went very still.

Who was it? Zephyr?

Maybe Orion.

Or was it someone else?

It was possible that this was a random Shade, doing some random sightseeing on a random day. That dark blur didn't necessarily have anything to do with me. There was no reason to think I was being followed.

If this sounds like wishful thinking, that's because it was.

I turned my gaze from the front door and the children gathered in front of it. I pretended to study the sculpture. Out of the corner of my eye, I saw the shadow glide away from the girl and bury itself in the greater darkness cast by the house itself.

I snapped my gaze from the statue and strode toward the river.

If I really was being watched, I'd find out soon.

It was easy enough to cross the river, though several cars speeding over the bridge nearly mowed me down. Traffic was picking up. Here, cars zoomed everywhere, and when I was several blocks east, getting closer to Lake Michigan and my meeting point with Conn, cars jammed the streets. I pretended to survey the bumper-to-bumper gridlock, then shot a quick glance down the street, in the direction from which I'd come.

A shadow was slinking through traffic. It seeped into the trunk of one car, spilled out the windshield of another. It was about fifteen feet away, but crept closer and closer.

Toward me.

I hurried east, down quaint wooden sidewalks, my feet rattling the planks. I touched the railing, ran fingers over carvings of flowers and flames, grateful for all this newness, this difference, this everything that made it easier to pretend that I hadn't noticed a shadow dogging my heels.

I had to lose the Shade. I couldn't be seen with Conn.

Street signs flew past, ones that should have read La Salle and Dearborn and State, but instead said Deacon, Wildfire, and Blaze.

It was when I reached Grant Park (here, 1871 Memorial Park) that I saw my chance: a farmers' market set up under bare trees. I pushed through the crowd, ignoring the sharp elbows and rude stares that would soon create yet another problem if those eyes got a little beadier and saw that I was a Shade.

I'm human, I'm human. I pressed deeper into the hundreds of people, hoping the shadow would lose me in the crowd. *Please believe me.*

I shuffled north past stalls of home-baked goods and winter vegetables and slaughtered chickens. Then the row of stalls ended and the crowd thinned.

I ran. Swung around a frozen pond and headed back to the city streets, to Michigan Avenue. Sprinted up the sidewalk, no longer caring who saw me, not even knowing what time it was or what I would do if Conn wasn't there, and what I would say to the Shade if he—or she—caught me and asked what I was doing and why I was afraid. I couldn't say, *You. You frighten me, because I'm like you.*

And then I was at the corner of Michigan and Van Buren. I stood still, panting.

Conn wasn't there.

Just a row of stately brownstones that didn't exist in my world.

My chest heaved, cold air stabbing into my lungs.

A door opened.

"Come inside," Conn called from the town house. "Quickly."

24

You're shaken." Conn shut the door behind us.

I didn't look at him. Instead, I cast a glance around the marble entryway, where an empty fountain stood in the center of the hall. Its silence seemed to make a lot of noise.

"Tell me," he insisted.

"I didn't think you'd be here." I tried to steady my breath. "I mean, I thought maybe. Maybe you'd come every Tuesday at the same time. To check."

"I came every day." He let his hand rest on the doorknob. "I practically lived here."

I walked down the hall into a bright white parlor. Conn had to be lying. Everything looked as if it hadn't been touched for years. Sheets covered the furniture. A fog of dust lay on the mantelpiece.

"It's not mine," he said. "This house belongs to the IBI." He stood behind me, far too close.

I edged away. Tossed my itchy wig on the grand piano, shoved my sunglasses in a coat pocket. I pulled a sheet off the sofa, revealing blue velvet brocade, and curled into its corner. Maybe it was the luxury that calmed me, or the quiet of the house, which felt like it had been quiet a long, long time. I felt suddenly safe, even with Conn there.

He pulled a chair in front of me and sat on its dusty sheet. But I knew that when things really mattered he'd rip off any sheet. He'd strip anything bare.

"Darcy, please say something. You have no idea what the past two weeks have been like for me."

"*I* have no idea? Me?"

"I only meant—" He stood. Something flickered across his features. On anyone else's face it might have been hurt. But this was Conn. His mouth hardened, and I remembered the word Ivers had used to describe him: ruthless. "You missed our meeting. You broke your agreement with the IBI. You are *required* to tell me why."

So I told him about meeting Orion, about my prison, my escape attempt, my trial. I shouted it, my voice ringing so loud my ears hurt. I rose to my feet, and so did he, and all the while his eyes looked into mine, when they didn't have any right. When they were, in spite of everything, too horribly beautiful to bear.

"*You* have no idea," I said. "You have no idea what you're making me do."

The room echoed with my words. It echoed with everything that was between us.

"I want that photograph," I said. "I need to know if it's really me."

"You haven't told me enough."

I stepped toward him, and even though he towered over me I felt my arm tense with the kind of power that could smash a man's face. "Give it to me."

His eyes narrowed. "Give me a location. You haven't said where the Society lives."

"I've told you plenty. Now you know *how* they live. You know about their customs. You know that there's infighting."

His expression turned scornful. "What makes you so sure this is news to the IBI?"

"Give me the photograph, or I walk out of here and you will never see me again. The deal is off."

He stalked to a bookshelf that had only appeared empty. Now I noticed a few books stacked on the lowest shelf, resting near an envelope.

Conn tossed the envelope onto the velvet sofa. "You can't keep it. You'll have to leave it here. Yes, I understand that I can't force you to listen to me. You've made your point. But if the Shades find that photograph they'll ask questions you won't want to answer, so make the smart choice. I'll give you your privacy," he added in a tone that made clear he was glad to get away. "I'll be down the hall in the kitchen. Find me when you're done."

When the oak door swung shut behind him, I sank down

onto the sofa. I touched the slim manila envelope and my arm went limp. It took a lot of strength to open the envelope, more than I would have thought possible, since this was what I had wanted: to find the truth about my past.

I shook the envelope, and the photograph fell into the palm of my hand.

The photograph was in color, but looked as if it had been taken in black and white, the girl's cheeks were so pale, her hair and eyes so dark.

And I remembered.

The little girl's birthday was soon. Right around the corner. I was going to be five years old. A baby tooth wiggled in my mouth and I wondered if it would fall out when I turned five, and who would remember my birthday here. I wanted to hold my mother's hand and press my face against her stomach, where she was soft, but she wasn't there and if she were she'd say what she always said, that I was too old for that. I needed to learn.

I gripped the photograph so hard that it bent and my image warped. The memory drained away before I could remember where "here" was, or why I was there, or what my mother's face looked like. I tried, but my mind got stuck. What I knew— without knowing how I knew—was that this photograph had been taken before I was abandoned in the Alter.

The girl's eyes stopped my heart. I hadn't known, until I saw the photograph, how I had really felt that day outside the Chicago firehouse. Over the years I had told myself a certain story about that girl. That she had downed the caseworker's hot chocolate and asked for more. That she hadn't minded the DCFS doctor's cold stethoscope because it was a lot less chilly than being outside. But the girl in the photograph had eyes stained with fear.

Me. I had been terrified.

I couldn't actually remember where I'd been when the photograph was taken, but I didn't need to. I knew the answer: the IBI.

I slid the photograph back into its envelope and smoothed a hand over its surface, as if soothing it to sleep. I looked up, because I had to look away from the memory of that girl, and noticed again the three books on the otherwise empty shelf.

Undusty books. New ones. Conn's.

I drew closer.

Two of them were about mechanics. Dense, complicated stuff with blueprints and equations that gave me queasy Pre-Calc flashbacks.

The third was the collected poems of T. S. Eliot.

It made sense. Conn was thorough, and passionate about his job even if he'd never truly been that way about me. And he saw a lot, much more than the simple fact that I cared about J. Alfred. Of course he'd studied the poem. Pretending that he cared about it, too, had been part of his cover.

This didn't explain, though, why he kept it with him still, now that he had nothing to fake, nothing to hide.

I set the book and the photograph on the shelf. There were mysteries I had to solve, I reminded myself. But not about Conn.

My boots made no sound on the hard hallway tiles. The kitchen door was wide open. When I entered, Conn was gazing out the window at the garden, where snowflakes drifted and swayed through the dead branches like silent white bees. Even though he was expecting me, he hadn't yet realized I was there, and the light silvered his face into something vulnerable.

"You were right," I told him. "The photo is of me."

He turned. The news did not make him happy.

"What?" I said. "What does that mean?"

"It means that you were taken into IBI custody. You were arrested."

"For *what*?"

He shook his head. "I don't know. Information connected to that photograph is classified."

"Unclassify it, then."

"It's not that easy. There's a file about that girl—about *you*— but it outranks me."

"Conn—" I don't know what I would have said, how I could have convinced him, but he interrupted. "I'll find out for you," he said.

I waited for him to add something, and when he didn't I crossed my arms. "What will I owe you for that?"

Anger flared across his face. Then it was gone, like every other trace of emotion he had ever shown me. "Nothing. But . . . don't get your hopes up. It'll take me a while to find anything out, and you might not like what I find. There are ways of getting around a classified file, especially in this case, because it's strange for the IBI to arrest a child Shade. That's one of the reasons the photograph caught my eye when I saw it in the database. People will remember that arrest. I can talk to some of the older agents in the Bureau, pull unclassified files from that year—"

"It was 1997. I don't remember much else."

"1997? You're sure?"

I nodded.

"All right," he said slowly. "This will take time. But I'll do my best."

The crazy thing was, everything that made me resent Conn was exactly what made me sure that his best was very good.

"Whatever you do," I said, "don't let a Shade catch you doing it. I'm pretty sure the Society is watching me, and I don't want them to have any reason to connect me to you."

"What do you mean, the Society is watching you?"

"I was followed by a Shade."

"When?"

"Just before I got here."

"And you're telling me *now*?" He was instantly alert, his gaze skittering into the corners of the room.

"Don't worry, the Shade's not here."

"You can't know that," he said. I watched his eyes transform the kitchen into a potential war zone. "Everything we said could have been heard. Everything."

"Trust me," I said, and explained how Shades cast shadows. "So some humans *could* see that Shades are there, even if they're incorporeal. That's what Orion said."

"That's incredible." It took me a moment to realize that the sound in Conn's voice was hope. "Why haven't we heard of this before?'"

I shrugged. "Maybe people doubt what they see. Maybe they think it's a trick of the light."

"But why some humans and not others?'"

"I don't know. You figure it out."

He fell silent, and I realized it was warmer in the kitchen than in the rest of the house, and slightly damp, as if water had recently been boiled to make tea or pasta. Pencils lay on the table of a breakfast nook for four, and there was a toothbrush in a glass by the sink. In a barely noticeable way, Conn *had* been practically living here. I felt a flicker of a feeling I couldn't name.

"Priming," he said.

"What?" I was less startled by the word than by my discovery.

"Priming is a psychology term." He caught my glance. "I'm trained in psychology. Agents have to be, for interrogation."

Whatever emotion I'd been feeling withered. "Of course you do."

"Priming is when the mind is prepared to understand something that would otherwise be too extraordinary to believe. Like interdimensional portals. Even if somebody in the Alter is standing by the Water Tower, he's not going to stumble through that portal into our world. He won't even see it, because he can't conceive that it's there. But if someone *told* him it was, or if his mind was otherwise primed for the possibility, he might see it. Maybe that's how seeing the shadows works."

"Like an optical illusion—the one everyone knows, that looks like a white goblet. Then someone tells you that, no, it's really two black faces in profile, and suddenly they're there."

"Exactly." He smiled. "This is valuable information, Darcy. Thank you."

"Valuable enough for me to skip town and head back to Lakebrook, courtesy of the IBI?"

His smile grew smaller. "Not quite."

"Then what is?"

"The exact location of the Sanctuary would be a good start."

"Excuse me if I don't leap at the chance to give the IBI the perfect site for a big bonfire. You'd wipe them out."

He made an impatient noise. "We're not monsters."

"Really. What about the Great Fire?"

"What about it?"

"Humans killed every last Shade in my world."

"Yes, in *your* world."

"So if there's a war," I said, "humans started it."

His expression was quickly growing angry. "It was more than a hundred years ago. Besides, you can't possibly blame *this* Chicago for something that didn't even happen here."

"This Chicago is drooling after the Great Fire."

His voice got dangerous. "Meaning?"

"You people are obsessed with it. You name streets after it. You make *art* out of it. Just because the Holocaust happened a long time ago in Europe doesn't mean it's okay for me to build a shrine to Hitler in my backyard."

"Street signs. *Street signs*," he hissed. "I forgive the Society, then. They murdered innocent people, but I forgive them, because now I understand that the street signs hurt their feelings."

I leaned back against the window and felt the cold glass against my shoulder blades. "I will never tell you the location. I don't trust you."

It was as if I had slapped him. Honestly, if I had known I'd get that kind of reaction from those words I would have said them earlier.

He turned. Walked out of the kitchen. Walked down the hall, picking up the pace. Then straight out the front door, letting it slam behind him.

Without mentioning when or where we'd next meet.

The IBI deal, it seemed, was off.

Well, I wasn't going to cry over it. As it happened, Conn had given *me* a piece of useful information, about portals. The IBI had never said *how* they'd send me back to my world, and they'd never claimed that only they could do it. It was stupid of me not to notice that before.

I'd find my own way home. In the meantime, I'd ask Orion if he knew anything about a five-year-old girl arrested in 1997.

I raised the hood of my coat and left the house.

There was no sign of Conn—and, really, that was for the best.

I headed north on Michigan Avenue, hugging my arms to me for warmth. I had a long walk ahead. One free of certain people and public transportation systems I despised.

The wind blew down the street, lifting a skeleton of ivy that trailed along a brick wall. It ruffled the tailcoat of a man walking toward me, the only other person on the street.

His footsteps quickened. His eyes darted to mine. I had just enough time to realize that my sunglasses were in my coat pocket and that I had forgotten the wig in the house when a gust of wind blew back my hood.

My black hair swirled in the air. The man stopped. Horror broke across his face.

I thought he would run.

And he did. Straight at me.

He slammed into my chest and caught me by the throat before I could fall.

25

Murderer!" he screamed. I scratched at his hands, trying to pry them from my throat, but he crushed harder. I couldn't breathe.

I fell to my knees and he raged down at me, his words getting so cruel and dirty that I was grateful when the rushing sound in my ears drowned out his voice. Lights spattered across my vision and I felt his spit on my face. The shock of it overwhelmed me, and things were starting to go dark when something rammed into the man's side and knocked him away.

Conn shoved him up against the brick wall, wrenched his arms behind his back, and cuffed him. The man struggled against the steel bracelets. He tried to break away as Conn hauled him to the nearest lamppost and chained him to it. "You traitor!" he howled at Conn, who stalked away.

Toward me. He knelt on the cold sidewalk and held my shoulders with hands that felt kind. Yet his face was furious. "Darcy—"

I shrank away. "I didn't do it," I croaked. "I couldn't have killed anyone."

"I know."

I let him help me up and lead me down the street, far from the screaming man. "Why did he do that?" I wiped at the wetness on my cheeks, which could have been the man's spit or my tears. "He doesn't know me. He can't know me."

"That doesn't matter." Conn's mouth pressed into a line so thin it looked like it could cut. "To most people, Shades are all alike. You're all murderers."

I was so dizzy and breathless that it was a full, long minute before I realized that Conn's arm was warm around me. I stepped away.

"*Most* people," he said. "Not me." As gentle as his words seemed, hostility flared from his body like fire. He reached for me.

"Don't."

His hand fell. "Are you okay?"

"I'm fine."

"Well, I'm not." He pressed his fingertips against his brow, hiding his face. I sensed the rage echoing behind his hands, even if I couldn't see it anymore. He took a deep, deliberate breath. His hands fell away. "We don't have much time," he said. "I have to go back there and deal with *that*." He tilted his head in the direction of the man. "Put this on." He handed me my wig. "When I went back to the house and saw that you'd left, that you were gone, I . . ." He stopped. "If something had happened, it would have been my fault. I was stupid. I was"—he looked away—"unprofessional."

I rubbed my throat. I couldn't believe that *he* was the one acting like it hurt to talk.

He said, "If I hadn't found you—"

"So is he another IBI agent?" I nodded at the man. "Like Michael? Did you pay him to do that?"

Conn didn't speak. He looked stricken, which was nice to see. "You should go," he said finally. "Meet me a week from this Thursday at the Jennie Twist Library, 118 Schiller Avenue, ten-forty a.m. Go to the third floor and browse for books. An IBI agent posing as a librarian will lead you to a private study room. I'll see you on Thursday?"

I shrugged. "You will if you find out more about that photo."

"I said you wouldn't owe me anything for that, but I've changed my mind."

Of course he had.

"You need to do something for me," he said. "You need to learn how to ghost."

AS DAYS PASSED, I should have been trying to meet Conn's requirement, but I could only think about how much I missed food, which was nowhere to be found in the Sanctuary.

The bottles of water did their trick, I guess. I was never physically hungry. But I was full of longing. I wanted fries so hot they'd burn the roof of my mouth. Spaghetti wound tight around a fork. Crunchy cucumbers. Toasted bread with a slick coat of butter. A bowl of ice cream as I curled up on Marsha's couch by the radiator.

When I asked Orion where they kept the real food, he said, "You mean human food."

"I just want something that tastes good."

He cocked one brow. "You don't have to search far for that."

"Orion."

"Darcy." He leaned against the large oak tree growing in the center of my new Sanctuary bedroom. It had been three days since I'd seen Conn.

"I'm serious." I reached for the closest branch and began to climb. "It's driving me crazy." My foot slipped against the bark.

"I heard that," Orion called from below. "You're going to fall." He almost sounded like he wished I would.

"I'm not worried."

"Only because you think I'll catch you."

I snorted.

"I heard that, too," he said.

I reached the top of the branches and surveyed my room with its shiny black marble floors. The large bed was draped with fine white linen, and lamps glowed from deeply set niches in the walls.

Orion appeared on a branch next to me. He lounged, swinging one foot in the air. "Why are you climbing this tree?"

"To make it rustle."

"To make it rustle?"

"The Society's given me this swanky room with a great big galloping tree growing out of the floor, and I can't sleep at night because it's too quiet. Trees *always* rustle, Orion. But there's no wind here, no windows, not even a draft."

"Hmm." Orion's midnight eyes grew thoughtful. "I understand. It's hard to accept what humans have taken away from us. We can't enjoy the world above—the trees, the sky—without feeling hunted, so we do our best to bring the world into our home. But you're right. It's not the same."

Orion hadn't understood, not really, or he would have realized that even though what I'd said was true, I'd also climbed the tree to place some distance between us. And now he was mere inches away.

"You only want food because you're used to it," Orion said. "And because you're always in your body. If you were a ghost, you wouldn't be hungry. That's why we don't bother keeping human food in the Sanctuary. It spoils, and we don't need to eat often. So we drink IBI water."

"Are you telling me the IBI never eats real food?" When Conn had given me that water in IBI headquarters, I'd thought it was supposed to be a quick fix, not a way of life.

I was right. "They use the water for military operations," Orion said. He propped an elbow on the trunk and rested his temple against his fist. "It's a recent invention of theirs, and a good one. We love stealing their supplies."

"If I ghosted, how long could I go without food?"

"As long as you needed." He paused. "I think you're

missing the point. When you ghost, your body ceases to exist, so *everything* that it does stops. You stop digesting food. You stop growing hair. You stop aging."

I nearly fell out of the tree. "Are you saying that Shades live forever?"

"We can live a very long time."

"So you could . . . put your body on pause, manifest ten years later, and still look exactly the same?"

"*You* could, too."

This meant that no one in the Society was the age they seemed. It meant that age had no meaning. I clung hard to the tree trunk. This was disorienting. It made my brain feel like a planet that had been zapped with an antigravity beam. All my thoughts were soaring off the ground and crashing into each other. Some things were starting to make sense, though, like how Zephyr could be in charge of the Council when she looked like a college student. "How old is Zephyr?"

"I think she's in her nineties."

"*What?*"

"Ninety-seven? Ninety-eight? I can't remember."

"Wait. How old are *you*?" Orion looked my age, but for all I knew, he could be a grandfather.

"You look faint. Maybe we should climb down and have this conversation on solid ground."

"*Orion.*"

"I'm nineteen." He studied me. "Does that make you see me differently?"

My mind skipped back to something he'd said earlier. That

I could look young longer, too. That I could prolong my life. That I— "Oh my God," I said. *How old am I?*"

Orion shrugged. "Probably more or less the age you think you are. You were abandoned in the Alter as a child, and most children can't control their shadows very well. They don't have the training or attention span. But since you can't remember your early childhood, we've no idea how much of your life, total, you've spent as a ghost. Nothing's certain."

I began to climb down from the tree. I was shaking. In the end, Orion did have to catch me. He was waiting at the bottom when I missed a branch.

"Told you so." He set me on the bed, then stretched himself on the blanket, a black, sinuous line against the white. "There. Now don't you feel better?"

I remained seated at the edge of the bed, but for once I didn't move away from Orion, because I was suddenly grateful that he was there to hold on to. If I wanted.

Which, you know, I didn't.

But I could.

"Every time I think I've gotten used to my new life, something *newer* happens," I said.

"How old your body will be is a choice, Darcy. There are Shades like Zephyr who want to get as close to immortality as possible. They think a longer life means more wisdom, and that more wisdom means more power. But the body has its powers, too, and its own ways of being wise.

"I've spent"—he glanced down at himself—"perhaps two years total of my life as a ghost. Even brief minutes out of my body add up, eventually. But two years is nothing. I need to know how to live in my skin if I'm to be ready for whatever humans might try next. They attack us when they can. A few months ago, a Shade was burned to death in the streets by an angry mob."

I knew the answer, but still I asked, "Why?"

"Why?" He gave a hard laugh. "Why *not*? Because he was there. Why were humans chasing *you*, the day we met?"

I would never get used to it. I'd never be able to believe that so many people wanted me dead. How terrible, to die. How worse, for my death to make someone happy. I touched the scar on my neck, and a memory almost quivered through me. Then it ebbed, and faded.

"Darcy." Orion's voice startled me. "Finding out what you can do is *good* news. The gift to ghost and manifest is your heritage. Do you realize how jealous humans would be if they knew?"

"They don't?"

"They did, long ago in the Alter, and look where it got us. The Society has tried very hard in the past hundred or so years to hide this from humans. When we're arrested, we give false names, false ages. Even if we're voxed."

With a sinking feeling, I realized that details I'd thought would be important about my photograph—like a name, an exact date—might be totally useless. It was as Orion said: nothing was certain. Unless Conn found out *why* I'd been arrested as a child, I'd get no closer to my past.

"How long can we live?" I asked.

"The oldest Shade in history died at almost two hundred. We don't get sick, but the body wears out eventually."

I gave him an incredulous look, which he misinterpreted as disappointment. "It's not forever," he said defensively, "but it's a long time. You should be glad."

His expression was growing troubled. The last thing I wanted was for him to think I wasn't stoked about being a Shade, so I smiled at him, though inwardly I kicked myself for letting this conversation go the way it had. I'd meant to talk to Orion about interdimensional portals. Now I realized that I couldn't do that without tipping him off to the fact that I wanted to lunge through one of them and head home. He was too sensitive to any hint that I was less than thrilled with Shadedom.

"Absolutely," I said. "Humans are lame. They can have their spaghetti with pesto made from fresh basil with lots of Parmesan and pine nuts. Who needs it? I'd much rather be able to ghost when I want and live how I want, however long I want."

"Bravo!"

"I bet you thought I was feeling sad or something, but—" I cast about for some kind of explanation and remembered how Orion had asked if learning his age had made me feel differently about him.

Insecurity. The realization was stunning. Orion, always confident, always outrageously flirty, had had a moment of insecurity. Because of how I might see him.

Because of *me*.

"I was worried that you think I look ancient," I said. "Worn out. Damaged." I showed him my hands. "I have these scars."

He sat up and took my hands in his. "You don't look worn out. You look like a warrior."

Not exactly what every girl longs to hear.

I felt the strength in Orion's long, thin hands and wondered if I dared to ask him what had been haunting me. Was it a safe question?

Was anything?

We used to sell Mexican jumping beans at the Jumping Bean Café. They were encased in plastic boxes, and hopped and danced like they were full of voodoo. They weren't really alive, but something inside them was. A worm. A tiny parasite that had eaten its way to the center of each bean. When it moved, the bean jumped.

I had an idea. It had burrowed inside me like one of those worms.

"I want to ask you something," I told Orion.

"You can ask me anything."

"Could my disappearance from this world . . . my memory loss . . . could it have something to do with the Ravenswood Medical Center attack?"

He dropped my hands. "What do you know about Ravenswood?"

"I know it happened in 1997. I was five years old then. It was the year I was abandoned in the Alter." It was also the year the IBI took my photograph. "Maybe it's no coincidence."

"Impossible." He shook his head. "The Shades involved in that operation died."

I remembered the sickening image splayed on the wall behind Fitzgerald. "So it happened. The Society really did it."

"Of course we did. I don't know much about Ravenswood, though. It happened when I was young, and many of the details are still cloaked in secrecy. Only a few people knew about the mission, and fewer still were directly involved." He gave me a shrewd look. "Is your memory returning?"

"Maybe." I couldn't tell Orion that the parasite in my mind had the voice of the screaming man. *Murderer*, he had called me.

I had lied when I told Orion why I couldn't sleep at night. It had nothing to do with the tree.

Murderer.

"I don't want to talk about Ravenswood anymore," I said. "I want to ask you a favor."

"Yes?"

"Will you teach me how to ghost?"

Orion clapped his hands and laughed. "Finally!"

26

I'd been trying for hours, with no sign of success.

"No," said Orion. "Don't breathe. You're supposed to stop everything. Your heart. The blood pumping in your veins. Even your breath."

We were in a room on one of the upper floors of the Sanctuary, with wide windows overlooking the Great Hall many feet below. Orion had said it would be too distracting for him to practice in my bedroom.

"I can't stop my heart from beating," I said.

"You can. You simply don't want to."

"What I want is for you to stop nagging me. Stop giving stupid advice. You're supposed to *help*."

"And you're not a child," he said. "In fact, children are easier to train than you, because at least they're thrilled to ghost. You act like your gift is a burden."

Orion was infuriating. He was also right. I'd gotten better at telling lies, though my voice always sounded brittle to me, like my words would shatter upon impact. Yet members of the Council had believed me, and so did Orion. Still, I hadn't figured out how to lie to myself.

I didn't really want to ghost.

I know. *I* had asked Orion. *I* had asked for this, and not because Conn had ordered me to. It was because of that screaming man.

In my dreams he grabbed me over and over again. In my dreams I died.

Murderer.

I used to think that at least I could rely on myself. That I was strong. Now I felt like someone with no control. Someone who fell out of trees. Who heard one word and was so paralyzed that she had to rely on the help of someone she hated.

This was Conn's fault. That afternoon at Marsha's house, he had broken something. Not only my trust in him. He had also broken my trust in myself.

"I thought learning how to ghost would make me feel stronger," I told Orion. "But I can't do this."

"Of course you can. You *have.*"

A memory trembled inside me. I heard my father's voice, rumbly deep, buried so far down in his chest that I wouldn't have been able to find it even if I looked really hard. *You need to learn,* he told me.

I looked at Orion. I *had* ghosted. Not just recently. Also long ago, long before I'd seen the Alter.

But I'd never been any good at it.

"You don't know how to control your shadow," Orion said. "That's all."

"Okay." I pressed a cold palm against my throbbing forehead. I tried to cling to the memory, yet it shredded and vanished. "*How* do I stop my heart?"

"You do it with what you have when your body's gone. You do it with your mind. You do it with your soul."

Pretty words. But they didn't help me either.

Finally, when my headache was raging and I didn't want to say so because Orion would tell me that if I ghosted, the pain would go away, I opened my eyes and looked around the room. Trunks were stacked against the black walls. "You said that this is a practice room. Practice for what?"

"Warfare."

I opened a trunk. It was filled with short metal batons. I'd seen these before, strapped to the hips of the guards in the truck. "That's IBI equipment. Those are flamethrowers. You brought *fire* into the Sanctuary?"

Orion shut the trunk. "Don't touch that."

"Orion." I paused. "Did you follow me?"

"What?"

"The other day, when I left the Sanctuary to explore the city. Did you follow me?"

"Why would I do that? You said you wanted to go alone."

"Well, someone followed me. I saw the shadow."

Orion's mouth pinched. "Contrary to what you might think, I don't push myself where I'm not wanted."

"I didn't mean—" This was going badly. Ghosting was going nowhere, now Orion was pissed, and I had just seen evidence of weapons that the IBI would like to know more about—a *lot* more about. And Orion was clearly in no mood to be milked for information.

It occurred to me that I was going to have to find other Shades to make friends with.

"I'm sorry," I told Orion. "I'm not thinking straight. My head really hurts."

"If you ghosted—"

"Hey, maybe you can give me some advice," I interrupted. "I want to get to know this Chicago, but the subway sucks." I explained what had happened on the train. "The humans didn't notice me, but I had no clue where to get off. I can't walk everywhere, and until I learn how to ghost—"

"You will," he said comfortingly, and I saw that if there was one thing he could understand, it was my frustration over not being able to control my shadow. "In the meantime, we're going to the Archives."

THE ARCHIVES WAS IN THE MOST basement part of the Sanctuary. It was a warehouse stacked with zillions of human objects—pots and pans, racks of clothes, umbrellas, wheelbarrows, knickknacks, bear traps, kayaks, and stuff stuff stuff, neatly labeled and arranged, stretching as far as the eye could see. It looked like a never-ending garage sale, and in front of it all was an elderly lady sitting at a desk.

"Oh." She took off her glasses. She let them dangle from the beaded chain around her neck and looked straight at me. "It's you."

She was the Council member at my trial, the one who had called me a security risk.

"Her access here is restricted," she told Orion. "*You* may come back another time, whenever you wish, so long as it's without her."

"You can only control her access because she can't ghost," said Orion. "You know perfectly well that any Shade can use any part of the Archives, if only because boxes and locks wouldn't stop us. Your job is to keep human objects organized, Savannah, not deny Darcy her rights."

She played with her glasses chain.

"We want to look at Section 7A," said Orion. "That's not a sensitive area."

Savannah stood, stiffly. "I voted against you," she told me.

"Surprise, surprise," I said.

She sniffed. "Fine," she said to Orion. "Follow me."

Our footsteps echoed in the musty air as she led us past some contraptions that I couldn't name but that Jims would probably go wild over. I half expected to see a rocket ship that delivered chocolate sauce propped next to machines that looked like they could either blow something up or vacuum out a car.

Finally, Savannah waved an irritated hand. "Section 7A."

Bicycles. Rows and rows of bicycles with rusted chains and colored chrome and sleek racing bodies. I even spotted a unicycle.

"Wow," I said.

"Pick one," said Orion.

It took only seconds for me to find the perfect bike. It was flashy. A candy-apple red with orange rubber handlebars and spokes so shiny that the wheels looked like exploding stars. A few weeks ago, I never would have chosen this bike for myself. But Lily would have.

Orion followed my gaze. "It's very bright." He squinted. "Don't you think you'd draw attention to yourself?"

"No. No, I don't." I knew he was right, but I couldn't say that I needed that bike, that I loved it because Lily would love it, and I loved her. I couldn't say anything he'd understand.

Savannah shrugged. "If you can get away with riding around Chicago on *that*, then what Orion claimed at your trial must be true: you can pass for a human like no other Shade. Maybe we *could* put her to good use."

"We don't want to get her killed before she's properly trained," said Orion.

"I'll be fine," I said. "Savannah's right. This bike will prove how much I can fool them."

Orion smiled.

"And—" Savannah hesitated. "It *is* pretty."

It was only then that I noticed that her glasses chain was strung with blue and yellow beads. At least one Shade, I realized, didn't see the world in black and white.

I was wheeling the bike toward the Archives' exit when my hand snatched something off the shelves. I'd grabbed it purely by instinct, out of some certainty that whatever it was, it belonged to me, and it was a moment before I really saw what I held. A box of oil paints.

"Can I take this, too?" I asked.

Savannah peered at it, pursing her lips. "It couldn't do any harm."

I tucked it under my arm. For the first time since I'd arrived in this world, I felt pleased. The box of paints reminded me that I wasn't a totally different person, even if I wasn't human. I still wanted to make beautiful things. And the bike made me think that Marsha had been right to give me a red sweater. Maybe it was time for me not just to seek beauty and color, but also to claim some for myself.

I gave the shiny bike an affectionate pat.

The only thing I didn't like about it was that it would take me to Conn.

27

I got totally lost.

As I biked south my brain kept getting fooled into thinking I knew where I was. Once I even thought I saw Lily, though that was crazy and impossible, and the girl had dark hair. Lily would never let her natural color show. Still, as I biked past I let myself pretend it was her, and that I was home.

It was a bright, bright day. The snow had melted, and the streets were streaked with sunny water. My bike tires swished through the puddles, water spattering my ankles as I wove through the city, trying to figure out how to get to Schiller Avenue. It wasn't easy. In the midst of all the bizarre differences of this Chicago—that metal rail running high along the buildings, the nauseatingly cute green lampposts, those decorated wooden sidewalks that Orion said raked in tons of money in tourism every year—I also had to keep an eye out for any stray shadows that might be following me. I almost crashed a dozen times.

But no humans spotted me as a Shade, and it didn't look like I was being tailed by the Society. At least, not today.

When I found the address Conn had given me, I parked the bike and bounded up the library steps, past the bronze lions with their shiny paws that had been rubbed by thousands of strangers. I was late. I was also, I realized, eager to see Conn.

Which made sense. He had information I wanted.

The Jennie Twist Library didn't exist in my Chicago (neither did Jennie Twist), but getting around the building was easy, thanks to a lifetime of navigating new schools. Plus, this library was super old-fashioned, down to its wood-paneled elevators. I got inside one of them and watched the golden arrow above the doors swoop past floor numbers. It occurred to me that Conn had chosen this place precisely because it didn't have any sci-fi techy gear for me to deal with. It occurred to me that I was grateful.

I got out at the third floor and headed for the stacks. Browse, I told myself. I was supposed to browse until an IBI agent posing as a librarian found me. I riffled through the shelves, which were massive oak things that would flatten me like a cartoon character if they toppled over.

I started with the A's. Alcott, Ardent, Austen. My hand stopped there. I was a pretty big fan of Jane Austen, and had read everything she'd written—which wasn't enough. I always wanted more, more, more. So imagine my delight when, nestled in between *Pride and Prejudice* and *Sense and Sensibility*, was something completely new: *Reservation*. I grabbed it off the shelf and was flipping through it when someone coughed. I turned to see a girl who was a few years older than me. She was very pretty. Angry, too.

"He's waiting," she hissed. She stalked away before I could respond, then paused and glanced over her shoulder. *"Follow me."* She rolled her eyes. "I can't believe he's wasting his time with someone like you."

I resisted the urge to whack her in the back of the head with my leather-bound book.

She whisked me toward a private study room, motioned for me to enter, then shut me in, alone with Conn.

He was sitting at a table, drawing something in a sketch-book that looked like a design for a machine. I instantly wanted to come closer, to see better, but reminded myself that I wasn't supposed to be curious about Conn. My heart wasn't supposed to stutter just because he lifted his tawny head and looked at me.

It made me mad. Even though my mind knew better, some part of my body couldn't forget the tug and pull of Conn.

He closed the sketchbook. "You're late."

"And you're obnoxious. But *I* won't always be late."

He blinked. Then he chuckled.

"You're not supposed to laugh," I said grumpily.

"It was funny."

"Not that funny."

"No, really." He smiled. "I'd congratulate you on it, but only nice people give compliments. Unfortunately, I'm doomed to always be obnoxious."

I had forgotten that he could be playful, and that when he was he almost glowed.

I wished he hadn't made me remember.

"What is *with* you today?" I demanded.

He opened his hands as if they were a box that was going to reveal something secret. "I'm just glad to see you."

I studied him suspiciously. "Act normal, Conn, or I'm leaving. You're weirding me out."

That wiped the smile off his face. "All right." He cleared his throat. "What's that?" He nodded at my book.

Even though I'd planned to come straight to the point and ask him about my photograph, for a moment I faltered, suddenly nervous about what I'd find out. So I showed him the book.

"Reservation," he said. "That's one of my favorites."

"This book shouldn't exist."

"In *your* world."

I shook my head. "The split between my world and this one is because of the Great Fire, so everything that happened in both places before 1871 should be exactly the same."

"That's right."

"But Jane Austen was writing way before then. It doesn't make sense that *here* she would have written an extra book."

"She didn't," he said. "But *here*, her lost manuscript of *Reservation* was discovered."

"Ahhhh," I said. "Okay." I leaned against a wall, recalculating my conception of how different this world was. "And Jennie

Twist? Who's she? I'm pretty sure I don't recall her from history class, and she's got to be important if a library's named after her. What'd she do? Eat twenty Shades for breakfast?"

"She's our first woman president."

I stared. "You have a woman president?"

"Not at the moment," Conn said. "Twist was elected in 1978."

"Well, at least you people got something right." I paused. "You know . . . has it ever occurred to you that there are probably more worlds than yours and mine? If the Great Fire caused some interdimensional split, what did the dropping of the atomic bomb do? Or the Civil War? There must be tons of worlds, zillions of worlds, where history and everything else is different."

He looked at me with an expression that seemed to be respect. "Not many people think of that. You're right, Darcy. There probably are more worlds than we can imagine. But the government keeps that information very close to its chest. Governments are like that. Yours, for example, knows full well about our existence. But they've kept it a secret for more than a hundred years. We have a treaty with them to protect that information. I don't approve, personally, but it's the law. As for this world, everyone here knows about the Alter, though they're not allowed into it."

I stared, and realized that my fascination about the world around me had sucked me into a much longer conversation with Conn than I really wanted to have. Conn was too easy to talk to. He always had been.

But of course he would be. He'd been trained in interrogation.

"Let's get down to business," I told him. "I want these meetings to be short."

For a moment he didn't speak. Then he nodded sharply. "Good," he said. "You're right. We're risking a lot to speak to each other. Every minute, we risk more. What do you have to report?"

"Nothing until I hear what you've found out about me."

He folded his large, scarred hands. "Have you met my requirement? Have you learned how to control your shadow?"

I braced my back against the wall and stared down at him. "Sure."

"Then ghost," he said. "Right now."

"Later."

He crossed his arms. "Now."

For a while, neither of us said anything. Then I caved. "I'm trying, all right? I can't do it. But I will."

He looked at me.

"I *will*."

Conn's eyes held mine. "I believe you."

I exhaled slowly. "So." I prepared myself for whatever might come next. "What did you find out about me?"

His mouth twisted. "Darcy. There's no easy way to say this. You're supposed to be dead."

For a moment, I wavered on my feet. The news didn't shock me so much as the way my memory reacted. *No one's supposed to know you're alive,* I heard a voice—a man's—say. *I'll keep your secret.*

I sat down hard, like my legs had been cut out from underneath me.

"I was looking at everything from 1997," Conn said. "Every file my rank allowed me to pull. Other Shade arrests. Transcripts of emergency phone calls." He rubbed tiredly at his forehead. "I even looked at traffic tickets. Then I came across your photograph, the same one, in a file from the coroner's office. It listed you as deceased, but the details of the file were sealed.

"I tried to find out more. The coroner—Dr. Green—has been with the IBI forever, and would have had to sign off on your autopsy—which obviously didn't happen—so I went to talk with her. Dr. Green claimed she'd never seen you, couldn't remember your case—nothing." He looked at me. "She's lying."

"How do you know?"

"Hours later, I checked the coroner's database again. Your file had vanished. I think it was a fluke that I'd found it to begin with. It was a loose end someone forgot to tie up."

"So go back to Dr. Green. Tell her the file vanished. See what she says."

"Confronting her won't do any good. I already tried that, with no luck. And whatever the IBI is hiding about you, it's something bigger than Anne Green. Information about you is buried so deep, only the highest ranking officers have access to it."

"But Green knows something. Make her talk."

"I can't *make* her," he said.

"Yes, you can."

"Darcy. I can't make people do things they don't want."

And there it was again. That kiss, throbbing across the tension between us.

There was a very long pause.

"Don't worry," Conn finally said. "Dr. Green's stonewalling me. Fine. That doesn't mean this is over. There are a lot of people in the IBI. A lot of people who know a lot of things. One of the secretaries invited me to dinner at her place tonight. Maybe that'll lead us somewhere. She likes me."

I felt a stab of an emotion I didn't want to examine too closely.

"I'm sorry I don't have more information," he said. "Now. What do you have for me?"

"Well," I said reluctantly. "The IBI might be right. Maybe the Society is planning something. But they could be planning an interpretive dance with IBI flamethrowers for all I know. Not necessarily an attack." Still, I told him about the little things Shades had let slip around me—the idea that I could be put "to good use" by passing as a human, that "now, more than ever," the Society couldn't afford a security risk. The flamethrowers, and how Orion had warned me away from them.

Conn's eyes sharpened. "Tell me more about Orion."

"He's . . ." It wasn't easy to sum him up. "Graceful. I think he must be one of the Society's best fighters. He mentioned something about training people. Well, he's training *me*, in fact. He's intelligent, and . . . passionate. So passionate that sometimes I think he doesn't always see things for what they arc. He doesn't see *me* for what I am, anyway. I think."

Conn leaned back in his chair, silent. A muscle pulsed along his jaw. "You should be careful around him."

"As if I'm *not*," I said. "Anyway, he's a nice guy. Sure, he doesn't *like* humans, but I've never seen him hurt one. Whenever hc's mentioned a Society terrorist attack, it's always been in a matter-of-fact way, like what they did is simply part of the past. And he's been good to me. I'd be in Society prison if it weren't for him, and he's been more welcoming to me than anyone elsc in this world." Something made me add, "He likes me."

"I'm sure he does."

"Can you please cut the sarcasm? I'm trying to tell you that Orion might give me some valuable information. The IBI wants me to spy. Hc's my best source."

"You can find other sources."

"I'm working on it." I frowned. "I really don't see what your problem is."

"It's just"—he ran a hand through his hair—"you're talking about using someone, and that's not an easy thing to do. I don't think you've ever done that before—use someone. Your friends—Lily, Raphael, Jims—"

I flinched, the pain of missing them was so sharp.

"I've seen how you are with people," Conn said. "Your friendships are true. You value people, and when they value you, you're true to them. That's a gift. I don't want to see you throw it away."

"Hey, I'm not spying for the IBI because I enjoy it."

"I know," Conn said. "But be careful," he repeated. "Especially if Orion has feelings for you."

I looked at Conn and decided I wasn't crazy about the turn this conversation was taking. So I changed it. "You were right about something. Sort of. Shades don't really need food." I explained what Orion had told me about ghosting, and how it could shut down hunger, pain, even aging.

Conn stared.

"I know what you're thinking," I said.

"I don't think you do."

"You're thinking about how different we are. You, a human. Me, the Shade."

"Actually . . . I think we have a lot in common. Though"—he smiled a little—"it's true that *I* can't live hundreds of years."

"So not worth it. What's the point in living that long if you can't *do* anything? Paint. Sleep. Ride a bike. Pet a dog." And kiss, I thought. Hurriedly, I added, "And food. Let's not forget about eating."

"Are you hungry?"

"Not technically, but I'd sell my soul to a minor demon for a candy bar."

"Tell me what you miss. What would you eat right now, if you could have anything? I mean, besides blueberry pancakes smothered with butter and maple syrup."

I glanced at him. That was what I had ordered at the diner the day we skipped class. "Chocolate-covered espresso beans," I said. "Veggie pad thai with lots of lime and crunchy peanuts. Pink apples. Fortune cookies. Roasted brussels sprouts with cracked pepper and rock salt . . ." I couldn't stop myself. I kept listing what I craved, watching Conn's face relax as if we were eating delicious things instead of merely talking about them. As I studied him, I couldn't help noticing how his features were lean and sharp but almost perfect. In fact (purely from an artist's perspective), they were handsome because they *weren't* perfect.

Conn looked noble. And treacherous, because the way he looked had nothing to do with who he really was.

But I couldn't tear my eyes away from that one feature that was off center. His one flaw. That broken nose. I glanced at his hands with their old nicks and cuts, and remembered Conn holding the X-Acto knife in my bedroom back home. I remembered him ramming into my attacker's side. And something made sense. "You got *that*"—I pointed—"fighting, didn't you?"

"This?" Startled, he touched the bridge of his nose. "No. I got it sleepwalking."

"You sleepwalk?" This was unlike Conn. He always seemed so in control.

"I used to, when I was little. One night I walked straight into a wall." He looked at me. "It was a long time ago."

"You don't sleepwalk anymore?"

"No." There was a flicker of a rueful smile. "Now I just don't sleep." His eyes were blue and hooded and sad.

After that, I got the details about our next meeting and left. The last thing I wanted was to feel sorry for Conn McCrea.

28

Training with Orion was intense and increasingly pointless. But he never gave up. He was certain that I only needed the right incentive to ghost, and alternated between getting bossy and playing the role of head cheerleader for Team Darcy. Frankly, I preferred it when he was bossy. I found myself making excuses to sneak away from the practice room. More often than not, I ended up in the Archives.

It was about a week after my meeting with Conn at the library, and since then I'd been stocking up on art supplies. The Archives had tons of them. Paper, colored pencils, primer, brushes. At first, Savannah grumbled at me from behind her desk, but one day she asked, "What are you *doing* with all that?"

"Nothing yet," I told her. Then I looked at her. "Would you help me?"

That's how I ended up painting Savannah's portrait.

"You're using an awful lot of color," she said as I dabbed a brush on the heavy paper fixed to an easel.

"That's why it's called watercolors. Water. Color."

She stood and stepped around her desk to peer over my shoulder. "You've put *yellow* on my cheek. My skin is not *yellow*."

I waved her away. "You're not supposed to do that. No looking. You said you'd wait until I finished."

"Don't tell me what to do. I'm on the Council. And I voted against you, remember that."

I rolled my eyes. "Yes, I remember. I remember because you remind me every single time I see you."

Savannah wasn't paying attention to what I'd said. She kept staring at the portrait. "And *blue*. You've put *blue* in my hair."

"It's not finished," I snapped. "I guess you think I should be painting you with India ink on rice paper. Well, you're not just shades of black and white, and neither am I. Do you think a cloud is white? If you do, you've been underground too long, because it isn't. It's lilac and charcoal and rose and tangerine. When the light strikes your hair, it casts a blue shadow. When it falls on your face, there's yellow."

"Don't get huffy." She returned to her seat. "I don't know why you want to paint me anyway."

I rinsed my brush in a cup of water and looked at the delicate wrinkles edging her eyes like lace. "Because you're beautiful."

"Now I *know* you're a liar and a fake."

"Believe what you want," I said coolly. "I'm telling you what I see."

For a while there was no other sound than the liquid whisper of my brush across paper, and as I painted, I thought about how the truth can sometimes sound like a lie because we're too afraid to believe it.

"Do I . . ." I tried again: "Do I remind you of anyone?"

"What do you mean?"

"Do I look like anyone you know?"

"Darcy, you're a Shade. You look like *everyone* I know." She looked at me, and her wrinkles deepened with a frown. "Ah. I see. You're asking if I know who your family is. Well, I don't."

"Maybe if you thought about it—"

"I have."

"Oh." My brush wavered, and a drip of purple went exactly where it shouldn't. I bit my lip.

"Everyone has." Savannah's voice was not unkind. "There has been a lot of talk about it."

"And?" I painted a curl of sheer black.

Savannah shrugged. "Silt thinks you belong to the wandering Shades, those who live in other parts of the country. He's probably right. That would explain why no one's stepped forward to claim you as family."

"Who's Silt?"

"He voted for you. Just barely, I might add."

The serious-eyed man. The one who had told Orion he was blind.

Savannah said, "It was the argument that you might help the Society by passing as human that convinced Silt. Now, Loam, on the other hand, was for you the moment you walloped him with . . . what was that metal thing?"

"A bed slat."

"Loam's all muscle, no brain. He kept calling you 'spirited,' said you were a 'true fighter,' which may be correct, but it hardly makes you less dangerous to the Society."

"And Meridian?"

"Oh, she and Loam are as thick as thieves. They lead the faction that wants the Society armed and on the offensive against humans. But Meridian's strategic. Even if she liked you—which, I believe, she rather does—she wouldn't hesitate to lock you up or even have you executed if she thought it served her purposes. But she chose your side the moment Orion stepped forward to defend you."

"Why is that?"

"As I said, she serves her goals by any means. In this case"— Savannah's mouth turned disdainful—"her goal was to make her son happy."

I lowered my brush. "Meridian is Orion's mother?"

"And he's a fool for you. Come, don't look so surprised."

I rubbed the bristles of the brush inside a little tub of periwinkle. "I'm not, I guess. But it's strange to hear some things said out loud."

Savannah gave a *hmph* of agreement.

Now that she'd said it, I couldn't help feeling a pleased flutter, yet it didn't heal my bruised heart or make me less wary to risk it again. "I don't understand why you're telling me so much, Savannah. You think I'm a security risk. Why are you even talking to me?"

"You *are* a security risk," she said. "But you're an interesting one. Anyway, I'm not telling you anything you couldn't figure out on your own."

"There are some things about the Society I never would have guessed. Like the freaky way we age—or *don't* age. What if my parents are really old? Or were. Like more than a hundred years old. And they left the Sanctuary a long time ago and wandered around this world by themselves. Then they had me, and somehow lost me. And maybe nobody here recognizes who I am because they're too young to have ever known my parents."

Savannah raised her brows. "Except maybe an old lady like me?"

I glanced at her.

"Zephyr's been around longer than I have," she said. "As Council leader she has access to a lot of confidential information. Why don't you ask her?"

"Yes, and why don't I play with a vat of vipers while I'm at it."

Savannah gave me a wry smile. "I'm sorry, Darcy. You don't look like anyone in particular, and you look like you could belong to anyone. And there have never been any reports of someone losing or abandoning a little girl."

What about a dead girl? I wanted to ask, but had no way of explaining such a weird question. "Not even in 1997?"

Savannah's fingers wrapped around her glasses chain. "1997." Her voice was halting. "1997 was a bad year."

"It disgusts me," I said in a low voice before I could stop myself. "Ravenswood. God knows how many other attacks. How many other murders. When I think too hard about what Shades have done, you all disgust me."

Savannah's hand snapped the glasses chain, and the beads struck the floor. Neither of us bent to pick them up. We sat there, frozen, as I stared in shock at the beads bouncing and rolling around like my stupid, stupid words. I'd probably destroyed any kind feelings Savannah had for me. I was probably about to get thrust right back into Society prison.

Savannah stooped to sweep some beads into the palm of her hand. "You know better than to say such things out loud," she told me. Then she straightened, returned to her desk, opened her catalogue of the Archives, and began writing.

I was dismissed.

"WE'RE GETTING NOWHERE," Orion was forced to admit when I met him the next day in the practice room.

"Yeah." I sighed in a way that I hoped sounded sad and not bored.

He leaned against the frame of one of the open windows that overlooked the Great Hall. "When you ghosted before, how did you feel?"

I shrugged.

"Don't you remember?"

"Memory and I aren't exactly best friends."

"I have a theory." He rested a knuckle against his lips and studied me over the top of his fist. "When you ghosted before, it was to save yourself, and there wasn't enough time for you to think about what you were doing while you were doing it. True?"

"More or less."

"So we need to risk your life, yet do so in a way that lets you really think about how to save it."

"Oh no." I backed away.

"Go on." He tilted his head toward the open window. "Jump."

"Unh-uh. No way."

"Why not? I promise not to catch you."

"Why not? Because you belong in a straitjacket. Because we need to book you a padded cell. Because I'm chicken."

"Well, little chicken"—he grabbed me—"it's time to fly."

He threw me out the window.

29

I tumbled through the air, too terrified to scream or do anything other than try to guess when I'd hit bottom and which body part would be the first to go crunch. Probably my spine. Or my skull? Either way, I was dead dead dead.

Then I remembered how pleased Orion's face had been when he'd chucked me out the window, and I decided I needed to pull it together and ghost. And survive.

So that I could strangle him.

The walls whizzed past. My hands blurred with speed.

Your heart, I told myself. Stop it. But it was rocketing in my chest, too fierce to ignore, and I knew that I couldn't do this, I couldn't deny my own body piece by piece. Not even to save it.

So how had I survived Marsha's knife? What had I done? Nothing.

When I'd vanished, it had been purely by instinct, the way I knew how thin or thick my paintbrush should be, and how hard to press my pencil when I sketched. I didn't think when I painted. It was a release. I never chose where my brush went. I let my desire lead me, sweep across the paper, nudge into the corners, plunge down in strong, hard lines. I just let myself go.

The stone floor rushed toward my face. I didn't close my eyes. I thought of nothing at all.

And fell through the floor.

I flew through someone's bedroom, where someone who was brushing her hair before a mirror frowned to see a shadow spill from her ceiling. "Privacy, please!" she shouted.

Then I fell through *her* floor.

And down, and down, until Orion appeared below me with a gleeful smile on his face. And suddenly I felt gleeful, too, because I had done it, and was no longer afraid of what I could do. I dropped straight into his arms and felt my weight hit hard against his bones.

"Brilliant!" He held me close. "You were brilliant!"

"I know!" I laughed, giddy.

He kissed me.

Now that I had my heart back it hummed in my chest. But each moment seemed to expand, grow slower and longer as I kissed him back, and when time dragged to a stop I realized that I was giddy only because I had triumphed over something, and not because of Orion.

Kissing Orion was like drinking IBI water. It only made me long for something else.

I pulled away and struggled to my feet.

"Darcy?" Orion murmured.

I could see his face clearly. Dreamy, inky eyes. A full, sensual, satisfied mouth. His body was relaxed against mine. He looked blissful.

After nearly killing me.

I remembered my plans to strangle him.

I shoved him. "You defenestrated me!"

Orion looked confused. "No, I didn't. I threw you out the window."

"That's what 'defenestrate' means, you idiot!"

"Darcy, you're not really mad." He peeked at me. "Are you? Because you were breathtaking. I admit what I did was a drastic measure." He spread his hands innocently. "But it worked."

I took a deep breath. Lectured myself about the dangers of yelling at my only ally. Tried to squelch the tiny thought that the person I really wanted to strangle was Conn, whose kiss had been a curse.

"Yeah," I told Orion. "I guess it did work."

"So you're not mad."

"I'll get over it. Let's risk my life again."

FALLING FROM GREAT HEIGHTS. Knives. A pot of acid flung across the room. Playing dodge ball in heavy traffic. The only thing we didn't try was fire.

Over the next few days I mastered my shadow, which proved to be far easier than keeping Orion at arm's length. "Business first," I always told him.

215

He grinned the first time I said it. "Pleasure later, then," he replied. But later was always later than that for me, and he grew sullen. I knew that I could change that, could heal the insecurity that shape-shifted Orion from a sly jester into someone who pouted. He pouted sexily and *looked* very kissable. Really, he was very everything. But he wasn't for me. In the midst of the lies I had to tell and secrets I had to keep and secrets I had to unearth, it felt important to be true to myself.

I wondered . . . would Conn take back that kiss if he could?

This was one of those positively demonic questions that made me want to tear my brain in half. There was no good answer. Both yes and no hurt too much to consider, so I locked the windows and doors and skylights of my mind and told thoughts like this to go far, far away.

I ghosted around town, nipping into the Swedish bakeries to steal plate-sized cinnamon rolls with gooey centers so dark with brown spice that my tongue tingled. Theft was easy, as long as what I stole was small enough to vanish along with me.

I snuck into people's homes and watched kids throw crayons at one another. Dads stirred spaghetti sauce while Moms deplored the state of the public school system. And nobody watched TV. It didn't exist in this world. Shocking, right?

I took the ways I knew to go between the Sanctuary and the city: the tunnel entrances hidden by gravestones and mausoleums. Sure, I could have ghosted my way through the layers of earth above the Sanctuary. But I wasn't *that* confident in my abilities, and I dreaded the thought of getting stuck along the way. Being buried alive wasn't high on my list of fun-filled activities.

Snooping around the IBI, on the other hand, was definitely a temptation. Who needed Conn? So what if information about me was classified way beyond his rank? I was invisible. I could unclassify anything. I could watch Director Fitzgerald floss her teeth if I wanted. I could pluck those red knots off Ivers's collar and fling them out the window like confetti at a ticker-tape parade. Point me in the direction of Anne Green. I'd haunt her morgue. Switch tags on the toes of dead bodies. Scribble on her charts. I would manifest when her back was turned, then ghost into shadow, quick as a snuffed candle. I'd spook her and poltergeist her until, when I demanded the truth about my "death," she'd give it up gladly, if only to make me leave her alone.

But when I thought about the IBI, I remembered the flaming glass box in solitary confinement. I remembered faces tight with hate. And, of course, I had told Conn that humans could see a Shade's shadow. What if someone in the IBI happened to see mine? Nothing riled the Bureau more than the constant fear that the Society was spying on them. I felt panicky imagining what would happen if I accidentally manifested and got trapped in the IBI. This time, I wouldn't be innocent. This time, the cuffs would stay on. Even thinking about it was so frightening that my ghost shivered and wobbled back into my heavy body.

I spent more time in the Archives, where Savannah didn't

shun me like I thought she would after my anti-Society outburst. She acted like nothing had happened. I helped restring her glasses chain and convinced her to add some sparkly vintage beads from Section 3Q.

I read *Reservation*—and reread it. It was delicious. Even better than *Pride and Prejudice*.

When I set the book aside, I painted my walls. I opened my box of oils and spread a jungle of color around me. Oils are too good to use on walls, too expensive, but I didn't care. They're gorgeous. They smell like gasoline, but have enchanting names like Permanent Madder Deep. They can be thick, rich, and cakey, or as sheer as silk.

I painted the sky I missed when I was underground. Rows of boring Lakebrook houses, abstracted to simple rectangles of blue, brown, and yellow. I painted Raphael as Hamlet, and Lily as herself. I dabbed at Jims's cheek with Cadmium Green, stepped back, and realized that I rarely saw him smile. He was always too busy making other people laugh.

"What's this?"

I wheeled around. Orion stood under the tree, his posture a little uncertain.

"It's Whatever I Want," I said.

"Oh." He was puzzled, which wasn't surprising since he knew nothing of my old life. He quickly sought familiar ground. "Meridian wants to see you tomorrow night."

My pulse jumped. If Meridian led the faction of Shades who wanted action against humans, this could mean something big. Something Conn, whom I was meeting tomorrow morning, would want to know about. "You mean your *mother* wants to see me."

"She's more than my mother. She's my commander. And she should be yours, too."

"So you have a mission for me."

"You're ready."

"Hmm."

"So you'll do it?"

I hesitated, barely. "I'll talk to her."

His mouth twitched with frustration. Clearly talking wasn't enough, clearly Orion expected me to stand and pledge allegiance to some plan that was possibly crackers and probably deadly. Before he could speak, I asked, "What does Meridian want?"

"I don't know. She has an idea, but nobody knows the full details except her. Some Shades are playing a part, but none of us knows what the big picture is or what the others are doing, and we are each sworn to secrecy about our roles."

Great. "So you're going to go ahead and do something even though you don't know the consequences."

"I trust my mother." Orion added, "She voted for you."

"I know."

"So . . . ?"

Carefully un-careful, I asked, "Do Shades ever visit the Alter?"

He gave me a strange look. "What does that have to do with anything? Why do you ask that?"

"I'm trying to figure out what happened to me when I was

five. How I got dumped there." I shrugged. "Maybe there's a booming tourism industry for Shades visiting other worlds. Maybe my parents were doing some Alter sightseeing and lost me, or forgot me."

"They wouldn't have *deliberately* left you there."

"Who knows what they would have done? All I know is that I was there and I was alone."

"Shades go to the Alter sometimes, but"—he shuddered slightly—"not often, and not for amusement. It's a pilgrimage, to pay respects to our dead. The Alter is a graveyard."

To destroy an entire people—to rub out even the memory of them—was a cruelty too large to imagine. Comprehending it would be like trying to swallow the sea.

"You *live* below a graveyard," I said to Orion.

"A *human* graveyard."

I looked at him, and felt—not for the first time—the weight of everything I could never say. I couldn't tell him to let go of the Great Fire. It was a long time ago, but Shades live a long time, and have a long memory.

"Well," I said, "if my parents did travel to the Alter, how did they get there?"

"Through a portal, of course. Any man-made structure that survived the fire in the Alter is a link between that world and ours, provided it exists here, too, in its original form. That's where the interdimensional border is soft, because of what both worlds share. Of course, the IBI has done their best to limit the number of portals so they can control interdimensional traffic. So in *this* Chicago they've razed or altered many of the sites that otherwise would have been held in common."

"Yes, but how do you go *through* the portals? The IBI must guard them all."

He blinked at me. "Go through them?"

I inwardly winced. Now Orion was going to see the obvious: that *I* wanted to go through a portal.

What I didn't realize was that my question was silly. That's what had startled him.

"You simply go," he said. "You walk right through it. Even a human could do that, if she knew where it was and no guards stopped her. And you are better than human. Darcy, now that you can ghost, what would stop you? IBI agents? They would never see you. Gates? You can slip through them like a knife through butter." He frowned. "It worries me, how you don't fully understand what nature has given you. I know allowances must be made. You're not used to thinking as a Shade. But you are what you are, and must embrace it. Darcy?" His expression changed to concern. "What's wrong?"

The blood drained icily from my cheeks. If possible, I had gone paler than I already was.

I realized that when I'd cut the deal with Fitzgerald, the IBI had had nothing to offer me. Nothing I couldn't learn to do myself. And Conn knew this. He must have known it was only a matter of time before I figured out how to go home.

"I haven't kept this information from you," Orion said hurriedly. "If you had wanted to go back to the Alter, we would have found a way to send you, even if you couldn't ghost. And now you can. Perhaps we've never talked about the portals before, but only because you didn't ask, and I assumed you knew. I assumed you *wanted* to stay here. You do, don't you?"

I couldn't answer. All I could do was stare at the boxes of art supplies stacked along the wall and wonder what color anger was, and what color betrayal. Which hue was hurt, washed by my own foolishness? If I knew, I could paint the story of how Conn had tricked me yet again.

30

I biked along the lakefront to the lone figure standing by an old pier.

Lake Michigan is huge, so big that it seems like an ocean, with choppy waves and miles of sandy beaches. On a cold, clear morning in the suburbs, you can look toward Chicago and see cloudbanks around the city because the lake is a little warmer than everything else, and it's so large it can change the weather. As my bike tires sped over the wet sand, I thought for sure dark clouds of hurt and fury were rolling off my skin. Conn should have been able to see them from far away.

He turned to me, pulling his gloveless hands from his pockets. I braked and let the bicycle fall to the beach.

"You lied to me." The words were thick and low in my throat.

He knew. He knew what I meant. I could see it in the sudden unhappiness that flashed across his face. Conn opened his mouth to speak, but the wind raked me with icy fingers and slipped below my hood to tug out black ribbons of hair.

Conn's expression changed. "Darcy, *your wig.* Pull your hair back."

"Don't tell me what to do!"

"Darcy—"

"How long did you and Fitzgerald think you had before I figured out that interdimensional travel didn't involve some IBI-only gizmo I'd have to hope and pray you let me use?"

His gaze cut to the lake. "We never said that."

"Never said I never needed you. Never said that once I learned how to control my shadow, I could be gone, out of this jacked-up world with its stupid war."

Conn kept his eyes trained on the churning waves. I seethed at his crooked profile, wishing his nose wasn't broken. Then I could break it for him. "Of course," he said finally. "You've learned how to ghost."

I hesitated, but only for a second. "No."

He looked at me. "Really?"

"I'm here, aren't I? Do you think I would have stuck around just for the pleasure of seeing you again?"

He thrust his hands back into his pockets. "Fitzgerald wanted to buy time and as much information as she could before you figured it out," he said. "And I didn't think that anything less than the promise to send you home would convince you to work for us. But I never banked on our promises. I never thought that *that*—or even researching your history—would keep you here, helping the IBI."

I crossed my arms. "Then what were you banking on?"

"You're a good person," he said simply. "You care. You meet with me because you don't want to see the Society destroy more lives. Maybe that's not the only reason. But it's one of them."

I blinked, because I suddenly realized I didn't know the answer to my own sarcastic question. Why was I still here, in this Chicago? And why was I *here*, on the beach in the dead of winter with Conn? I looked at him, and some part of me, the artist part, thought that if I were to paint him with oils, his eyes were the color of King's Blue Light.

At least, they were today.

But I would never paint him.

As my anger cooled, my mind began to tick. Something didn't make sense. Conn had asked me to learn how to ghost. He had *demanded* it. I'd thought he wanted me to become the IBI's Top-Notch Invisible Spy, and maybe that was the case, but it still didn't seem like a smart move if Conn had wanted to keep me from portaling home.

Conn glanced down the beach, and I saw it, too: a man jogging toward us, a golden Lab at his side. "Darcy, please pull your hair back."

I tucked it into the hood. I sighed, admitting to myself that Conn had to have known that by controlling my shadow, I'd gain independence from the IBI. Yet he had still asked me to do it. And what he'd said was true: I didn't want the Society to attack again, though I wasn't so sure that made me a good person. If you do things because otherwise you wouldn't be able to live with yourself, isn't that selfishness?

"Meridian wants to meet with me," I said. "She's the leader of the Shades who call themselves 'warriors.'"

"About what?"

"That's the thing. There *is* a plan, Conn, and since it's Meridian's, it's probably a scary one." I told him what I knew, which wasn't much.

Conn became . . . *intense.* He didn't speak or pace or even budge. He went electric. "So you're meeting her tonight?"

"Midnight."

"Agree to whatever she asks."

"What?"

"Agree."

"You're crazy, Conn. Totally non compos mentis. What if she wants me to blow up your lousy subway? Which, if I may say so, is a pretty good idea as long as nobody's in it."

He was humorless. "Obviously I don't want you to blow anything up. Just agree, and see what you learn."

"They'd never blow anything up anyway. They don't like fire."

"No," said Conn. "They attack with gas."

"Then why were there IBI flamethrowers in the practice room?"

"I don't know." He shook his head.

"Orion probably knows."

"And he's part of Meridian's plan." Conn's lip curled into a sneer. "I thought he was supposed to be so very *nice.*"

"He doesn't even know what the plan is. Come on, Conn. Maybe we're being apocalyptic. Maybe the Society is planning a parade and Orion's in the color guard. Meridian's his mother, you know. It's hard to tell your mom no. At least, that's what I hear."

"You're defending him." Conn was incredulous.

"I'm saying we don't know the whole story. We're assuming the worst."

"Because Shades have *done* the worst."

We fell silent as the jogger and his dog passed us, kicking up sand. Masochistic jogger. It was December. It was *freezing*. The wind cut through my clothes, and I thought that now would be a good time to get out of the cold. Now would be a good time to ghost. If, that is, I felt like giving Conn one of my few, precious secrets.

I stayed solid.

"Have you found out more about my arrest in 1997?" I asked.

"Not yet. I'm sorry."

"What, your pretty little secretary had nothing to say?"

"My pretty . . . ?" He looked at me quizzically. "What are you talking about?"

"You said you were having dinner with a secretary who might know something."

"Yes, but she's not *my* secretary."

"Conn, you better not be withholding information from me."

"But I'm not. And she's not—" A strange expression flitted

across Conn's face. His eyes rested on me, considering, seeming to order the world into different patterns and possibilities. Then something shut down. "I have nothing to tell you because there's nothing to tell. I've hit a dead end with your case. No one knows anything, or they don't want to talk." He checked his watch. "I have to meet Fitzgerald. I hope I'll have something for you next time, Darcy. I really do."

"Next time."

"Yes . . . I thought we could go to the Art Institute."

My heart flared. I couldn't speak.

"That's not what we call it here, of course," he said. "But it's a good museum. Great collection. A *different* collection from the one you know."

I stood, breathless. Tantalized. "When?"

"As soon as we can after your meeting with Meridian. The weekend begins tomorrow, and the museum's too busy then for you to walk around unnoticed. So Monday morning, 9:00 a.m. Just walk through the front entrance."

"The Art Institute's closed on Mondays. In my world."

"It is here, too. To the *public*. We'd have the museum to ourselves." His smile was so small it looked almost like a wince. "What do you say?"

I almost snatched at his offer with both greedy hands, but only because my brain was so flooded with eagerness that I had forgotten to think. Then I remembered that I was a Girl with Options. If I wanted to see the Art Institute's alter ego, I could ghost through the doors during the busiest time of day, no problem. No fee. I could break in under the full moon.

I could probably even steal a van Gogh. I didn't need Conn and his blatant bribe.

And yet . . . the bribe—the *perfection* of it—touched some tender spot in me, one that hadn't realized he knew me so well. If I squinted my eyes and looked at his offer, it seemed to be a gift, one as smooth and shining as the silver planet he had once tipped into the palm of my hand.

But my eyes were open now. This *was* a bribe, and if he knew me well that was all the more reason to be afraid. Suspicion knotted in my chest.

"Darcy?" Conn's smile, small as it was, had vanished.

How badly did I need to find out about my past? I'd been okay without it before. And forget seeing a bunch of paintings. I could see Lily, Raphael, and Jims tonight. All I had to do was find the Water Tower.

Sure, humans here had problems, and I'd protect them if I could. But how much could I really do? How much were Conn's problems my problems?

"I don't know," I told him.

Conn seemed to expect this. He nodded. He looked back out at the lake again, pulled up his coat collar to block the wind, and said, "I'll be there." Then he turned and began to walk up the beach, shoulders hunched against the cold.

What I did next was unethical.

It was also inevitable.

31

I followed him.

After he'd dwindled to a faraway dot on the long stretch of sand and I was reasonably sure that if he hadn't looked back yet, he wouldn't look back at all, I stashed my bike behind a clump of pine trees and ghosted.

I flew after him.

He kept to the edge of the surf for some time, as if he liked this beach, enjoyed it despite the bad weather—or maybe because of it. Then he abruptly turned away from the lake. Conn quickened his pace, taking a path through a park. He stepped out onto a busy street and walked toward a subway plate. I rushed forward, close to his elbow, and down we went.

The roller-coaster ride was okay this time. Orion had promised that physical problems like green-sick nausea wouldn't bother me if I didn't have a body, and thank God he was right.

Conn leaned against the subway car wall, unfastened the top button of his coat, and slipped a notebook out of an inside pocket. It was the same one he'd had in the library, the one with drawings of gears. He clicked a pencil and began to sketch amazingly even lines for someone rattling along on the subway ride from hell. He held the book firmly open, resting it on his left forearm, his fingers clasping the top of the pages. He was drawing a machine. It was nothing like my sketches, with free lines dashed across the page. Conn's pencil was careful. Serious. And what was unfolding, I realized, was a design for something that looked like a motorcycle, but way scarier.

Then his chin tilted up suddenly, and my pulse jumped. Could he see my shadow? I oozed toward a tall woman, hovering almost inside her body, pooling my shadow into hers.

But Conn's eyes were on the subway plate in the center of the car. His stop must be coming up. My breath (if I'd had any) hitched with relief, and when he stepped forward I slipped behind him onto the plate. My shadow mingled with his.

It was a short walk from the subway to the IBI, and when Conn set his foot on the first of those twenty-seven steps, I quailed. Of course, he *had* said he was going to meet Fitzgerald. That's why I was stalking him. But when I actually saw the building, fear bloomed inside me, and I remembered all of the very good reasons I shouldn't go inside—all of them, that is, except the best reason, the one that I *couldn't* remember, the one that had brought me here when I was almost five.

But Conn mounted the steps, and without thinking I followed as if an invisible string tied me to him. We went inside.

Agents called cheerfully to Conn, who chatted with them about some sport named wicket that was apparently all the rage here. He took off his long coat and slung it over an arm, revealing his IBI jacket. Conn's stance was easy, sure. He was in his element. He belonged here.

Which, I reminded myself, was all the more reason to dislike him.

Conn wove through a section of the IBI I hadn't seen last time. A warren of offices. Finally, he stepped into a waiting room and hung his coat neatly on a hook.

A middle-aged woman in a brown wool dress looked up from her desk. "Conn." She smiled.

"Hello, Helen." He stepped toward her. "Thanks again for dinner the other night."

Oh.

This was the secretary he'd talked about. This kind-eyed woman with an actual lace handkerchief peeking out of the purse that sat open on her desk.

"Sweetie." Helen flapped one hand. "You should come over more often. The kids love you."

Conn smiled. "They love wrestling me to the ground."

"It's good for you. You work too hard and spend too much time alone."

"Speaking of work . . ." Conn's eyes flicked meaningfully toward the closed door.

"The Director's in. I'll let her know you're here." Helen stood from her desk and was turning toward the door when she paused and leaned close to Conn. "I'm sorry I couldn't help you," she murmured. "You know, with your question about that girl."

Conn shrugged. "It's all right."

"No," she said with sudden sternness. "It's not. None of it's right, Conn. You should leave 1997 alone. It'll only bring grief."

"Helen," he said. "Please."

But she walked toward Fitzgerald's office, knocked, and when she heard a muffled "yes," cracked open the door to say, "Agent McCrea to see you."

When Conn walked past her, Helen raised her hand to rest it briefly on his tall shoulder. "You're a good boy," she said, and returned to her desk.

"Sit," Fitzgerald told Conn as he stepped inside her office. The leather chair sighed under his weight but not under mine as I glided over it to blend my shadow into the leaves of a potted ficus tree.

Fitzgerald settled onto the couch across from him, her posture straight, almost stiff. Her gray pants had sharp creases ironed into them. "So?" she said. "How's the Jones Project?"

Conn rubbed his brow. "Frustrating."

"You asked for this, McCrea. Begged for it, I might add."

"I know."

"Need I remind you of how you stormed into my office, interrupting a sensitive meeting with the mayor, demanding that I hurry to witness your debrief with Ivers?"

Conn was silent.

"You're lucky I didn't put you on probation," Fitzgerald

said. "Had you been any other agent, I certainly would have. But you're one of our finest. And, given your history, if *you* were willing to give a Shade the benefit of the doubt, I suppose I had to listen to your rather extraordinary plan. I gave you what you wanted. So don't whine. Give me results."

Conn told her about my upcoming meeting with Meridian, but I didn't pay attention. I could only think of Conn's defiance to Ivers, who had been ready to torture me. I remembered Conn's urgent voice as he had rushed me away from him, down the IBI halls to solitary confinement. I heard Conn's promise that he would be back. And I suddenly understood that even though he'd thrown me headlong into trouble, he'd saved me from it, too.

Fitzgerald said, "We need to know Meridian's plan. Jones needs to make that meeting."

"Yes . . . but I'm not sure she will."

"Please tell me that I misheard you."

"She knows that as soon as she can ghost at will, there's nothing to stop her from using any portal she likes."

Fitzgerald leaned back, exhaling. "Well," she said. "I suppose we should be grateful she didn't discover this sooner. It was only a matter of time. But"—she raised one finger—"Jones *does not* know how to control her shadow."

"No."

"Thank God for small favors. That means we still have some leverage. Work it, McCrea. Milk her for all she's worth while we can."

Conn looked at her.

Fitzgerald widened her eyes in disbelief. "Unless, of course, you'd like to see Ravenswood happen again."

"No."

"Good. When's your next meeting?"

"Monday. If she comes."

"She'd better. When she does, make her a promise. Tell her that we're pleased with her reports, and that we'll send her home soon—as soon as we know Meridian's plan."

"And if she gives us partial information?"

"I do not need to tell you how to string someone along. Just do it." Fitzgerald stood. "That will be all."

Conn didn't reply, but there was a rebellious glint in his gaze. Then he stood and headed for the door. For a moment, I couldn't move. I felt rooted in place, like I had truly become part of the tree and would grow with it, like my perception of Conn was growing, changing, putting out tender new twigs, green vines, baby leaves tightly curled.

The sound of the doorknob as it turned in his hand jolted me out of my trance. I floated toward him.

"Don't screw this up, McCrea," Fitzgerald called. "Ivers would be glad to have your hide, and if you fail me, I'll be glad to let him."

Conn glanced over his shoulder and we were suddenly face-to-face. I pulled back, unnerved, but his eyes stared right through me, focusing on Fitzgerald.

"I'd expect nothing less," he told her, and walked out of the office, grabbing his coat and waving at Helen as he passed her desk.

Then it was back through the carpeted offices, down a narrow hall that gave way to iron and gray marble. Conn opened a wooden door. I was already following him into this new room when he shifted, and I saw the sign his body had blocked.

He stepped forward. The door swung shut behind him.

MEN'S LOCKER ROOM, the sign said.

I took a deep breath. Then I slipped through the door.

32

I swooped after Conn, because if I didn't move fast my hesitation would get the better of me and I'd end up pacing outside the locker room, missing the kind of revelations I'd just heard.

Conn halted in front of a locker, and I flew into him before I could stop myself. His feet stood right below me, as if they were my feet. His hand reached out as if it were my hand and pressed a thumb to a pad exactly where a spin lock should go. It occurred to me that if I lost control of my shadow now, my body would come alive inside Conn's.

I jerked back.

Lockers whined, banged open, banged shut. Men were seated along the wooden bench, pulling off the polished boots of the IBI uniform. Others were walking across the room with towels draped around their hips, hair wet, bare feet slap-slapping on the floor. I heard the hiss and whistle of showers not too far away.

Joking with Lily about being a fly on the wall in the boys' locker room was one thing. This was real. It was *too* real.

I decided to focus on the contents of Conn's locker. Jeans and a stone-colored sweater. Very uninteresting. Very non-distracting. Very unhelpful.

"McCrea." A young man leaned against the lockers next to Conn's. "Punching out early?" he asked in a mock disapproving tone.

"So are you, Paulo."

"It *is* Friday. Got plans?"

"Yes."

Catcalls came from nearby men.

"I've got to get out of this thing." Conn yanked at the top button of his uniform. "Why do they have to make the collars so tight?"

"To make me look good." Paulo grinned.

Conn rolled his eyes. Then he shrugged off his shirt, balled it, and pitched it into a laundry basket.

If I'd had any breath, I would have lost it.

The strong wings of his shoulder blades. The ribbon of his spine. A narrow waist. The faded tattoo of a circle marking his upper right shoulder.

I'd seen this all before, in the back of the truck rumbling toward the IBI. But I had hated him then.

A thought cracked delicately inside me like a frail egg that spilled out a secret I had been keeping from myself for some time now.

I didn't hate him anymore.

Conn's skin looked new because he was new. Because he was a stranger again, someone who had fought to save me from the situation he'd created, who had broken his nose as a boy, who had asked me what I longed to eat and offered art I longed to see. He was someone I wanted to understand.

He unbuckled his belt.

My gaze fell to the floor. My entire body would have blushed, if I'd had one. I examined the tiny white floor tiles and listened to Paulo talk about traffic tickets.

Then he said, "Conn. *What* are you wearing?"

I glanced up. Conn had pulled on the jeans and sweater. "I got it in the Alter."

"No no no," said Paulo. "If you're going out tonight, you're not looking like an Alter-addled weirdo."

"It's comfortable."

"Flannel trousers. A nice, sharp tailored suit. It's the fashion."

"It's not the law."

Paulo held up both hands as if to show he had no weapon. "Hey. *You* want to commit sartorial suicide, you go right ahead." He shut his locker and leaned against it. "About the Alter . . . how's your project?"

"Project?" called a new voice. It was Michael, strutting down the aisle.

"None of your business," said Conn.

"Project *Jones*," Michael drawled. "I'd like to project *her*."

Conn flinched. Then he bit his lip, hard, and pulled on his coat.

"You're sick, Mike," said Paulo. "Shades and humans do *not* mix."

"Oh, I know," said Michael. "Seriously, McCrea, I'm surprised you signed up for this. Kind of twisted, isn't it? Interrogating her must be like talking with your worst nightmare. Why do you do it? Halloween was almost two months ago."

"That's right," Conn said coolly. "So then who let you out of your cage?"

Michael's eyes flashed.

"Now, Mike," said Paulo. "It was a joke."

"No," said Conn. "It wasn't." He held his body ready, to take a blow or strike one of his own.

"Hey," Paulo said to Michael, smiling, "some of us are going out to Allegri's after. Wanna come?"

Michael scowled at Conn.

"Conn's got plans," Paulo said easily.

"Yeah, sure," Michael mumbled. "Meet you there." He stalked away.

As soon as the locker room door had swung shut behind him, Paulo turned to Conn with a big, sarcastic thumbs-up. "Good job, Conn. You've made an enemy out of Ivers's lapdog."

"He made an enemy of *me*," said Conn, and stalked toward the door.

I was floating after him when I noticed someone watching from a far bench. He was middle-aged, with a hefty body and prematurely gray hair. His eyes were on Conn, and had been for some time, I thought. Given the tense expression on his face, he seemed to have listened to the entire exchange.

That was not what startled me.

I *remembered* him.

I stared, trying to unclog my memory, yet the more I struggled, the more it fought back. And beneath it, fear bubbled like black tar.

I wanted to remember. Some part of me, though, *didn't* want to, and would fight tooth and nail to keep it from happening. Maybe it was the wisest part of me.

I heard the door swing shut. Conn was gone.

I looked at the door. I looked at the man. The choice was clear, and I knew what I should do.

But then the invisible string that tied me to Conn tugged on the line, and I didn't even really decide. I simply followed him.

HE GOT OUT OF THE SUBWAY at an area that sort of looked like the Ukrainian Village. Through the twilight, I could see tall, old Victorian houses, and when Conn rested his eyes on one of them his shoulders relaxed, and I wondered if he was glad to see whomever he was visiting, or if maybe this was his home.

It was the kind of house I used to dream about when I was little. It had gables, bay windows, fresh paint. Every window in the house glowed, and I could see a dog hurtling through the living room to jump at the front door. I heard glad barking. A little girl was sitting on the couch, her legs too short to reach the floor, a book open on her lap.

Conn pulled a set of keys from his pocket. He was home.

But he didn't walk up the front steps. He went around to the backyard, where a swing set sang in the wind. The back of the house had one dark window and a weathered door. Conn set his key in the lock and went inside.

It was a studio apartment, completely separate from the rest of the house.

The walls were white and bare. A bar partitioned the main room from a tiny kitchen with a two-plate stove and a clean, empty sink. A stool stood at the bar. Books were stacked on the floor along the walls of the entire main room, except where a mattress lay on the floor, pushed into a corner. At the center of the apartment was a table cluttered with tools, gears, and blueprints.

Conn walked into the kitchen to open the narrow refrigerator, then went to the living room with a sandwich on a plate and a glass of water, which he rested on the only clear spot on the table. He pulled the stool from the bar, lowered it, and dragged it up to the table. He sat, poring over pages of mechanical designs as he ate. When he finished, he leaned to set the empty plate on the bar, brushed his hands, and picked up a pair of pliers and something that looked like a carburetor. He settled back and proceeded to take the thing apart.

For some time there was no sound except a bare branch scratching at the dark window, the jingle of metallic parts, and the clunk of the pliers hitting the table when Conn dropped them to pick up a screwdriver. His face softened and filled with peace. I had never seen him look like that before.

Conn showed no intention of doing anything else than tinkering all night long. This, it seemed, was his big Friday night plan.

The screwdriver slipped, stabbing into Conn's other hand. He swore and dropped the part, which thumped onto the table and then onto the floor, where it broke apart and scattered.

For a moment, Conn stared at the gears rocking on the floor, at the screws spinning on their heads like little break-dancers. Then, with a movement so sudden I nearly jumped out of my invisible skin, he flung out his arm and swept everything off the table. Metal hit the floor with the jangle of a thousand tuneless bells. Conn dropped his head into his hands.

He pressed the heels of his hands against his eyes, shoulders tight, body frozen, breathless.

Enough. I felt as if *I* had destroyed something. He never would have shown me this. He never would have shared anything I had seen and heard. I had stolen it.

Guilt sickened me as I glided toward an outside wall, ready to fade away.

Conn's head snapped up, and his eyes zeroed in on me. They went wide with disbelief, then livid with rage.

He could see my shadow.

He vaulted off the stool and grabbed something from the pile of metal on the floor.

A flamethrower.

With a click, it came alive, spitting a stream of fire. Conn lifted it like a blazing sword and stepped steadily toward me.

33

My mind disintegrated at the sight of fire, babbling *Run run run* and *He doesn't know it's you, he can't know it's you. Go, go now!*

If I stayed, fear would melt my body into being, and then he would know that *I* was that shadow. He would *know*.

That thought was more terrifying than fire.

Yet . . . I chose to stay.

I poured myself back into my skin, feeling flesh cloak my bones and adrenaline spike my blood so strongly it felt like poison. "Conn." I swallowed. "It's me."

He lowered the flamethrower. "You," he said slowly, as if the word was part of a foreign language. "You." He switched off the flames, and I almost sighed with relief. Then I saw his face. It was worse than before. There was still rage, yes. But also betrayal.

"How long?" he whispered.

"How—what?" I stammered.

"How long *have you been here?*" he shouted.

My lungs swelled with everything I couldn't say. I closed my mouth. Drew back.

"Since the beach," Conn said through gritted teeth. He nodded. His knuckles clenched white around the flamethrower before he flung it to the floor. "You've followed me since the beach. The whole time."

I forced myself to speak. "Yes."

"How dare you?" he hissed.

"You wanted this," I said, suddenly frightened. Not of him, but of what I had done. "I mean, not *this* this, but you wanted me to learn how to ghost. You *demanded* it. Didn't you want me to spy on people? Not on you, of course, but—"

"I wanted you to be safe!"

I fell silent.

Conn's hands opened and closed, and he stared at them as if something should have been there yet now was gone. "My— you heard—" His voice broke. "You saw—" His mind was really working now, tunneling through the shock to remember every moment, every detail since he'd walked away from me on the beach. "Oh God."

"Conn." I groped for my courage, because there was something I had to know. "What upset you?"

"What *upset* me?" He made a sound too harsh to be a laugh.

"No, not what I did. What upset you before you saw me, when you dropped the part you were working on?"

"The truth," Conn snarled. "That's what. The fact that nothing turns out the way I plan. Nothing is the way I want it to be." He glanced at the metallic ruins around his feet and then simply stared, as if counting all the broken things.

I was counting them, too. "I'm sorry," I said. "I shouldn't have spied on you, and I won't do it again, I swear. I'm sorry I hurt you. I didn't know that I could be this sorry. But, Conn." It took me a moment to speak again. "You hurt me, too."

The anger drained out of him. He looked at me, and he looked lost.

"Conn, please tell me. What happened to you in 1997?"

He sank to the edge of the mattress and sat there, feet heavy on the floor, arms limp and resting on his knees.

Finally, in a low voice, he said, "My baby sister, Moira, had a fever." He paused, then started again. "She was three months old. My mother couldn't bear the thought of anyone else taking her, and my father didn't want my mother to go alone, so they went to the Ravenswood Medical Center together. I was eight. I knew what it meant to visit the doctor. Long waits. Nowhere to run. I wanted to stay at home and play with my cars, so they asked a neighbor to look after me.

"It's strange. I only remember pieces of my parents. The sound of my mother's slow heart. My father's hands showing me how to use a socket wrench. He was a mechanic, and

I wanted to be one, too." Conn's shoulders slumped in defeat. "I didn't want Moira, when she was first born. But then my mother put her in my arms and I fell in love. She smelled like milk. And she's the one I remember perfectly. So curled and soft and fuzzy-headed, like a caterpillar. I always held her carefully. Sometimes she would fall asleep in my arms, and then I was proud.

"Here, orphans become wards of the state. Well, that was true for you, too. But here there is no foster care system, no adoption. All of us are tattooed with an O—" He tentatively raised a hand to touch his shoulder, and his eyes asked me if I had seen it. I looked away. Nodded. Conn shrugged a little. He said, "I was put into a school with other children like me, and when I was twelve years old, a professor from the department of education visited our class. We expected him. We knew that our careers would be chosen for us that year, and we'd be sent to different schools—special ones, where we'd practice to become whatever the government wanted us to become. I was very nervous. There was only one thing, then, that I wanted to be. And after my evaluation by the professor, I thought I was lucky. I was going to get exactly what I hoped. I was sent to the IBI Academy."

Conn gazed up at me. "When I met you, I wanted to destroy you. I didn't understand your game. Why you stayed solid. Why you spent time with humans. Had you recruited them? For what? Something deadly, I was sure. Something cruel.

"You seemed so smug, tight in the center of your three

friends, who circled you as if *you* were the weakest of them, as if *you* were the one who could be hurt, when I knew full well you were nothing of the kind.

"I needed information. Taylor Allen and her crowd were more than happy to give me some." He made a disdainful noise. "A lot of petty gossip. But nothing about strange disappearances, or cases of you being aggressive to other students. This made you seem even more dangerous. It was clear that you were so serious about whatever plan you had up your sleeve that you wouldn't slip into typical Shade behavior until the moment suited you.

"The trick to catching Shades is to lull them into a false sense of confidence. And to be close enough to them when that happens, and quick enough. I had to get close to you."

"'The Love Song of J. Alfred Prufrock,'" I said.

"'The Love Song.'" He nodded. "It didn't make sense that you'd play through the charade of being my class partner, but then you'd already played through every charade high school had to offer, and you didn't know what I was. Yet . . . the more I talked with you, the more I began to doubt what I knew. You were either the most deceitful person I'd ever met, or"—his voice dropped—"the sweetest. Quick. Funny. Passionate about what touched you, sensitive to small details. And when you told me about your past, and I read your file—"

I winced.

"—I had an insane thought." Conn's eyes held mine. "I wished I could be like you. Because I saw that you hadn't let your past rule the person you'd become. You were not bitter.

In fact"—he gave a short, hollow laugh—"you seemed to think that most of your foster parents were *good* people. You cherished your friends and your art, and you weren't angry at your life. *I* am angry, Darcy." He rubbed at his hand, at the blood where the screwdriver had cut him. "*I* am bitter."

"You arrested me."

"I . . . I was living in a topsy-turvy world where my enemy was my friend and insanity seemed like the most perfectly sane thing. I asked myself if what I felt was worth another Ravenswood. I decided it wasn't." Conn looked up to where I'd been standing, motionless, the entire time. "I can't ask you to forgive me. But I want you to understand."

I lowered myself to sit on the floor. Then I reached across the distance between us to rest my scarred hand on his. "I do," I said.

34

Conn looked at my hand with astonishment, so I drew it back. A silence fell between us, one that didn't end until he lifted his gaze to meet mine and it occurred to me that he might be longing for his privacy after having had so little of it. He might want to be alone in this apartment that was perfectly oriented around the needs of one person. He probably didn't want to see my face, which must have been a constant reminder of everything he had lost. But Conn wouldn't be the type to say so.

I cleared my throat. "I have to go. My meeting with Meridian is soon."

He nodded and seemed like he might speak.

"I'll see you on Monday," I told him. "At the museum."

"You will?" There was a catch in his voice.

"Yes."

* * *

AT THE SANCTUARY, I discovered Orion pacing in my bedroom.

I placed my hands on my hips, annoyed—though, admittedly, this did seem like karmic punishment for *me* entering where *I* wasn't wanted. "Did I say you could come in here uninvited?"

"You never minded before," he said, sulky.

And that was true, for I had been lonely and the Sanctuary always felt empty—so large and quiet and spattered with shadows that were only echoes of people who never showed me their faces. Not like Orion. He had always been real.

But that was not enough.

"Where have you been?" he demanded.

I bristled. "Out. Do I ask *you* how you spend your days?"

"I wish you would. It would be a sign that you cared."

"Orion." I sighed. I had been hoping for some time to calm my nerves. Time to sort through everything I had learned that day, and through my own raw feelings. The last thing I needed was *this*. "What's wrong?"

"You're cutting it awfully fine."

"What?"

"Your meeting with Meridian." He folded his arms and drummed the fingers of one hand. "I thought we could celebrate beforehand."

"Celebrate *what*?" I stared. "Do you . . . do you mean Meridian's *mission*?" I couldn't keep the anger out of my voice. In my mind, I saw babies gasping for air as gas pumped through hospital floors. People choking and twisting and *knowing*, knowing what was happening to them, knowing that they were going to die. It was as if Ravenswood had been a shadow, and after I heard Conn's story, it had become flesh and blood. I couldn't pretend anymore that Meridian's plan might be innocent. It couldn't be.

"Of course," said Orion. "You're about to become a contributing member of the Society. It means you will truly be one of us."

I stood still, trying to school my face into a glad expression. *Prepare a face to meet the faces that you meet*, J. Alfred Prufrock says. Yet I had seen pure honesty today. I had stolen Conn's privacy and still he had chosen to open himself up to me, to let me see everything I had asked for, even if it hurt.

Truth was like an exploding star: violent, glitteringly beautiful. Now that I had seen it, felt it, it was impossible to settle for anything less. Yet I had to pretend.

"Yeah," I told Orion. "It's great. I can't wait."

Relief washed across his face. He slipped a hand around my waist, dragged me forward, and covered my lips with his.

I squirmed and tried to tell him to stop, but his mouth garbled my words, making them sound like they came from underwater. Then Orion laughed, and the sound cut through me, because I realized why he was laughing.

I was acting like a human.

I vanished from his arms and reappeared at a safe distance.

"I *taught* you that!" Orion cried. "I have helped you and helped you, and now you cast me aside!"

"No," I said. "*Help* is freely given. You did something else. My body isn't a bargaining chip. It's not yours just because you want it, or because you think I owe you something."

"I do want you," Orion said. "But not like you say. Not only that." He took a step forward.

I took a step back. "No."

In a resentful voice he said, "There's someone else."

My mind reeled with the sudden fear that Orion knew. That he had been following me all along. That he had seen me with Conn. "But . . ." I groped for something to say. "That's impossible. Since my trial, I've seen no one but you and Savannah. It's not as if the Sanctuary is crawling with people our age—or people who *look* our age."

"Oh, they're here. I told them to stay away from you."

"You did *what*? Do you have any idea how . . . isolated I've felt? How much I've needed friends?"

"Yes," he said, and that word was his revenge.

I looked at the art supplies lined along the wall, wishing for a pot of black paint so I could pour it over Orion's face. "Take me to meet Meridian," I said. "After that, I don't want to see you again."

"WELCOME, WELCOME!" Meridian spread her hands as if they could hold the entire practice room. The trunks that had once been filled with IBI flamethrowers, I saw, were flung open and empty. Orion slipped into a corner of the room, where he brooded.

Meridian was flanked by Veldt and Loam, the hulking

Shade who had voted for me at my trial. "I hear you've been making great progress, Darcy," he said.

Veldt asked, "Are you ready to do something for your people?"

"Sure," I said.

"Don't worry." Meridian smiled at my expression. "It's easy. Unless you want something more challenging?"

"Easy's good."

"All right. We want you to—"

"Wait a sec." I shot a glance at Orion. "I thought this was supposed to be top secret," I told Meridian. "No one else is supposed to know about my task. Orion should leave."

"Orion's my son," Meridian said. "He already knows everything."

"You *do*?" I narrowed my eyes at him. "You said you didn't."

He shrugged.

"Ah." Loam chuckled. "A lovers' quarrel."

"Now, Darcy," said Meridian. "I appreciate that you're eager to be part of the mission. Of course you're curious. But you're involved on a need-to-know basis. Orion's right to keep details from you, despite your relationship."

"There *is* no relationship," I said flatly.

Meridian glanced at Orion, who shrugged again. She paused, seeming to reorder her understanding of the situation at hand. "Then you shouldn't resent his secrecy," she said. "Can we count on you to emulate it?"

I turned so that I couldn't see Orion, not even out of the corner of my vision. "Yes."

"Excellent," she said. "I understand that you enjoy exploring Chicago, and have visited some of the tourist sites downtown."

Orion could have told her this, of course, but a gleam of certainty in Meridian's eyes made me gasp. "*You* followed me, that first day."

"The Society does have strict regulations about spying on our own kind," she said, "but I hope you'll agree that what I did was necessary. I wanted to make certain that exploring was *all* you were doing. And given my son's interest—" She paused. "Well. Regardless. I was pleased to see how shocked you were by Cecil Deacon's home, and the way humans revere the Great Fire. And Orion had been right when he suggested at your trial that you could easily disguise yourself. No one on the streets looked at you suspiciously, not even when you were elbowing your way through the farmers' market. It's almost uncanny." Her eyes measured me. "You carry yourself like one of them. There's a certain . . . *weight* to the way you stand. It's not exactly attractive, but it will help you complete your task."

"You want me to pass as human."

Veldt said, "Specifically, we want you to pretend to be an IBI officer." He misread my expression. "Don't worry, we have a uniform for you."

"And these." Loam handed me a pack of contact lenses with green irises. "They're contraband, exactly for the reason that we're giving them to you. The Society makes a lot of money by bringing them from the Alter and selling them on the black market."

"Even humans can be born with dark hair and eyes," Veldt explained. "Not Shade black, of course. There's nothing like that. But those human fools don't see the loveliness in darkness. They dye it. They hide it."

"But what am I supposed to *do*?" I said.

"You will direct the flow of humans," said Meridian. "It's very simple. All you have to do is tell the human herd where to go."

"Where, exactly?"

"We will tell you that the day of."

"Day of what? When?" I said, frustrated.

The three exchanged glances. "I think she should know that," Loam said. "She needs to prepare herself."

Meridian nodded. "New Year's Eve."

That was barely two weeks away. "But what will *happen*?" I said, hopeless for any real answer.

Meridian smiled. "We're going to throw a party."

35

Conn was waiting for me inside the doors of the empty art museum, his face framed by a pane of glass. I manifested at the top of the museum steps, yet Conn didn't notice me until I knocked at the door, and then he startled.

He opened the door. "You could have ghosted your way inside."

"This was more polite. More human," I said, stepping into the lobby. "I appeared on the steps so you'd see me coming."

Conn shook his head. "Someone else might have noticed you. Next time, just come right in, okay? Don't expose yourself, especially not for my sake."

"You didn't see me anyway."

"No," he said. "I was thinking."

"About what?"

He smiled. "You. I was thinking about you so hard I didn't even see you."

I didn't know what to say to that, and when Conn sensed my awkwardness he hastened to add, "Don't mind me. I'm in a strange mood."

"Like when we met in the library?"

"Yes," he said. "Exactly like that."

His words echoed, then murmured, then vanished. We stood in a high-domed chamber with curved walls that swept around us in a perfect circle painted the color of lace or bone. The dome was robin's egg blue. I could see frosted doors on the other side, which I assumed led to the galleries. No art hung on the walls here. It was a bare space. Vast. Yet also somehow intimate, maybe because the only sounds we could hear were the ones we made with our bodies and our words.

I groped for a way to explain how the room made me feel. "It's like we're inside an egg, and are going to hatch."

"Yes," he said. "It's an in-between place."

I cracked open the frosted doors.

We entered a hall lined with statues, and I recognized some—not from the Art Institute I knew, but from books. In my world, those sculptures didn't belong in Chicago, but in galleries far away, like one classical statue of the goddess Diana that I was pretty sure should have been in a collection in New York City.

The works after 1871 were fascinating. Most were completely new to me, but some were made by artists born soon before the Great Fire, and I almost recognized these sculptures, except for little twists of difference. Rodin's famous statue "The Thinker" was called "The Dreamer" here. The sculpted man sat, his chin propped on his fist like the one I knew, but in this world he was looking up, not down.

"I suppose I should give you my report," I said with reluctance and also some surprise that Conn hadn't asked for it already.

"Yes," he said slowly. "Let's get that over with. I wish we could just enjoy the museum. I wish we didn't have to talk about the Society. But we should."

I told him what I knew about the task Meridian had given me, and her plans for New Year's Eve.

"A party?" Conn said. "You're supposed to . . . *herd* humans?"

"I know. Doesn't sound good, does it? They already made me practice yesterday afternoon. I dressed up in the IBI uniform and stood in the middle of a street intersection, stopping cars and telling people when they could cross the street. The humans obeyed. None of them looked at me twice. Meridian was thrilled."

Conn furrowed his brow. "And she hasn't said anything else about this . . . *party.*"

I shook my head.

"No one else in the Society has offered more details?" he asked.

"No."

"I would have thought that you'd ask Orion."

"Things with Orion, um, went a little south."

Conn's face grew stern. "Define *south*."

"Well . . . let's just say he thought we were more than friends, and now we're not even that."

Several emotions fluttered across his features, too quick for me to identify even one. "You're not."

"No."

He paused. "This is dangerous, Darcy. *He* could be dangerous."

"Not necessarily."

"You're too willing to believe the best of people," he said shortly, "until they disappoint you and the damage is done."

"Orion can't hurt me."

"Because he can't touch you?" He gave me a dark, skeptical look.

Conn was right, of course. There are a million ways to hurt someone without ever lifting a finger.

"I can handle Orion," I told him.

For a moment, it seemed like Conn would argue. Then he nodded.

"Hey," I said. "Don't worry about me. I broke your ribs, remember?"

The corner of his mouth lifted. "Oh, I do."

"I'm sorry I only brought bad news."

"Don't be," he said. "This is important. Now we have a date for the attack: New Year's Eve. We have an idea of what the Society will do."

"I won't do what they're asking of me."

"I know you won't. And . . . you *didn't* bring only bad news to this meeting. You brought yourself."

A silence fell. I tore my eyes from his (they were green today, like spring grass). I turned back to the art and noticed a series of four statues. They were of the same life-sized figure— a boy leading a horse—yet each was made from a different material. One was carved from wood, another from marble. The third statue was cast in bronze, and the last was chiseled from limestone. There was something arresting about the series. Maybe it was the way the horse dipped his nose to brush the boy's shoulder. Or how their limbs were carved into fluid motion, so that they looked like one elegant creature. Or maybe it was the sheer fact that the different materials completely changed the way I saw each statue, even though they were of exactly the same thing. The bronze sculpture made it seem as if the boy and horse were entering battle. The limestone glittered, like the boy and horse were mythic. The stuff of stories.

I stepped close to the wall to read the placard. The artist was named Moré, and the date was 2009. I read the title out loud: "*Te Panta Re*. What is that . . . Italian?"

"Greek," said Conn. "It means 'Everything flows.'"

"You know Greek?"

He laughed. "No. But I know these sculptures. They're famous here, so if you live in Chicago you end up learning a bit about them, like people in the Alter know about that architect, Frank Floyd Wright."

"Frank *Lloyd* Wright."

"Right," said Conn. "Anyway, a Greek philosopher was talking about a river when he wrote 'Everything flows.' He said that you can't step into the same river twice. Even if you set your foot in the very same spot, nothing is the same. Everything is different. *You* are different. The river has gotten warmer. The sun shines with a different light."

"So what's that supposed to mean? That there are no second chances?"

Something flickered in his eyes. "What do you think? Are there?"

I thought about it. "Yes. That sculpture is made of bronze and the other one is marble, but they're still a boy leading a horse."

"Ah, but maybe you like one more than the other."

"True . . . I like the marble better. It looks softer. More alive. Not the color, of course. But the texture of the stone looks like skin. Like if I touched it, it would sink beneath my fingertips."

"You could touch it. There are no guards to stop you, and"—he gave me an impish grin—"I won't tell."

I hesitated, because breaking the Do Not Touch museum taboo isn't so easy when you've trained yourself for years to obey it. Then my hand stretched out before my mind said that it could. I would have touched the boy—his arm, or shoulder—but felt suddenly shy, and swept my hand down the horse's back, then patted its nose. It was hard and cool, but smooth.

"Good boy," I told the horse, kind of foolishly, but everything seemed a little too serious and also . . . magical. I had to say something. Who knew what Conn thought of me, stroking a horse as if it were real? Maybe, for him, this moment wasn't special. Better to make some kind of joke, even if it was lame.

"Which is your favorite?" Conn waved a hand to include all four statues.

"This one." I gave the horse a final pat and let my hand fall from its side. "And you?"

His answer was immediate. "I like the one you like."

"Well, let's say I've changed my mind, and now I like the wooden one best."

"Then that's the one I prefer."

"The limestone. The limestone sculpture is my favorite."

"Then it's mine, too." Conn smiled.

"Now you're just being silly."

"I know." He laughed. "Isn't it great?"

"I want a real answer, Conn."

"Really, truly, the marble. But what if I *did* like it best because you do? That would only mean that you've changed the way I see something. Isn't that . . . isn't that what friends do? They change our perspective on the world. Part of why we care about them is because we love that feeling. The feeling of being changed."

I studied the series, choosing my words carefully. "Okay," I said. "There are second chances. But maybe it's also true that things can never be the same, and that you have to decide whether the second chance lives up to the first."

"It could be even better."

I looked at him. "Yes," I said, achingly aware that we weren't talking about art. "It could."

Conn reached for my hand as if it were the most natural thing in the world to curl his fingers into mine. "Let's go see the paintings," he said.

Happiness swirled through me, spiraling from my fingertips. "Perfect." I felt my face light up. "That's exactly what I was going to say."

He gently tugged me in the direction of a flight of stairs. We walked up, our feet hushing into the silence.

And neither of us let go.

We strolled through a hall of old masters. I tried not to be distracted by the way Conn's hand in mine made me feel as if I were wrapped in rough fur—warm and sort of prickly all over. "You're not bored by Renaissance art, are you?" I asked. "I know not everybody likes the old stuff. But I've been trying to work with oils lately, and these artists could teach me a lot about that."

"They definitely knew a lot about the interplay of darkness and light," he said in a confident tone, yet also with a quick sideways glance at me, as if checking to see that he was right.

"Yes . . . but how come you're giving me that funny look?"

"Oh," Conn said sheepishly. "Well, maybe I did a little studying."

"On art? Conn, you're not trying to *impress* me, are you?"

"No. Um . . . yes. I mean, did I?"

"You didn't have to do that."

"I just thought I should read up on the museum's collection. I want you to have a good time today."

"I *am* having a good time." I tightened my fingers around his.

"Good." He ran a thumb over my knuckles, and the sensation rippled through me.

"Let's . . ." I started. I tried again. "Let's go see the Impressionists." With sudden wariness, I added, "Impressionism happened in this world, didn't it?"

"Yes."

"Whew." I pretended to wipe my free hand across my brow. "You're lucky, you know that?"

Conn smiled down at me. "Yes."

As we walked down the hall, he said, "Are you upset about what happened with Orion?"

I let go of Conn's hand—not because I wanted to, but because I was startled and felt like I needed to concentrate to answer his question. There was no way I could do that while a small part of me touched even a small part of him. "Honestly? Yes." I saw his expression change and hurried to say, "It's not what you're thinking. It's just . . . it was nice to have a friend here."

"*I* am your friend."

I was silent. I didn't know what to say, and it was hard not to sense how my hand already felt homesick for his.

"Darcy." He rubbed his brow. "I've thought a lot about what happened on Friday. How you followed me. I was furious. One thought kept looping through my head: How could you invade my privacy? *You.* Of all people. The last person who should see me unguarded. But then I realized that's exactly what I've wanted, for so long."

Conn's words unleashed such a rush of feeling in me that I wanted to offer him something. Give him something. But I didn't know what. Or, to be perfectly honest, I didn't know what I could risk giving away. Finally, I said, "On Friday, I saw someone I remembered, from when I was arrested in 1997." I described the man I'd seen in the IBI locker room.

"That's Kell," said Conn. "You're talking about John Kellford."

The name plucked at my memory, striking a chord that panged and throbbed. "Yes," I said.

"He was young in 1997," Conn said thoughtfully. "A bit older than me. He was a rising star back then. Everyone thought he'd shoot through the ranks, maybe even become director one day, but he stagnated. No one knows why. Maybe the reason has something to do with you."

"I want to talk with him."

Conn mulled this over. "You'd spook him," he said after a long pause. "Don't get me wrong," he spoke over my noise of protest. "I'm not saying you *shouldn't* talk to him. Spooking Kellford might be a good thing. The shock of seeing a Shade—especially a Shade from his past—might rattle him, might make him more willing to share what he'd otherwise try to hide—try to hide from *me*, for example. The only thing is . . . once you manifest in front of him there's no going back, and afterward he might try to cover up important information. That's exactly what happened when I approached the coroner who signed your death certificate. I know this is asking a lot, but could you wait before going to Kellford? I might be able to dig up something on him first."

His logic was, well . . . logical. But I was reluctant.

"A week," he said. "Give me a week."

I still had that urge to give something to Conn, and when I looked at him squarely I realized that he was almost pleading with me. This was important to him. *Helping* me was important to him. I had waited eleven years to discover how I'd ended up outside those firehouse doors. Could I wait one more week?

"Okay," I said.

"Thank you."

"But I want his home address."

Now it was Conn's turn to look resistant. "That sounds risky. We don't know how he's going to react."

"Well, I'm not going to talk to him at the IBI."

Conn saw the sense in that. His co-workers weren't exactly my biggest fans. "All right," he said. "I'll get it for you."

For a while, I couldn't focus on the art and stared blankly at a Midwestern painter's cornfields. Gold waves under a pink slice of sun. But I didn't really absorb it, because the name John Kellford kept stabbing into the darkness of my memory, and hit nothing but shadows.

Conn touched my shoulder. "I want to show you something." As we strolled into a new wing of the museum, he asked, "Do you like John Singer Sargent?"

"Eh . . . not so much. He was an awesome painter, but

obsessed with painting pretty, rich women. That gets old. Sargent was kind of the *People* magazine of the late nineteenth century, except boring."

"In this world, he painted a very controversial portrait. I promise you'll find it interesting."

Conn guided me to a canvas that was taller than me, with a heavy, silvery wooden frame. As we drew closer, I was about to say to Conn, "Told you. Just another pretty girl." Then I saw that I was wrong.

The background was gray with hints of pink—typical Sargent, who was wild about this color, which looked like a misty dawn or certain kinds of shells. And yes, it was a portrait, and yes, the girl stood in a classic Sargent pose. Slightly turned away from the viewer, her eyes glancing back at me over her shoulder.

But she was a Shade.

Her black hair was swept back, held in place by one fringed swan feather. A string of pearls rested in the hollow of her throat, so close to the color of her skin that the pearls only stood out because of their shape and shine. An inky silk dress belled from her hips, flowing out onto the canvas until it faded away where the girl's feet should have been, but weren't. It looked as if she were ghosting slowly, disappearing from the bottom up. She floated there, looking at me, unsmiling. But her black eyes gleamed with a joyful secret.

"There," said Conn. "You see?"

"Why . . ." My voice trailed off. "Why is this controversial?"

Conn's eyes held mine. "Because she's beautiful."

We stood still, and I wondered if my face was full of the same secret as the Shade's. I asked, "When will I see you again?"

"I thought . . . Friday night, if you're free."

"Where?"

Conn hesitated. "Why don't you come over to my place? I'll cook dinner for you."

It took a moment for my mind to translate those words. Then I understood.

He was asking me on a date.

And this—this trip to the museum—this was a date, too.

The beach, the library, the beautiful old house. Conn had chosen all of those places.

He had chosen them to please me.

I gazed back at Conn unwaveringly. "Yes," I said. "I'll come. And when I do . . . I have a favor to ask."

"Name it."

"Can I paint you?"

36

In my Sanctuary bedroom, I sat beneath the quiet tree, my back resting against its bark. I closed my eyes and kept seeing the boy and his horse, the Shade in her dress, Conn's face.

I'd always thought that "counting the days" was a cliché people like Marsha used when waiting for the season finale of their favorite TV show. But I was doing exactly that: counting the days until Friday. Three days. After tonight, two. And then it would be one.

And then I'd be there.

Something flickered in the corner of my vision. A shadow, grazing over my bed.

I jumped to my feet. "Get out," I said. "Or when I find out who you are I will make you pay."

The shadow turned to flesh. It was Orion, and I can't say

I was surprised. "That's my girl." He perched at the edge of the bed, silkily swinging one foot. "Miss me?"

"No."

Orion's grin grew hard. Bright and glassy, like something that would break, and when it did, it would cut. "Can't you even pretend?" he asked, but didn't wait for an answer, because the answer was clear. "I'll still give you another chance. One last chance to prove yourself to me."

Well, *that* sounded icky. But before I could reply, Orion was gone.

I hated having no sense of privacy in the Sanctuary. Even when I wasn't being watched, I *felt* as if I was, and my skin itched at the thought of those unseen eyes. As Orion got less flirty and more pushy, less graceful and more snakelike, more demanding, more vindictive, I longed for my closet-sized room at Marsha's, where I could shut a door and block out whomever I wanted to block out, and let in whomever I wanted to let in.

Sometimes I really missed being human.

So I went down to the Archives with the thought that prowling around the human junk would be comforting. Like wearing pajamas and eating warm chocolate chip cookies, which was something Marsha and I did together a lot last winter.

Savannah was not glad to see me. "I hear Meridian's roped you into her scheme," she said.

I opened my mouth, then clamped it shut. I was supposed to keep that scheme secret—and *should*, if I wanted to stay on Meridian's good side and learn more about New Year's Eve. "I don't know what you're talking about," I said to Savannah.

She snorted. "Try again, Darcy. What's Meridian up to?"

"*If* Meridian was up to anything, and *if* I knew, then obviously she wouldn't want me to say anything, and she could have asked you to grill me about it, just to test me. To make certain I'm loyal to the cause."

"*Test* you? You are testing my patience! Do you have any idea how hard it's been to keep the Society from lashing out at the humans these last eleven years? Meridian and her crew are going to wreck everything Zephyr and I have worked for."

"What do you mean? What are you working for?"

Savannah folded her hands on her desk. "Citizenship. Shades have no place in human society. But we should. *We* should have a place at the table. In government. In the halls of justice. We want rights, Darcy, and to sue for them we had to disarm, but how do you disarm when your very body is a weapon? When Zephyr was elected head of the Council, she had a mandate to try for a period of peace with the humans, so that when the time was right we could point to our reforms as proof of our good intentions. Zephyr has cracked down on rebellious plotters within the Society, and she's mostly succeeded. There have been no terrorist attacks since Ravenswood. The IBI can't refute that, and they are fools if they think it's because of their increased surveillance and advances in technology. Oh, sure, they've made improvements. They've arrested some of our people. But we have *let* them."

Could I really be on the same side as *Zephyr*, that power-hungry, youth-obsessed shrew? "Zephyr despises humans."

"Of course she does," said Savannah. "But she doesn't

want to destroy them. And given that there are more of them than us, we need to find a way to live with them." Savannah crossed her arms. "It only takes one Shade with a bottle of poisonous gas to destroy our plans. *One* Shade. I would think that you, Darcy, with your obvious fondness for human things"—she waved a hand at the Archives—"would want to prevent that."

"You and Zephyr voted against me," I pointed out. *"Because* I was raised by humans."

"We voted against you because you are an unknown element. As such, you are a risk to security at a time when security is paramount. Prove that we're wrong. Help us, Darcy."

I hesitated. "What makes you think Meridian's planning an attack?"

Savannah gave me an irritable look that accused me of playing innocent. "In the past few days, there have been reports that Veldt is training Shades not to be afraid of fire. To *use* it."

I remembered the IBI flamethrowers in the practice room. I remembered how, when I first met Orion, he'd been impressed by my (mostly faked) nonchalance over torches. "Fire freaks me out, Savannah. Sometimes I lose my mind when I see it. Even the *smell* . . . what makes you think I'd ever play with it?"

"All I know is that if Meridian has a plan, Orion's part of it. And if he is, you are," she said meaningfully.

I smacked a hand against my forehead. "Why does everyone think we're a couple?"

Savannah blinked. "That's what he's told everyone."

"Well, we're *not*."

"Then you should have no problem telling us what he's planning with that troublemaking mother of his."

I studied Savannah. I liked her, and liked what she was saying. I got wistful at the thought that humans and Shades in this world might find a way to live together, that Conn and I could actually go *out* on a date. We could grab some deep-dish pizza and nestle into a puffy-seated booth and let the whole world see us together.

But Savannah's words still could be a trap. She could be working with Meridian, and this could be a lie designed to lure me into betraying myself. Even if it wasn't, there were a lot of shadows in the Archives. A lot of places for Shades to hide.

"Sorry," I told her. "I really don't know anything. Can I look around in Section 8L?"

Savannah slammed her hands down on the desk. "Do whatever you want. But don't think you fool *me*."

I slunk guiltily away, ducking down an aisle and out of Savannah's sight as quickly as I could. I rummaged through a tray of silver spoons, hoping that the noise might convince Savannah that all I cared about was finding more stuff to decorate my room. My fingers plucked out a spoon painted with a bird.

I missed home. I'd always thought my life was messy and hodgepodge, something pieced together by a year here, a year there. Now, though, my old life looked pretty simple. I studied the bird spoon and thought about that roll of money stuffed into Marsha's tea tin. I thought about who got second chances, and who didn't, and why. I wondered if Marsha would give me a second chance. Maybe she'd take me back. Maybe I could help *her*. Help her save up for whatever it was. I could set aside some of my money from working at the Jumping Bean. Marsha probably wanted to buy a new car, I bet. Hers was a heap of rust.

I slipped the bird spoon into my pocket and tried to focus on hopeful things.

Friday, I thought, and Conn.

But there was a problem with counting down the days until I'd see Conn. The closer I got to Friday, the closer I got to New Year's Eve and Meridian's plan.

37

A light snow was falling through the dark when I knocked at Conn's door, and I could feel individual snowflakes as they tingled on my skin. I focused on that, on each cold pinprick, instead of on my nervousness, which seemed ready to eat me alive from the inside out.

Conn threw open the door, and lamplight from the studio poured onto the back porch. "Come in," he said in that stiff, formal way that I now recognized meant something was troubling him and he was trying to hide it.

Conn's apartment was warm. He had cleaned the gears and tools off the table and packed them into an open cardboard box that lay next to the mattress on the floor. A primed, stretched canvas rested against a wall, and on the floor beside it was a can of turpentine and a wooden palette. Exactly what I had asked for. I set my box of paints and brushes on the table.

Conn ducked into the kitchen and bustled around like someone trying to make noise. "I wasn't sure what you'd like," he said, "so I got lots of vegetables." He tugged open the little refrigerator and began stacking eggplants, zucchini, and tomatoes on the bar.

"Conn, what's wrong?"

"Nothing. Um. Actually . . . I'm a horrible cook. I once set this kitchen on fire." He clapped a hand over his mouth. "I did not just say that."

"Conn, you can *talk* about fire around me." I studied him. Was . . . whatever it was . . . anxiety about cooking? Maybe that was part of it, but I got the sense that Conn was playing that up in order to distract me from something more serious. "Tell me what's going on."

He set a cutting board on the bar with a clatter.

"I can leave," I offered.

"No," he immediately said. "It's . . . well. It's Kellford."

"Just say it."

"In 1997, Kellford was part of the Vox Squad."

I couldn't find my voice. "Torture," I finally said.

"Yes," said Conn. "Voxing . . . it's a separate division of the IBI. Field agents don't usually do it." His eyes begged me to understand something.

"*You* don't do it."

Relief flashed across his features. Then it disappeared.

"No, but what does it matter?" he said bitterly. "I've made arrests. I knew what might happen after."

Ruthless, that's what Ivers had called him. I remembered the Conn I'd seen on the first day of school, when he was a nameless stranger who had radiated a danger I had willfully ignored.

But he was different now, and so was I.

Weren't we?

"Kellford joined the squad in 1995," Conn said, "and was promoted the following year. Apparently"—his voice was hard—"he excelled at his job. But in the winter of 1997, he was put on probation. He was stripped of his rank and exiled to desk duty for a long time. It's only been in the last few years that he was allowed back in the field. Whatever he did wrong, it's classified. But it happened right after Ravenswood."

I choked out, "You think I had something to do with Ravenswood."

"No. Darcy, *no*. You were a child. You couldn't have been part of the attack."

"You don't know that."

"I know *you*."

"Then what *do* you think happened to me?"

He set his palms on the bar. Took a deep breath. "There was a dragnet after Ravenswood. For months, the IBI did anything and everything to pull in as many Shades as they could. It's easy—*easier*—to arrest Shade children, but it's usually frowned upon. They're children, after all. It looks bad to the public—even to people who think that there's no such thing as an innocent Shade, because if the IBI hauls in kids it looks like we can't handle someone our own size. But the city wouldn't have cared about any of that after Ravenswood. I think you got picked up. I think that Kellford . . . hurt you, and that's why you can't remember."

I shook my head. "That's not possible."

Conn leaned across the bar, grabbed the collar of my shirt, and roughly pulled it aside, exposing the scar on my neck. "Then what is that?"

"I don't know," I whispered.

He let go, his fingertips brushing my collarbone. His hand fell to his side.

"The DCFS did a medical exam," I said, because something had to be said or my face would betray how his brief touch shimmered inside me. "Psych exams, too. I was fine. Amnesiac, but fine."

"If you can't remember what happened to you, you clearly weren't *fine*."

"Well, the only way I can know is to talk to Kellford. Did you get his address?"

"No."

Conn wasn't the type to forget a promise. Now, was he the type to tell a lie in order to prevent some damsel-in-distressing? Oh, yeah.

"I don't believe you," I told him. "And I *will* talk to Kellford. Either it'll be at his home or at the IBI, surrounded by your oh-so-friendly co-workers."

Conn hesitated. Then he grabbed a small pad of paper,

scribbled on it, and ripped off the top sheet. He offered it. "Consider taking me with you."

"I'll consider it." I slipped the paper into my pants pocket, where it rested against the bird spoon I'd taken from the Archives.

I sat on the stool at the bar. "Do you need help?" I pointed at the vegetables and cutting board.

"Um."

"Don't be too proud to beg."

Conn relaxed, maybe as glad as I was to send the topics of Kellford and Ravenswood back to their shadowy corners. "Well," he said, "I could use a little direction. Maybe you could . . ."

"Boss you around?"

"Please?"

"Sure," I said. "First, don't lie to me. Even if it's in the name of some totally pointless chivalry. *If* I decide to let you tag along to see Kellford, and if any kind of fracas goes down, *you* are going to be the one at risk, you with your skin and bones and flesh. Not the girl who can ghost."

"You're not invulnerable."

"Conn."

He sighed. "Okay."

"Second, let's see what you've got in those cabinets." I hopped down from the stool and went into the kitchen. It was a small space, and I could smell soap on Conn's body. Something earthy, yet light. Green tea, maybe. I breathed it in. There was a slight crisp scent, too—mint—and below all this was something rich and elemental and uniquely Conn. The scent seeped inside me.

This close, his skin had a glowy damp quality. Fresh from a shower.

I went still, and the same aware stillness came over Conn. He watched me with darkened eyes.

I turned away. I stood on tiptoe to open a cabinet door, and my bare arm brushed Conn's shoulder. He shivered.

Steady, I told myself. That shiver could have been mere surprise. Even if it wasn't . . . it was hard to block out the memory of our only kiss and how it had twisted into disaster. "I see." My voice was oddly even. It didn't sound the way I felt. "You've got pasta, pasta, and"—I opened another cabinet— "more pasta. I guess we're making pasta." I eyed the two-plate stove. "What is that, gas or electric? I don't do gas. No open flames."

"It runs on magnetic energy."

"Of course it does. You'll handle that, then. In the meantime, chop the eggplant into one-inch cubes and salt them. I'll be mixing paints."

Conn humbly accepted his servitude. I fetched the palette and turpentine, then pulled the stool up to the table, where I squeezed oils out of their tubes and onto the thin platter of the palette. I blended colors, mixing in turpentine to thin the paint. The chemical tang cleared my head.

Conn stood in the kitchen at the bar, chopping. "How'd you learn to cook?" he asked.

"The house mothers at my group home taught me when

I was about thirteen. They were really big on survival skills. Cooking. Cleaning. Doing laundry. Sewing buttons onto clothes. That kind of thing. Sounds very 1950s housewife, I know, but it was partly to give us something to *do*. Some of those girls had problems—serious problems, not like me—and they would go off the rails if they didn't have chores and a structure to their lives. And those girls taught me some pretty useful skills, too."

"Like what?"

"How to hotwire a car. Steal. Commit credit card fraud. Break into—or out of—locked buildings."

Conn's knife paused in mid-chop.

"Relax, Officer." I rolled my eyes. "I didn't *do* that stuff. Er . . . most of it. But it's good to have lots of tools in your toolbox, you know? In case sewing buttons can't bust you out of an underground jail cell guarded by inhuman creatures."

Conn gave me a narrow look. "Underground. So the Sanctuary is underground."

I winced. I shouldn't have let that slip. Conn could never know the location of the Sanctuary, because as much as I wanted to trust him completely, I couldn't. Not only because he had once betrayed me. I now knew that Conn had an honorable streak in him a mile wide, and if he decided that giving the location to the IBI and helping them mount an assault on the Sanctuary was the Right Thing to Do, he might choose that over any . . . attachment, or whatever, to me.

I used to be afraid of Conn. Now I was afraid of his Right Things.

"Don't ask," I told him. "I won't tell you."

There was a silence.

I broke it. I sailed right past any more discussion of the Sanctuary. "The house moms also wanted us to learn how to take care of ourselves," I said, picking up the thread of our earlier conversation, "since when we turn eighteen, we're on our own."

Conn swept the eggplant into a bowl and doused the cubes with salt.

"Work the salt in with your fingers," I told him. "Spread it evenly."

He shook his head.

"What?" I said. "You *told* me to boss you around."

"It's not that. It's just that the foster care system in the Alter sounds horrible."

"*Our* system sounds horrible? What about yours? They *tattooed* you, like you were a member of a gang. The Orphan Crips, or something."

"That's for our own good."

I spluttered.

"Really," he said. "It's to help bring runaways home. What happens to runaways? The same thing, in your world and mine. Abuse. Prostitution. Homelessness. Sometimes they get arrested, and then they claim they've got no one to take care of them, because they *feel* alone, and they're too proud to admit that the state is their legal guardian."

"Fine. That tattoo is great for runaways, but what about you? You've still got ink on your skin and I'm betting that O comes with a stigma."

"I don't mind." Conn shrugged. "It stands for orphan. That's what I am."

"And in this world, you never had the chance to be anything but that." I was getting angry on Conn's behalf. "You said that adoption isn't allowed here. So no family for you. Ever. Plus, they *made* you become an IBI agent. They took away your chances to be anything but what they wanted you to be. How can you possibly say that the DCFS is worse?"

Conn stabbed into a tomato. "When I graduated from the Academy, I had a career. When you turn eighteen, you'll have a high school diploma and nowhere to live."

That sounded stark and dire . . . and kind of mean, too. I inhaled sharply, ready to say something starker and direr and meaner. But then it occurred to me that maybe I already had, and that the resentment in Conn's voice was *for* me. It seemed as much on my behalf as my anger had been for him.

I let out my breath. "You are massacring the tomatoes."

He glanced down at the mess on the cutting board. "Oh. Sorry."

"It doesn't matter." I turned back to the blobs of paint fanned out on my palette, which was starting to look like a flat, lopsided flower with multicolored petals. I gave Conn a few more culinary commands, and soon the pasta sauce was bubbling on the stove.

"Come here," I said. "Sit on the bed."

"The bed?"

"You have only one stool, and I need it." I dragged the stool into the middle of the room, propped the canvas against it so that it served as an easel, and sat cross-legged in front of it on the floor, with a good view of Conn on the mattress when I peeked around the edge of the canvas.

"You should sit on the bed," he said. "I'll sit on the floor."

"I like the floor. It's good for my posture."

"Your posture's perfect."

"Conn. Sit still." I reached for a stub of charcoal.

"But—"

"I thought I was the one giving the orders tonight."

"That was just for cooking."

"I seem to recall that I offered to boss you around, *generally*, and you said, 'please.'" I sketched the rough outlines of the portrait, my charcoal rasping against the canvas.

Conn leaned back on one elbow. The look he gave me was downright roguish. "All right. I'll do whatever you say tonight."

"Anything?"

"Anything. Except—"

"There's always an *except*."

"In exchange, I'd like for you to do one thing *I* ask of *you*."

My charcoal skidded to a stop. "One thing?"

"One thing."

"I'm not going to tell you where the Sanctuary is."

"I'm not going to *ask* you where the Sanctuary is."

I pushed the canvas aside so I could look Conn full in the face. "Then what is it?"

"I'll tell you later."

I narrowed my eyes. "You can't make me do something if I don't want to."

"I know."

"All right," I said. "Deal."

He smiled, and my charcoal leaped to the canvas to capture the curve of his cheek.

I pulled the canvas back in front of me so that he couldn't see my face.

"So . . ." I heard him say. "What do I do for the portrait? Should I . . . I don't know. Sit in a certain way?"

"No, just sit. You can move around for now. I'll tell you when you can't." I traced the line of his neck, the shadow of his jaw, that tricky quirk of his broken nose. Straight brows, almond-shaped eyes. Sometimes I glanced up at him. My eyes always danced away first, back to the canvas and the other Conn coming to life underneath my fingertips.

Then I dipped my brush into pale gold and began to paint.

Thin washes of color, shining wetly on the canvas. Broad strokes. Shadows. The way the light shifts a color out of itself, back into itself, and then into something entirely new. I listened to the smooth slap of my brush and Conn's quiet rustles as I fleshed out a face I almost didn't recognize. And of course I didn't, not yet, because I was only painting the base layer, so all I had then were vague shapes of color.

Conn and I were blanketed by a cozy kind of almost silence. The radiator hissed and clanked, the sauce simmered, and my brush swept over the canvas. I settled into a trance.

Then Conn asked, "Why are you painting the portrait in oils?"

My fingers paused. There were several ways to answer that

question. I switched my brush for a thinner one, making a fuss over the selection, stalling for time.

"You could have chosen something else," he said. "Acrylics, watercolors, Conté crayons."

I teased, "You've been studying again, haven't you?"

"Or fingerpaints. Why not fingerpaints?"

"You're not a fingerpaints kind of person."

"Hmm," he mused. "But I'm the oils kind."

"Oh, yes."

"What does that mean? To you."

I set down my brush and turned away from the canvas to look at him. I was arrested by his gaze, entranced by it as fully as painting entranced me. The words flowed out of me before I could stop them. "I used to be afraid of painting with oils. It's risky. Easy to make a mistake, hard to correct it. They're expensive—no, it's more than that. They *feel* expensive, like I'm squeezing my blood out of those tubes. But when I see oil paintings by great artists I know that they felt that way, too, and that it was worth it."

"Why?"

"Because it shines with light even when the paint is dry. It gleams like a jewel. It's treasure."

Conn eased himself off the bed. His lips parted.

Then we heard the distinct sound of sauce spattering onto the stove.

"Yikes." I dashed into the kitchen, muffled my hand in a towel, and pulled the pan off the hot plate and onto the cutting board. I was grateful for the interruption. I felt a sharp certainty that that stupid oils speech was enough heart-on-sleeve wearing for the rest of the evening—for the rest of my life, even. "It's too hot."

Which wasn't such a bad thing, since the steam from the sauce could be a plausible reason for the blush burning in my cheeks.

"Let me." Conn fiddled around with some wacky-looking knobs on the stove and transferred the pan back to the hot plate. The sauce began bubbling again, but gently. "What now? I await your orders." He smirked, and I was glad—glad that he was striking a lighthearted tone, glad that if I'd made a fool of myself he was overlooking it.

"Well." I was still flustered. "Spices always go in last, but I didn't see any dried spices in the cabinet, so—"

"Ah. I forgot." He opened the refrigerator door and pulled out a bunch of basil tied with string.

"Shred it, all of it, and put it in the sauce. We'll put the pasta on to boil, and eat in ten minutes."

"Yes, ma'am."

"It's a good time for a break, anyway. The paint needs to dry before I add the next layer." Something made me add, "I've painted my friends with oils, too, you know. Lily and the boys."

"Oh," he said, and fell silent.

And stayed silent, even when he spooned the pasta and sauce onto two mismatched plates.

We both sat on the floor this time. The pasta was simple but perfect, and piping hot. I was so eager to eat that I burned my tongue. After two months of drinking water and stealing the occasional cinnamon roll, it was *amazing* to eat a real meal. To bite. To taste different flavors in my mouth. To swallow and feel heat radiating through me. "Mmm," I said.

"It's delicious. How did you do that?"

"*You* did it."

His eyelids lowered in a skeptical, be-serious way. It was a little too scary, though, to be serious with Conn. Like talking about painting. Art is so much a part of who I am, so close to the very essence of me, that it always makes me show things I'm not sure I'm really ready to show.

But since I couldn't think of any not-serious topic, I ate in silence, and so did he. When we finished, Conn took my empty plate, stacked it on his own, and tilted his head toward the canvas. "Back to work?"

I nodded. We settled again into our triangle: Conn, the canvas, and me.

I used a thinner brush this time, dabbing on paint with short strokes that made a *push-pat, push-pat* sound. Dark ochers filled out the planes beneath Conn's cheekbones. A mix of blues and browns blurred into the hollows under his sleepless eyes. A touch of crimson brought out the warmth of his skin.

I had to use my finest brush for his lips, which were thin yet exquisitely defined. I held my breath for this part, trying to keep my hand steady, steady. Then I made the mistake of glancing at him. I had only meant to look once and look away, but I couldn't. I was hypnotized by the memory of his mouth on mine.

My fingers shook, and the brush wavered across the canvas.

I swore.

"What's wrong?" Conn asked.

"I made a mistake," I growled. The painted line of the mouth had gone wrong, had sloped and wiggled. Frustrated, I rummaged through my box for a palette knife and used it to scrape paint off the canvas, clearing away as much as I could of my error.

Conn started to get up.

"No!" I said. "Don't. I don't want you to see."

"Okay, but can I do something?"

"Of course not. What could you possibly—" I broke off. This wasn't Conn's fault. It was mine, for looking. Mine, for not looking away. Mine for trembling to my very core. I focused on the blotch on the canvas, trying to squeeze my feelings into something small, something I could easily hide. "Do you have a rag, or a shirt I can use?" I asked in a calmer tone. "Whatever you don't mind me ruining."

Conn went to the closet, swept aside a few hanging shirts, and tossed an IBI jacket onto the floor.

That startled me out of my anger. I raised one brow.

"I have others," he said.

"It was the *way* you did it."

He returned to the edge of the bed as I dipped the jacket sleeve into the can of turpentine, wrapped it around the end of my brush, and dabbed at my mistake.

He said, "I'm going to quit after New Year's Eve."

What was left of the wiggled line slowly faded. The mistake hadn't been as bad as I'd feared, and I could blend what was left of it into the natural shadow at the corner of Conn's mouth. Carefully, I said, "Are you really sure that you want to quit? It seems like this job has been important to you for a long time."

He shrugged. "People change."

"One thing's for sure: you're seriously slacking. You haven't even asked me for my report."

"Right." He rubbed his eyes. "There was Kellford . . . and then, I guess I was just having a good time. I didn't want to . . . pump you for information, and—"

"See? You're slipping. Well, there are only two things you need to know: one, Meridian and her pals are training themselves to handle fire, and two, Zephyr, the leader of the Society, and most of the Shades have managed to quash terrorist plots against humans since Ravenswood, and they are going to demand full citizenship. Equal rights with humans."

"I find both very hard to believe. Fire makes Shades insane. It's an instinctive, primal fear. You—" he glanced at me.

"Yeah, I know. It unhinges me. But I've gotten used to it, a little."

He continued, "As for Shades wanting *equality* with humans, that's a fairy tale. The Society has never valued human life or human anything. There haven't been any attacks since Ravenswood, true, but that's because of the IBI's vigilance."

"Savannah said that's what the IBI would think." I set aside the turpentine-soaked IBI jacket. "Why is it so hard to believe that the Society—well, most of the Society—wants a truce? It's not like it's in our DNA to hate humans. *I* don't."

Conn loosely folded his hands and rubbed a thumb against the opposite palm. "You're the reason I want to quit."

"Me?"

He looked up. "The Society is the IBI's enemy. You're a Shade. I can't . . . I can't handle being part of something that makes you my enemy."

I almost reached across the short distance between us. "Then don't. Don't be a part of it. But you don't have to quit the IBI. You could change it."

"Change it?" Conn said incredulously. "Change the way the IBI feels about Shades? What the IBI feels is pure, cold, unadulterated hatred. I know. I've felt it. And you think I could wish *that* away from the hearts of hundreds of people? I don't have that kind of power, Darcy."

Part of me couldn't believe I was trying to convince Conn to stay in the IBI, yet I still said, "You could try."

"Impossible."

"Consider it," I insisted. "You said you would do anything I asked, tonight."

Conn grew quiet. "I'll consider it."

I'd said those same words earlier, when I promised to think about taking Conn as backup to meet John Kellford, but I hadn't meant them. Conn, though, wasn't me. There was an earnest set to his jaw that made me believe him, and so I raised my brush and tried to paint that expression into his face—something daunted . . . and yearning.

My brush slowed, stroked the contours of his face as I wondered if I was painting what I saw, or what I wanted to see. It
was hard to know, as hard as it would be to say, *I'm not your
enemy, but I need to be more than that, more than your friend,
and more even than that, and more, and more.* It was easier to
paint and not talk, and not look at him again. I began to rely
completely on my memory of his face. A silence grew, one so
solid and looming that it seemed larger than us.

I left Conn's eyes for last. They weren't gray or green or
blue but somehow all three, and yet none of them. I doubted
I could do it. I couldn't capture the light and fragility of his
eyes.

Still, I painted.

Then it happened: recognition. It flared inside me, and when
I stared at the canvas I saw that I had painted the right color.
I had no name for it. But I had found it.

I tore my gaze away from the canvas and dared to look at
Conn. Yes, it was true.

My heart was a cage that swung wide open, and I saw,
I knew.

"Darcy?" he asked softly. "What is it?"

I shook my head. "Nothing." I wiped my brushes on the
IBI jacket and packed them in their box.

"You're finished?"

I avoided his gaze. "For now."

"You're not leaving, are you?"

Then I did look at him. "You're tired," I said, and he was.
Beneath the unreadable emotions rippling across Conn's face

was weariness, the kind of bone tiredness that comes from many nights without sleep. "You should go to bed."

"I *am* in bed."

"Conn." I closed the paintbox. "You should go to *sleep*."

He stood, took two steps, and drew aside the canvas and stool. I stood, too, so that he couldn't tower over me and make me feel smaller than I already felt. Yet that didn't change the way Conn gazed down at me. That didn't change how inescapable he suddenly seemed. "All right," he said. "I will. But I want my one thing from you."

I paused, and wondered how something I longed for could be so terrifying. My heart thrummed in my throat.

"I'll go to sleep," he said, "if you stay."

"What—what do you mean?"

"Stay with me."

His hand slipped to my waist. Nestled there, large and warm, his fingertips touching the skin of my spine below the edge of my shirt.

Somehow I said yes, and somehow our feet slow-danced to the bed, somehow the lamp switched off and I lay tight against the heat of Conn's body in the dark, feeling the scratch of his sweater against my face, smelling the wool of the blanket pulled over us, and the sweet piney scent of crushed basil rising from Conn's hands as he stroked my hair away from my cheek. His hand slid down my back, and I bit my lip against the feeling. He gathered my hair into a rope and gently held it. "You'll stay?" he asked. His breath fluttered against my throat.

"I will," I whispered.

Conn's cheek grazed across mine, and his lips hovered close for a second, only a second before my heart kicked with fear and I pulled away.

I remembered. Conn holding a knife. Broken glass handcuffs, and my hands full of fire. Him shoving me onto the bed.

I turned away from him, onto my other side. I would have slipped from the mattress, but Conn's arms held me, drew me to him so that my back pressed against his chest and his knees were tucked up underneath mine. "Darcy, please listen." I felt his words against the nape of my neck. "When I came over to your house to finish our project, I didn't know what to do. My orders were clear: I was supposed to arrest you the moment I saw an opportunity. But I couldn't imagine doing it. I had begun . . . dreaming about you, when I was able to sleep. Dreaming about you, even when I was awake. When you kissed me, it was like you had ripped the world away and all that was left was the only thing I wanted. And *that* was the moment I decided. *That* was the moment I betrayed you. Because the intensity of what I felt scared me." There was a long pause. "Please forgive me."

I sighed. I said, "I forgive you." But forgiveness doesn't heal everything.

"Don't leave." His arms tightened.

"I won't," I promised. My eyes traced the shape of his small apartment, saw through the window that the snow outside was coming down hard now, reflecting the city light so that it glowed into the dark room.

Conn's body relaxed. I felt him burrow his face into my

hair and breathe deeply, breathe me in. Then his breaths grew longer, and slower, and deeper. His arm became heavy around me. A lovely weight.

He was asleep.

My eyes found the unfinished painting resting against the stool in the snowy light cast by the window. Anybody who saw that painting would see. They would see what I saw. They would know what I knew.

I loved Conn.

There were many reasons not to. They didn't matter. They crumbled like sand under a wave.

Then why wasn't it enough? Why was I still afraid?

Maybe, some part of me whispered, *you're afraid of yourself. Of what Conn might do when you do something unforgivable, something that won't let him forget what you are.*

I remembered what I'd said to him, *You think I had something to do with Ravenswood.*

He'd denied it, and he could have meant it, but as I lay in his arms I realized that *I* thought I had something to do with Ravenswood, that *I* was almost sure of it, and if I hadn't found evidence to that effect it was because I'd been asking the wrong questions. Why hadn't I asked Savannah if she knew something about a dead girl in 1997? I could have come up with a reason to ask that, even if it was a strange question. If Orion hadn't been willing or able to tell me about the Shades who'd planned Ravenswood, why hadn't I turned to Savannah for the truth, or even tracked down Zephyr?

I hadn't wanted answers. I hadn't wanted anything to tie

me to Ravenswood. Yet John Kellford did. John Kellford, whom I recognized. Who had been kicked off the Vox Squad so soon after the attack.

Conn shifted in his sleep.

I had to talk with Kellford. I had to know.

Now.

I slowly turned so that I could see Conn's face. His closed eyes with their dark lashes. His mouth soft, somehow fuller with sleep. He seemed to stir, and his hand closed over my shoulder.

I vanished.

38

John Kellford lived in a three-bedroom apartment north of Conn's place. I ghosted up to the top floor of the building and through Kellford's apartment until I found the master bedroom, and him sleeping next to his wife.

My feet hit the floor, my body manifested by Kellford's side of the bed, and I took stock of the room. Then I said, "Wake up."

His wife made a small noise and rolled onto her side. Kellford slept soundlessly, his head tipped back on the pillow, his strong, brutal chin raised as if in defiance.

"Wake up." I switched on a lamp.

Kellford winced against the sudden light, his wife murmured, and then Kellford's eyes snapped open and he saw me. He jolted upright, head slamming back against the headboard.

He swore and scrambled for something in his nightstand drawer.

"Don't bother," I said, waving the flamethrower I'd taken moments before.

Now his wife was up. Her eyes went wide, and she sucked in her breath. Just before she screamed, Kellford clamped a hand over her mouth. "Laurie, no." He glanced meaningfully at the door.

"The kids are sound asleep," I said. "I took a peek at them a minute ago. You don't want to wake them, right? Let's keep things quiet."

Laurie whimpered behind Kellford's hand. Tears trickled down her cheeks and over his knuckles.

"They're fine," I said wearily. "I didn't do anything to them." She made a muffled sob. She didn't believe me.

I sighed. "Go check on them yourself. But Kellford's staying with me, and don't even think about calling the IBI, or . . ." I paused. I was a monster. What would a monster say? "I'll kill him."

Laurie glanced at her husband, who nodded. She burst from the bed and ran from the room, her bare feet pounding down the hall.

I was watching her go, but I still caught a glimpse of Kellford's leg slipping from the covers, down to the floor, ready to spring. "Stop." I pointed the flamethrower at him.

"You can't use that," he sneered. "You don't have the guts to turn it on."

"All I have to do is keep it away from you. I can do that."

The fight didn't go out of him, but it retreated. I had to hope things would stay that way. Despite what I'd boasted to Conn about facing Kellford on my own, I wasn't ready for a Shade-versus-Human throwdown. But Kellford—beefy Kellford, with decades of IBI service under his belt, plus a talent for torture—probably was.

"What do you want?" he demanded.

"I want to talk."

He scoffed. "Right."

Then we both heard it: the sound of the front door whining shut and several sets of feet clattering down the wooden staircase outside. Kellford relaxed, and his face grew bold.

I was a fool. I should have played the vicious Shade until the end and held his family hostage until I'd gotten what I'd come for. Now it was too late.

He stood up from the bed, broad and threatening.

I forced myself to hold my ground. If I showed an ounce of fear, it was over. I said, "Do you know me?"

Uncertainty altered his face. He squinted at me like he *almost* saw something, *almost* thought something. Then he bit out, "How the hell would I know you?"

He advanced, and I couldn't help it: I stepped back. This might be my last chance to ask, so I spoke quickly. "On February 16, 1997, I was left outside the West Armitage firehouse in the Alter. I was five years old. How did I get there?"

Kellford halted, rubbing at his brow like he'd walked into a spiderweb. A new expression dawned on his face.

I gathered the shreds of my courage and put some backbone

in my voice. "Soon before that, I was arrested by the IBI. Do you know why? Tell me. Tell me, *please*."

Kellford sagged. He shuffled to an overstuffed chair in the corner and lowered himself into it. He was too big for it, and he let his arms hang down over the chair's sides as he looked up at me with resigned eyes.

Sad eyes.

"You," he said. "It's you."

"But who's *me*?" I cried. "Who am I?"

He gave a gusty sigh. "You were arrested, along with your parents, for the murder of 763 people at the Ravenswood Medical Center."

His words poked a hole deep inside me, and some feeling began to slowly leak out. Something that felt like poison. It was filling my lungs. I was drowning in it. "No," I whispered.

Yes, said my memory.

"Who were my parents?" I said. "Tell me their names."

He gave me a strange look.

"I don't remember," I said. "I don't remember anything."

"Mistral and Hart."

Yes.

"Who am *I*?" I begged again.

"You don't know?"

"No."

"Your name is Skylark."

That strange feeling gushed through me. "Yes." The word spilled past my lips. "But everybody calls me Lark."

And I remembered.

39

But I want to go, too!" I shouted at my parents.

"You can't," said my mother.

My father sank to his knees and looked straight into my eyes. "Lark." He tucked a lock of hair behind my ear. "Wild girl. You need to learn patience. Someday we will be proud to take you with us, but right now you're too little."

"I'm almost *five*." My birthday was in a few days.

"Lark, you can't even ghost."

"Yes, I can."

"Stop pouting," my mother told me. To my father she said, "We need to leave, Hart. We don't have time for this."

"But . . ." I wanted to wash that look away from my mother's face. Hard and bright, the way she stared at me whenever she brought me cold, chewy little squares of human food called ravioli. My favorite. I would almost swallow them whole, I was so hungry, and then she would look at me and the food would get stuck in my throat because I knew what she would say, and she did: "You're too old for food."

I knew what made her happy. So now I made my voice sweet and clear, and said, "But I want to do something for the—the glory of the Society. That's what you said. I heard you say it last night, when I was supposed to be asleep."

"Did you?" She went still, and I liked that, because it meant she'd stay for a little while longer. She didn't like to manifest, which was sad because she was so pretty that it calmed my insides just to look at her. If we were human, people would think she was my sister, not my mother, because she seemed so young, and sometimes I would play a game in my head where I pretended she *was* my sister, and I would wonder if things might be better that way.

"What else did you hear?" My father's voice was stern. This surprised me. He was the one who'd explained that humans eat ravioli when it's hot, and then he stole a strange box for heating up food so I could try it that way.

"Nothing," I said.

They exchanged a look. I guessed what it meant, because as soon as I saw it, my face relaxed in the same way. Relief. That's what I felt, because my lie had worked, and that's what they felt, because they believed it.

"Sorry, little bird," said my father. He kissed my cheek. "Goodbye."

They ghosted.

It always hurt when they did that, and sometimes I would chase after their shadows. This time, though, it hurt worse, and this time I let their shadows float away.

I *could* ghost. I'd been practicing. I would show them, I would help them, and then they would be proud.

I'D HEARD SOMETHING ELSE stand out from their whispers the night before: Ravenswood Medical Center. I knew where that was, and that's where they must be going.

No one noticed me as I left the Sanctuary. I cast a small shadow when I ghosted.

I didn't know the medical center was so big. I mean, I *knew*, because I'd followed my father there last week and watched his shadow wait across the street from the building, hovering until I realized that he *wasn't* waiting. He was looking. He was studying the building. So I did, too, my shadow buried in the bigger one thrown by a mailbox.

But now I was inside the building, and I didn't feel so brave anymore. It had many floors and was busy and noisy and crammed with humans. I would never be able to find my parents in this mess. My shadow flickered with fear.

No, I told myself. *Not again.*

That day I'd followed my father, he'd finally drifted away from the medical center, down the street. I was going to go after him when a man smoking a cigarette walked up to the mailbox and dropped in a letter. His thumb flicked against the end of the cigarette and its flaming tip sparked and fell off, hissing down to where my feet should have been.

And then they *were* there, and I yelped and jumped back from the little hot coal, tangling into the man's legs.

He yelled in surprise, then cut the sound short, gazed down at me, and clamped his hand over my arm. I was expecting worse, but he was a brave human. He had a look on his face like how I'd felt when I went to the zoo to see the baby tiger.

I held my breath and tried to ghost again. I tried to be light. I tried to free myself from my body, like my mother always said I should, but my heart was rattling in my chest and it was too hard to do.

The man laughed, then glanced around to see if anybody had noticed us. No one did, and he let me go. "Scat," he said.

I did.

My father always said there was no such thing as a kind human, but I thought maybe this man was.

Now I hovered invisibly in the lobby of the medical center, watching all the humans walking, getting on elevators, talking. They made so much noise. Even when Shades are manifest, we never thump around like that. Thinking that made me feel better. I could do this. I would find my parents' shadows. I wished I knew why they were here, though. It would help if I knew what they were going to do.

But I didn't know, and if I'd had shoulders I would have shrugged them like I had seen my uncle Bear do sometimes. He was a great shrugger, and when he lifted his shoulders and scrunched his mouth he looked like he wasn't afraid of anything.

Floor by floor, I decided. I would look for my parents floor by floor.

I didn't see their shadows on the second floor, or on the third, or the fourth, or the fifth. The fifth floor was full of children. Some were strapped to beds on wheels that were pushed by nurses, and I watched them roll by. There was a room with children who looked so sick it was hard to tell they were still alive. They were skinny and had no hair and their eyes looked like bruises. This was strange to see, because Shades never get sick. We only get hurt.

Humans don't live long, I knew that. But when I looked at the sick children I thought this was unfair. They should at least live longer than this. I felt something inside, something like a balloon filled with heavy water. It grew, and got heavier, and pushed at where my heart and throat and stomach would have been. I realized it was sadness.

I didn't want to stay in that room.

A long hall brought me to a sort of cheerful place. There were bright chairs and sunny windows and children tumbling around with toys. They were sick, too, but not very sick. Some of them made coughing sounds, like dogs barking, and smeared runny stuff from their noses across their faces. Parents read magazines. A woman looked at the clock and made an angry sigh. She tossed aside her magazine and walked up to a man behind a desk. "We've been waiting for over an hour!" she told him. "My son had an eleven o'clock appointment!"

"I'm sorry," he said, "but we're backed up. It's flu season, and we had several walk-ins today. Would you like to reschedule?"

She sighed again, sounding angrier this time, and returned

to her seat. She sat next to a woman rocking a baby. The baby was the smallest person in the room. The loudest, too. The baby screamed and screamed.

"Shh, my little girl," the mother said. "Shh, Moira."

The baby was pink and dimply and waving her arms like she had no idea what to do with them.

A man walked up, holding a steaming cup. He smiled at the mother. "Trade you," he said, and offered the cup.

She smiled back. "Thanks, honey." She passed the baby to the man, who cuddled her into the crook of his arm. He was the baby's father, then. "Coffee's just what I needed. Did they have anything else in the cafeteria?"

He made a shudder that was supposed to be funny. "Nothing you'd want. Why don't you take a break and read for a while? I'll walk around with Moira. Maybe that'll calm her down."

It did. I floated after them. I shouldn't have wanted to look at the baby. She had reddish hair, almost like the palest color of fire, the very edge of a flame. I shouldn't have liked to see anything that reminded me of that. But then I decided that no, her hair was the color of a flower petal. More pink than red. I was surprised at myself, that I had been able to change my mind and think of a flower instead of flames. I realized that I wanted to look at this baby very much.

It was because of how her father held her. That was why.

He was very tall, with eyes that were sort of blue but not really, and hair the dark gold color some leaves turn in autumn. I watched him hold the baby and wondered if my parents had held me like that when I was that small.

I followed the father down the hall until he reached the end, where he stood in front of a person-sized window that was like all the windows in the medical center, with no latches or any way to open them for fresh air.

I decided to go to the sixth floor, the last floor. My parents had to be there. I might have missed them, but I didn't want to think that, and I didn't think my parents would try to hide their shadows like I had hidden mine from my father last week. Humans almost never see our shadows, and my parents didn't know I was there, so why would they hide?

I was right. I was on the sixth floor for only a minute when I saw two shadows darting over the shiny floor tiles. They were going fast, so fast that I worried I wouldn't be able to keep up, and suddenly I was desperate to see their faces, even if they were mad at me, even if it was stupid of me to have come here.

That longing was a mistake, because it poured me back into my body.

I heard someone scream. A human had seen me.

"Wait!" I cried, running toward the shadows.

They stopped. They turned and rushed back to me. My parents manifested, and then the world seemed to speed up and break apart at the same time. There were more screams now, louder ones, and shouts for the IBI, and an alarm began blaring as humans fled.

When I saw my mother's face, things got worse, because I saw something I had never seen there before: fear.

I looked at my father. It was on his face, too.

Everything inside me began to tremble.

"Lark." My mother gripped my shoulders. "You've got to ghost."

I tried.

"Lark!"

"I can't!"

"Yes, you can," my father said. I could hear the effort it took for him to speak calmly. "I didn't see you a minute ago, did I? But you were here. Think back to a minute ago."

Someone flung a chair at us. My father yanked me to his chest and blocked the chair with his back.

I began to cry.

When my father spoke again, he had lost his fake calm. "Mistral," he said to my mother, "we've got to get her out of here."

She did something strange. She sniffed the air.

I did, too. A bitter smell itched at the back of my throat.

"There's no time," she said in a low voice like a sob. "It's too late. We blocked the fire escapes. We're on the top floor. We'll never make it to the lobby in time."

In time for what? I wanted to ask, but instead I gripped my father's shirt and pretended I was that baby on the fifth floor and that I was safe.

"There's got to be a way," my father said, and I heard the desperation. He did not think there was a way.

The smell in the air grew stronger, and I coughed, and that cough turned into a choke. I saw a human at the far end of the hall fall down, and at first I thought he'd tripped, but then another one fell, and another.

My father pressed my face against his shirt. "Hold your

breath," he told me, his voice raspy and tight. He coughed, too.

"The window," my mother said suddenly. I looked up at her, and my bones went watery with relief, because her face was fierce now, her eyes almost sparking with urgency. She looked at my father, and he glanced back, and in that split second I saw he understood whatever she wanted to do. He nodded.

She grabbed the chair that had fallen to our feet, ran at the large window at our end of the hall, and beat the chair against the window until it cracked and large chunks of glass fell at her feet. She stuck her elbow into the frame and raked her arm against the shards. A piece of glass flew through the air and cut my neck.

Cold air rushed in, the pain in my throat got better, and I saw some humans lift their heads from where they lay on the floor. They began to crawl toward the window.

"Go," she told my father. "I'll catch her." Then she ghosted.

My father held me tight against him, pinning me so that I couldn't even squirm, and ran at the window. My mind had been foggy from that ugly smell in the air, but now it cleared up fast as I realized what he was about to do. "No!" I struggled against him. "We'll die!"

He jumped.

We fell, and it was cold, so cold, and the air filled my ears and I would not look, I could not look at the ground. Then my father disappeared and I was alone.

I squeezed my eyes shut.

"Lark!" I heard my mother call, and I opened my eyes to

see her standing on the ground below me. I smacked into her arms and heard one of her bones break. I sobbed with terror, even though I wasn't falling anymore, I was on the ground, she was holding me, and my father appeared and wrapped his arms around both of us. He touched my chin. "Breathe, Lark. Breathe. You're all right. Everything's fine."

But my breath hitched and hiccuped and I was right to cry, because everything was not fine, not fine at all. When I raised my eyes I saw we were not alone.

We were surrounded by the IBI.

THEY SEPARATED US. At first I thought my parents would fight them, but the IBI had flamethrowers and they pointed them at me. A woman stiff and tall in her gray uniform wrenched me out of my mother's arms and put firecuffs on me. I went still. I had heard about them. I knew what they could do.

My mother's mouth opened, and I saw that she was going to say something to me, but then a man twisted her broken, bloody arm behind her back.

She clamped her lips shut. She didn't cry out.

But I did.

THEY SHOVED ME INTO A SMALL, dark cell where the only light was the flame flickering in the firecuffs. It made me rigid with fear, but I couldn't stop staring at it. My eyes were sore, but I didn't close them and I couldn't sleep. I didn't want to sleep, because I didn't want to wake up here.

The cut on my neck closed. Time passed. I wasn't sure how

much time, but it was enough for my body to start to trick me. My fingers relaxed and my legs went heavy, even though I told them they had to be ready. Ready for everything I didn't know was coming.

But things went fuzzy. I had one last thought before slipping into sleep.

This was all my fault.

I WOKE UP TO THE SOUND of voices outside the door. They murmured at first, and I caught only a few words.

". . . vox her?"

". . . unusual situation . . . child . . . orders . . . we wait."

"Wait?"

The voices got louder, because they were angry, and they rang clear.

"My cousin died in that attack! Everybody in that building died except for a few people on the sixth floor, and that's only because the Shades blew out the window!"

"I know the casualties. *You* better know how to follow orders. Director Martinez told us to wait. So we wait."

Before, when the flame in the firecuffs seemed to burn my brain, I used to pretend that it was that baby's hair, the one from the fifth floor, and then I would pretend it was a flower, and then I felt better.

I stopped doing that.

THEY STARTED TO COME IN, one by one, to ask me questions. There were five of them, and I began to know their faces.

Who else was involved in the plot? they asked.

What was your role in it?

Where do Shades live?

What other crimes have your parents committed? They are your parents, right?

What is your name?

Come on, you can at least tell us that.

We can be very nice to you. You know that, don't you?

Are you hungry? Thirsty?

I was, but I didn't say so.

They asked, How old are you?

My birthday had come and gone, I was pretty sure, even though I couldn't really keep track of the days. I was five years old, but I didn't tell anyone.

I had my own questions for them.

Where are my parents?

When will I see them?

But I didn't ask. I didn't say anything. I knew the rules. You don't talk to the IBI.

ONE OF THE GUARDS was bigger than the others. He had to stoop to get through the door, and when he was in the cell it felt like there was no room, not even for me. I tried to be brave with the other guards, because that's what my parents would tell me to do if they were here, but when he came into the cell I shrank into the corner.

He always paused before asking questions, and that pause scared me because I didn't understand it. The faces of the other guards were hard with hatred, but at least I expected that. I didn't expect whatever was on this man's face. Maybe it was something worse than hate.

He began his questions. Most of them were old, some of them were new, and I stopped listening to all of them.

Then a noise interrupted him. It was my stomach, rumbling.

I felt so ashamed. For being hungry. For having a body. For being trapped. Tears leaked out of my eyes.

The man stood suddenly and walked out the door.

I didn't think he would come back, so I didn't bother to stop crying. But he came back.

He held out a roll of bread and a glass of milk. "Quickly," he said.

I hesitated. Then I tore my teeth into the bread and swallowed the milk.

He took the empty glass, and I studied him.

I couldn't tell what the look on his face meant. I had never seen it before, and it didn't seem like anything I had ever felt. But I knew that his face was different from the other faces here. This didn't seem so frightening anymore.

He had dark eyes and dark hair with streaks of gray. If I squinted at him and pretended, he almost looked like my uncle Bear.

I would call this man Bear, I decided.

BEAR CAME EVERY DAY, and he didn't stop asking me questions or say anything different from what the other guards would say, nothing like that one word, and whatever was in his voice when he'd said it: *Quickly*.

But he always brought me something to eat.

He was there when they came into the cell, all five of them, and he wouldn't look at me when the thin-nosed woman said, "We're going to try something new today."

Fear broke into my mind and began to crumble it to pieces, because Bear was not looking at me.

I ran at his legs. I couldn't wrap my cuffed arms around them, so I leaned against them like they were a tree trunk, the last tree in the world.

There was a shocked silence. Then someone laughed. I heard a man say, "Well, well, well. Look who's made friends."

Bear's hand came down heavy on my shoulder. "You're coming with us," he said, and his voice sounded just like the guards'.

THEY TOOK ME to see my parents.

The room was a metal box, and my mother and father were strapped to metal chairs. My mother's arm was twisted and lumpy and swollen, and my father had burns on him.

I started toward them.

"No." Bear held me back.

"Nobody in this room seems to like our questions," said the thin-nosed woman. "But this time, when we ask, we *will* get answers." She switched on her flamethrower, and I began to shake. I searched my father's face, but he wouldn't look at me.

My mother did, and her black eyes were shiny and wet. She said, "Caged skylarks don't sing."

But then the woman thrust the blowtorch in my mother's face, and I opened my mouth, and sang and sang and sang.

40

I stared at Kellford, my throat aching as if I had been really screaming instead of only remembering it.

"You . . . clung to me," he said. "Called me Bear. And all I'd ever done was give you a bit of bread."

It took me a moment to speak. When I did my voice was hoarse. "Are my parents alive? I never saw them after that."

He shook his head. "Mistral died in prison and Hart was sentenced to death. As for you . . ."

"You saved me."

"You were such a tiny thing," he said helplessly. "Huge eyes. A soft, serious face. That day, in the interrogation room, the way you looked at me when—" He broke off.

I didn't want to talk about that either. "How?" I asked. "How did you get me out of the IBI?"

"You don't remember?"

"I do . . . now. But there's a lot I don't know, or understand."

Kellford sighed heavily. "The IBI wanted to lock you up forever. Director Martinez said you were a gold mine. There would have been tests, experiments . . . and I know for a fact that the Vox Squad was biting at the chance to get at you, *really* get at you. You still hadn't given up some information that would have been invaluable to the IBI, like the location of the Sanctuary. In the interrogation room, you would have told us anything, anything we wanted, and we got a lot, but Valerie—the head of the squad—wouldn't stop. The more she voxed the prisoners, the more you gave us, but the more you lost. You lost it. Began talking gibberish. Finally, we stopped. When we brought you back to your cell, you were numb. You didn't speak a word after that. You didn't even blink.

"I went to the coroner. I knew Anne from the Academy. We weren't friends anymore, because she knew what I did for the IBI and I knew that she was soft on Shades. She agreed to sign your death certificate. Officially"—he glanced at me—"I tortured you to death."

"Why would you say that?" I whispered. "You could have . . . you could have said I broke my cuffs, and ghosted."

"Your firecuffs were set to kill you."

"You could have claimed there was a malfunction. Why would you accuse yourself of such an awful thing?"

Kellford looked out the dark window. "It was more forgivable to the IBI than what I actually did. More forgivable, even, than negligence. A prisoner dying under interrogation? It happens. It happened to your mother. And I *wanted* to get kicked off the squad. The Society has done terrible things to humans, but we do terrible things right back."

"Why did you bring me to the Alter? You could have let me go."

"What, and let you find your way back to the Shades? So they could twist a sweet girl into a monster? I'm sorry for what happened to you, Lark. I believed—*everyone* in that room believed you had nothing to do with Ravenswood, but your parents were bloody monsters."

I didn't know what to say to that because, of course, he was right.

And he was wrong.

"The Alter was Anne's idea," Kellford continued. "It was a good one. I knew that the IBI would hunt for you, and you'd be safest in that world. It would give you a chance to become your own person." He rubbed his forehead into a mass of wrinkles. "I hope I did the right thing."

With his gray hair, he looked weary, as weary and unsettled as anyone would if an old ghost had come to visit him.

"Thank you, Bear," I said.

He looked down at his big hands. "I am not a good man."

"You're good enough for me."

I saw the city with new eyes. Well, new-old eyes, since now there were streets and sites and buildings that I recognized from the past two months, and that recognition was layered

MARIE RUTKOSKI

over an older one, the one that had been buried inside me. The one that had begun to emerge when I was in Lakebrook. That had crept into my sketchbook when I had drawn all those cityscapes.

I used to think of the Alter as my Chicago, and this one as an impostor, but the truth was that this Chicago had been mine, too, all along.

When I left Kellford's apartment, I glided through the coming dawn to Graceland Cemetery.

I touched the scar on my neck, a mystery no more. I looked out over the gravestones and wondered if any of the Ravenswood dead were buried there. Then I boxed that thought, shoved it away from me. Going to Kellford had been a mistake.

I wished I'd never known. I'd gained only grief and guilt and a name that I didn't want to be mine.

And there was a lot I had lost.

The hope that I would discover my parents, get rid of the orphan in me. I hadn't even known I had hoped for this. I had let myself assume they'd abandoned me in the Alter and had taken off. One of the wandering Shades, like Savannah had said. I hadn't searched for them. I'd shrunk my hope into something the size of a dust mote, something I couldn't see. It was one of those hopes you only know had been there when they're gone.

And I missed my innocence. Before, the bad things that had happened to me had simply *happened* to me. They were not my fault. Now, in some ways, they were.

Among all the things I had lost, surely I had also lost Conn.

320

Don't think about him.

Don't think about how much he looks like his father did, holding his baby daughter on the doomed fifth floor.

Don't think about how you can't lie to him.

Don't think about how he would never love you if he knew the truth.

He wouldn't even like you.

He would hate you.

Don't think.

I let my mind glaze over and watched the snowy cemetery glitter in the rising sun. I hovered there for some time. Then, as I was staring at a mausoleum, I realized in a disconnected way that my last drawing in the sketchbook I'd tossed on Marsha's carpet on that day in Lakebrook had not been of a small, stone house, as I'd thought. It had been a mausoleum. And not just any mausoleum—it was a portal, *the* portal Kellford had brought me through in 1997, one that he must have chosen because it was out of the way, or badly guarded, or ignored.

Maybe it was finally time to go back to Lakebrook.

I thought I could remember my way to the mausoleum, and it would be a far better choice than the only other portal I knew about, the Water Tower. Conn knew I knew about that one, and he might decide to look for me when he woke up. I couldn't risk seeing him. Even if he couldn't see me, I couldn't bear seeing him.

I could go home.

Then I caught myself. I shouldn't think of Lakebrook in that way.

But then, I thought as I glanced at a Sanctuary entrance, was *this* really my home?

What was?

My mind was exhausted and battered and sore. I reminded myself that I wasn't supposed to think, and so without thinking I drifted into the Sanctuary.

I manifested in the Great Hall. I listened to my footsteps and recalled the echo of my smaller feet almost twelve years ago.

Suddenly, I wanted to see Savannah and tell her everything. She would know, wouldn't she, what I should do? What I should feel?

I had started toward the Archives when Veldt appeared before me.

"Where have you been?" He almost seized my arm before he remembered—as I now remembered—the taboo about touching another Shade unless you're certain that touch is welcome. "We've been searching for you. We need you."

If I'd been my old self, I would have done what I wanted, which was to walk away from Veldt and go straight to Savannah. But I wasn't my old self, so I stayed silent and followed him.

We ended up in a bedroom that I guessed was Meridian's, since black clothes too small for anyone else in the room were strewn across the floor. The usual suspects were there: Meridian, who was poring over a pile of maps on a small table, and Loam.

And, of course, Orion.

He didn't look up when Veldt and I entered the room, but

flinched. Then he covered it by running a hand through his hair and leaning over the table. "There," he said, and pointed at the map.

But Meridian looked up at Veldt and me. "Ah," she said. "Perfect."

Orion stubbornly gazed down at the map, and Meridian noticed. "Orion?" she said. "This was your idea."

"Yes." He finally met my eyes. "It is."

I drew closer to the table, because my old self knew that I should see those maps. They were of city blocks downtown, close to the home of Cecil Deacon, the man who had started the Great Chicago Fire.

"Idea?" I repeated woodenly.

"I'll be frank with you, Darcy." Orion had recovered his cocky attitude and was now resting lightly on one hand pressed against the table. "The task we assigned you is too easy."

"Necessary, of course," Meridian said. "We want to maximize casualties."

"But we can just as easily herd the humans by scaring them," Orion said. "They'll go where a Shade cleverly disguised as an IBI agent"—he waved a hand at me—"tells them to go, but they'll also flee from a pair of terrifying Shades"—he pointed at Veldt and Loam—"and run where we want them. The truth is, we wanted to give you something to do. To make you feel part of something big, something for the glory of the Society."

"The glory of the Society," I muttered.

"And, of course, you're inexperienced." Orion's voice became cloying. "We didn't want you to get hurt."

"So . . ." I tried to figure out where all this was going, and relaxed when I hit upon the only thing that made sense. "You don't need me anymore."

Orion smirked. "We need something *more*."

"Our intelligence indicates that the IBI has beefed up security for this Friday night," said Meridian. "I suppose they finally realized that there are going to be thousands of stupid sheep milling around the downtown area, eager to count down to the New Year together, outside in the freezing cold."

Orion rolled his eyes. "Humans."

"So the IBI has appointed a head of security," said Meridian.

"He's good," said Orion. "We want you to eliminate him."

"You—" I stuttered. "You want me to *kill* someone?"

Orion snapped his fingers and pointed at me like I'd guessed a trivia question and was about to win a prize. "Exactly," he said. "His name is Connor McCrea."

41

"onn—" I stumbled over his name. "Connor McCrea?"

Veldt shot Orion an outraged look. "I know who you're talking about, and I know that you're setting her up to fail. I can't believe you're using the greatest moment in our history for a personal vendetta." He turned to Meridian. "I can't believe you're letting him."

"The elimination of McCrea serves the Society," she said smoothly. "He's one of their most promising young agents and is personally responsible for the arrest of several Shades."

"Yes," said Veldt, then added sarcastically, "Since we're assigning impossible tasks, we may as well tell Darcy to kill Fitzgerald, too."

"Fitzgerald is *old*." Orion gazed steadily back at Veldt. "Old trees topple on their own. It's the strong saplings you need to worry about."

Veldt crossed his arms. "Like I need to worry about you?'"

"Darcy should be *eager* for this task," said Orion. "McCrea was the one who arrested her."

I looked at Orion. Fear frosted my heart. "How do you know that?"

"I read the arrest docket. I've been . . . curious about certain things. Yesterday, I decided to do some research at the IBI, and discovered that McCrea's debrief after your arrest is highly classified. In fact, the level at which information concerning Darcy Jones is protected seems, well, *unusual*. Even *I* wasn't able to find much, which makes me suspect that the IBI is taking care to hide this information from Shade eyes. Of course, with due time, I could delve much deeper into this mystery. Unless"—he lifted a hand toward me, palm up— "Darcy would like to fill in the blanks."

I swallowed. "I have no idea why the IBI would classify anything about me." Orion's smile told me I was going to have to try harder. "Well, I'm a Shade, right? I guess the IBI keeps most Shade arrests under wraps. For, um, reasons of national security. And in this case, I was a Shade raised by humans. Maybe, since I was . . . different, they found that interesting."

"Interesting," said Orion. "Do you know what *I* find interesting?" He turned to address everyone in the room. "The fact that the one thing I overheard about Darcy Jones's arrest—a little thing, a bit of gossip one IBI agent mentioned to another over a cup of coffee—is that, in the Alter, when she still thought she was human, she and McCrea were dating."

There was a gasp. It might have come from me. "That's not true," I said.

Sweetly, Orion said, "I don't believe you."

"We were class partners, but that was an assignment, for English class, which is totally normal in high school. In the Alter, at least. Obviously I didn't *know*—"

"Shut up," Orion snapped. His faked easy manner was gone. "If you did care for him, that's all the more reason for you to kill the man who tricked you. If you did not, you should have no problem doing this small favor for the Society. If, that is, you are truly one of us."

Veldt, whose expression had tightened when Orion had said the word "dating," muttered, "If we have a viper in our midst, better that we know it now."

"Indeed," said Meridian. "Well, Darcy? What is your answer?"

I knew what Conn would want, if he were here. Say yes, he'd tell me. Say it, because if you don't you'll never learn anything else about New Year's Eve. Your cover will be blown. They will guess the truth lurking under Orion's accusations.

The truth that somehow, some way, a Shade had fallen in love with a human.

"Will you kill him?" Meridian pressed.

It was one lie I couldn't bear to tell.

"No," I said, and ghosted before they could seize me.

*   *   *

I FLEW THROUGH the city in a daze, watching the silver sun climb in the sky. It was only when its light struck the skyscrapers downtown and transformed them into shining icicles that that brightness cut through my misery.

I had to warn Conn, I realized. If I couldn't do anything else, I had to do that.

But not in person. I didn't have the strength for it.

It was Saturday, so I couldn't count on him not being home. The coward in me wanted to wait until a workday, when he'd be at the IBI, but who knew what Meridian and Orion might try before then?

I waited until noon, when I wouldn't cast a shadow. Then I went to his house.

I'm not sure what I expected, but it wasn't what I found. Conn was sitting on the back porch without a coat on. He was wearing the same clothes he'd had on last night, as if the moment he'd woken up and discovered I wasn't there he had walked right out of the apartment to wait.

To wait for me.

Conn's face looked fragile, like something that might break. And when I saw that, something broke inside of me, and I almost appeared, almost called to him.

I caught myself. His expression might have had nothing to do with me.

And if it did?

He wouldn't look that way if he knew what my past really held.

I glided toward a tree, and as the sun slipped down the sky my shadow mingled with the ones thrown by a network of branches. I waited, and he waited, and I wondered if he somehow knew I was there, breaking my promise never to spy on him again.

At dusk, when all the shadows had blended into darkness, he burst from the porch in a furious movement. He leaped down the steps and stalked across the snow to the street. Then down the street and around a corner.

He was gone. He had given up.

I told myself that this was a good thing.

I slipped into his apartment, and the scent of it knocked me back into my body. Turpentine. Basil. And Conn.

I wobbled on my feet and caught my breath.

I didn't want to stand on his wooden floor, to feel and hear the creaks echoing the ones we'd made last night as our feet found their way to his bed. I didn't want to see the undone blankets. I didn't want to climb inside them, touch his pillow, and press my face against it.

But the universe didn't seem to really care about what I wanted.

I forced myself not to look at the painting in the center of the room—I'd never finish it now—and went into the kitchen for the pad of paper Conn had used last night to write down Kellford's address. I tore off a sheet. Every word hurt to write, because they were the last words I would say to him, so I wrote as few as possible.

*I think Meridian's attack will take place near Cecil
Deacon's home. I'm not part of their plans anymore, so
they'll probably send Veldt and Loam to cause a panic
that will herd humans into danger.*

*Convince Director Fitzgerald and the mayor to cancel
any New Year's Eve celebrations. Impose a curfew. It's
the only thing you can do, because Meridian's counting
on thousands of people being in the streets.*

Please do it. They want to kill you, too.

Be careful.

> *Goodbye,*
> *Darcy*

I folded the sheet of paper and set it on the bar. Then I left.

FOR DAYS, I stayed a ghost. It was weird to think that every
hour I remained like this was another hour padded onto my
life, but that was definitely the lesser of two evils. The greater
evil would have been to have a body that made me really *feel*,
made my heart cramp in pain and my stomach clench with guilt.

You can't cry if you don't have any tears, or eyes, or lungs.

One downside of ghosthood, though, was that I never got
tired, and every time night came I couldn't help wondering if
Conn was sleepless, too.

When Thursday dawned, I had had enough. Why was I lingering in this world, anyway? There was nothing for me here
but bad memories, and I'd done what I could to help the IBI.
As for Conn . . .

Conn would be all right. I couldn't contemplate any other possibility.

I floated north over Lake Michigan, then picked up speed when I reached what in the Alter was Lincoln Park, and what in this world was another cemetery. I darted through the graves, looking for the mausoleum that had taken me to the Alter and would take me there again, to whatever kind of life I'd have there.

When I saw uniformed IBI agents standing in front of one of those small, stone mausoleums, I knew I had found the portal.

And I found something else there, too.

Someone else.

A girl, flirting with one of the guards.

A brown-haired girl, tall and radiating sexiness, even though her body was completely swaddled in a camel hair coat.

It was Taylor Allen.

I nearly went solid with shock. "Taylor? What are *you* doing here?"

42

Taylor screamed.

"Oh, sorry," I said, remembering that it *is* a little scary to hear disembodied voices. I manifested.

The guards screamed.

"Argh!" I ghosted again.

The guards kept yelling and fumbled for their flame-throwers, one of them smacking into another, Three Stooges style. None of them looked older than me, and I felt a burst of thankfulness that this portal seemed to be a kind of training ground for rookie agents.

Then they switched on their flamethrowers, and I stopped feeling so grateful. I just had to hope that none of them was primed to see my shadow.

"Taylor," I hissed in her ear. "It's me, Darcy Jones."

"I know," she snapped.

"What?" One of the guards swiveled to look at her.

She gave a short, irritated sigh. In a quavering voice, she wailed, "I know the IBI will protect me!"

"Don't worry," said the guard. "You're safe with us."

I couldn't tear my eyes away from the flames, and my shadow began to tremble. I had to get out of there or I would go solid. I whispered again in Taylor's ear, "Cover for me, please. I'll explain everything later. Tell them you see me somewhere else, okay? Then walk away—slowly, so they don't think anything's weird. I'll be right behind you."

"Oh, joy," she muttered through gritted teeth. Then she surprised me by doing exactly what I'd said. "There!" she shouted to the guards, and pointed. "I saw her behind that tree!"

They took off running, and she sauntered in the other direction, toward the cemetery gate. I floated after her. "Thanks, Taylor."

"Stop doing that! I will not have a conversation with someone I can't even see."

"It's safer this way. Listen, I know this will be hard for you to understand, but I'm—"

"I know exactly what you are."

"You . . . do? But how? And how did you get here? *Why* are you here?"

"If you want answers you'll have to follow me home, and you will not—I repeat—will not talk to me until we get there, because I don't relish the thought of everyone in public seeing me babble at myself like some straitjacket asylum psycho. Got it?"

I hovered and glanced back at the unguarded portal.

Taylor kept walking. "You'd better be behind me," she called.

In a second, I was.

I followed her into the subway, where Taylor seemed to have no trouble finding her stop, if only because she laid a mittened hand on the arm of a college-age boy and purred, "Will you please tell me when we reach Old Town?"

Taylor's trim, heeled boots rapped confidently down the streets of Old Town as if she owned all the luxury around her: the gorgeous Victorian brownstones, the intricate weavings of wrought-iron fences, the sidewalks meticulously swept clean of snow. My curiosity spiked when she took a key from her alligator skin clutch and walked up a stone front porch. She entered the mirrored vestibule, shaking snow from her coat.

"So, Taylor—"

"Later." She opened her clutch, plucked out a lipstick, and began to apply, peering at one of the mirrors. Then she snapped her purse shut and walked up the gleaming wooden staircase, past numbered apartment doors. She flung open the door on the third floor and stepped into a living room with eleven-foot ceilings and elegant furniture, including deep armchairs and a high-backed sofa turned tastefully away from the entrance.

"Guess who I found," Taylor sang.

A disheveled head popped up from behind the sofa's back. "You didn't!"

It was Jims.

I manifested. "Jims?" I breathed.

"Darcy!" He sprang up and over the sofa, and spread his arms wide. "You crazy Shade, you. Come over here and give ol' Jims some sugar."

43

I ran to him. I couldn't believe I had ever forgotten, even for a
few days, how good it is, how important it is, to have arms to
hold someone tight.

"Um," Jims wheezed. "I love you, too. I also love breathing."

I felt something press against my cheek and pulled away. I
reached into Jims's suit jacket (Jims was wearing a suit?) and
plucked a stick of beef jerky out of his inside pocket. I laughed.
"Even in another dimension, you still managed to find this?"

"It's not a Slim Jim," he said, "but it *is* teriyaki flavored,
with enough MSG to grow me a third arm." He snatched it
back and peeled open the plastic wrapper. "Delish."

I heard doors slam and feet bounding down a hall. Raphael
burst into the living room, with Lily right behind him. Raphael

reached me first, swinging me into the air with his strong arms, murmuring something in Spanish that I hoped meant he'd never let me go.

"Hey, man." Jims poked Raphael in the shoulder and nodded at Lily.

Raphael set me down.

Lily was standing there, stock-still, her hands balled into fists at her sides. Then her hands slowly unclenched and lifted to cover her face. Her shoulders shook.

She was crying.

"No." I hugged her. "Lily, don't." I smoothed a hand over her hair—which, for once, wasn't dyed. It was her natural black. It occurred to me that maybe I *had* seen her, that day I biked to the library. And that if I'd stopped and let myself believe the impossible, I would have found my friends so much earlier. Lily lifted her face, and I saw she hadn't lost her love for blue mascara. I wiped away her blue tears.

"We were so worried," she whispered.

"I wasn't," said Taylor.

There was a silence as we watched Taylor nonchalantly throw off her coat and settle into an armchair. Finally, she noticed our stares. "What?" Taylor said. "She's a Shade. She can't get hurt."

Jims narrowed his eyes. "You seem to have forgotten some of the finer details of Shade biology."

"You really know." I looked around the room. "All of you."

Raphael nodded.

"Have you always known? About me? About this world?"

My thoughts got very jumbly. "Am I the last one to find out about what I am?"

"It's not like that," said Lily.

"We figured it out once we got here," said Raphael.

"Which is when? And how? And . . ." I looked at Taylor. "Why is she here?"

"Thanks a whole bunch," she said.

Lily glanced at her. "We needed the ride," she told me with a shrug.

"Somebody please explain," I begged.

Lily began. "When you called me after Conn attacked you, and we got cut off, I ran across the yard to Jims's place and hauled him out of his cave."

"Interrupting an intense online gaming session, I might add." Jims glanced at me, then threw up his hands defensively. "Which I totally did not mind, under the circumstances."

"Then we called Raphael and told him to meet us at Marsha's."

"Now that you're safe," Jims asked me, "can I say how impressed I was by the damage? It was a wreck."

"*Marsha* was a wreck," said Lily.

"I got there around the same time as the police," said Raphael. "Who were oh-so-helpful."

"Jerks," said Lily.

"They made a call and discovered that Conn had no registered address, or record of birth, or social security number, or *anything* that would indicate he actually existed," Raphael continued. "And even though you'd think *they'd* think this was worth investigating, they kept telling Marsha there was nothing they could do until you'd been missing for at least twenty-four hours. That's when Lily began screaming at them."

"And Raphael looked like he'd punch someone," Lily added.

"And Jims told Mr. Officer of the Law where he could put his nightstick," said Jims.

"That snapped Marsha out of it," said Raphael. "She began soothing ruffled feathers. She buttered up the police officers until they cared at least ten percent more than the zero they started out at. They agreed to drive her to the station so she could file a report, and we said we'd stay at her place in case you came back. Since the cops couldn't be bothered to do their job, once they'd left with Marsha we searched the house for clues."

"Anything," said Lily. "Anything that might tell us where Conn might have taken you, or at least where he'd come from."

"In your bedroom, we found *this*." Jims pulled a small, leather-covered rectangle out of his jacket pocket.

I took it. It was an ID card with a holographic image of Conn framed by a metallic raised crest. *Interdimensional Bureau of Investigation*, it read. Below Conn's photograph were his name and the words *Agent, First Class*. "His badge," I said. "I remember . . . when he first brought me into the IBI, they gave him a hard time for losing this."

Raphael said, "When Jims saw the badge, he went wild. He kept claiming that it explained everything. He was like, 'I knew it! I knew there were other dimensions!'"

"They thought I was completely crazy," said Jims.

Taylor sniffed. "Like he's not."

"Then Lily found your sketchbook on the living room floor," said Raphael.

Lily shifted uncomfortably. "I know that's private," she said to me, "and please believe that normally I'd never look in it without asking you, but I couldn't help remembering how edgy you'd seemed when you talked about your latest sketches. How you kept drawing cityscapes that looked like Chicago but weren't, and how it didn't feel like you were inventing a new city, but that you were drawing from memory. As I looked through the sketchbook, I saw that you were right. The sketches *did* look like another version of Chicago."

"And that made you believe Jims?" I asked.

"No," said Lily. "I still thought he was crazy. But when I turned to the last sketch . . ."

"I recognized it," said Raphael. He walked over to the fireplace, and I noticed my black sketchbook resting on the mantel. He returned with the book and flipped it open to the last sketch I'd drawn: the mausoleum. "After the Great Chicago Fire, the city began a wave of big civic projects, and focused on building Lincoln Park. There used to be a cemetery there . . . well, like the one here. In our world, Chicago officials convinced every family with someone buried in that cemetery to let the city move them somewhere else—every family, that is, except the Couches. This"—Raphael pointed at the sketch— "is the Couch Mausoleum. It's famous."

"So famous only Raphael had ever heard of it," Jims drawled.

"It's a piece of Chicago history," Raphael shot back, then continued. "The Couch family got into a snit, said that no way would they ever move their dead. So the city built Lincoln Park anyway, around the mausoleum."

"The Couches had to have known it was a portal," said Jims. "I mean, *some* people back home must know about this world. It can't be a secret from everyone."

"Luckily," said Lily, "Raphael knew what it was, even if he didn't know what it could do. Thank God he recognized it."

"It's right by the Chicago History Museum," he said. "I go there all the time."

"You know," said Taylor, "it's really cliché for an immigrant to be obsessed with American history."

"I am not an immigrant," Raphael said. "My *parents* are immigrants."

"Whatever."

"Can we get to the part where somebody explains what Taylor's doing here?" I said.

"Raphael"—Taylor glared at him—"called me to ask if I wanted to rehearse for *Hamlet*, and could I *please* pick him up at Darcy's house?"

"If I'd told you what was really going on, you never would have come," Raphael protested.

"I pulled up, and the three of them crammed into my car, bullying me into driving around Lakebrook looking for you, as if I had nothing better to do on a Saturday afternoon."

I studied her with an unfamiliar curiosity. "But you did it."

"Well . . ." Taylor looked down at her pink lacquered nails. "They were pretty upset."

"We searched the neighborhood for hours," Lily said, "but you were gone, and I could *feel* that you were gone. So we decided to drive to the Couch Mausoleum. I guess it was silly to think we'd find you there, but we couldn't do *nothing*, and we didn't know what you maybe hadn't told us about the time you'd spent with Conn."

"Remember when you ditched class?" said Jims.

"We thought it was possible that, at some point, you'd gone into the city with him, and had drawn the mausoleum from life. So maybe the place meant something to you, or to him, and maybe we'd at least find a clue about what had happened to you."

"They were grasping at straws," said Taylor.

"When we got downtown, everyone had gone silent. We parked at the Chicago History Museum and walked toward the mausoleum, and none of us could talk. Not even Jims."

"That didn't last long," said Taylor. "As soon as we got to the mausoleum, Jims began babbling about its doorway, how it looked wavy around the edges. And then he said he could see *through* it, and that it looked like there was an entire cemetery inside the mausoleum."

"Jims was primed," I realized.

"Primed?" said Lily. "What do you mean? Like a canvas is primed?"

"Sort of. When we say a canvas is primed, we mean that it's

ready to be painted. Conn said—" I took a breath. It hurt to say his name out loud.

My friends had noticed how I'd paused over Conn's name, and their faces hardened into cold masks.

Well, except Taylor. She still seemed mostly bored.

"Conn said that 'primed' is a psychology term," I continued, "one that describes how the brain is able to accept information that on the surface seems insane, like the existence of an interdimensional portal, as long as it has been prepared—primed—for the possibility."

"Ooh, I like that word," said Jims. "Jims Lascewski: Primed and Ready for Action."

"Jims kept insisting he saw something," said Raphael, "and we got mad. It wasn't the time for his stupid games. But then Lily saw it, and then I did, too."

"Guess who was last," said Taylor.

"We walked through the doorway, and all hell broke loose. Suddenly, we were surrounded by guards pointing weapons at us."

"And who saved the day?" said Jims. "Go on. Who?"

"Jims did," Raphael and Lily chorused wearily.

"That's right. I whipped out McCrea's badge and began waving it around, telling them I was Agent McCrea, returning from an important mission, and I outranked them, and they'd better shut up and let me bring my prisoners back to the Interdimensional Bureau of Investigation."

"Didn't they notice that you look nothing like Conn?" I said.

"I held my thumb over the photo. It always works in movies."

Lily said, "We settled into the city and spent every day looking for you. We were afraid to go to the IBI, because that's Conn's home ground. Plus we didn't want anyone to recognize us from that stunt we pulled at the mausoleum and decide to boot us back home—or worse, arrest us. Then we heard about Shades. And we knew."

"Did Marsha tell you what happened at her house?" I asked. "How she threw a knife at me—accidentally—and I vanished?"

"No. She never mentioned that."

"Then . . ."

"It's because of the way you *look*, dummy," said Taylor. "It was obvious."

I felt suddenly tired. I sank down onto the sofa with Lily next to me, while Raphael and Jims arranged themselves into armchairs and Taylor coolly watched us. "You don't . . . care about what I am? You're still my friends?"

"How can you even ask that?" said Lily.

"Shades are mass murderers," I muttered.

"But you're not. A few Shades have done some awful things, but that doesn't mean they're all evil."

Which was the point I'd been making to Conn.

"People here have lost perspective," she continued. "Shades are the monster under the bed."

"Frankly," said Jims, "I think you're *awesome*. Aside from fire being your obvious kryptonite, you're practically invulnerable."

In a low voice I said, "I don't feel invulnerable."

"That's okay," said Jims. "You've got us. We'll play Robin to your Batman."

Lily looked at me. She knew I wasn't talking about physical weaknesses. She leaned comfortingly against me.

"I still can't believe you're here," I said. "I can't believe we ever found each other."

"We hoped you'd make it back to the Couch Mausoleum," said Raphael, "and try to go home. Of course we wouldn't have been able to see you, but you'd at least notice one of us. So we took shifts watching it around the clock."

"Except Jims," said Taylor. "Jims didn't have to stand around in the cold. At night. In the *snow*."

"Jims has a job that keeps the roof over our heads," said Jims.

I glanced around the swanky apartment, then back at him.

"That's right," he said. "Daddy's bringing home the bacon."

"Please stop calling yourself that," Lily moaned.

"Exactly what kind of job do you have?" I paused. "Are you a drug dealer?"

"Close," he said. "I'm a Storyteller."

"This world has no television, no movies," said Raphael, "but it's big on the performing arts, like theater, ballet, and—"

"—role-playing games," Jims finished. "I happen to be a very talented Game Master. I run about fifty games a week, and I am *rolling* in money. Oh, and can we please talk about my social life?"

"Jims," said Lily.

"The ladies here *love* me."

Lily rolled her eyes.

"I am a thousand volts of deliciosity," Jims insisted.

"I've heard more than I ever need to on this subject," said Taylor. "I don't want to talk about it. I want to know what Darcy's been up to."

"Taylor," warned Raphael.

"No, seriously. We deserve some answers. So." Her hazel eyes bored into mine. "Spill."

"Taylor, shut up," said Lily.

"Why? We told her everything that happened to us."

"She'll tell us if she wants to!"

"I do want to," I said quietly. "But not tonight, okay? Tonight I just want to be happy. I want to hang out with my best friends."

"Done." Jims stood and clapped his hands once. "How about dinner? Darcy's cooking. Right, Darcy?"

"For you guys? Anything."

AS WE SAT AROUND the table in the dining room with steaming plates of curried veggies in front of us, Jims opened a bottle of champagne. "We were saving this for tomorrow night, but I guess in the morning we'll pack up and head home. Unless you want to stick around for New Year's Eve, Darcy? It could be fun."

I shuddered at the thought of my friends in the heart of Meridian's catastrophe. But it wouldn't happen. It couldn't happen. The mayor would cancel the celebration. Even the thought, though, upset me. "No," I said.

"Any special reason why not?" Taylor speared a carrot and inspected it before eating.

"If you're worried about getting a kiss at midnight," Jims told me, "I'm sure someone here will do the honors."

"I just want to go home," I said.

Taylor heaved an irritated sigh. "I can't stand this sentimental secrecy. Get over whatever's bothering you, Darcy. It can't be that bad."

A silence fell, and I watched Taylor eat.

She caught me staring. "What?" she asked, lowering her fork. Then, with an understanding air, she dabbed her lips with a linen napkin and said, "It's *good*, okay? The food tastes absolutely yummy. God, this is what I get for living with a bunch of nerds in another dimension. You're all so insecure."

"That's not it," I said. "It's . . . well, I can't figure out why you're still here, Taylor."

"And they say *I'm* rude."

"I didn't mean it like that. What I meant was . . . I'm surprised. If it was only the three of you doing shifts at the mausoleum while Jims worked, that means you spent eight hours a day waiting around for me to show up. And we were never friends. I'm grateful, Taylor. Really grateful. But I'm surprised, too."

"Well." She played with a lock of her hair, searching for nonexistent split ends. "Beats being in school."

"Oh God," I said. "*School.*" A sick feeling of crisis swept over me. You wouldn't think the sudden realization that I'd missed a ton of class and my finals would freak me out after everything I'd been through, but believe me. It did.

"Now, now," said Jims. "Don't tell us you're crying salty tears over missing the fetal pig dissection in Bio."

"But my grades," I said. "My GPA. I hoped . . . I hoped to get a scholarship." I wanted my old life back, my old dreams, and now I saw my chances of going to the School of the Art Institute shrink to zero.

"Don't worry," said Lily. "I'm sure we're all going to end up in summer school together—"

Taylor buried her face in her hands.

"—but everyone at Lakebrook High will do their best to help you. As far as excuses go, getting kidnapped is pretty airtight. Marsha saw Conn attack you."

I felt a little better, but still . . . "Marsha."

"She'll take you back."

"You think so? I don't know. She saw me ghost—disappear— right in front of her. I'll have to explain that. Unless . . ." I glanced around the table hopefully. "You didn't let her know somehow, did you? Maybe you popped back home through the portal to tell her I was a supernatural creature, and got her reaction?"

"Nah," said Taylor. "We thought about it but decided not to. They were afraid she wouldn't take you back."

"Taylor!" said Lily.

She spread her hands innocently. "It's the *truth*."

"Hey, Taylor," said Raphael, "why don't you take the sofa tonight, and let Darcy sleep in your and Lily's room?"

"Excuse me?"

"It's a two-bedroom apartment," he explained with more

patience than I would have thought possible. "Darcy and Lily need to catch up, so—"

"But why me? Why don't *you* sleep on the sofa?"

"Are you saying"—Jims snaked an arm over her shoulders—"that you want to share a bedroom with *moi?*"

Taylor shot out of her chair. "Fine! I'll take the sofa," she shouted, and stormed from the dining room.

We laughed. Little bursts of happiness fizzed and sparkled in me like the champagne, and as we ate my friends told me about their interdimensional escapades. I remembered, as I looked around the table, what I'd said to Aunt Ginger long ago on her blueberry farm, when she'd asked me to confess my greatest wish: *I want a family.*

Why, make your own, she'd answered.

And I had.

After dinner, the boys volunteered to clean up and Lily took me to her room, where she gave me a set of pajamas and said I could use her toothbrush. "I'd only do that for you," she said as we washed our faces at the marble double sinks in her and Taylor's private bathroom.

I climbed into Taylor's bed and Lily slipped into hers, and we lay there, silent in the soft glow of the lamp. The sheets smelled like Taylor's perfume: exotic and a little outrageous. The perfume was nothing like the scent of Conn's skin, but I still remembered it, still couldn't block out how it had felt to be held by him. Even though I hadn't meant to say anything to Lily tonight, the pressure of everything that had happened in the past months swelled inside me.

It wasn't all about Conn. I knew that. But it had started with him and somehow ended with him, too. I cleared my throat. "Conn—"

"I want to kill him," Lily said flatly.

"Then you're not going to like what I have to tell you."

44

I told Lily everything. When I finally stopped, my throat was sore from speaking.

I pulled the blankets up to my chin and waited for Lily's reply, looking at her somber face, wondering if I'd said anything unforgivable. There was so much, from me spying for the IBI to my murderous parents to Meridian's plot to my stupid, impossible love for Conn. I didn't know what might be too hard for her to understand.

She sighed. "Why does it have to be *him*? What about Raphael?"

I sat up in bed and stared across the room at her. "What *about* him?"

"Oh, please. That boy has been carrying a torch for you since—"

"Can we please not talk about torches, even metaphorical ones?"

"Darcy, don't avoid the point."

I turned it over in my mind, considering this possibility. It seemed as startling as the existence of another world. "I can't," I said. "I can't think of Raphael that way. Maybe I could have, before. But . . ."

"Conn," she said with disgust.

"You don't know him."

"You don't even know how he feels about you. Just because he tried to get you into bed—"

"It wasn't like that."

"Honestly? You two sound like a pair of misfit toys who are going to end up breaking each other."

"Well. We'll never know. We're going home tomorrow."

Lily hesitated. "Are you sure about that? I mean, I can't believe I'm advocating anything that might throw you and Conn together again, but maybe you could help stop the attack."

"It's not going to happen. The mayor will cancel the celebration."

"I haven't heard anything about that. You'd think he would have announced it already."

"Maybe it'll be a last-minute thing."

"Look, if you want to go home tomorrow, that's what we're going to do, okay?"

"Yes," I said, and turned off the light.

We lay there, talking in the dark until our voices grew tired and our sentences farther apart.

"Doesn't it bother you?" I finally asked. "What my parents did?"

She paused. "Yes. But *you* didn't do it. You're not your parents."

That was a kind of comfort.

The silence stretched. Then, drifting near the edge of sleep, I murmured, "Lily? How come your hair's not purple? Or pink?"

She chuckled. "It probably would be if black wasn't so bottom of the fashion barrel. People here drive me crazy, the way they demonize Shades. It's racism, you know."

"I don't think we're a separate race. We might be a separate species."

"Still." She paused. "Anyway . . ."

I closed my eyes, and Lily's words began to weave into the threads of a dream.

". . . it reminded me of you."

I smiled and fell asleep.

A STENCH WORMED INTO MY DREAMS, bitter and thick and searing, like poisonous gas, though I knew that wasn't it. It was the smell of destruction. It was the smell of things being eaten alive. It was fire.

I saw flames flash down the streets. Fire bloomed in my mother's face.

Then I was awake, on my feet, too terrified to scream, and running down the hall, because there *was* a fire, there was a fire *here*, and I had to put it out. I had to save my friends.

I chased the smoke to its source. The living room.

Raphael was reading in an armchair pulled up to the fireplace. A small flame writhed behind the iron grill.

"Darcy?" he looked up. "What's wrong?" He followed my wide-eyed gaze. "Oh, crap. I'm an idiot." He scrambled to his feet. "I totally forgot. I'll put it out."

I found my voice. "No, don't. That'll make it smell worse."

He opened a window, and cold air rushed in, clearing my head. "I'm so sorry," he said. "I'm not used to thinking of you like—"

"It's okay. And . . . I need to get used to fire. Shades can, you know. Sometimes I think I'm getting better." The burning wood popped, and I jumped. "Or not."

"Sit with me over here," Raphael took my hand and pulled me toward the sofa, which was far from the fire. "I'm really, really sorry," he said again.

I steeled myself against the fire, pretended it didn't exist. "You can't sleep?"

"Nope. Too happy, I guess."

"Where's Taylor? Shouldn't she be sleeping right here? And snoring. I bet she snores."

"She went out. To a club, or something. She'll probably be back by dawn. You know . . ." He paused. "Taylor's all right. We did need a ride, the day we left Lakebrook, but that's not why I called her. We needed someone like her. She's tough."

"I got that." I didn't particularly want to talk about Taylor, so I picked up Raphael's book. "*Hamlet*? But the fall play . . .

it's over," I realized. "You missed the performances. Oh, Raphael."

He shrugged. "There'll be other plays."

"Thank you," I said.

"Hey, I'm right where I want to be."

I looked at his face glowing in the firelight and thought about missed chances, and other lives, and how you can't go back. Or I couldn't.

My thumb fanned the pages into a flipping arc. "Why're you reading this, then?"

"It's a good play."

"Sure, if you like tragedies."

"That's the thing. It didn't have to be a tragedy. I mean, yeah, it sucks that Hamlet's uncle killed his dad and married his mom, but that doesn't mean everyone had to be poisoned or drowned or stabbed by the final act. Sometimes I like to read *Hamlet* and think about how everything could have gone differently. Hamlet and Ophelia could've run off and lived happily ever after." He smiled.

I held the book with both hands. "Raphael . . ."

Understanding flashed across his face, then disappointment. "Don't," he said.

"It's just that—"

"Please." He found his smile again, though it was different now. "Hey, weren't you sleeping? Didn't I thoughtlessly wake you? You should go back to bed." He glanced at the fire. "I'll stay up until it goes out." He added, "And pour water over the ashes. I promise."

355

"Okay."

Raphael hugged me. I wished my brain could tell my heart what was good for it.

"I'm glad you're here," he said.

WE ALL SLEPT IN. It was almost two o'clock in the afternoon when I went into the kitchen to make blueberry pancakes. One by one, the others straggled into the dining room, their faces gleeful at the sight of stacks of pancakes. Even Taylor. Everyone heaped butter and maple syrup on top, since they knew that's the best way to eat them, except for Jims. He ate his with peanut butter.

"So good," he mumbled with his mouth full, and the others agreed, but the bready, sweet smell of pancakes couldn't quite mask the lingering odor of last night's fire. The pancakes tasted like ashes to me. Then I remembered eating blueberry pancakes at the Lakebrook diner with Conn and wished I'd never made them.

Jims finished eating. "Now it's time for some dessert," he said. "I'm going out for pastries. You kids start packing. And pack *only*"—he glared meaningfully at Taylor—"what you can carry. We still have to figure out how we're going to get past the guards."

The apartment whipped into chaos, with Taylor spreading her clothes across the living room, trying to figure out how to make everything fit into a rolling suitcase, Lily telling her to get on with it already, and Raphael stacking maps and books about this world's history on the kitchen table. I kept them company and helped when I could, since all I had to bring back home with me was the Society-issued black clothes I wore and the silver spoon in my pocket.

Then Jims came back with pastries and a newspaper, and the pastries turned into a very late lunch. Lunch turned into coffee, and more packing, and more coffee, and it wasn't until I was sipping a cappuccino out of a porcelain cup that I glanced at the paper resting on the table.

I dropped the cup, and it smashed against the floor.

"What's wrong?" asked Lily.

I stared at *The Chicago Tribune*. The headline read, "New Year's Eve: The Biggest Celebration in Chicago History."

"They didn't cancel," I said. "It's happening."

"What is?" Raphael stood, a map in hand.

I looked at the map, then at the paper. The sinister smell of last night's fire taunted me, and I remembered my dream of blazing streets, of fire radiating across the city in a steady, planned pattern, swallowing everything in its path.

"Of course," I whispered. "Meridian's going to start the Great Chicago Fire."

45

I snatched the map out of Raphael's hand, but it didn't have what I was looking for. "Do you have one with city firehouses on it?"

"Um, probably."

"Find it."

As Raphael sorted through his pile of maps, Taylor said, "Is this the part where you tell us what's going on?"

"Yes. But briefly, because I need your help." I almost shook with the effort of deciding how to explain in the quickest way possible. "What happened at Marsha's . . . Conn arrested me. More or less just for being a Shade. After he brought me here, I agreed to help the IBI find out more about a rumor that the Society was plotting an attack."

"You agreed?" said Raphael. "After he did that?"

"Wow," said Jims. "You're like a double agent."

"The point is," I continued, "there *will* be an attack. Tonight. I think—no, I *know*—that four Shades are going to set Cecil Deacon's house on fire, probably at midnight, when thousands of people are gathered there to ring in the new year. Have you seen those wooden sidewalks near his house?"

"Sure," said Raphael, holding out a map with the firehouses. "They're a big tourist attraction."

"And *flammable*. Give me that." I took Raphael's map and opened it on the table. "If they set fire to the house, it's going to spread to the sidewalks. They'll burn up like straw. The fire could destroy most of downtown, and people are going to die. The Shades will make certain of that, by steering them right into the path of the fire. This world never had a Great Chicago Fire. Meridian's going to make certain it does."

There was a silence. Then Lily said, "How can we help?"

"Are you sending us on a death-defying mission?" Jims's eyes got round. "Listen, if something happens to me and I end up on life support, don't pull the plug, okay? I can get better. And if I die, don't embalm my body and don't put me in a coffin. Putting me in the ground is fine, but I want a very shallow grave."

"Jims—"

"I can get better," he insisted.

"Jims! You won't have to claw your way out of a grave. You'll be fine. Look." I grabbed a pen and drew a wide circle around Deacon's house and the wooden sidewalks. "Go to all the firehouses inside this circle. Split them between you, and tell the firefighters they need to be on the scene and ready to put out the fire. Jims, use that IBI badge. The rest of you . . . be convincing. It's"—I reached for Lily's wrist and checked her watch—"eight o'clock? How did it get so late?"

"Um . . . we're lazy?" said Jims.

"Never mind. We still have four hours till midnight. Plenty of time. Will you do it?"

"Why not?" Taylor shrugged. "Firemen are hot."

"What're you going to do?" asked Lily.

"I'm going to see Conn."

HE WASN'T AT HIS APARTMENT. I thought that would be the case, but I still had to check, since it was on the way to where he almost certainly was, and where I certainly didn't want to be: the IBI.

Once I got there, though, I cursed myself for having wasted time stopping at Conn's house. I moved fast as a ghost, but not *that* fast, and it was well past nine o'clock when I began hunting the halls of the IBI for him.

Precious minutes ticked by, and I threw increasingly panicked glances at clocks sitting on desks and mounted on office walls. The IBI was busy for a Friday night, and as I wove through gray-jacketed agents I began to think that Conn must have already left for downtown. How would I ever find him on the streets?

It was almost ten-thirty.

Then I saw someone I recognized. Michael. Not the person

I would have picked, but I was running out of time and couldn't afford to be choosy.

We were in a crowded hallway, so I sidled up to him and whispered in his ear. "Michael."

He jumped and spun around. A few passing agents gave him a curious look.

"Don't freak out," I hissed. "It's Darcy Jones. I need to find Conn. Do you know where he is?"

Michael muttered, "He's getting ready to leave with his division. He's head of security for New Year's Eve." He slipped into a quiet corner office set apart from the hallway traffic, and I followed.

"Take me to him."

Michael had recovered from his surprise, and now his attitude got cocky. "Well, sure, if you want him that bad. Why don't you manifest, Darcy, and we'll take a stroll together, like two civilized beings? I hear you're very civilized."

"Nice try. Do you think I'd give you the chance to slap firecuffs on me? Just lead the way."

Somewhat to my surprise, he did. He also didn't attempt to trick me, as I'd feared when he led me downstairs into the wing of training rooms, interrogation rooms, and prison cells. Once, he glanced behind him and grinned. "So it's true," he said. "I *can* see your shadow."

"Find Conn," I reminded, and Michael shrugged, turned back around, and led me directly to him.

Conn was in a training room with dozens of IBI agents. He

walked among them, checking their flamethrowers and other gear I didn't recognize and didn't want to. He looked alert, his body moving in quick lines. Clearly skilled. Clearly ready.

He was intimidating.

This was the same Conn I'd seen in the truck on the day of my arrest. Yet I almost manifested, almost let my longing fling me back into my body.

"McCrea," Michael called.

Conn glanced up in surprise. "Michael? I don't really have time to—"

"Someone here to see you." Michael jerked his head toward the empty air behind him.

Conn's eyes fell on my shadow and an emotion flashed across his face. Then his expression went dangerously calm. "I see," he said. He turned to another agent, presumably his second-in-command. "I'll be back in a minute."

Without another word, he stalked out of the room and down the hall.

Michael followed, and I followed, my gladness eroding into something else.

46

Conn opened the door to what looked like an interrogation room—one for humans, since it didn't have iron walls or the iron chair I remembered from my conversation with Ivers.

"Leave us," he told Michael.

"Hey. You're welcome." Michael shut the door behind him.

Conn folded his arms and waited. "Well?"

I manifested.

He leaned back against the wall as if the sudden sight of me had pushed him there. "What do you want?" His face was hard, armored. Completely closed off.

Something was wrong.

I had been afraid as I'd flown through the city to find him. But I hadn't been afraid of this.

"Well . . . I . . ." I stammered.

"Yes?"

My thoughts got shaken up. I tried to reorder them, but the most important thing didn't come out of my mouth first. "Why didn't you cancel the New Year's Eve celebrations? I told you. I told you to tell Fitzgerald and the mayor. In my letter."

"Your letter," he repeated.

"You got it, didn't you?"

"I did."

"Then why . . . ?"

His eyes flickered with impatience. "It's an election year. The mayor didn't want to show any sign of weakness."

"That was a mistake," I said. "A big mistake. Meridian's going to set fire to Deacon's house, the sidewalks, too, I'm sure of it."

A stunned expression appeared on his face.

"I sent my friends—"

"Your friends?"

"Yes. Lily and the others. They're here—it's a long story— and I sent them to the firehouses in the area, to warn them."

"And you are here . . . ?"

"To warn you," I finished lamely.

"Well." He nodded. "Thank you." He turned to leave.

"Wait," I called.

He looked back at me as if I was chaining him to the room and he wanted nothing more than to walk out the door and never see me again.

"Why are you acting like this?" I demanded.

"I'm not acting like anything," he said coldly.

"You *are*." Then I understood. The knowledge bored into me, flooding me with horror. And loss.

"You know," I whispered.

"Do you mean"—he raised his brows—"I know what Kellford told you? What he told me?"

"He told you."

"Yes." He opened the door. "Are we done?"

"Listen, I know how you must feel—"

"No." He slammed the door. "You don't. You don't know how I felt when I woke up, and you were gone."

"Conn—"

"I waited for you. I waited for you all day. Were you there? Were you watching?"

"Yes, but—"

"Do you think I'm stupid?"

"*No.*"

"Do you think that I wouldn't have figured out that you'd gone to Kellford on your own? I went there, Saturday night, and he told me everything."

"He can't have," I shot back with anger of my own. "He can't have told you everything. He can't have told you how it feels to have been the cause of my parents' deaths, and how confusing it is to love two people who could do something so horrible. I saw them tortured, Conn." I stared at him and felt accusation mount in my face. "You are being unfair. This is hard for me, too."

Conn closed his eyes, and when he opened them they looked desolate. "You have no faith in me," he said in a low voice.

"You think I blame you for what happened. For something you didn't do. I read the transcript of your interrogation, Darcy. After I talked to Kellford, I moved heaven and earth to dig up that document. Anyone reading it would understand that you were in the wrong place at the wrong time, that you were just a five-year-old girl who adored her parents. Because if you'd been anything else, you would have confessed it. You were saying *everything*. You were telling the Vox Squad that you had a loose tooth, that it was your birthday, that you had an uncle who gave you crayons, what your favorite color was . . . all of that mangled and mixed with the real information they wanted until everything got so mangled and mixed they gave up. They *broke* you. Couldn't you trust me a little, enough to know that *that* was what I'd care about?"

"I do trust you." Only then did I realize it was true.

He kept speaking as if he hadn't heard. "And then there was that letter. That impersonal, empty letter. There was nothing of you that I could hold on to. Nothing. You just vanished. You were gone. It's been nearly a week, and I had no idea where you were. No idea what had happened to you. You could have been hurt. You could have been dead, killed by Orion or Meridian or God knows who else. Or you could have decided I simply wasn't worth it."

"Conn, no." I groped for the right words. "I was afraid you'd hate me."

"Hate you?" He shook his head. He started to say something, then stopped. A silence stretched.

When he spoke, his voice was even but sad. "I shouldn't

have said this. I'd take it back, if I could. You're right. Of course you're right. Kellford's news can't be easy for you. I only wish . . ." He glanced down at the cuffs of his uniform. "I've got to go."

"Wait. Listen. I *do* trust you. I didn't come here just to warn you. I need your help."

His brow furrowed.

"We could stop the attack," I said. "Zephyr would never let it happen if she knew about it, and she could command the entire Society to track down Meridian and the others to stop them. Only a few Shades are involved in the plot, and I think the rest of the Society would be against it, especially if they could believe in Zephyr's plan for peace. If they could believe there is a way for humans and Shades to live together. Come with me to the Sanctuary and help me convince them. We still have time. The Sanctuary's not far by car. It's beneath Grace-land Cemetery, and there are entrances a human could use, below gravestones—"

"I think that's about all we need to hear, don't you, Michael?" said a new, metallic voice broadcast into the room by a speaker.

Conn looked suddenly sick with the same sinking feeling I had.

Seams appeared in the wall, forming a rectangle that turned into a door. It slid aside, and Ivers and Michael walked into the room.

"Really, McCrea." Michael smirked. "An interrogation room? It's like you were begging us to listen in on you. Frankly, I don't get the fuss everyone makes over you. You're sloppy."

Conn ignored him and turned to Ivers. "Sir, we need to adjust our strategy for New Year's Eve—"

"We? Must? There is no 'we.' Because *this*"—his thick finger waved between Conn and me—"is a sickness, and I sure as hell am not going to catch your disease. Thank God Michael came to get me when he did. Now we have the chance to strike a big blow for the IBI. Can you imagine? I'll be responsible for the destruction of the Sanctuary." He switched on his flamethrower, and Michael did the same. I stopped breathing.

"Darcy, ghost," said Conn.

"Darcy, *don't.*" Ivers pointed his flamethrower at Conn. "He'll burn as easily as you."

I stayed where I was.

Ivers smiled. "I probably won't hurt you two, if only because I don't have the time. But if you don't do as I say, I'll *make* time. Got it?"

"Yes," I said.

"Then follow me."

Ivers led us to the room down the now-deserted hall, with Michael right behind us. Ivers opened the door, and I backed into Conn when I saw what was inside.

It was solitary confinement.

Conn held me steady. "Ivers—"

"Shut up, McCrea."

Michael leaned forward and danced his flame into the ends of my hair. It caught fire, and I clamped down on my scream as Conn put it out with his hands. I went dizzy from the smoky stench.

"You see?" said Ivers. "See what happens when you don't listen? Now"—he pointed at the tall glass box in the center of the room—"get inside. Both of you."

"Remember," Conn murmured in my ear.

Nothing here could hurt me.

I remembered, but my memory only made things worse as Conn and I walked toward the large box.

Ivers pushed us inside and turned to Michael. "Take McCrea's agents," he said, "and call up six more divisions. We've got a Sanctuary to burn."

"This is the wrong move," said Conn. "The last thing we need is for the IBI to start a fire. We need to *stop* one—"

Ivers sealed us inside the coffin. "Bye-bye, McCrea. Enjoy yourself, and later on you can thank me."

He and Michael left the room. Then there was a hiss and a click and everything burst into flames.

47

I couldn't close my eyes. Flames thumbed my eyelids back, burrowed into my mouth, my ears. The fire was climbing inside me.

I had to get it out.

I tore at my skin.

But something grabbed my hands.

"Darcy."

Something was holding me. Something hard and strong.

No. *Someone.*

I shoved back, struck out, felt my hand connect with solid flesh. I hit again. He didn't move.

"Darcy," he said. "This is an illusion. Remember?"

I remembered fire burning my mother's hair, and I sobbed.

"Shh. Nothing here can hurt you. I won't let anything hurt you."

His hands folded over mine again, and the panic in me eased a little. *My hands are safe,* I thought. *The fire can't reach them now.*

That sense, that *certainty,* that at least part of me was protected helped chase away the red-orange blindness that filled my eyes. I saw a network of fingers. I focused. I knew those hands on mine. Large and long and kind of messed up. Lots of old cuts. A vague memory stirred, and I realized that, once, I had wanted to touch every single one of those scars.

The fire continued to flicker at the edge of my vision, but as I blinked clarity began to return. I went still, and could feel that those hands felt my stillness, and that the worry in them lessened.

I glanced up. There was a face that I knew was dear to me, that sometimes slipped into my dreams. When I would wake up all I wanted was to sleep again. "Conn?" I whispered.

A shudder of relief went through him. "Yes," he said. "The fire can't touch us, Darcy. You know that, don't you?"

I considered this. The fire tried to drag my gaze away from Conn's face, but I stared back into his lake-colored eyes and thought about that: a lake. Dark and deep. "Yes," I said.

"Ivers and Michael locked us in, but we won't be in here forever, someone will come eventually . . ." Conn began to ramble. I remembered enough to know this was odd behavior for him. Conn did not ramble. *He's trying to distract me,* I realized.

"I know," I told him, though I didn't mean it. I had wanted to comfort him, and his comfort seemed so dependent on mine. Then, as soon as the words left my mouth, I *did* know. I remembered how we had gotten here. Everything became clear.

Conn's gaze dropped to somewhere near my neck. His eyes immediately met mine again, but I had noticed. I touched the skin beneath my collarbone. It stung, and my fingers came away bloody. "I did that," I said. "I thought the fire was inside me."

"It—"

"I know," I stopped him. "It *isn't*. I'm okay, Conn. Really. Just a little case of temporary insanity."

He smiled faintly.

"I thought I was learning how to handle fire," I said, "but it's worse now that I remember my parents." I swallowed against the parched feeling in my throat. "It's so hot in here."

"Try to ignore it."

The flames kept mesmerizing me. It was hard not to look at them.

"Close your eyes," Conn said.

I did.

Fingertips touched my face like rain. Cool palms were on my cheeks.

Water.

Conn.

My mouth opened with relief.

I felt the sudden intensity in Conn's body, and the hesitation. I pulled him to me. A softness covered my lips, and

I breathed into it, and it was like the first breath after none at all.

Conn was the rain, he was the water. Those were his lips on mine. I drank him in. I tasted my own urgency. I tasted his.

Our kiss fluttered and tugged, and it was strange, so strange to sense that the fire had won, that it had somehow slipped inside me, and that it was one I would never want to put out, even if it ravaged me whole.

Conn pulled away for a heartbeat, looked at me with hazy eyes, and lowered his mouth to my throat.

"Uh, Conn?" said a new, faraway voice.

We broke apart in confusion.

The voice spoke again. "Why are you in solitary confinement . . . making out with a Shade?"

Conn peered through the flames. "Paulo!" he shouted. "Cut the fire!"

"Yeah, well, is that a good idea? It doesn't look like that Shade's cuffed. I mean, she had her hands all over you. What is this, some new interrogation technique?"

"Paulo, just do it!"

The fire died. I ghosted out of the box to reappear at Paulo's side, and he jumped, his hand skittering away from the control panel set into one of the iron walls. "You're Jones," he said. "You must be."

"Let Conn out."

Paulo threw his hands up defensively. "Okay. I was going to do that anyway."

When Conn stepped out of the box he strode up to me and

Paulo, who said, "What is going on, Conn? I've been looking for you everywhere. Do you know that Ivers has reassigned your division to attack the Sanctuary? He's practically emptied the building of agents."

"Does Fitzgerald know about this?" asked Conn.

"Doubt it." Paulo spared a nervous glance my way, but I stayed very still. It didn't seem to be a good idea to spook Conn's only current ally in the IBI. "Fitzgerald always spends the holiday with her family, so unless someone's contacted her—"

"That's exactly what you're going to do. You know what this is, don't you, Paulo? It's a coup. Ivers may outrank me, but he's breaking regulations to take agents assigned to me by Fitzgerald. He wouldn't do that unless he knows he won't pay for it, and the only way he won't pay for it is if tonight he has a victory so big he can topple Fitzgerald and seize the directorship. You go to her and tell her that. You tell her that if she doesn't stop the assault on the Sanctuary, she won't have a job tomorrow."

"But Ivers will get to Graceland Cemetery any minute now."

I almost seized Paulo. "What time is it?"

"About eleven-thirty p.m."

Conn said, "We've got to go, Darcy."

"But, Conn," said Paulo, "if our agents surround the Sanctuary, the Shades are going to notice, and if the IBI *doesn't* attack, the Shades will."

"We won't let that happen. Just reach Fitzgerald. Promise me you'll do that."

Paulo hesitated.

"Unless you want to see Ivers running the IBI."

Paulo let out a resigned sigh that seemed a good enough promise to Conn, because he took my hand and began to run.

As we raced down the corridor, I said, "Is that true? Is that what Ivers is trying to do?"

"I don't know. But it'll make Fitzgerald act."

"*If* Paulo calls her. *If* she gets there in time."

Conn didn't say anything to that, and as the word "time" echoed in my head I realized something that almost stopped me in my tracks. "We don't have time to do both."

Conn glanced at me and began to run even faster.

"It's impossible," I said desperately. "We can't stop Meridian from burning Deacon's house *and* keep the IBI and the Society from tearing each other apart at the Sanctuary. Deacon's house and Graceland Cemetery are at opposite ends of town."

We jumped down a flight of stairs.

"It's too late," I said. "Everything's too late."

Conn paused before a door and pressed his thumb against a lockpad. The door swung open. "It isn't," he said. "Not if we split up."

"Bad idea." I followed him into a garage. "No way."

"It's the only way." He stopped. "Darcy. There are two tasks. We are two people."

"Then I'll go to the Sanctuary." It seemed more dangerous, the place where anything could happen. It was the place where Conn would most likely get hurt, even killed.

He shook his head. "Let me go. Please."

"*No*. The Society *will* attack if it's to defend their home."

"I think I can stop them."

"How? With your two bare hands? You're insane."

"I'll talk to them. I'll convince the Shades not to attack."

"Conn—"

"I know what to say." He cupped my face in his hands. "Do you trust me?"

"Yes, but—"

"Good," he said. "Now, realistically, Meridian's fire will happen. The only thing you can do at this point is damage control—and you've already started that, since you're brilliant. You alerted the firefighters. As for Deacon's house, it's just a tourist attraction no one lives in. It can burn." Conn handed me a small, square object the size of a quarter. "This is a sort of megaphone. Talk to the crowd. Keep them from panicking. That will save lives."

"Me. You want me, a Shade, to keep humans from panicking." My voice rose and echoed in the cavernous garage. "The very *sight* of me will make them panic."

"They'll trust you. Like I do. You will make them trust you. Okay?"

That word felt like a harness loaded with the world. But when I looked at Conn his eyes held a strength that helped me find my own. "Okay."

"Let's go. I'll drop you off midway."

It was then that I looked over his shoulder and saw the machine behind him. "What is that? Is that a motorcycle?" As soon as I said that I realized that *this* was what Conn had been drawing in his sketchbook.

"No," he said. "It's a hypercycle."

"Conn, did you *make* this?"

"Come on." He reached for the helmet hanging by its strap from one of the handlebars and straddled the machine.

"Well," I said, "at least I get a helmet this time."

He laughed. "You don't need a helmet, Darcy, and you never did. This is for me."

I climbed up and held on to him tight.

The engine caught with a roar and we peeled out of the garage.

48

I found out why Conn needed his helmet, and why he hadn't worn one on our trip to the railroad tracks in the Alter.

It was because, for him, riding a motorcycle was like riding a bike.

And the hypercycle absolutely was *not*.

The machine screamed down the street.

We scraped around a corner and hit heavy traffic—all the partygoers, the cars cramming the streets to get wherever they wanted to be by midnight. It filled me with frustrated despair to think that this—*traffic*—was going to stop us. But then Conn's helmeted head turned skyward, and I followed his gaze and noticed, as I had on my first day exploring this Chicago, that odd metal rail looping high around the buildings. I had just enough time to wonder why Conn was looking at it and what it had to do with escaping this demonic snarl of traffic, when he jerked at the handlebars and the hypercycle kicked beneath us. It rocketed into the air and slammed its wheels down on the rail, then swung to ride along at a right angle with the building, the machine parallel to the ground.

I probably yelped or did something similarly unheroic. I mean, hey, I'm practically invulnerable, but more than a decade of human living is pretty hard to shake. Humans like their spines. They like them attached to the rest of their bones. They usually don't like being a hundred feet in the air, hurtling along at killer speeds, their bodies hanging over the streets below.

Then I saw that the city block was about to come to an abrupt end. We were reaching an intersection, and the buildings we were driving on were going to sheer off into thin air.

The hypercycle sped toward the edge. I clung to Conn's waist and buried my face against his back. I wasn't sure I wanted to see this.

But before I could decide whether to close my eyes, the hypercycle kicked again and we launched across space to slam onto the rail waiting for us on the other side of the street.

Another thing about humans—and I wasn't entirely sure whether this was true for Shades, too—is that they can get used to almost anything. I'd been human long enough that after about fifteen minutes on the hypercycle I relaxed enough to have an idea. "Hey!" I yelled near Conn's ear. "Can you hear me?"

He nodded.

"Most people die of smoke inhalation in fires," I shouted.

"Not from the fire itself. If you can stop a battle over the Sanctuary, ask the Society for help. Shades can ghost up high buildings to smash windows for fresh air. They can tell firefighters where people are trapped. If the Shades can handle being near the fire. If they're willing."

We jumped over another street, and I could feel Conn thinking as we arced through the air. Then we hit the other side, and he nodded.

Soon after that, the engine seemed to fail. I clamped my legs to the sides of the machine and hung on to Conn for dear life—whether his life or mine, I didn't know. They felt like one and the same.

The hypercycle hovered, its wheels spinning in place, and Conn flung up the visor of his helmet and turned to look over his shoulder at me. "Here," he said. "We have to split up here." He took one hand off the handlebars—a suicidal move, if you ask me—and pointed west. "That's Deacon Street. Head that way, and it'll take you straight to the celebration."

I didn't know what to say, because everything I wanted to tell Conn felt more dangerous than fire.

"Darcy?" he said.

"Be careful."

He gave me a half smile. "You, too."

For a moment, I wondered if all the things he wasn't saying were the same things I wasn't saying. Then I ghosted, and turned so that I wouldn't have to see him speeding away.

The streets below swam with people, the crowds getting thicker and louder as I flew toward Deacon's house. I could see the nineteenth-century sidewalks radiating from the house like spokes from the center of a wheel.

I passed an old clock tower—11:55 p.m. Five minutes till midnight.

In front of Deacon's house was a low stage. Dancers in flame-colored leotards leaped and spun across its surface as a man who I guessed was the mayor watched from a chair seated at the far end of the stage. I glanced at the clock, and saw another clock in my mind, the sculpture that Conn and I had made for "The Love Song of J. Alfred Prufrock." It struck me then that the poem wasn't simply about love, but about how love demands the risk of one's whole self. Could I really do that? Could I shake my identity to its foundations? Could I put my life on the line?

I looked out into the sea of strangers who would recoil the moment I appeared. Of course they would. I was a Shade. My name was Lark. Yet I was also Darcy Jones, and somehow I would have to love both parts of me, or I would never be able to save anyone, and would never know the answer to this question:

> *Do I dare*
> *Disturb the universe?*

There wasn't time for me to think about what to say—or even what to do. I simply did it. I manifested in the center of the stage.

A dancer screamed, then another, and then they poured off

the stage, running away as fast as they could. Some secret service types pounced on the mayor, protecting him with their bodies, while someone in the crowd yelled, "Assassination! It's an assassination attempt!"

"No!" I shouted into Conn's micro-megaphone, and was shocked to hear how loud my voice was. People blocks away must have been able to hear me. "I'm not trying to kill your mayor. I just want to talk."

There were more screams, and calls for the IBI. Panic was brewing—exactly like I'd told Conn it would.

"The IBI isn't here," I told them, "so there's no one here to protect us. We're going to have to protect ourselves. Because you're right: something bad is about to happen."

Not the smartest thing I've ever said.

It made the mayor's bodyguards lunge at me. I ghosted and reappeared a few feet away. "Where are your basic math skills?" I shouted. "Can't you count? I am one person surrounded by thousands. I am *way* more in danger of you than you are of me."

This didn't seem to calm the crowd much—or the bodyguards. One of them snagged my arm and slapped a firecuff around my wrist.

I wriggled away and darted to the very edge of the stage.

The bold guard slipped toward me warily, but he needn't have worried. I was frozen, staring at the flickering bracelet around my wrist. I fought to fill my lungs with air.

Yet this is what they need to see, a tiny idea whispered inside. *That you can be as vulnerable as they are.*

I forced my free hand to move. Almost as if it didn't belong to me, it reached for the dangling half of the firecuffs. Then I cuffed myself.

There was a gasp. It might have come from me. Or the people who had seen what I'd done. The guards hung back, astonished that their prey had practically hand-delivered herself.

Soon. They would seize me soon. As soon as the shock wore off. I had to find the right words to convince these people. I had to find them now.

I held up my wrists so everyone could see the flame coursing through the glass cuffs. Now my hands cupped the megaphone as if lifted in prayer, and as I saw the minute hand on the clock tower swing toward midnight, I searched for my voice. It came out shaky, throaty.

Afraid. Afraid of what I'd done to myself. Afraid of what I probably wouldn't be able to stop. "I know you're thinking I'm part of some plot to kill you," I told the crowd, "and that even cuffing myself is an act. You're standing there, torn between running away and stampeding me, because you don't know what to do. You don't know what *I* am going to do. And that's because *you don't know me*. You have no idea who I am. Think about that. Think about the fact that if you don't know me, then you can't *know* that I'm out for your blood. I could be a halfway decent person. I could even be trying to help you. And I am.

"Four Shades are going to burn down this house"—I pointed as best as I could with my cuffed hands—"at midnight. In *one minute*. The sidewalks you're standing on are going to catch fire. I'm sure those Shades are watching us right now, and they are counting on you to let them frighten you, to let them steer you into the fire. Don't let them. Be smart, and listen to me.

"I'm not asking you to like me. I'm just asking you to get off the sidewalks. Trust me that much. Trust me enough to stand in the streets. Put your feet on concrete. Get away from anything that can burn."

The crowd muttered to itself, the mutters building to a low roar. Then someone stepped into the empty street and everyone fell silent.

It was Lily.

I saw Raphael step into another street, and Taylor did the same, and so did Jims, who (bless his big, loud mouth) shouted, "Listen to her!"

Slowly, miraculously, people began filing into the streets.

Then the house exploded behind me.

49

I went blank. The fire was so big. I was dimly aware that people were now fighting to get off anything wooden, and that claws of flame tore at the stage, but I couldn't move. I couldn't think. It was like my brain had ghosted out of my body.

Then someone with huge arms grabbed me from behind. I snapped out of my trance and began to struggle.

"Don't," said a voice in my ear. "You'll break your cuffs. I'm here to help you, Darcy. I know you're on our side."

I went still. I glanced down and saw that the man was wearing a thick uniform. Not IBI. The fire department?

"Agent McCrea told me to get you," he said.

My heart soared. Conn was all right.

But how had he gotten here so quickly?

The fireman shoved through the crowd, carrying me in his

arms. When he reached a fire truck, he set me down in front of Jims.

"There she is, McCrea," said the fireman.

"Good work." Jims clapped him on the back. "The IBI will be pleased. Very pleased."

I went numb again.

Jims chattered at me, but I couldn't hear anything he was saying. I kept my eyes on the fire, because that shut off my mind, and if my mind couldn't think it couldn't imagine Conn bleeding on the snow of Graceland Cemetery.

It had been stupid to think that he could thrust himself between two armies and live.

Why had I let him go?

I watched the fire.

It devoured the sidewalks, but firemen from the nearby precincts were there to contain it, and a lot of people who'd been standing on the wooden sidewalks had already moved into the streets before Deacon's house blew up. The rest quickly decided that it was wise to do the same thing. As for the firemen, they barked the crowds into more or less orderly behavior.

There was no sign of Meridian, Orion, or the others.

Then the fire crept up a nearby building and the faces of the firemen changed. They weren't so cocky anymore. I heard one of them curse. "An apartment building," he muttered. "Hundreds of people in there."

The firemen suited up to enter the building, and Jims was tugging at my sleeve, saying something like, "Hey, this is a job for the professionals. Let's be professional cowards and get out of here."

I ignored him, leaning against the fire truck. Finally, Jims gave up and did the same.

Just as the firemen were ready to go inside the burning building, dark figures appeared on the roof, settling at its edge like a flock of crows.

Shades.

Zephyr and Savannah manifested in front of the firemen, who staggered back with surprise. But even from a distance, I could see that Zephyr was at her most intimidating, pointing at the windows of the building, then at the Shades, and then in the fire chief's face. Whatever she said must have been convincing enough to make the chief nod before he moved his men into the building. Zephyr and Savannah ghosted. Shades burst in and out of being around the apartment building, clinging to ledges, smashing the windows.

It took a moment to realize what they were doing, even though this had been my idea. I had suggested this to Conn, remembering how my parents had broken a window in the Ravenswood Medical Center so that I could breathe. The Shades were helping.

Which meant that Conn *had* talked with them, and they had listened. If they had listened, surely they wouldn't have hurt him.

Hope slowly crept back.

The wail of an IBI siren grew nearer, and cars pulled into the street. Fitzgerald stepped out of one of them, and I began running toward her, so glad to see her harsh face, because it was good that she was here, good that the Shades were here. This meant that Conn must have succeeded. He had to be okay.

But I didn't see the hypercycle, and he didn't get out of an IBI car, and he wasn't with the other agents.

I kept running anyway.

My cuffed hands threw me off balance, and I ran awkwardly. I stumbled, but didn't fall, when Conn stepped out of the crowd and saw me.

I thought the expression on his face was relief. I thought it might be delight. But it vanished so quickly that I couldn't quite tell, because suddenly there was nothing there but anger and a sick horror.

He rushed forward and caught me by the shoulders, holding me at arm's length.

"Conn." My giddiness at the sight of him drained away with the knowledge that he clearly didn't feel the same way. "What's wrong?"

"Who did this to you?" he demanded.

"What?" I followed his gaze to my wrists, and the firecuffs. "Oh." I laughed, because now I understood. "I did."

Conn took my hands in his, inspecting the cuffs. He went pale. "Darcy. Don't move."

It was the first time I ever saw his fingers tremble. He carefully deactivated the cuffs, and the light in them vanished. Yet even when he slipped the cuffs from my wrists, Conn still looked like he couldn't breathe.

"The cuffs were set to kill you," he said finally.

I didn't really care, because, well, I *wasn't* dead. And he wasn't either. I wanted to spring up on my toes to kiss him, I wanted to touch him with hands that were free, completely free.

"No big deal," I said.

He shook his head. "Only you," he said with a faint laugh. "The Sanctuary's fine, you know."

"How did you do it? How did you stop the fight?"

"I talked to them."

"That's it?"

"Well"—he smiled—"and how did you save the day, Darcy Jones?"

"I, um, talked to them."

"In the end," said Conn, "it was easy. Fitzgerald showed up in time and reined in the IBI. As for the Society, I knew exactly what to say to them."

"What?" I asked. "What did you say?"

His smile deepened.

Then his eyes lifted away from mine, glanced over my shoulder, and grew serious. "I'll tell you later."

"Well, Ms. Jones," said a voice behind me. I wheeled around. It was Director Fitzgerald.

"Come with me," she said.

50

Conn shot me a warning look.

Fitzgerald darted sarcastic eyes between the two of us. She opened her mouth to say something, but the mayor stormed up to us, asking furious questions about the lack of security.

Conn pulled me behind a fire truck as I heard pieces of Fitzgerald's calm reply: ". . . warned you . . . Ivers . . . no lives lost . . ."

"Ivers was fired," Conn told me. "Michael, too."

"What about Fitzgerald?"

"The mayor won't replace her, because if he does she'll go public with the fact that he pushed for this celebration despite our intel." Conn paused. "It may not seem so right now, but in the end tonight is going to be a victory for the IBI. For the first time, the Society is working *with* us—under certain conditions.

There are going to be a lot of changes in this world. But, Darcy . . . they're not going to happen overnight. Fitzgerald wants you. She won't imprison or harm you—if only because you're going to be a hero in the eyes of everyone here. But she will use you. She will use you to get advice about how to bargain with the Society. Advice about any secret weaknesses Zephyr has, or Savannah has, or anybody else on the Council. If I were you—" He broke off, then started again. "If I were you, I'd go home now. Tonight."

"Now?"

"Don't you want to go back to the Alter?"

"Yes," I said, because it was the truth. But I said it slowly, since I hadn't heard Conn mention anything about coming with me. It was becoming painfully clear that I had my world, and he had his. Neither of us fit in the other.

Conn nodded. His face was firm. Convinced. I saw that he had decided that this was the Right Thing to Do.

The gladness inside me withered. "Fitzgerald can't force me to do anything."

"Trust me," he said. "She'll find a way."

"I don't see why I have to sneak away like some kind of criminal."

"You're not." He frowned. "Why are we arguing about this? You said you wanted to go, and I think you should."

I couldn't speak.

"You should ghost," he said, "before Fitzgerald wrangles herself away from the mayor. The Couch Mausoleum portal won't be guarded right now. Even on a good day it's badly monitored, and tonight practically every agent has been brought here. The dispatcher will have pulled all agents from unimportant posts, and that'll include the Couch guards. I'll find your friends and tell them to meet you there. Once you're together, don't waste time. Just go."

"And you?" I managed.

"McCrea! Jones!" we heard Fitzgerald shout close by. "Where are you?"

Quickly, he said to me, "I've got to stick around. I'll see you later, okay?" He touched my cheek. His fingertip sent a shard of ice into my heart.

I didn't say, *Why are you pushing me away?*

I didn't say, *How soon is later?*

"Yeah," I said. "Sure."

I ghosted.

TAYLOR WAS, PREDICTABLY, the last to arrive at the mausoleum, and when she did the sun was rising and she was lugging her suitcase.

"You stopped at the apartment?" said Lily. "Conn said not to waste any time."

"Since when do we obey his every word?" Taylor replied.

"Don't you have a ton of clothes back home?" said Raphael.

"Yes, but they're not imported from *another world.*"

Lily sighed. "Let's get out of here."

Which was what we were going to do, when Savannah appeared.

"I am very angry with you," she told me.

I winced. "I know. I'm—"

"Sorry? For lying, spying, and giving up the location of the Sanctuary? I don't think 'sorry' cuts it. You could have come to me, you know. If you'd told Zephyr and me about Meridian's plot, we would have stopped it. Now we have to *negotiate* with the humans."

"But . . . isn't that what you wanted? You wanted to become citizens. Doesn't that mean, you know, laying foundations for how humans and Shades will deal with each other? You would have had to do that at some point."

"Don't get smart with me!"

"And won't the human population be grateful to the Society for what they did tonight? No one died, did they?"

"Zero. That's not the point. The point is I don't forgive you."

There didn't seem to be anything I could say to that, so I muttered something lame like, "Well, okay. Goodbye, then," and turned to leave.

Savannah stopped me. "I'm surprised to see you taking off so soon, though I suppose your young man is rather persuasive. Among other things."

I stared at her. "You were spying on us?"

"Turnabout is fair play. How do you think I knew you were here?" Then Savannah said impatiently, "Oh, just go. But when you visit me—"

"Visit?"

"Yes, visit. That's what people who share an acquaintance do. They visit. That"—Savannah pointed at the mausoleum—"is a perfectly decent portal, and if you don't use it I will be even angrier than I already am. When you visit, you can work on getting back into my good graces."

I thought about how easy it would be to ghost through portals to this world, and things no longer seemed so grim. I realized that I had an uncle here, somewhere. Maybe he was someone I'd want to find. Plus, there was Savannah.

And Conn. "I will," I said.

"It won't be easy. You will probably have to come back many times before I even speak to you."

"Like you're not speaking to me now?" I laughed. "Okay, Savannah." I echoed Conn's words, which no longer seemed quite so empty. "I'll see you later."

WE WERE QUIET ON THE DRIVE back to Lakebrook, until Taylor cranked some Cuban rap I swear Raphael must have given her. Then that noise became a different kind of silence.

I couldn't stop fidgeting, even though it was making Lily crazy. All I could do was wonder whether Marsha would be home when we got there.

That became too hard to think about, so I stared out the window once Taylor got off the Route 355 exit ramp and we began driving through the strip malls and near-identical houses of Lakebrook. I saw the skeletons of deserted playgrounds. Spindly winter trees. Cars huddled around a grocery store. Everything looked as sleepy as it always did on Saturday mornings. Everything seemed the same. Yet it felt different.

I felt different.

A light was on in Marsha's house when we got there, but it was the living room lamp she left on twenty-four hours a day. "I hate coming home to a dark house," she'd say. "And what if I wake up in the middle of the night and want a snack and some TV?"

She wasn't there.

Without saying a word, my friends settled around the living room, waiting with me. I sat on the sofa and glanced at Taylor. "Don't you have better things to do?"

"Nah," she said. "I want to see what happens."

We heard a car chug up the driveway, and a door slam.

Marsha was home.

51

D arcy?" Marsha clutched a grocery bag to her chest, and a rip split the brown paper. Her eyes cast about the living room, blinking as she registered each one of us. "All of you. You're here. And you?" Her wide forehead furrowed at the sight of Taylor. "Who are you?"

"Everyone's always so glad to see me," said Taylor.

A pint of ice cream squeezed out of the torn grocery bag and hit the floor. Raphael scooped it up and grabbed the bag from Marsha. "We'll take care of the groceries. Right, Jims?" He set the bag on the kitchen table, and he and Jims hustled out the front door to unload the car.

As soon as Marsha's hands were empty, she glanced down at her palms like she had no idea what to do with them. Then she looked straight at me. "You're okay?"

"Yes."

"You're not hurt?"

"I'm fine."

She sat down next to me on the sofa and pulled me into a big hug. "What *happened* to you?"

"I . . ." My voice was muffled against her soft shoulder. I thought about how easy things would be if I didn't answer that question honestly. If I told some crazy horror story about being held captive for two months. I could pick up right where Marsha last saw me, assaulted in her own living room. I was kidnapped, I could tell her.

I vanished? No, I didn't *vanish*. Your eyes tricked you, I'd tell her.

She would believe me.

I'd fool Marsha, and then maybe I could move back in like nothing had happened.

No.

I put my arms around her. Marsha wasn't a fool, and I couldn't bear to make her into one. If I lied to her and she took me back, she wouldn't be sharing her home with *me*. She'd be living with a stranger. When you're a stranger to people you care about, you become a stranger to yourself.

I said, "You're not going to believe me—"

That made her mad. She pulled away. "Don't give me that. Do you have any idea what I've been through these past two months? I have been going *out of my mind*."

I cowered, sinking into the corner of the sofa. "Well—"

"Don't 'well' me, young lady. I want answers, and I want them now."

Jims and Raphael came back through the door and plunked more grocery bags on the table. "I think that's it," said Raphael.

"Hey," said Lily, looking between Marsha and me, "why don't the rest of us get some takeout for lunch? We'll get Thai food."

"Or I could cook," I said, a bit desperate at the thought of them leaving me alone with Marsha. "There are groceries."

"No," said Lily. "I want Thai. We'll get your usual. Pad thai with extra lime and peanuts, right?"

"Yes, but—"

"Come on, guys," she said to the others.

"You're all in big trouble," Marsha told them. "Your parents—"

They looked at each other with dread.

"—are going to ground you within an inch of your lives."

"Just so long as they don't spank me," said Jims. "I hate it when they do that. I only like getting spanked by—"

"We'll be back." Lily grabbed Jims and then all of them were gone, the front door banging behind them.

It was hard to face Marsha, so I looked around her house—at the water-stained carpet where the fish tank had been, that ridiculous raccoon painting. I fumbled into my pocket and pulled out the silver bird spoon. "I got this for you." I offered it to her. "Now your collection's complete."

Marsha stared down at the spoon, at the word "Alaska"

inscribed in cursive letters across the bowl, and the bird perched on the handle. "I don't understand," she said. "Have you been in *Alaska*?"

"No, I—"

"That's not the willow ptarmigan. That's not the Alaskan state bird. I don't know *what* kind of bird that is."

Of course.

I had clung to this spoon for weeks like it was a talisman, some magical object that would win Marsha's heart and make her keep me forever. And of *course* Conn's Alaska hadn't chosen the same state bird.

Hopeless. This was hopeless. I couldn't explain to Marsha. She would believe a lie, but she'd never understand the truth. I dropped the spoon, stood woodenly, and began to walk toward the front door.

"Darcy Jones, you get your little butt right back here!"

I stopped.

"You *owe* me an explanation."

I did. I owed her more than that. So I told her the truth, because that was all I had to give her.

Though I might have toned down some of the Conn-related stuff.

She interrupted me once, to ask me to ghost and manifest in front of her. I did, and she was only a little freaked out, I guess because the last time she saw me vanish things were more dramatic. When I finished telling her everything that had happened since she'd thrown the kitchen knife, there was a long silence.

"Well." She let out a big breath, and her hands flopped to her sides. "I see I have my work cut out for me."

"What do you mean?"

"I am going to have to lie until the cows come home. To the DCFS, the police—" She caught me staring. "No one would let a crazy person be a foster parent, and if I told the truth I'd sound like a nutcase, wouldn't I? I suppose you could prove that you're not human, but you're better off keeping that to yourself."

"Doesn't it bother you . . . what I am?"

"Darcy." She gave me a firm look. "I have always known exactly what you are. You are a good girl."

A feeling bubbled up inside. "Does that mean you're not kicking me out?"

"Kicking you out would get in the way of *punishing* you, which is exactly what I'm going to do once I figure out how many chores I need done around the house."

I couldn't help it. I laughed. "You know, getting kidnapped wasn't really my *fault*—"

"Zip it. You could have come home a lot earlier, and you know it."

Then Marsha, having learned that there was another dimension and that her foster kid wasn't exactly human, did what I should have guessed she'd do. She began unpacking the groceries. I helped, putting everything where I knew it should go.

When I opened a cabinet to put away some sugar plum herbal tea, I paused. I pulled out the Lapsang souchong tea tin and turned to Marsha. She saw what I held and stopped unpacking.

"I know what's inside," I said. "I found the money months ago, back at the start of school. I wasn't *looking* for it. It was an accident. But I've been thinking . . . I could help you. I could help you save up, whatever you're saving for. I've got some money from the coffeehouse, and if I can get my old job back I—"

"Darcy," she interrupted.

"Please let me. Please. You don't have to tell me what it's for, but—"

"Darcy." She took my hands and held them tight around the tea tin. "You're going to go to a good college."

"What?" I looked down at my hands and her hands. Then I understood. The label on the tin began to wobble, and the letters got fat and watery. Tears spilled from my eyes.

I sobbed, and Marsha's arms were around me, and I couldn't believe how lucky I was, how good it was, to have a home.

She held me until I got to the hiccupy end of my tears. "Look at you," she said. "You're a mess. You don't want your friends to see you looking like that, do you? Go on, wash up." She shooed me toward the bathroom, and I went.

Some people's eyes change color when they cry, but not mine. I splashed cold water on my face and patted it dry with one of Marsha's purple hand towels, looking at myself in the mirror. My skin had gotten red and puffy, but my eyes blinked back at me, black as ever. Steady and unchanging.

I happened to glance at the plaque hanging over the toilet:

Desiderata. I began reading it again for the millionth time, and stopped when I reached a certain line:

You are a child of the universe, no less than the trees and the stars. You have a right to be here.

Those words were like brushstrokes inside me, painting a picture. A portrait.

It was a portrait of myself.

I looked in the mirror. *This is me,* I thought.

I smiled.

"Darcy," Marsha called. I heard the front door opening, and footsteps, and the high and low voices of Lily, Jims, Raphael, and Taylor. "Your friends are back."

"I'm coming!"

WE TORE INTO THE THAI FOOD, and the sunlight from the living room windows stretched and lengthened and faded. The sun was going down early, as it always does during winter in the Midwest. It was almost dark when there was a knock at the door.

One by one, everyone in the room turned to me.

They knew who it was. *I* knew who it was. My entire body did. My pulse quivered.

There was a second knock, but no one said anything. It was as if we were afraid to speak.

Except Jims.

"Look, Darcy." He dropped his white fork into an empty take-out carton. "I'm not going to list the ways in which I don't like your boyfriend."

"He's not—"

"—all I'm going to say is that I don't think you two are going to traipse off into the sunset and have fat, happy babies."

"*Jims.*"

"But that's not what everyone wants. The question is: what do *you* want?"

I took a shallow breath. It didn't seem like my lungs were working properly. Or the rest of me. Certainly not my heart.

I stood and opened the door.

Conn.

"Hi," I said.

He was framed by the deepening sky. Night was falling around him in smudges of lilac and gray. "I came as soon as I could," he said.

"Oh. Um." I glanced back at the warm yellows of the brightly lit living room, at Marsha and my friends. "Do you want to come inside?"

"No. I mean, I'd rather talk to you out here." His face was arranged into my least favorite expression. The completely unreadable one.

I didn't bother to get my coat. I stepped outside, and we walked to the edge of the driveway. He stood in the dry gutter and I stood on the curb. That way he wasn't so much taller than me.

"There was a lot to mop up after the fire," Conn said. "I decided to listen to what you told me, the night you came over to my place. That I could do some good if I stayed in the IBI. That's what I want to do."

I had a hard time responding. "Good."

"But that meant I couldn't leave the crime scene. There was a search for Meridian, Orion, and the others—*that* didn't go anywhere—and then there was Fitzgerald, and the mayor, and . . ." He trailed off, looking at me searchingly. "What's wrong? I said I would come later. I thought you wanted me to."

"I did. I do."

"Really?"

It occurred to me that it might always be like this with Conn. I might always be searching for my courage. But I said what I wanted to say. "Very much."

He let out a nervous breath. "You looked so . . . strange."

"So did you. And I *felt* strange. You said you'd see me later, but I didn't know *how* much later, like weeks, or months, or years—"

"Darcy," he chided, "when I said that, the only kind of *later* I wanted was a second later. A millisecond later. A nanosecond. Faster than the speed of light."

"Oh." I smiled.

He studied me through the darkness. "You've been crying."

"Happy tears."

Conn's hand lifted my chin, and he gently kissed my eyes. I shivered.

He began unbuttoning his coat. "You're cold."

"Not really."

Conn pulled me inside his coat and wrapped it and his arms around me. I pressed my cheek against his chest, burrowing into the cocoon we made together. "You know," I said, "there is such a thing as a long-distance relationship."

"And an interdimensional one?"

"I think it could work."

"I think so, too."

I pulled away and looked at him. I don't think I had ever seen pure joy on his face before. I saw it then.

He chuckled. "I'm a little disappointed. I hoped you were going to ask me again what I said to the Shades. How I convinced them not to fight."

"Slightly off topic, but all right. Tell me, Conn. What did you say?"

He gazed down at me, and his eyes were the color of heavy weather. "That I love you."

When I kissed him, his mouth tasted like warm rain. My heart crashed, and I knew that this would not be easy. It never would be easy. It would be rough and stormy.

And beautiful. Beautiful, too.

Like a tornado spinning down from the clouds.

I know. Most girls want their skies to be sunny.

But I'm not most girls.

ACKNOWLEDGMENTS

Thanks to—

Mark Beirn, Cathy Meyer, Nina Orechwa, Becky Rosenthal, and Dan Wolfe, for helping me get through high school.

The teachers of Bolingbrook High School 1991–1995, especially E. J. Bronkema, who was very kind and influential.

Brian Shallcross and Brooke Tafoya, for discussing the Department of Children and Family Services with me.

David Moré, for an excellent talk about painting with oils.

Dave Elfving, for suggestions about how to incorporate Chicago history, particularly the Couch Mausoleum (though I fudged some details, since the cemetery the Mausoleum used to be part of was moved after the Civil War, not the Great Fire).

Doireann Fitzgerald, for Irish names.

ACKNOWLEDGMENTS

Cat Keyser, for discussing "The Love Song of J. Alfred Prufrock" with me.

Lila Davachi and Kevin Ochsner, for giving me the term "priming."

Marilyn Rutkoski, because I love your raccoon painting and spoon collection.

Andy Rutkoski, for advice about motorcycles and the kinds of tools Conn might use.

Robert Rutkoski, for explaining Lake Michigan cloudbanks.

Thomas Philippon, for helping me invent the hypercycle and suggesting Shades cast shadows.

My son, Eliot, who was a newborn in my arms when I began this story, and his babysitter, Shaida Kahn, for giving me time to write it.

My stellar editor, Janine O'Malley.

The wonderfully supportive Charlotte Sheedy, Meredith Kaffel, and Joan Rosen.

All those who read drafts or portions of drafts: Betsy Bird, Heather Duffy-Stone, Gayle Forman, Daphne Grab, Jenny Knode, Mordicai Knode (who influenced the character of Jims and let me crib from our conversations), Marilyn Rutkoski, Jill Santopolo, Eliot Schrefer, Rebecca Stead, Natalie Van Unen, and especially Donna Freitas, for encouraging this project, reading it as it grew, giving great suggestions, and saving me from plenty of mistakes.

And last, to Chicago and Bolingbrook, Illinois, with love.